PLAYERS IN PARADISE

Eleanor . . . A stunning young lady surrounded by danger and chaos, she grew to womanhood determined to possess life's most wonderful treasures.

Charlotte . . . Eleanor's governess, so plain she often felt invisible. But underneath was a soul of courage, goodness, and passion.

Owain . . . A darkly handsome Welshman whose ambitions were matched only by his all-consuming love.

Lord Evan . . . A bully, a giant and a tyrant they called him. Yet one woman found the courage to love the gentle man within.

Lord and Lady Athmore . . . He was a depraved artist and aristocrat who seduced and abandoned women remorselessly. His wife was breathlessly beautiful, utterly mad, and would stop at nothing, not even murder, to satisfy her desires.

Driven by their love, they would search the world to find . . .

A DIFFERENT EDEN

KATHERINE SINCLAIR

A DIFFERENT EDEN

JOVE BOOKS, NEW YORK

A DIFFERENT EDEN

A Jove Book / published by arrangement with
the author

PRINTING HISTORY
Jove edition / August 1988

ISBN: 0-515-09699-7

Jove Books are published by The Berkley Publishing Group,
200 Madison Avenue, New York, New York 10016.
The name "JOVE" and the "J" logo
are trademarks belonging to Jove Publications, Inc.

PRINTED IN THE UNITED STATES OF AMERICA

10 9 8 7 6 5 4 3 2 1

1

ELEANOR HATHAWAY CROUCHED under the rain-dampened coats in the guest closet, her fist rammed against her teeth to keep from making a sound.

She could hear her grandfather bellowing her name up and down the hall. His voice bounced back off the marble floor, louder than the sporadic rumble of thunder from the storm moving up the river.

His footsteps advanced and retreated, then went clumping up the oak staircase, followed by the lighter step of Charlotte Briggs. Eleanor's nanny pleaded in her gentle but surprisingly firm English accent for her employer to please rejoin his guests and allow her to find her charge.

"You bring that granddaughter of mine to the drawing room within five minutes, or you're dismissed, Briggs. I'll find somebody who knows how to discipline that self-willed brat."

"Eleanor is a very well-behaved child," Charlotte's voice protested. "She is afraid of Mr. Yarborough. She doesn't want to recite for your guests because he's here."

"Mr. Yarborough is my biggest depositor and my closest friend. You'd better knock some manners into that child, or I'll do it myself. I won't have her insulting my friends."

Their voices faded into the upper reaches of the house, and Eleanor uncoiled her stiff limbs and crept out into the hall. She went to the foot of the stairs and sat on the bottom step to await Charlotte's return.

Her beloved Charlotte mustn't be dismissed on her account.

1

She would just have to go up to the drawing room and recite. Terrifying Mr. Yarborough would look at her and lick his oily lips, wanting her to give him a good-night kiss. Her grandfather would make her obey, and Mr. Yarborough's big hands would squeeze as he hugged her. Eleanor would feel sick. Once, he had pulled her onto his lap, and that had been the worst of all. She didn't know why she was so afraid of him, because all of Grandfather's friends liked to kiss and hug her, exclaiming what a pretty little thing she was, but some sixth sense told her that Yarborough's touch was evil.

Eleanor wrapped her arms around her knees, trying not to shiver in anticipation of Yarborough's touch and of her grandfather's threatened punishment for hiding from him.

Grandfather had never liked her, although he grudgingly admitted that she had a nice way of reciting poetry and, for a nine year old, quite a stage presence. Eleanor wasn't sure what that meant, but Charlotte said it was a compliment. More often, he demanded to know when her father was going to present him with grandsons.

Nor did Grandfather particularly care for her mother, Eleanor sensed. A feeling of anger like a heavy black cloud hung in the air whenever they were in a room together. Was that why Mother and Father had left? They said they couldn't take her with them because of redskins on the warpath, and bandits and outlaws, but that they'd be back to see her, maybe by Thanksgiving, certainly by her tenth birthday in November.

"Ah, there you are, Eleanor." Charlotte's relieved voice floated somewhere over her head. Looking up, she saw her nanny descending the stairs.

At first glance, Charlotte Briggs appeared to be a pale, plain little woman, her fragile features weighted by a heavy coil of brown hair. But there was about her a sense of purpose, evident in the direct gaze of her true gray eyes, and her determined stride. She never strolled aimlessly, or stared into space, or indulged in gossip with the servants. She treated Eleanor as if she were a real person, rather than the silly child her grandfather said she was. Charlotte never spoke down to her, or ignored her, and she always carefully considered her opinions, as though they really mattered to her. She had been hired when Eleanor was only two weeks old, and despite Grandfather's threats to dismiss her, they had never been separated. But that was because Amy—Eleanor often thought of her mother by her given name simply because Amy was too beautiful to be anyone's mother—interceded on Charlotte's behalf. But now Amy and Father were gone, and who would protect Charlotte from Grandfather's wrath?

Reaching the foot of the stairs, Charlotte drew Eleanor to her feet and into a comforting embrace. "I'll go with you into the drawing room, and stay there until you're excused. I shan't be more than an inch away from your side, I promise."

Taking Eleanor's hand, Charlotte squared her thin shoulders and marched back up the stairs to the second-floor drawing room where Stansfield Hathaway entertained his guests. Just before they reached the landing, Eleanor whispered, "You don't have to go in with me. I'll be brave, I promise."

Charlotte smiled reassuringly. "But I *want* to go in. Don't worry, it will be all right."

It wasn't all right, of course. From the way her grandfather glowered at Charlotte, it was clear that he disapproved of the presence of a mere nanny among his guests. She was a servant in his eyes, although Charlotte had told Eleanor that in her native England, a nanny enjoyed a special position in the household. Before he could speak, Eleanor quickly bobbed a curtsy. "I'm sorry I'm late. I'd like to recite "Song of Hiawatha" for you."

She moved to her favorite spot beside the grand piano and Charlotte stood behind a large candelabrum that cast a silver reflection on the gleaming rosewood surface. " 'By the shores of Gitche Gumee, By the shining Big-Sea-Water, Stood the wigwam of Nokomis, Daughter of the Moon, Nokomis.' "

As always, Eleanor soon forgot the watching, listening circle of grown-ups, even the huge, ugly Mr. Yarborough with his nasty leering eyes, greasy smile, and big, red hands. She lost herself in the magic of the words she spoke, feeling transported to another place and time, even to a different body.

" 'The Wrinkled old Nokomis, Nursed the little Hiawatha, Rocked him in his linden cradle . . .' "

Sometimes Eleanor cast Charlotte in the role of Nokomis, because, like Hiawatha, Eleanor had been taught much by a wise and loving nurse. " 'Many things Nokomis taught him Of the stars that shine in heaven . . .' "

Charlotte wasn't old and wrinkled like Nokomis, but she was just as kind, never finding fault with her, never requiring more of her than simply to *be*. When Grandfather raged and roared, and her father withdrew into his tightly closed shell, or Amy's restless spirit was too intent upon her own secret longings to sympathize with childish problems, then dear, kind Charlotte would be there, fiercely protective, warmly loving.

" '. . . Showed the Death-Dance of the spirits, Warriors with their plumes and war-clubs, Flaring far away to northward In the frosty nights of winter . . .' "

Mr. Yarborough leaned forward in his chair, one elbow on his immense thigh, his bulbous-nosed face propped on a hand with fingers like radishes. His other hand hung over the chair arm and Eleanor faltered, no longer in the wigwam of Nokomis, as that hand opened and closed, slowly, like a drifting octopus. Oh, how she hated his hands! They seemed to take the form and shape of everything on earth she detested. And worse than his hands was that mouth! Even from across the room, Eleanor could see spittle glistening on his chin.

She was breathless by the time she finished reciting "Hiawatha." Charlotte moved instantly to her side and took her hand. Before anyone could suggest good-night kisses, she briskly said, "Eleanor is a little feverish tonight. You will all please excuse her now. She's going straight to bed. Say good night, dear."

"Good night, Grandfather, good night everyone," Eleanor said, not daring to catch his eye. Charlotte led her to the door, and, once outside, they exchanged conspiratorial grins and raced for their rooms on the third floor.

Charlotte lit the bedside lamp and helped her into her nightgown. "You mustn't worry about your grandfather punishing you, dear. I'm going to have a long talk with him after the guests leave. I don't like the way that Mr. Yarborough touches you, and it's got to stop."

"I love you, Charlotte," Eleanor said. "You won't ever leave me, will you? You won't go away like Mother and Father did?"

Placing a kiss on her forehead, Charlotte said, "No, my darling, I'll always be with you. Now, I'm going down to the kitchen to fetch you a glass of nice, warm milk and some biscuits. Then I'll read a story to help you go to sleep."

Eleanor snuggled under the blankets, feeling warm and cared for. Charlotte sometimes used the wrong word; biscuits, for instance, really meant molasses cookies. "I'd like you to read some more about New Mexico, where Mother and Father are."

The merest hint of a frown creased Charlotte's pale, smooth forehead, but she nodded. "I'll stop by the library and get the book." She paused. "Perhaps there'll be a letter from your mother tomorrow.'' She didn't sound as if she really expected one.

After Charlotte left, Eleanor felt suddenly drowsy. Battles with Grandfather and reciting for guests always made her tired.

She was almost asleep when her bedroom door creaked slowly open. She gasped as Mr. Yarborough lumbered into the room like a big, black bear. Before she could cry out, he was beside the bed, one hateful hand over her mouth, sweaty, smothering, terrifying. His other hand ripped away her covers, then grasped her cotton nightgown and yanked it upward.

Twisting her body, kicking, she felt like a little stick figure in the clutches of a giant as he imprisoned her ankles with one knee. Her wildly flailing fists could not reach beyond his arm, but she beat a steady, desperate tattoo on his coat sleeve.

Now he had one hand on her belly, moving it in widening circles, upward, downward. Somewhere over her head in the shadows, his face floated like a monstrous moon. He never spoke, but she was aware of little sounds, deep in his throat, like the rumbling of an earthquake about to split open the ground.

Now his probing fingers really hurt her, and she arched her body in a violent spasm. Stars danced dizzily in front of her eyes, and there was a rushing sound in her ears.

Yarborough suddenly crashed down on top of her, crushing the air from her lungs. A second later he rolled off her, landing on the floor with a thud.

Sobbing, trying to catch her breath, Eleanor looked up to see Charlotte standing over Yarborough's prostrate form. In her hands, her nanny grasped a heavy, silver tray that had recently held milk and cookies. Yarborough's face lay in a pool of spilled milk. Eleanor flung herself into Charlotte's arms.

Stroking her hair, speaking soothingly, Charlotte calmed the child. ''We must go downstairs,'' she said at last. ''Before he comes to his senses.''

''He isn't dead?'' Eleanor asked, disappointed.

''No, but he'll have a nasty headache when he wakes up. Here, let me help you put on your dressing gown and we'll go and bring your grandfather to see where his fine friend is—and what he is.''

Charlotte stared in incredulous disbelief at Stansfield Hathaway. His dark eyes burned beneath a high, domed forehead, and his mouth curled in an almost sharklike grimace. In his youth, he'd been handsome; his features hinted that once they had been as well-carved as those of his son, Hugh. But the years had dealt harshly with Stansfield, leaving broken veins, sagging jowls and a proliferation of mottles and warts that seemed to be nature's revenge for the man he'd become. The dashing young hero of two wars had changed into a mean and grasping banker, without compassion or soul, or even the vaguest empathy for his fellow-man. More than once, Charlotte wondered what had brought about such a metamorphosis.

He repeated, "The matter will never be mentioned again, do you both understand that?"

Charlotte's arm tightened around Eleanor's still shaking shoulders. "No, sir, I do not understand. Criminal charges must be filed against Mr. Yarborough. I insist upon it."

"Oh, you do, do you? Well let me tell you something, you dried-up old maid. You'll be lucky if *he* doesn't bring charges against *you*, for assaulting him. How dare you strike one of my guests? How dare you put filthy ideas into a child's mind? He only stopped by her room to bid her good night, because you rudely dragged her from the drawing room. So much for your English manners. You're finished here, miss. Return my granddaughter to her room and go and pack your things. You won't spend another day under my roof. I want you out of here first thing in the morning."

"No, Grandfather!" Eleanor found her voice at last. She clung to Charlotte. "Mr. Yarborough was hurting me, just like Charlotte said. He pulled up my nightgown—"

Stansfield's hand swished through the air and slapped the child's cheek. Charlotte reeled, feeling the pain of the blow herself. The old man growled, "If you ever repeat such a lie again, I'll wash your mouth out with lye soap."

Charlotte picked up the little girl, who buried her face in her neck, and stumbled from the room.

The butler and Cook's husband had already carried Yarborough from Eleanor's room, but Charlotte rushed into her own room with the child.

Placing her down on the bed, she whispered urgently, "Listen to me, Eleanor. I can't stay here now, but I can't bear to leave you here unprotected. Having got off scot-free tonight, there's no telling what Yarborough might attempt in the future. I learned today that your grandfather sent your father to establish a bank in the New Mexico Territory. Mr. Yarborough's railroad has crossed into the territory and the two of them are intent upon establishing western empires.''

"But if Mother and Father are staying out west, why didn't they take us with them?''

"As your mother explained, there are hostile Indians and desperadoes in the territory.'' She added hastily, "But, of course, your parents will be safe since they are going to be in town. However, they felt the West is still too raw and unsettled for a child your age. You are to go to school in the autumn, here in Boston.''

"And live with Grandfather?'' Eleanor was aghast. "Oh, no!''

"My dear child, you know I love you as if you were my very own flesh and blood. I would never let any harm come to you. But if I am to protect you, we must leave Boston. We must run away tonight. Eleanor, it's a big decision I'm asking of one so young . . . but will you trust me? Will you come with me?''

Eleanor's thin little arms went around her. "Oh, yes, Charlotte. Take me away with you, please. Let's go quick, before Grandfather comes and locks me in my room like he did when I tried to go with Mother and Father.''

2

STANSFIELD HATHAWAY LISTENED impassively as his butler relayed the grim news. "We found the boat capsized, floating about ten yards offshore. There were a few other things in the water . . . a child's shoe, a woman's handbag, some articles of clothing. I've put them in the kitchen."

"When do the police think their bodies might wash up?"

"Maybe the next tide . . . could be days, or maybe never. There's a lot of mud and underwater debris in that area. They haven't had much luck dragging for bodies in the past, but of course, they'll try as soon as it's light."

"Where the hell was the Briggs woman going, do you suppose? Why would she attempt to cross the river?"

"I don't know, sir. Perhaps she thought it was the one means of transportation you wouldn't expect her to take, so you wouldn't follow. It was a bad night, what with the rain and wind. The water would have been choppy, hard for a slip of a woman to handle the oars on such a night."

His employer was silent for so long that the butler coughed discreetly and asked, "Will you be wanting to send a telegraph to Mr. Hugh, sir?"

"No. Not yet. We can't know for sure if the two of them drowned. It's possible they may attempt to follow my son and his wife to New Mexico. Let's wait and see if any bodies wash up. After breakfast have the carriage brought around. I'll go to the Pinkerton Agency and hire one of their detectives to assist the police with the search."

Stansfield crossed the drawing room and went out onto the second-story wrought iron balcony. The thunderstorm of the previous night had washed the air fragrantly clean. As he watched, a silver sunrise peeled back the night from the horizon and steam began to rise from glistening foliage. Around him the homes of his neighbors on the hill lay serenely sleeping. None of them were as fine as his four-story house with its arched Georgian doorway and handsome Corinthian portico. The purple-tinted window panes gave the house a mysterious, brooding air. Often when he approached it with the sunlight at a particular angle, he felt that his secrets were concealed behind those lavender windows. That if he were to take a stone and hurl it through the glass, everything that was rotten would escape and he'd be free of those old demons forever. But then, of course, the source of his rage against the world would be out in the open for all to see.

Were they dead, his granddaughter and her nanny? Or had they run away, as once his wife had run away and, he suspected, as Eleanor's mother had often contemplated running away? Indeed, Amy would have, had it not been for her financial dependency. Damn every woman on earth, they weren't worth the trouble they caused.

He'd learned firsthand of female perfidy long ago. His wife had taken their baby son and left him, accusing him of caring more about money than his family. Scant months later she had sent Hugh home because she became ill. She had died in a charity ward, preferring a pauper's grave to the wealth and comfort he could provide.

But Hugh had been the ideal son, more than making up for his mother's treachery. Until Amy came on the scene. She might have been a copy of Hugh's mother, beautiful, selfish, and willful. Amy had never wanted to move into the family home, and it had taken all of Stansfield's powers of persuasion to get Hugh to remain in his house and business.

Perhaps he had played on Hugh's sense of guilt about what had happened to his mother, pointing out that it had been his birth that caused her to become temporarily deranged. It was a well-known fact that women often acted strangely in the postpartum period. But Stansfield's actions had been necessary, otherwise Amy would have destroyed a promising career, not to mention separating father and son.

Then, a month ago, they had dropped their bombshell. Hugh announced that he and Amy had decided to migrate west. She could no longer tolerate, as she put it, the fact that her husband was his father's lackey. Nor did she intend to go on living under the roof of a disagreeable tyrant.

The resulting battle of wits lasted for days, but for once, Hugh was adamant. If he didn't go west, Amy would leave him. No, it wasn't sufficient merely to move to a new house in Boston and continue working at the bank. She wanted a fresh start, and a thousand-mile buffer between her and her father-in-law. In desperation, Stansfield had come up with the idea of establishing another Hathaway bank out west, in order to keep a connection between Hugh and himself. His close friend Franklyn Yarborough was building a railroad over the Raton mountains into the territory, and he pointed out that a seemingly endless supply of silver poured out of local mines. There was gold in the Mogollon mountains, turquoise in the Burro mountains, and iron and copper everywhere, not to mention the cattle ranches that were springing up. Fortunes could be made out west, and bankers were needed to preside over them.

Yarborough had also been the one to suggest that the child Eleanor remain in Boston, suggesting that it was a way to prevent the total alienation between father and son that Amy obviously wanted. Amy had been tearful, angry, unwilling to be separated from her daughter, but had given in when she heard the news of the terrible Geronimo and his renegade Apaches breaking out of the reservation and terrorizing settlers in the Southwest.

The French door behind him opened and his butler gave a discreet cough. Stansfield turned and asked, "Have they been found?"

"No word yet, sir. But Mr. Yarborough is here to see you."

Evidently Franklyn had fully recovered from his blow on the head the previous evening, since he was pacing back and forth in the library. The instant he saw Stansfield he asked, "Have you heard?"

"Yes, of course. But how did you know?"

Yarborough blinked. "I own the damn railroad. Why wouldn't I know?"

"Railroad? Are we talking about the same thing? I was referring to the fact that Briggs and my granddaughter ran off last night and might have drowned in the river."

Yarborough's mouth dropped open. "Oh, good God, Stansfield . . . not Eleanor, too! You'd better sit down. I'll pour you a brandy."

"Never mind the brandy. What happened?"

Yarborough's pudgy fingers plucked distractedly at the buttons of his jacket, then unfastened them, releasing his paunch. "We overlooked the danger of spring flooding from the Rio Grande. A cloudburst can send a wall of water thundering into the dry arroyos. In the last few weeks several trains reported the tracks were underwater. But we never thought . . ."

"Flooding? Trains? What in heaven's name are you getting at?"

"A bridge washed out. A train plummeted off the end of it."

Stansfield felt a chill. "Not—"

"It's too soon to tell, but there are very few survivors. Stansfield . . . it was the train Hugh and Amy were taking to Silver City."

Somewhere in the fog that blurred his vision, Stansfield heard Yarborough say, "Perhaps Eleanor isn't dead. You fired the nanny. She may have taken the child away with her. Stansfield, you must find out for sure. Eleanor is all you've got left."

Charlotte Briggs carefully tucked a blanket around the sleeping child, worrying for a moment that the pitching and rolling of the ship might dislodge Eleanor from the bunk. Then she decided the wooden rails were probably sufficient to prevent such an occurrence. Picking up a lightweight shawl, Charlotte slipped it over her shoulders and left the cabin.

The tinkle of glasses, music, and muted laughter drifted down from the first-class section as she walked quickly up the companionway to the second-class promenade deck. At the polished, wooden rail in the stern, she looked back at the halo of light on the horizon that was all that remained of New York harbor. If they'd sailed from Boston they could have saved six hundred sea miles, but they might have been caught if Stansfield Hathaway had seen through the ruse of the "accidental drowning" and had had the outward-bound ships watched.

Now that the last streak of land was rapidly vanishing into a starry night, Charlotte exhaled a long sigh of relief. So far so good. It hadn't even been necessary to lie about her relationship to Eleanor. Everyone assumed they were mother and daughter. And why not? After all, who had raised the child from infancy?

Strolling passengers, couples mostly, passed her without glancing in her direction. She gazed at the phosphorescent wake of the ship, accustomed to being overlooked. Having grown up in a country vicarage with a preoccupied father, and a mother forever taking care of the "poor unfortunates" at the expense of her husband and daughter, Charlotte had no delusions about her importance in the scheme of things. She had not been allowed to speak unless absolutely necessary. "Children should be seen and not heard" was the creed in the Briggs' vicarage. But apparently no one had wanted to see a plain, painfully shy little girl, either. They looked through her rather than at her. As a little girl, she had often surreptitiously glanced in mirrors, windows, even puddles of water, to make sure that she did, in fact, exist.

"A nice evening, isn't it," an Oxford-accented English voice spoke at her elbow. She jumped, startled.

Turning, she was astonished to see a tall, extremely good-looking man dressed in evening clothes, also leaning against the rail. Instinctively, Charlotte glanced about to see if he was addressing someone else, but there was no one near. She cleared her throat awkwardly and murmured, "It is, indeed, a pleasant evening."

"Nothing like the feeling one gets as a ship leaves one shore and the other is days away, is there? Past problems have been left behind and any possible future ones not yet reached, therefore not worth worrying about. Being at sea is a glorious sort of limbo, don't you think?"

"If one is leaving behind problems, or anticipates confronting some," Charlotte answered cautiously. "Yes, I suppose so." She fought an urge to run, feeling unequipped to deal with a handsome man of obvious breeding, who amused himself by slumming in the second-class section of the ship. She privately hoped he wouldn't also visit steerage dressed like that.

"My name is Stephen Meadows, by the way."

Charlotte hesitated, then said, "I am Mrs. Danforth." It had been her mother's maiden name, the one under which she and Eleanor were traveling.

"You have a very pretty little girl," he added. "I saw the two of you walking around a lower deck as we sailed."

A knot of tension formed in Charlotte's stomach. No man ever noticed her, so it wasn't surprising that it had been Eleanor who caught his attention. The memory of Franklyn Yarborough was too fresh in Charlotte's mind for her not to suspect any man of unhealthy thoughts about a child as pretty as Eleanor. Besides, it would be unwise to risk even a passing acquaintance with anyone who might deduce that she and Eleanor were running away.

Stephen Meadows said, "The reason you stood out so was that every other passenger aboard was hanging over the rail, waving good-bye to someone." He lowered his voice sympathetically. "I also noticed that you were wearing black and I wondered . . . if you might be a widow?"

Stansfield Hathaway had required her to wear black, as all of his servants did, and her slender savings hadn't stretched to buying any new clothes before sailing. She glanced about, again considering flight, and Meadows said, "I'm sorry, I'm being terribly presumptuous."

"No, not at all. Yes, I am a widow."

"He was an American?"

"Who?"

"Your late husband."

"Oh . . . yes, he was."

"So you decided to go home to England. Do you have family there?"

"No. Eleanor—my daughter and I are quite alone in the world. If you will excuse me, Mr. Meadows, I must go and see that my daughter is all right."

"Of course. Good night, Mrs. Danforth."

He watched her disappear into the shadows, her thin little body rigidly erect, shoulders squared, head held high. Her steps on the rolling deck were careful but unwavering. Still, he knew she was running away from him.

After a moment he turned and went back up the companionway to the first-class grand saloon. Passengers who had just finished dining were now enjoying liqueurs. Men in dinner jackets and women wearing pastel satins and iridescent brocades with diamonds glinting on throats and wrists, reclined in plush armchairs, as stewards moved unobtrusively among them, serving drinks in crystal glasses. The contrast between the appointments here and in second class was quite marked, but it was the memory of his foray into steerage that depressed him.

Zoe regarded him over the edge of her champagne glass as he approached. She wore a midnight blue gown of whispering silk that seemed to move even when she was sitting still. Her black hair, dramatically swept back from her brow to call attention to her distinct widow's peak, gleamed with a bluish sheen. The contrast of dark hair against her pale, translucent complexion was quite striking, and he saw several men covertly watching her. Tonight she appeared calm, he was thankful to note. He darted a quick glance of assessment at her eyes and hands, the usual indicators of her state of mind. Her hands were still and her gaze level.

He sat down beside her and she raised perfectly shaped black eyebrows. "Well?"

"Steerage is half empty. I expect there are more of the lower classes traveling from England to America than vice versa. I saw no one who would be suitable. But on the way back up here I strolled around the second-class promenade deck. Do you remember the plain little woman with the extraordinarily pretty little girl? We saw them when we sailed, and you remarked that the woman must have an exceedingly handsome husband, since the child hardly inherited her looks from her mother."

"Yes," Zoe said. "I remember. No one had come to see them off. But surely, you don't think . . ."

"The woman is widowed and I don't think they're too well-off. Her clothes are cheap quality, almost like those worn by a servant. I learned she has no family in England—probably none in America either, or surely they'd have stayed with them. But she is a gentlewoman, and sounded educated. If, as I suspect, she must find a way to support herself and her child when they arrive in England, then . . . she could be the person we're looking for."

"But what about the child?"

Stephen tapped his forefinger against his lips thoughtfully. "She could be an asset. If you were a poor widow with a little daughter to support, wouldn't you like to see her brought up at Glendower? With luck, little Mrs. Danforth would stay forever."

Zoe shrugged. "Well, we have to find someone to replace Francesca before we return. She will have finished serving her notice by the time we dock at Southampton and she'll be off to Spain . . . that is, if he hasn't killed her in our absence."

Stephen Meadows looked less formidable without his evening clothes, Charlotte decided, but no less handsome. She saw him coming toward them across the deck the following morning wearing a loose shirt, a sketch pad tucked under his arm. A breeze ruffled his dark hair, giving him a carefree air that was at odds with a strangely haunted look in his eyes that had been hidden by the darkness the previous evening.

"Don't run away, Mrs. Danforth," he called to her as he approached. "I'm really quite harmless."

She had been poised for flight, she realized, and had immediately seized Eleanor's hand protectively. "Good morning," Charlotte said uncertainly. "May I present my daughter. Eleanor, this is Mr. Meadows."

The little girl bobbed a curtsy and Stephen said, "I am honored and delighted to make your acquaintance. You see, my dear ladies, yours are the only faces aboard ship that have inspired me to bring out the tools of my trade. I had not thought to work again until I returned to England. I feared a voodoo spell had been placed on me while I was in New Orleans."

"You are an artist," Charlotte said, feeling a tremendous sense of relief. Of course, no wonder he was so taken with Eleanor. Her exquisite features would be an inspiration to any artist.

"If I could persuade you to pose for me? I'll make some sketches and promise not to keep you longer than you feel disposed to stay."

"Oh, let me, Charlotte," Eleanor begged. "I could send a picture to . . ." She broke off, turning pink as she realized she had almost given the game away.

But Stephen apparently hadn't noticed, as he was saying, "Actually, I'd like to sketch both of you."

Astonished, Charlotte said, "Oh, really, you don't have to invite my participation merely to be polite—"

"My dear Mrs. Danforth, while your daughter is lovely, I am just as interested in sketching you. How fortunate it is that we have the whole voyage ahead of us, since I find it impossible to capture a likeness without first getting to know my model."

Charlotte hesitated, unsure how to deal with the situation. She was intrigued yet uneasy. Why had he sought out Eleanor and herself when the ship was filled with women and children who would have been delighted by the attentions of a handsome man? Every instinct urged her to turn and flee. Yet would she not arouse more suspicion by refusing? Anyone would be flattered that an artist wished to sketch them, and she could hardly plead that other duties demanded her attention.

Stephen walked to the ship's rail and pointed at the gray swells of the ocean. "If you refuse," he said in a dramatic tone, "I shall be forced to make you walk the plank."

Eleanor laughed and Charlotte felt some of her tension dissipate. "Well . . ."

"Good. We'll begin at once. The light is perfect. Now, Mrs. Danforth, I want you to relax. That furrow between your eyes is interesting and your attitude of impending flight intriguing, but for the sketch we can do without either. Limbo, remember? Nothing that we do, say, think or feel is of any consequence for the length of the voyage. While at sea we can be anyone we wish . . . simply decide upon your temporary self and I shall capture it in your picture.''

"I shall be the ancient mariner's little daughter, accompanying him to sea," Eleanor declared dreamily, posing prettily against the polished wood rail, "to keep him company.''

"Goodness, must I then be the ancient mariner?'' Charlotte asked, joining in the fun even as she chided herself for her foolishness. Perhaps it was the limbo of being at sea, but she thought it more likely to be the sheer charm of Stephen Meadows.

Eleanor sat on the edge of Charlotte's bunk, her eyes wide. "You're wearing your Christmas dress!"

Charlotte smiled. "Today feels a little like a holiday.'' She fastened the last of the tiny pearl buttons and surveyed her reflection in the mirror. The dark red, velvet dress had been a Christmas gift from Amy Hathaway the second year of Charlotte's employment. It had been worn only for Christmas dinner each year since. The dress was really quite unsuitable for high summer wear, but as the ship neared the cooler English clime Charlotte thought perhaps it would be appropriate. Besides, she had nothing else but her drab, black day dresses. Dinner with a man in evening clothes in first class, at the captain's table, demanded something a little more festive.

"You'll remember everything you do and eat and what Mr. Meadows says, won't you?'' Eleanor said. She paused, her eyes clouding. "But . . . if he asks you to marry him . . . what will become of me?''

"Eleanor!'' Charlotte was shocked. "There's absolutely no possibility of such a thing happening—either that he'd want to marry me, or that I would ever desert you.''

She peered into the mottled mirror, noting that a pink flush suffused her face. Or perhaps it was caused by a reflection from the red velvet. Certainly she had never considered the possibility that Stephen had sought her out and enjoyed her company. No, as soon as she learned he was an artist it was clear that what he really wanted was to paint a portrait of the exquisitely beautiful child.

Still, during this most breathlessly exciting week of her life,

Charlotte had risen each day with a keen sense of anticipation, because Stephen would again leave the luxury of first class to visit their more Spartan surroundings. Tonight, their last-night at sea before landfall, Charlotte had been astonished when Stephen invited her to dine with him. She'd protested that it wouldn't be allowed, but Stephen laughed and said, "Nonsense. You must never let the petty rules and regulations of others stand in the way of what you want, Charlotte."

They had moved quickly and easily to a first name basis, and he hadn't seemed surprised that Eleanor called her Charlotte rather than "Mother."

"You'll be all right, dear? You won't be lonely?" she asked Eleanor.

"Too sleepy," the child replied, rubbing her eyes in exaggerated fatigue.

"You know where the bell is, to summon the steward if you need anything? Very well, into bed and I'll tuck you in."

"Charlotte . . . will Mother and Father be waiting for us in England?"

"No, dear. You must be patient. It will be some time before they come."

"We should have gone to them." A fretful note had crept into Eleanor's voice. Charlotte bent and kissed the child's cheek. "They would have simply sent you back to your grandfather's house, dear. You know you can't be with your parents out west, there are too many dangers. Not only from the Indian wars, but also from the desperadoes in the territory. I could never let you go there until law and order has been established."

"But I miss her . . . Father, too."

"I know, my darling. But we'll have a wonderful time in England, you'll see. The days will pass quickly until they come."

Stifling her qualms, Charlotte reminded herself of what could have happened had she not removed the child from that evil man. As soon as they reached England she would send a letter to Eleanor's parents in New Mexico, explaining why she had taken such drastic action. But there would have to be assurances from them that the child would not be returned to her grandfather and Yarborough. At the back of Charlotte's mind was the nagging question as to whether Amy and Hugh, like Stansfield, would refuse to believe what Yarborough had done, discounting the story as the wild imaginings of a child fueled by the sexual frustration of an old maid.

But as she went to meet Stephen on the promenade deck, her worries were temporarily forgotten. Charlotte chided herself that her heart was beating a trifle too fast for a respectable spinster thirty years old.

He was waiting for her, standing with his long legs astride, feet braced on the rolling deck, watching the companionway from which she would emerge. During the times he sketched Eleanor and herself, Charlotte had studied every detail of his appearance, from his smooth, dark hair to his gracefully tapered fingers. The hands of an artist, the mournful eyes of a poet, and the fearless demeanor of an adventurer all combined to devastating effect. That such a man had even deigned to speak to her was perhaps enough to create memories for the rest of her life.

His eyes, blue-green like the sea, lit up when he saw her. The effect was rather like sunlight gilding the ocean, since usually there was that haunted quality to his gaze, which seemed to indicate he was privy to the darker aspects of human nature and sought to counteract them with his artistic talent.

"How charming you look! And what a pleasure to see you in something other than dreary black. I trust this means your mourning period is at an end?"

She had completely forgotten her pose as a widow. "Oh . . . yes."

He slipped her arm through his in a proprietary gesture that both thrilled and alarmed her, because of the rush of awareness his proximity caused. A tingling sensation swept from her fingers to her throat. "Good. I have an artist's appreciation for color, and besides, the world is dim enough. We must strive to brighten it whenever we can."

Charlotte thought that Stephen Meadows brightened the world by simply being in it. She fixed her gaze on the damp planks of the deck and walked at his side as though she belonged there.

She was dazzled by the splendor of the first-class dining room, and immediately felt out of place at the captain's table. Eight passengers were dining with the captain and his first officer, and Charlotte's red velvet dress, that seemed so grand on Christmas Day, now looked old-fashioned, a little worn, and definitely out of season beside the other women's pastel silks and satins. The men rose at her approach, and Stephen introduced her. Wine was served and conversation resumed. Everyone was excited at the prospect of tomorrow's landfall. After a glass of wine and the fish course, Charlotte began to relax and enjoy herself.

One of the other male passengers suddenly asked Stephen, "And where is the stunning Lady Athmore this evening?"

"Zoe is a little under the weather," he replied easily, taking a crusty roll from a basket offered by a steward. "She decided to rest this evening so that she'll be ready to disembark tomorrow." Turning to Charlotte, he said, "You didn't say where your final destination will be. Will you be staying in Southampton?"

"No. I thought I'd return to Sussex. That's where I was born and brought up. My parents were missionaries in India when they were young and were content to remain in the parish in Sussex all the rest of their lives. I suppose they'd had enough of foreign places."

Stephen had changed the subject so deftly that Charlotte wondered why. Surely he didn't think she would be upset by the mention of another of his shipboard friendships? After all, he'd spent only an hour or two a day in the company of Eleanor and herself. Lots of time to be with others. The *stunning* Lady Athmore. *Zoe,* Stephen had said, with familiar ease, in the same manner he called her Charlotte. Perhaps a woman with designs on him would have suffered an attack of immediate jealousy, but Charlotte had no such pretensions about either him or herself.

Dinner progressed to the next course, and Charlotte realized from the conversation of the other passengers how long it had been since she had set foot in the land of her birth when so few of the names mentioned, whether in the world of the arts or politics or science, were familiar to her. She decided Stephen must be a successful artist, not only because he could afford to travel in such luxury, but also because of the deference shown to him by their companions.

Charlotte spoke little, out of the long held habit of unobtrusiveness, but she listened intently.

Stephen turned to address her frequently, and it amazed and thrilled her that within the group, the two of them seemed to be a couple. The others were courteous and attentive also, and her lowly station in life and worn velvet dress were forgotten. Heady visions danced at the back of her mind, undoubtedly conjured by the wine and the magic of a captain's dinner aboard an ocean liner. She experienced a dreamlike sense of unreality. How right Stephen had been, that first evening, when he said that being at sea was like being in limbo. She no longer worried about someone guessing they were running away, nor did she even seriously contemplate what she would do when the ship reached

England. She seemed to have caught Stephen's insouciant attitude toward the voyage.

The conviviality of the evening was suddenly shattered by a woman's shriek. Conversation abruptly died, and everyone turned in frozen disbelief toward the beautiful black-haired woman who stumbled into the dining room. She crashed into tables and clutched at passing stewards, all the time screaming unintelligibly. She was stark naked.

Charlotte, who had never even closely examined her own body, let alone seen that of another woman, felt her cheeks flame at the sight of round, bouncing breasts and a triangle of dark pubic hair.

Quick and agile as a panther, Stephen arose and ran across the slightly sloping deck. He whipped off his dinner jacket and wrapped it around the woman, who clawed at his face. He swept her into his arms and walked quickly from the room.

For a few seconds everyone remained immobilized. The captain had half-risen but he settled back into his chair, clapping his serviette over his mouth, perhaps to smother his embarrassment. At Charlotte's left a rather learned-looking gentleman murmured awkwardly, "Well, he did say she wasn't feeling well." Someone else whispered, "She must be drunk. How dreadful for him."

Apparently, only Charlotte realized that the woman had been shrieking in French. She had cried: *Devil, monster, defiler,* and lastly, *whore.* Was it Charlotte's imagination that the woman's dark eyes seemed to be fixed on her as she uttered that last invective?

3

STEPHEN CAUGHT UP with Charlotte as she ushered Eleanor out of the customs area toward the waiting line of hansom cabs. A misty early morning drizzle fell on the Southampton docks, but patches of bright blue sky and a rising breeze promised a fine summer day to come.

"Wait . . . please," Stephen said. "I must explain."

Charlotte, clad in her somber black, a shabby bonnet doing little to disguise the dark circles under her eyes, had resumed what she saw as her proper role, that of a plain and dowdy little nanny. All delusions of grandeur had been erased in that revealing moment after the enactment of the brief drama in the ship's dining room the previous evening. Into a lengthy silence that had fallen at the captain's table, she had uttered the foolish words, "How very kind of Mr. Meadows to rush to the poor lady's assistance."

They had all stared at her in amazed disbelief. Someone murmured, *"Mister* Meadows?" making it sound like a question. Eventually the captain said gruffly, "The lady in question, Mrs. Danforth, is Lord Athmore's wife. His lordship uses the nom de plume of Stephen Meadows for professional reasons."

Now on the dock on a blustery English morning, the man she knew as Stephen Meadows seized Charlotte's arm to prevent her from hurrying away from him. "You were gone when I returned to the dining room last evening, and you wouldn't open your cabin door to my knock this morning. Now, damn it, you *will* listen to what I have to say."

21

"I did not intend to be rude, Lord Athmore," Charlotte said quietly. "And I do wish to thank you for your many kindnesses to Eleanor and me on the voyage. I simply felt you would wish to be with your wife during her indisposition."

His blue-green eyes reflected the turbulence of sea and sky, regarding her in silent appraisal for a moment. In the misty rain he seemed, if possible, even more handsome, more tormented. The anguish she had sensed behind those seeking eyes, and his controlled desperation that she had mistakenly interpreted as artistic awareness, had their origins in the tragedy of his marriage. Charlotte felt overwhelming pity for a man shackled forever to a madwoman, but at the same time she felt betrayed. He should have told her about Zoe and warned her what might happen.

As if reading her thoughts, he said, "Zoe can be quite normal for much of the time. It's been months since she had an attack. The episodes are erratic, as is their severity. Sometimes it's no more than an extravagant shopping spree when she buys articles she cannot possibly use. Or she will give incomprehensible orders to servants—to smash all of the crockery, for instance. Once I returned after going up to London on business to find she had had all of one wing of the house painted scarlet—walls, ceilings, furniture—"

Embarrassed, Charlotte held up her hand to stop the recital. "Please, spare me! It's quite improper to reveal such intimate family secrets to anyone, least of all to me."

"I have good reasons for wanting you to know. If my wife had not chosen last evening for one of her lapses, I would have told you then. Charlotte, you're a widow with a young daughter, traveling second class with little in the way of luggage, returning to England after a long absence, and there's no one here to meet you. It doesn't take a great deal of analysis to understand your situation. You are, I take it, going to look for a position in order to support yourself and your daughter?"

"Why do you ask?"

"I want to offer you one. I want you and Eleanor to go to Glendower."

"Glendower?"

"*Glyndŵr*," Stephen said, "to give it the correct Celtic pronunciation. Our estate in North Wales. I had intended to return there also, but in view of my wife's behavior last evening I've decided instead to take her to London to see yet another doctor. I'd hoped that taking Zoe for a holiday in New Orleans, which is where she was born, would perhaps forestall another attack, but obviously I was wrong. Every time I think she is cured, something like last evening will occur, although this was the worst of all. Fortunately, outside the family and servants, no one else has witnessed my wife's lapses.''

Charlotte took Eleanor's hand. ''I really don't think—'' She began to walk again, toward the dwindling line of hansom cabs. Stephen fell into step beside her. ''Charlotte, I realize you must be frightened by what you saw, but I'm not asking that you take care of my wife. You wouldn't even have to live in the main house at Glendower with her during the times we are in residence. The position I'm offering you is that of housekeeper to my uncle. There are plenty of servants to do your bidding, but it's necessary to have a buffer between them and my uncle, who is inclined to bully them. I feel that you would not allow Evan to bully you. For one thing, you're better bred and more educated than anyone else we've found. He's something of a recluse, and doesn't entertain, so the position is not terribly demanding. You'd have a pleasant home for yourself and your daughter, with time for your own pursuits.''

Charlotte glanced toward a waiting cabbie, thoughts tumbling through her mind. Even if they traveled by second-class rail and moved into the cheapest boardinghouse she could find, she had only enough money left to support Eleanor and herself for a few weeks. Could she find another position in that length of time? It would be difficult, especially since she'd have to keep Eleanor with her. The child was too young to be left alone. Charlotte now wished she had followed her first instincts and sailed in steerage aboard the ship, but having crossed to America that way herself she hadn't wanted to subject Eleanor to such discomfort. Still, it would have left more money to tide them over until she found a means of supporting them.

Drawing a deep breath, she said, ''Of course, your uncle might not agree with your choice of housekeeper, but I am willing to go to North Wales to be interviewed.''

On the long journey from Southampton to North Wales, which entailed many changes of train and waits in dreary stations, Charlotte had time to feel apprehensive. She wondered why Stephen had asked so little about her background and qualifications for the position of housekeeper. Though the position was evidently secondary to the main housekeeper, as it was for a relative who occupied a guest-house on the estate, Charlotte nevertheless felt that Stephen's disinterest was strange.

From her childhood in the vicarage, with several wealthy family estates in the parish, Charlotte was familiar with country house life. She knew that vast houses involved large numbers of servants. Surrounded by parklike grounds filled with herds of deer, woods stocked with pheasant, and stables with horses, most country houses had a constant stream of guests. Usually, these estates were self-sufficient, baking their own bread, brewing their own ale, and washing their own laundry. They had their own craftsmen for repair and maintenance and for making anything needed for the house and grounds. Behind the luxurious way of life of family and guests there existed a subculture of those who made it all run smoothly. This was the realm of kitchen, butler's pantry, dairy, brewhouse, workshops, sawpits, coach house, harness room and maids' closets. Most wealthy families never came into contact with the majority of their servants. They issued orders to either their butler or housekeeper, who were like captains of great ships.

Since Charlotte had been employed only as children's nanny, she did not have the experience to run a great house. After her first impulsive statement that she would go to meet Stephen's uncle at Glendower, she had informed Stephen of her lack of qualifications, without mentioning her former position.

He had assured her that a very able butler took care of the estate, in addition to a housekeeper for the main house, and that he was sure Charlotte would be comfortable in his uncle's smaller house. That her life as the wife of a Bostonian was all the experience she needed. Eleanor, sensitive child that she was, had said nothing to dispute what little Charlotte was forced to divulge about her former life.

They were both exhausted, despite the fact that they'd broken the journey and spent the night at an inn near Chester, when at last they arrived at the tiny railway station in the Welsh town of Llanrys.

Alighting from the train, Charlotte caught her breath at the beauty of the Welsh mountains rising majestically around them, jagged peaks piercing a clear blue sky.

"Look, Charlotte," Eleanor said. "We're the only ones who got off the train. That carriage must be waiting for us."

Charlotte dragged her gaze reluctantly from the wild and wonderfully untamed vistas that surrounded what was little more than a village of stone cottages, chapels and small shops, to glance at an ornate brougham harnessed to a fine pair of horses. "I don't think so, dear. The carriage is on the other side of the railway lines, which means they're either boarding or meeting a train coming from the opposite direction. Lord Athmore suggested we ask the stationmaster to find someone to drive us out to Glendower. There wasn't time to send word that we were coming."

She patted her valise, as though to reassure herself that the letter of introduction Stephen had written to his uncle was still there. She continued to think of him as Stephen, and had to remind herself that should she accept this position, she must forget that he had allowed her the liberty of addressing him as anything but Lord Athmore.

As they walked toward the stationmaster's office, Charlotte saw the driver of the brougham lift a trunk and several bags down to the platform, then help a young woman to alight. She was dark as a gypsy and looked frightened.

The stationmaster came out to greet them in his lilting Welsh accent and when Charlotte explained she needed to be taken to Glendower, he exclaimed, "Well, there's lucky that you are, madam. For that's a Glendower carriage on the opposite platform bringing the Spanish lady to catch her train." He waved excitedly to the driver of the brougham. "I've a couple of passengers for you, Owain *bach,* for the return trip."

The driver, a swarthy young man, called back in Welsh, to which the stationmaster responded in the same language.

"It's all arranged, look you. Davies will take you back with him. Soon as he's put the Spanish lady on her train. You can sit on the bench here and enjoy the sunshine. You won't have to wait long."

Charlotte sat down and Eleanor nestled into her side. On the opposite platform the departing woman paced restlessly, glancing frequently down the line to see if the train was coming. She must be the departing Francesca, mentioned briefly by Stephen when he took Charlotte and Eleanor to the railway station in Southampton. The woman looked too young and pretty to be a housekeeper, but if she were indeed Francesca, then according to Stephen she had been prevailed upon to stay until he and Zoe returned from America. Had they not gone to London, they would have arrived today. It was curious that Francesca was departing before they returned. She must be very anxious to leave.

The grinding of wheels on track and the hiss of steam announced the arrival of her train. The opposite platform disappeared from view as the train came to a halt. The stop was brief. A whistle blew, there was another burst of steam, and the train moved out. Francesca and her luggage were gone, and belatedly, Charlotte realized that she'd missed an opportunity to ask about the Athmore family. But perhaps it would have been bad manners to do so.

"Davies will be across to get you," the stationmaster said, from somewhere behind her. "He'll just trot up to the bridge. My now, there's a pretty little girl you håve, madam. Will she be staying at *Glyndŵr* with you?"

Charlotte nodded wearily.

"Well then, I hope you'll find everything up at the house to your liking."

Despite his melodic, singsong voice, something in his tone suggested he thought it was highly unlikely that everything would be to their liking.

The Athmores' driver loaded their baggage, which was considerably less than that of the departing Francesca, and helped Charlotte into the carriage. The young man, who had what to Charlotte seemed a rather brooding Celtic manner, regarded her silently for a moment after she was seated. "There's another train in an hour. It will be the last of the day. Why don't you get on it?"

Unsure she had heard correctly, Charlotte said, "I beg your pardon?"

"I don't want to be the one to take a poor widow and her daughter to work for that beast. I'll wager Lord Athmore never told you what to expect of his Uncle Evan did he?"

Outraged·at his insolence, not to mention his disloyalty to his employers, Charlotte drew herself up stiffly. "Kindly take us to Glendower, and spare us any further comments."

Still the young man hesitated, one hand on the carriage door. "There's a little village with an inn, a couple of miles from Glendower. I'll take you there. Stay at the inn tonight. Ask the people there about Evan Athmore."

"You will either drive us to Glendower, or we shall leave your carriage and find another," Charlotte said coldly.

He slammed the door and climbed onto the driver's seat.

The little town of Llanrys was quickly left behind and the

carriage rolled along steep and winding lanes that cut through a dense forest, crossed nearly barren moors, went through a tiny village consisting of a few cottages, a chapel, a general shop and an inn, and came at length to a bridge over a rushing river.

Soon after crossing the river Charlotte noticed a change in the scenery. It became tamer, like a rather large and untidy garden that was loved but sometimes neglected by its keepers. A deer darted across a meadow, and she saw the iridescent flash of a pheasant's wings in a copse of trees. They were now on the Athmore estate, she was sure.

As if in confirmation of the thought, they rounded a bend in the lane and the house came into view. Charlotte was at once impressed by the sheer sprawling size of the structure, and disappointed that it conformed to no known architectural style. A portion of the roof, in the center of the house, was at odds with the rest of the building, suggesting that the original house had been added to, perhaps several times, in order to achieve its present size. There was no courtyard, nor did the gravel driveway reach the house. Instead, it ended abruptly at the edge of a steeply inclined lawn, suggesting that visitors were not welcome.

She had not realized they had been climbing so steeply until she saw that the house overlooked a verdant valley enclosing a shimmering lake.

Davies stopped the carriage, jumped down and opened her door. He offered his hand and she stepped down onto the springy turf. "Front door's over there." His head jerked back toward the center of the house. "I'll take your bags around to the tradesmen's entrance."

"Wait," Charlotte said. "I don't think we should go to the main house. How do we get to the residence of Lord Athmore's uncle?"

"I wasn't told to bring him a new housekeeper and I'm not about to do so without his permission, look you. You go see Whitcombe, the butler. He'll tell you what to do."

He lifted Eleanor down beside her, jumped back onto the carriage and was gone before Charlotte could protest.

The child glanced at the house and whispered, "I'm frightened, Charlotte. Please, let's go home now."

Stifling her own apprehension, Charlotte gripped Eleanor's hand. "There's nothing to be afraid of. We shan't stay if we don't feel comfortable. But we've come too far to turn back now."

They walked across the lawn, which was even wider and more sloping than it had at first appeared. The front doors were set in the center of a stone terrace reached by means of half a dozen steps. The minutes seemed endless between the time Charlotte rang the bell and the doors opened.

"Mr. Whitcombe?" Charlotte asked of a tall, bony man dressed in a black morning suit. "I am Mrs. Danforth and this is my daughter, Eleanor. I have a letter of introduction from Lord Athmore."

The butler nodded and held the door wider for them to enter. He didn't seem surprised by her unexpected arrival. "If you'll wait in the library, madam, I'll fetch Mrs. Carmichael, our housekeeper."

They waited in a well-stocked but somewhat gloomy library for half an hour. Eleanor refused to let go of Charlotte's hand, and both of them jumped when the door finally opened. The woman who came into the room carried herself well and moved briskly, despite her fifty or so years. She wore a chocolate-colored bombazine dress with a froth of ecru lace on the bodice, and her silver hair was elaborately coiffed. Her eyes, however, were small and cunning, and her expression showed no sign of welcome.

"I have read Lord Athmore's letter and sent it over to Mr. Evan. He's just sent word that I'm to take you both to the grange. Follow me, please."

They followed her across a magnificent entry hall, along vaulted corridors to a door that led to an inner courtyard. On the far side of the cobbled yard stood a somewhat smaller house, almost hidden behind several aged oaks.

Mrs. Carmichael said, "Go on. He's expecting you."

Since she obviously did not intend to accompany them further, Charlotte led Eleanor across the courtyard. A young housemaid stood at the door of the grange, smiling nervously. "Mrs. Danforth? This way, if you please."

Inside the house, Charlotte was first struck by the tremendous height of the ceilings, and secondly by the fact that the doors leading from the entry hall were all twice the size of ordinary doors. The housemaid knocked timidly on one of these colossal portals, and a deep voice from within called, "Come in."

The maid whispered to Charlotte, "Go in by yourself. I'll take the little girl to the kitchen with me. It will be better for her."

Charlotte was about to argue when the voice inside the room bellowed, "Where the hell are you, woman?"

Handing Eleanor over to the maid, Charlotte drew a deep breath and went into the room.

Nothing registered in her numbed brain except the man who sat in an enormous wooden armchair in front of the fireplace. Even seated, he towered over Charlotte's diminutive frame. From the size of his powerfully built torso and the length of his legs, she estimated he must be well over seven feet tall.

4

EVAN ATHMORE WAS not a monster. His features could even be described as pleasing, despite a heavy jawbone, ferocious steel-blue eyes, and a tendency to scowl. His body was muscular, arms and legs well proportioned, and only his hands and feet seemed slightly larger than necessary, even to go with that massive frame. Despite their size, his hands were as beautifully shaped as those of his artistic nephew. Still, it was instantly obvious to Charlotte why Stephen's uncle was feared by servants and villagers. He was a giant. That was obvious, even though he didn't rise when Charlotte entered the room.

As she stood before him, waiting for him to acknowledge her presence, she recalled one of her teachers answering her questions about *Jack and the Beanstalk* by telling her that legends of giants were based on fact; but she had never met one in the flesh.

He continued to stare at her, and she returned his gaze unflinchingly. At length he said, "Mrs. Danforth." His voice was deep, booming.

Charlotte cleared her throat. "Lord Athmore."

"You will address me as *Mister* Evan. I understand you have a child. Where is she?"

"There is no reason for my daughter to be present during this interview."

His eyes flashed angrily. "I do not eat small children, Mrs. Danforth, no matter what you might have heard."

"I merely meant, sir, that should we both conclude I would

make a suitable housekeeper, my daughter would be kept out of your way and would pose no problem in regard to my duties.''

He digested this silently for a moment. "What have you heard about me?''

From his tone, his glowering expression, and the way he leaned back in his chair, half-turned away from her, Charlotte was convinced that the outcome of this interview was a foregone conclusion. Therefore, there was no reason either to be intimidated or to avoid telling the truth. She replied quietly, "That you are a bully and a tyrant who cannot keep servants.''

There was a long silence, then he placed his huge hands on the carved wooden arms of his chair and rose to his feet.

Standing, he was at least four or five inches over the seven feet of height she had estimated. Charlotte, at barely five feet one inch, did not even reach to his jacket pockets. She tilted her head to look up at him and didn't move as he took a step closer to her.

Slowly he walked around her, studying her diminutive figure as though it belonged to some rare and previously undiscovered specimen. While still behind her, he spoke suddenly, "Why would you *want* to work for a bully and a tyrant?''

She was glad she hadn't jumped, although she felt as if her nerves were quivering inside her skin. "Your nephew—Lord Athmore—also described to me the beauty of Glendower. Few people are privileged to live in such splendor, and certainly a poor widow with a child could never hope for such accommodations, if indeed an employer were even to allow her to have the child on his premises.'' She paused, and since he didn't respond, she added, "I need a position quite urgently.''

He stepped back in front of her, towering over her like the largest of the great oak trees that guarded his house. "And I need a housekeeper quite urgently. I need one who will not flinch every time I speak to her, or run and hide rather than spend a moment longer than necessary in my presence.''

"If you are asking if I am afraid of you,'' Charlotte replied, "I will answer that I do not know you well enough to have formed an opinion as to your character. I have never paid any heed to hearsay.''

"And what about your daughter? Will she scream in fright when she sees me?''

"Not unless you act in some manner that is frightening.'' Charlotte lowered her head, partly because a cramp had formed in the back of her neck and partly because she wasn't sure how Eleanor would react, since the child had never before been confronted by a giant. But Eleanor was bright, and she would perhaps remember discussing legendary giants after they read *Jack and the Beanstalk,* just as Charlotte and her teacher had.

"Then let us send for your daughter to see," Evan declared, reaching for the bellpull.

"No—wait!" Charlotte said quickly. "I refuse to allow you to test her. It would only be fair for me to go and bring her to you, after first telling her what to expect."

His eyebrows came down over his eyes in the fiercest glare of all. "And what *should* she expect? What will you tell her?"

Raising her head, Charlotte looked him straight in the eye. "That you are much, much taller than ordinary men."

"And that she should pity me for my extraordinary physical size?" he asked quickly.

"Of course not. One reserves pity for a person with a physical handicap."

He gave a small, explosive laugh. "And you think my size *isn't* a handicap? Very well, Mrs. Danforth, you can go and fetch your child, and if she doesn't hide in your skirts at the sight of me, the position is yours."

Charlotte turned to leave and he added, "One other thing. Lord Athmore doesn't spend a great deal of time here. He's too caught up in being Stephen Meadows, famous artist. So if he induced in you a mistaken belief that if you came to Glendower he would continue to romance you, you will be disappointed. He reserves his well-known charm to get what he wants, and what he wanted in your case was a housekeeper to keep me from straying over to the main house because all of my servants have fled."

Feeling the color flood upward over her face, Charlotte didn't turn around, or respond. Evan went on, "In his letter of introduction he stated that you are aware of his wife's malady. I'd warn you also against allowing yourself to dramatize the pity you feel for the cross he apparently bears. Zoe is perhaps the most beautiful woman in Europe, just as she was the belle of her native New Orleans. Never doubt, Mrs. Danforth, that men forgive a great deal if a woman is beautiful."

Charlotte answered in a low tone, "I would not presume to feel pity for Lord Athmore. Nor did he, as you put it, 'romance me.' I believe it was my daughter's beauty that appealed to his artistic eye originally, and later my availability for employment that led him to enlarge upon our acquaintance.''

She felt a prickling sensation down her spine as she left the room.

From the rear of the grange, on the third floor where Charlotte's rooms were situated, she could stand on a small balcony and look out across the valley to the lake that lay like a shining silver cape tossed there by some careless god.

The late afternoon sunlight cast a million sparkling jewels on the water, dappled the trees, and warmed the air like a lover's breath. But Charlotte's gaze never strayed from the man who walked in an endless circle around a gazebo that had been built on the highest elevation of the Glendower grounds in order to take advantage of the view. Stephen had been pacing that same circle for nearly two hours.

He and Zoe had arrived from London the previous day, one week after Charlotte and Eleanor moved into the grange. Charlotte had been informed of this by the grange servants, as Stephen had not yet visited his uncle.

The French window leading from Charlotte's tiny parlor to the balcony opened and Eleanor came bursting out like a small comet, her long, golden hair flying. "Charlotte! Guess what Lizzie told me.''

Wrenching her eyes from the solitary stroller circling the gazebo, Charlotte slipped her arm about Eleanor's shoulders. "And what has our parlor maid and chief gossip revealed now?''

"She said there's going to be a—a *Gymanfa Ganu*. It's a singing festival. She said it will be in Llanrys, and people will come from all over North Wales. She said the big house will be full of guests and there'll be parties and balls for a whole week while the festival lasts.''

Charlotte placed her hands on Eleanor's cheeks, looked down at that earnest, lovely face and read what was in the child's heart. "You've been rather lonely here, haven't you, dear?''

Eleanor shook her head, but her lip trembled slightly. "Will they ask me to recite for them—at the parties? Like I used to for Mother's parties . . . and Grandfather's?''

Charlotte sighed. "I don't think so, dear. But I'll ask Mr. Evan if I can take you to the singing festival in Llanrys. I've heard the *Gymanfas* are wonderful. It seems that every Welsh person sings like an angel. Now why don't you run along and play outside, it's such a lovely afternoon.''

Her heart ached for the little girl as she disappeared through the French window. The trouble was, there were no other children to play with on the estate. Even the gardeners, laborers, and cowmen who occupied a row of tiny cottages on the outer perimeter of the grounds had no children, probably because no one would bring children where they might encounter the terrifying Mr. Evan. Some of the laborers and craftsmen employed at Glendower lived in the tiny village situated a mile or so beyond its periphery. Perhaps they had children, Charlotte thought. She wondered how many villagers threatened their offspring that if they didn't behave they would be given to the giant.

Eleanor, mercifully, had accepted him on sight, after Charlotte's careful explanation that he was simply a man who had grown bigger than other men. He was not a gentle, fumbling giant, an object of mirth, nor a ferocious man-eating one, as portrayed in children's literature. When Charlotte presented the child to him, he had spoken quite gently to her, explaining that she may have the run of the third floor which accommodated the upstairs servants, also the lawns and woods to the rear of the grange. She was not to go near the main house, or even the courtyard that separated the house from the grange. He then dismissed her by adding that he did not expect to find her under his feet. He asked Charlotte whether she intended to send the child to the village school; she replied that she would tutor Eleanor herself.

Turning to look out at the gazebo again, Charlotte was disappointed to see that Stephen had disappeared. A moment later, Eleanor appeared on the lawn below. The child walked slowly, shoulders slumped disconsolately, dragging her feet. Charlotte felt her heart turn over. Eleanor had been so brave and uncomplaining and had entered wholeheartedly into the masquerade of being her nanny's daughter. But was she, Charlotte wondered, expecting too much of a nine year old? Eleanor had begun having nightmares, shortly after her parents departed for New Mexico. The nightmares still continued, and Charlotte was sure they were caused by Yarborough's abuse.

The first thing Charlotte had done upon establishing herself at Glendower was to write to Eleanor's mother in Silver City, New Mexico, telling her where the child was and why. Given the length of time involved for letters to travel so many thousand miles, by sea and overland, it could be months before they could hope for a reply. In the meantime, all Charlotte could do was care for the child and protect her. Charlotte didn't dare think about having to give up the little girl, or what the consequences of her actions would be. A prison term? Worse?

In the periphery of her vision, Charlotte caught a flash of movement. A horseman came cantering from the direction of the woods, cutting across the lawn directly toward Eleanor.

Charlotte caught her breath, knowing that to scream a warning would be useless, since Eleanor would not be able to hear it from this distance.

The horse was reined, perilously close to the child in Charlotte's opinion, although perhaps the rolling lawn distorted her perception of the distance. As the rider jumped down, grabbing the reins to lead the horse, Eleanor straightened up, then she bounded over to the young man with obvious joy.

Frowning, Charlotte now recognized the young groom, Davies, who had taken Francesca to the railway station and brought the two of them to Glendower that first day.

Owain Davies was only eighteen years old, but there were times when he felt he had lived a hundred years. Born the third son of a collier in South Wales, he had watched his father die of the black lung and a year later his two older brothers perished in a cave-in. His mother had kept a vigil at the pithead for three long days in an icy rain, while the miners attempted to reach their trapped comrades. A week later, she succumbed to pneumonia, and Owain, at age thirteen, was alone in the world.

After her funeral he went to the pit, where he'd worked for three years. He looked at the dirty slag heaps, the pall of smoke hanging over stanchions and girders. The pulley wheels turned and the steel cage carrying its miserable cargo dropped into the bowels of the earth. Those men would not see the sun, for it had not yet risen, and would be long set before they were hauled back up to the surface. They would spend this and every other day in that dark hell below.

Owain, like the other boys his age, and the smallest of the men, would spend his shift lying on his back along a narrow ledge, hacking coal from the face above. Dust and grit would invade every part of his body, but worse was the constant menace of that slimy black roof, sweating like a demon, just waiting to swoop down and crush the life out of him. There were a million tons of shale and stone and clay over his head, and fear in his belly. The pit had taken his father and brothers and, indirectly, his mother. Owain threw down his pick and turned his back on it.

He walked for six days until he found a farmer willing to take him on as a stableboy, in return for his keep. Owain knew little about horses, but he'd always been drawn to the pit ponies, and felt a special compassion for the ones blind from years below ground. He slept in the stable, worked sixteen hours a day and was beaten by his master when he did something wrong, but he learned a great deal about horses. He also became an expert rider and, by the time he was sixteen, proficient at handling a carriage and team.

One day as he was taking the farmer's favorite stallion to the blacksmith, Owain saw a carriage hurtling down the lane toward him at reckless speed. As he drew closer he saw that the eyes of the horses were wide, their ears laid back, manes flying, and there was froth on their mouths. They were bolting; the carriage behind them rocking alarmingly. It would surely overturn on the next bend and perhaps plunge over the edge of the lane to a gully some thirty feet below.

As the carriage reached him, Owain turned his mount and plunged alongside the bolting team, grabbing for the dangling reins. He managed to halt them just before the bend in the lane, and then saw that their driver was slumped in his seat, immobilized with fear. As Owain talked soothingly to the frightened horses, loosening their bits and gently stroking sweating flanks, a deep booming voice came from inside the closed carriage. "I am indebted to you, young sir. A fox darted across their path and they bolted. They were too much for my poor old coachman to handle."

Owain watched in incredulous disbelief as a great giant of a man emerged from inside the carriage. He offered his hand and Owain's fingers disappeared into an enormous grip. The giant surveyed him for what seemed an eternity, then asked, "Are you intimidated by my size?"

"No, sir. I'm impressed by it," Owain said, truthfully.

"Then let's go on to the village and have a tankard of ale. I hate to go to strange places alone."

Before the day was over Owain had been offered, and had accepted a job as groomsman on the Glendower estate in North Wales. It was a grand opportunity to care for fine riding horses and show horses and racers, instead of the plow horses of the farmer. Owain had been riding the only horse on the farm capable of catching up with runaways.

A month later he presented himself at Glendower. Within two years he had risen to head groom, answerable only to the stablemaster. His only disappointment was that Mr. Evan had not proved to be a man to look up to figuratively as well as physically. Owain had taken a score of terrified women to the railway station in Llanrys and had heard enough stories of the giant's murderous rages to take care to keep out of his way. Not that Mr. Evan ever left the grange nowadays. That trip south had evidently been his last venture out into the world. Owain remembered very well the reception he'd received at the local inn. Everyone cowering away from him and regarding him with frightened stares until eventually the innkeeper had haltingly requested that they leave because he was losing business.

Most distasteful of all to Owain, who had an inbred quixotic attitude toward women, were the rumors that many of Mr. Evan's female servants and especially the housekeepers found by Lord Athmore for his uncle, had departed because of his amorous advances. It was even whispered that a couple of them had been in the family way when they left.

He'd tried to warn Mrs. Danforth, and when she refused to listen, he'd hoped that she was too plain to inspire lust in her employer. Certainly she was nothing like the exotic Francesca or any of the other lovelies Lord Athmore had brought to the estate, often to serve the double purpose of posing as models for the portraits he painted. Perhaps at last his lordship was learning some sense in regard to the women he selected to be his uncle's housekeepers.

The child Eleanor, pretty as a rose, was mercifully too young for any man's carnal appetite. Such a lonely little thing. A couple of days earlier the child had wandered down to the stables wistfully looking for a way to pass the hours, and, feeling sorry for her, he'd shown her the horses. The gossipy Lizzie had informed him that she'd heard the child sobbing in her sleep every night since they arrived.

This was the reason that on this particular afternoon Owain sought out the child. "Ellie, *bach*," he called to her. "Look, this is the gentle mare I showed you the other day. Would you like to sit up on her back and I'll walk you down to the copse?"

"Oh, yes, please, Owain. I've forgotten her name."

"We call her Dreamer, because that's what she is, look you."
He lifted the child onto the unsaddled mare. "Just grab her mane
and hold on. We shan't go fast."

Eleanor regarded him with shining eyes and did as she was
told.

He led the mare carefully, one eye on the little girl all the time,
and wondered how long it would be before she trusted him
enough to confide in him. If that great bully were mistreating her,
or scaring her in any way . . .

Owain had never spent much time with children, and was
surprised by the feelings of protectiveness he felt toward Eleanor.
Such a formal name for a small girl, so he called her Ellie and
added the Welsh endearment, *bach*.

"You know, Ellie, *bach,* if your mother will agree, I could
teach you to ride Dreamer. We could find a lady's saddle small
enough, I think. I could ask Mr. Friars, the stablemaster, to
speak to her. Would you like that?"

"I would," she said, and the radiant smile on her face nearly
broke his heart.

A moment later, he saw her mother striding determinedly
across the lawn toward them.

"Look Charlotte," Eleanor cried. "I'm on a horse."

Her mother was not a pretty woman, but she had expressive
gray eyes and what they expressed at this moment was love, pride
and fear. She said quietly, "Lift my daughter down, please,
Davies. You had no right to endanger her like this."

"She was in no danger," he said, but immediately lifted
Eleanor from the back of the horse. Charlotte seized the child's
hand and marched off with her.

Owain watched them go, wondering if she would complain to
Mr. Friars, or worse, to Mr. Evan. He wondered, too, about the
subtle differences in the way mother and daughter spoke, their
accents not quite matching, and asked himself what sort of
strange modern fad was it for a child to address a parent by her
first name instead of calling her "mother."

He arrived back at the stables at the same time a footman from
the main house appeared. "Her ladyship wants a horse saddled
and ready at the house in five minutes. She says you're to be
mounted yourself, to accompany her."

Owain handed Dreamer's reins to a waiting stableboy, and,
vaguely uneasy, went to comply with the order. Why did Lady

Athmore choose such an odd time of day for a ride, with long shadows already heralding the evening?

The lovely Zoe, according to the house staff, periodically acted in a very irrational manner, but Whitcombe the butler and Mrs. Carmichael the housekeeper guarded their mistress's reputation zealously. Every man and woman on the estate knew it would cost them their job to breathe a word of her malady to any outsider.

There had been a troubling incident when Owain picked them up at the station after their return from America. Her brilliant black eyes had flickered, almost imperceptibly, from his face to his feet and back again. She murmured, "Why, Davies, you've shot up and filled out nicely while we were away. You're quite a young man now, aren't you? Tell me, how many of the village girls do you have waiting for you on lovers' lane on starry nights?"

He had merely touched his forelock respectfully and opened the carriage door for her, but Lord Athmore had given her a reproachful glance and said to him, "Her ladyship is only teasing you, Davies. No comment from you is needed."

Owain's instincts warned him that it would be well for him to keep out of her way as much as possible, in case she was about to go off on another of her tangents. But when she emerged from the house clad in a perfectly tailored black riding habit and he held her horse's head while she placed a dainty booted foot in the stirrup, she appeared to be calm and detached, in the usual manner of the aristocracy. She wanted to ride down to the lake, she said. Ladies didn't ride alone and no doubt her husband was otherwise engaged, so it was natural that Owain, as head groom, would accompany her.

He kept his mount several paces behind hers and tried not to think of the wild stories he'd heard about what the house servants called "her ladyship's fits." Somewhere back in time, before Owain's arrival, it had been suggested belowstairs that Zoe's moods were the direct result of having to put up with her husband's fearsome uncle, that each time she went off the deep end it was because of some evil thing Evan had done that his nephew had managed to cover up. Zoe was popular with both the staff and the villagers, since she frequently handed out small gifts for no reason whatsoever. Besides, it was difficult for anyone, man or woman, not to pay homage to her beauty. But Owain remembered the way Zoe had looked at him upon her return from America, and worried about the message he'd read in her eyes.

Owain had grown to love Glendower. He knew every tree and stream and blade of grass on the estate, loved every one of the horses, got along well with the rest of the staff. He now had his own comfortable room in a cottage he shared with the stablemaster, and thought of it all as his home. He'd already risked losing it because of his compassion for a lonely little girl, and must be careful not to upset the volatile Zoe in any way.

Close to the lake the willows grew in dense profusion, forming a screen that hid the grassy bank from view. The lake was part of the Glendower estate and, except for an occasional poacher, rarely frequented by anyone other than the Athmores or their guests.

Zoe dismounted, snapping her fingers for Owain to follow suit.

Owain took the reins of both horses and prepared to wait, but Zoe said impatiently, "Leave them here. I want to walk by the water and I want you to come with me." She turned and looked at him over her shoulder, lowering her long, black eyelashes slightly and allowing the merest hint of a smile to curve her full lips.

He had seen that look on the faces of girls in the village and in Llanrys, and knew very well what it meant. A knot formed inside him and his throat constricted. His fingers tightened on the reins. "I'd better stay with the horses, Lady Athmore. They might run off."

"Nonsense. Come with me."

"I'm sorry. I don't think it would be proper."

Her face drained of color and her eyes flashed like black mirrors. "Come with me, *at once!*"

He swallowed. "No, milady. I can't be alone with you on foot."

"How dare you disobey me?" She still held her riding crop and, without warning, raised it and struck him across the face.

He swayed slightly, his cheek stinging from the blow, but looked her straight in the eye, knowing full well that a servant's gaze should always be lowered.

"Why you insolent . . ." The pupils of her eyes dilated and he saw that the riding crop in her hand was shaking. She raised it again and this time he put up his arm and deflected the blow.

She screamed, *"Meprisable! Diable!"* and continued to strike him while he took the brunt of her rage on his hands and arms. When at last her anger was spent, she grabbed the reins of her horse and, when Owain bent down to take her foot in his hand to help her mount, kicked him viciously in the groin.

He reeled backward, biting his lip to stifle a cry of pain. Zoe climbed into the saddle and tugged sharply on the reins, startling the horse and causing him to rear up on his hind legs. Owain had to jump aside to avoid being trampled.

Watching through a red haze of anger as she galloped away, Owain silently cursed whatever fates had caused the mistress of Glendower to cast a seductive eye on a lowly groom. No doubt his job was doomed from the moment she noticed he'd grown to manhood. Had he accommodated her lust, she would eventually have tired of him and had him dismissed. His rejection of her advances merely eliminated the waiting for the axe to descend.

As he dejectedly remounted and cantered back toward the house, he realized that instead of worrying about finding another position, or thinking about how much he would miss Glendower, his mind was filled with nagging fear for the little girl, Ellie. What would become of her here if there was no one to watch out for her during Charlotte's long absences when she attended to her housekeeping duties?

5

"STAY!" EVAN THUNDERED, his hand striking the dining table, causing crockery and crystal to rattle.

Charlotte stopped, halfway to the door. "Is there something wrong with your meal, sir?"

"No. I wish you to stay with me while I eat it. Is that asking too much of you?"

"Not at all." She returned to the table and stood with her hands folded in front of her.

He rose, walked around the table and pulled out a chair. When she was seated, he returned to his own mammoth chair at the head of the table. Gesturing with his fork toward a platter of roast beef, he said, "Help yourself."

"Thank you, but I've dined with the servants."

"You're a liar. The servants don't eat until after the beast has been fed."

"I meant that I usually dine with them."

"Tonight you'll dine with me. Wine?"

A memory flickered in the back of her mind, of sparkling wine and Stephen smiling at her at the captain's dinner. "No, thank you."

His knife slashed through a thick slice of roast beef. He glanced across the table at her. "Good. Done just the way I like it, with the blood following the knife."

The huge pile of potatoes and gravy, carrots and parsnips, cabbage, peas, and Yorkshire pudding, began to disappear, along with a great quantity of beef. He paused only to say, "Eat, damn it."

She took a tiny portion of vegetables and the smallest slice of underdone meat she could find, managing to swallow a little of the combined mashed carrots and parsnips.

"Where did you meet him?" Evan asked abruptly.

"Aboard the ship returning to England," Charlotte answered, then immediately realized her mistake, and flushed.

He gave her a knowing glance. "I know where and why you met my nephew. I meant your late husband."

"In America—Boston."

"And how did you come to be there?"

"I'd heard English women were in demand as governesses and nannies. I had been unable to find a suitable position in England."

"So you set off on your own for a new country. That required courage. But perhaps it was merely courage born of desperation? How interesting it is to watch the puny human animal clambering aboard life's merry-go-round, hopping off here, jumping on there, riding a carrousel of bewilderment and never seeming to realize that he—or she—is going nowhere but in a circle. That ultimately we'll all go back to where we came from . . . to oblivion."

Charlotte said, "I don't believe it is where we're going that gives life meaning, but whom we meet and how we change each other's lives. Whether we connect with one another in love and compassion, or contempt and hatred."

He laughed, tilting his head backward as though inviting the gods to join in his mirth. "As I live and breathe! A female Don Quixote! Surely such altruism must be a facade?"

"As your cynicism is a mask to conceal your need for human companionship?" Charlotte asked out of anger at his ridicule, then was appalled that she had done so. All her life she had held back, been "seen and not heard" as her parents had instructed her. How could she be so foolish to challenge the man on whose largess her very existence depended?

Evan stopped laughing and his huge face contorted. "I have never needed anyone, nor shall I ever."

Some heretofore unknown demon goaded her still further. "Then why did you order me to dine with you?"

He flung his cutlery down on the table. "I *invited* you. It was *not* an order. Damn you, don't you realize that if I so desired, a beautiful woman would be seated in your chair, wearing a pretty gown and enough jewels to brighten even this dreary room. There are plenty of comely young things willing to endure the company of the giant when the Athmore wealth is dangled in front of their noses. Go, get out of my sight. Your presence offends me. I asked you only out of pity. What other reason would there be for a man to want to look at a little gray dove of a woman forever clad in somber black?''

Charlotte rose and, unhurried, walked from the room. She felt no resentment for his insult, instinctively recognizing that he had spoken out of pain and loneliness. At least he had not dismissed her permanently. Intuitively she now knew that he would respect her more for refusing to accept his jibes meekly, that if she could find the courage to stand up to him, then she and Eleanor would have a place here for as long as it suited them.

She went belowstairs to await the bell from the dining room summoning her to take the dessert, along with the crackers, cheese, and fruit that would complete Evan's meal. He had decreed that only Charlotte was to wait on him, which suited the other servants very well, since he'd been known to hurl any dish that displeased him at the walls, door, or their retreating backs.

They were already seated about the scrubbed wood table in the kitchen, gossiping and ladling thick vegetable soup into their bowls. Lizzie and two other upstairs maids, Cook, a pair of scullery maids, a footman and Evan's personal valet. Nine of us, Charlotte thought, not to mention the contributions of the main Glendower staff, to care for one man. Yet he would probably gladly change places with any one of us, poor soul.

Lizzie looked up as Charlotte entered the kitchen. "Your little girl is crying again. I heard her when I went up to my room a little while ago."

"Thank you, I'll go to her as soon as I've served the master's dessert." Charlotte sat down, trying not to think about Eleanor crying alone in her bed.

"It's on account of young Owain Davies," Lizzie volunteered. "He's been given notice to leave at the end of the week."

"Who goes or who stays at Glendower has nothing to do with my daughter, nor with any of us," Charlotte responded, secretly relieved at the news. There was something about the young groom that worried her. It was more than his wild Celtic good looks. There was a look in his fierce, dark eyes that reminded her of an animal in a cage, not yet tamed, watching for an opportunity to devour its captors.

Strangely, tonight the bell demanding dessert did not ring. Charlotte had Cook keep the suet pudding and custard hot for nearly two hours before they concluded Mr. Evan did not want anything further. By the time Charlotte tiptoed into Eleanor's bedroom, the child was asleep.

Charlotte entered Evan's bedroom just as Lizzie finished smoothing the plain burgundy-colored quilt on the oversize four-poster bed. The room was as austerely furnished as the rest of the grange, with a few simple pieces of gargantuan size. The windows were uncurtained and the wood floors bare. The only decoration, if it could be called such, was that one incongruous item, roughly nailed to the wood paneled wall behind the bed.

"I was hoping to catch you in here," Charlotte said. "I wondered if we could take down the leopard skin. It's very dusty and the nails have rusted and are splitting the paneling."

Lizzie's eyes flew wide open. "Oh, no, look you! It would be more than our lives are worth to touch that old hide."

"Surely we could at least have it cleaned and properly mounted, then rehung?"

"No, Mrs. Danforth," Lizzie said firmly, picking up the soiled bed linen and backing out of the room. "Mr. Evan said we're never to touch it."

Charlotte decided to mention the leopard skin when she served Evan's lunch. Clearing her throat, she began, "I noticed that the . . . trophy on the wall in your bedroom needs cleaning—"

"Leave it alone. Exactly the way I nailed it up there."

"But—"

"Did you hear me?"

"It will rot if it isn't cleaned."

He looked her directly in the eye. "I hope it does rot. It's all I have to remind me of a time and a place and some people in my life who taught me a valuable lesson, about life, about myself. While that skin hangs there I won't make the same mistakes again."

Puzzled, Charlotte stood aside as he rose abruptly and left the room, his food untouched. Minutes later she heard the front door slam.

She was in the kitchen discussing his evening meal with Cook when Eleanor came running in. The little girl wore a puzzled, close-to-tears look that caught Charlotte's attention instantly. "What is it, Eleanor, what's wrong?"

The child flew into her outstretched arms. "I don't know, Charlotte. He just made me feel so sad . . ."

"Sad? Who made you feel sad?"

"Mr. Evan."

"Darling, you were supposed to stay out of his way."

"I know. But we didn't think he'd come to that old tree behind the big barn. He just walked by and stopped and he was looking at me in this . . . sad way, as if it hurt him to watch me swing."

"Swing?"

"Owain made a swing for me and hung it from the tree branch and I can swing ever so high."

"And Mr. Evan found the swing and was angry about it?"

"No, not angry, I told you. *Sad*," Eleanor explained patiently. "I don't think he was even looking at me. He was looking at the swing." The little girl sighed. "I don't think I like the swing anymore. Now I feel sad, too."

"But you felt sad before. Because Owain has to leave in a few days. I'm sure you're mistaken about Mr. Evan's feelings, dear. Perhaps he thinks the swing should be placed in a more secluded place."

Eleanor shook her head. "I'm going to ask Owain to take it down. It's too awful when a great, big man like Mr. Evan is sad."

Although Charlotte told herself that Eleanor had a vivid imagination, she couldn't help wondering if the swing could possibly have recalled to Evan some unhappy event in his life. He never mentioned it to her or anyone, but then Owain took down the swing that same day.

Lizzie bustled into Charlotte's office adjacent to the kitchen as she was going over the household accounts. "You're wanted over at the main house. At your earliest convenience, the footman said." Lizzie's plump face was animated with curiosity. "What do you think they want?"

"I have no idea," Charlotte answered, closing her ledger. A nervous flutter in her stomach was surely due to apprehension, she told herself, not to the possibility of seeing Stephen again. "My daughter is studying in her room. Will you tell her where I've gone and see that she has lunch, Lizzie?"

"Yes, mum. Is she allowed to go for her riding lesson after lunch?"

"Yes, I suppose so." Charlotte had agreed to allow Owain Davies to give the child lessons. He was leaving tomorrow, so there was no point in distressing the child by forbidding her to see him.

Charlotte walked across the courtyard to the main house through a mellow August sunshine. She went to the tradesmen's entrance and a footman conducted her to a drawing room furnished in delicate pastels. Her heart fluttered as she saw that both Stephen and Zoe awaited her there.

She had not yet been formally presented to Lady Athmore, and as Stephen greeted her and made the introduction, it was difficult for Charlotte to associate the beautifully gowned woman, who sat gracefully upon a Queen Anne sofa, surrounded by marble statuary and a priceless collection of porcelain vases and figurines, with the naked and screaming harridan who had burst into the ship's dining room.

Over the handsome, Italian-marble fireplace hung an enormous full-length painting of Zoe. The artist's rendering—was it Stephen's?—was so vibrant that it created the illusion that she might step down from the gilt frame and join her twin on the pale pink sofa.

Zoe's oval face and perfect features were so flawless, they seemed to belong to some distant goddess. She wore a dramatic jade green gown, decorated with black embroidery and a design of jet beads that glittered darkly, disturbingly similar to her large obsidian eyes, which seemed to gaze right through Charlotte, as though her presence were of no consequence. She said offhandedly, "Ah, here's Mrs. Danforth." Her smile didn't reach her eyes, but she added with a faint degree of graciousness, "My husband's uncle thinks very highly of you. Such a relief to us all to have a competent housekeeper looking after the grange."

"Indeed, yes," Stephen said warmly. "Evan is quite delighted with you."

He certainly hadn't acted delighted, Charlotte thought, but she murmured that she was happy to be of service.

"There are a couple of small matters to take care of, however," Zoe said. "Evan finds your clothes a little drab. My housekeeper's dressmaker will take your measurements and provide you with a suitable wardrobe." She glanced at her husband, as though waiting for him to continue.

Stephen's sad eyes were fixed on Charlotte and he wore a small, enigmatic smile, as though endeavoring to send her some unspoken message. She felt her knees quiver slightly, and she lowered her gaze.

"Darling," Zoe prompted. "Are you forgetting the main purpose for Mrs. Danforth's visit?"

He said, "Your daughter came to see me early this morning."

"Eleanor?" Charlotte asked, startled and confused. Eleanor was usually such an obedient child, and she knew she was not supposed to come to the main house. She must have slipped away while Charlotte was discussing the day's meals with Cook.

"It seems that she's become quite fond of Davies, our head groom," Stephen explained.

"Yes . . ." Charlotte responded uncertainly. "He's been giving her riding lessons. I assumed he had permission. I will, of course, forbid Eleanor to—"

"The child came to plead for Davies to be retained at Glendower. He has been dismissed," Zoe put in impatiently. "He is to leave tomorrow."

Stephen said, "The child meant no disrespect, I'm sure. Please don't be too hard on her, Mrs. Danforth. I personally think it's rather admirable for one so young to risk the adults' wrath on behalf of a friend. And Davies surely had no idea of what she intended to do."

"Nevertheless," Zoe said, "Davies leaves the estate tomorrow. Mrs. Danforth, we would appreciate your explaining to your daughter the position she . . . and you, occupy here."

"I'll do so at once, Lady Athmore."

Stephen looked uncomfortable. He asked, "Is there anything at all you need over at the grange, Mrs. Danforth?"

"Nothing, thank you, sir. We're very comfortable."

"If anything troubles you, please don't hesitate to let us know."

Zoe pulled the bell cord and a moment later Whitcombe, the butler, appeared. She said, "Conduct Mrs. Danforth to Mrs. Carmichael's office. She has an appointment with the dressmaker." To Charlotte she added, "The cost of the dresses will, of course, be deducted from your salary."

Before the door closed behind her, Charlotte heard Zoe say, "Lord, what a skinny little sparrow! So plain, so dowdy. I can't imagine why Evan is so taken with her!"

Charlotte pressed her fingers against a knot of tension between her eyes as she followed the butler to the servants' wing. She spent the next two hours with the Glendower housekeeper and her dressmaker, and when at last she emerged from Mrs. Carmichael's office and started along the corridor toward the tradesmen's door, she was surprised to see that Stephen was waiting for her, alone. Silently he beckoned with his finger to indicate that she was to follow him. He led her back into the family wing, along a vaulted corridor to a door leading to a flight of stairs.

The spiral staircase led to a long attic room with sloping

dormer windows all along one side that opened to a parapet on the roof. The room was filled with canvases in various stages of completion, several easels, and all of the artist's paraphernalia. The smell of oil and turpentine hung in the air and the clear northern light fell on numerous portraits of Zoe, including, to Charlotte's embarrassment, a full-length nude.

It was a moment before Charlotte realized that on one of the easels there was a half-finished picture of herself and Eleanor, posed against the rail of the ship with the ocean in the background.

"Do you like it, so far?" Stephen asked.

Charlotte could not find her voice to speak. He had captured Eleanor's quicksilver glance, her lively smile and the perfection of her features. The face was so realistic she half expected Eleanor to toss her golden curls and laugh out loud. But it was not Eleanor's likeness that astounded Charlotte, it was the way in which he had painted her own face.

Surely he did not see her like that? Since his perception of the child was so true to life, then how could he possibly have seen her own face so enhanced as to be almost unrecognizable, even to its owner? That heavy coil of brown hair was hers, she supposed, and the eyes that regarded the world with a brave and fearless gaze were perhaps a little like hers, but so exaggerated . . . huge gray orbs set off with lustrous lashes and well-defined brows. The forehead was smooth, the chin firm, the mouth composed, yet not forbidding. He had not made the face pretty, yet he had given it a quality more arresting, and perhaps more enduring than mere prettiness.

Charlotte whispered, "I don't know what to say."

"It's not finished, of course. I've a lot of work to do yet. But I think I've captured your faces, don't you?"

She turned to look at him. "Do you really see me . . . like that?"

"Isn't that how you see yourself? It's the expression you present to the world, believe me. My reputation for realism in my portraits is well-known. Does my rendition offend you?"

"Oh, no," she breathed. "Far from it. I'm immensely flattered . . . that you perceive me so. I've always considered my face to have the plainest of features."

His hand fell lightly on her shoulder. "Then you have made the same mistake other people perhaps make when first seeing you. They have certain set standards in their minds by which at first glance they measure the beauty, or lack of it, of another person. Then they forever see that person in that way. An artist never begins his sketch until he has studied his subject for many hours, and then he is often surprised at how wrong his first impressions were. Your face, my dear Charlotte, possesses a serenity that comes from true inner beauty, and more than that, reflects courage, compassion, integrity. Most of all, a quiet strength.''

Her shoulder burned under his touch. He had again addressed her as *Charlotte*. She was afraid to turn and look at him, in case he saw the happiness in her eyes. When she spoke, her voice was low, shaking with emotion. ''Thank you. I . . . can't believe that is my face on your canvas, yet with all my heart I want it to be.''

Smiling, he placed his forefinger under her chin and turned her face toward him. ''I have not begun to do you justice, believe me. That morning on the dock in Southampton, when I thought I should never see you again, I had such feelings of opportunity lost as I cannot describe.''

Her heart thudding against her ribs, Charlotte stepped backward, away from his touch, from the heat radiated by his nearness. To cover the utmost confusion she felt, she turned her back to study a portrait of Zoe, propped against the wall. ''I feel so foolish that I spent hours with you aboard the ship and did not know you were such a famous and talented artist.''

He moved to her side. ''Not really famous, alas. It seems to be the curse of the artist that he acquires true fame only after his death.'' He paused. ''Charlotte, those companionable hours we spent at sea were very precious to me. How can I tell you what it meant to me to be with a quiet woman?''

''Oh, please, Lord Athmore!'' Charlotte couldn't look at him. ''I don't know how to respond to such a remark.''

''There's no need to. Tell me only that you forgive me for not warning you about my uncle.''

Charlotte could not help smiling. ''It would perhaps have been less intimidating had I known in advance of his rather awe-inspiring stature.''

''Oh, his height is probably less of a problem than his temperament. I hear he's yet to send you fleeing to your room in tears, and for that I admire you tremendously. I suppose you've heard by now about all of his previous housekeepers?''

''I never listen to gossip.''

''Then you plan to stay? I'm so glad.''

His eyes seemed to caress her, and she felt a swimming

sensation, as though she were floating in the depths of a misty lake. It was a moment before she realized that she was lost in Stephen's blue-green eyes. She said quickly, "I must return to the grange."

He was at once businesslike, the hint of romantic longing disappearing from his tone. "I need you and Eleanor to pose for me again. As you can see, although I've succeeded in capturing your faces on canvas, I need bodies to go with them. I'll speak with my uncle when he joins us for dinner tomorrow night, but I wanted first to be sure it would be acceptable to you."

"Yes, of course. We'd be delighted. Lord Athmore—"

He smiled sadly. "When we are alone, would you address me as Stephen? It would remind me of our happy hours together, when we were in limbo—having left one shore and not yet reached the other."

"Stephen." His name fell from her lips like a prayer. Confused by the intensity of her feelings, for a second or two she forgot what it was she had been going to ask him. Then she remembered the main reason she had been summoned to the house. "I wondered . . . about Owain Davies. He isn't being dismissed because he befriended Eleanor? Because of the riding lessons?"

His eyes clouded. "No. He's being sent away because he insulted Lady Athmore. He's always been a diamond in the rough. Far too outspoken and arrogant for a servant. We only put up with him because he was Evan's protégé."

The instant Charlotte entered the grange, which seemed empty and bereft as a tomb after the luxuriously furnished main house, she heard Evan's voice booming from the direction of his study on the ground floor. "I don't give a damn what Lord Athmore said. I hired you and I'll be the one to dismiss you. You can have a room in the servants' quarters here at the grange."

Pausing, Charlotte wondered if she could walk past the open study door without being seen. Then she heard Owain Davies's lilting Welsh accent reply, "I think you should know, Mr. Evan, that I tried to talk your new housekeeper out of coming here. I felt the grange was no place for a lady like her, or a little girl."

There was a pause. "Why are you telling me this?"

"So you'd know my opinion of you."

Evan's booming laugh rang out. "I've known that for some time. Doesn't change my opinion of you."

"But, sir—"

"No buts. I'll speak with my nephew later. Go now and fetch your things. As soon as Mrs. Danforth returns, I'll speak with her about finding a room for you."

Charlotte started to cross the entry hall and at the same time the study door swung wider and the two men appeared. Although Owain was fairly tall by ordinary standards, he appeared short and slightly built beside Evan. "Ah, there you are, Mrs. Danforth. Would you come in here for a moment?"

Owain nodded to her as he went by, and Charlotte followed Evan back into the study. The room, like all of the others in the grange, was massive in proportion, but sparsely furnished. There were no figurines or statuary or ornaments of any kind. The walls were bare and the wooden shutters at the windows were not softened by curtains. She had already learned that he could not abide clutter in any form.

He sat down immediately. Charlotte was beginning to realize that this was a form of courtesy on his part, since she then did not have to strain her neck by looking up at him. "Davies is moving into the grange. There's an empty room next to that young footman's, isn't there? See to it, will you?"

"He will be staying here permanently?" Charlotte asked, although she already knew the answer.

"Yes."

"Will that be all, sir?"

"When will your new wardrobe be ready?"

"The dressmaker says she hopes to have something ready before the guests arrive for the *Gymanfa Ganu.*"

"Good. No black dresses, mind. Now, I'll tell you about your daughter. She climbed the beanstalk and bearded the giant in his lair."

Charlotte blinked. "I beg your pardon, sir?"

"It was Eleanor who informed me that young Owain Davies had been sacked. I admire the child's courage. You may inform her that I'll never allow Lord Athmore to send her friend away."

She didn't doubt him but couldn't help wondering about the relationship between Evan and his nephew that permitted him to dictate the affairs of the estate. After all, the title, lands, and wealth belonged to Stephen, by right of inheritance from his father, who had been a firstborn son, just as Stephen was. According to Lizzie, prior to the present Lord Athmore, the men of the family had spent little time on the estate, having been soldiers and empire builders. In fact, no one in the village had even been aware of Evan's birth, which had taken place abroad, or of his affliction, until the estate passed into Stephen's hands and he brought Evan to live there. Evan was Stephen's father's younger brother, only eight or nine years older than Stephen, having been born to his grandfather late in life.

Evan was peering at her with an intense and probing gaze. "You look flushed, excited. What happened over at the house? Did Stephen look at you with those melancholy eyes of his and manage to convey his unspoken longing for you?"

"There is no need to taunt me in such a manner," Charlotte replied with as much dignity as she could muster. "I assure you I have no delusions about my place here."

He leaned forward. "Let me tell you about Stephen and Zoe. Just so your eyes will be wide open before you stumble into anything."

"I shan't stumble, as you put it, into anything."

"Stephen and Zoe," Evan mused, as though she hadn't spoken. "Zoe and Stephen . . . Think of them as climbers on the sheer face of a mountain, roped together. If one falls, they are both lost."

Zoe raised her hands and unfastened the combs holding her hair, which cascaded like a dark waterfall about her shoulders. She wore a silk kimono of brilliant scarlet, and the feel of the material against her bare skin caused a tingling of her breasts as she leaned closer to her dressing table mirror to outline her eyes with kohl, making them appear even larger. She dipped her finger into a small pot of cochineal and dabbed her lips, then reached for a cut crystal perfume bottle.

Crossing the polished oak floor of her bedroom, she hesitated for a moment before opening the connecting door to her husband's room.

He was standing in the window alcove, his back to her, staring out across the courtyard that separated the main house from the grange. Zoe felt a familiar stab of resentment. She said, "He should have been drowned at birth, like an unwanted puppy. A great, big, monstrous hound puppy. Damn him, damn him to hell!"

Stephen spun around, too quickly to replace the tortured look on his face with the seductive smile she expected her appearance to elicit. He said, "Please, let's not talk about Evan tonight. Come here, I need to hold you."

He extended his arms and she went into them, laying her face against the cool, smooth satin of the lapel of his smoking jacket. He stroked her hair and pressed his lips to her forehead. Zoe whispered, "Send him away. Before the guests arrive for the *Gymanfa*. He could go to the London house. Better still, the villa in Florence."

"I can't do that. He hasn't left Glendower for years."

She pulled away. "He'll spoil it for all of us. No one knows how to behave—he terrifies everyone. All of our parties will be ruined . . . Oh, God, what if he wants to come to the ball again, like he did two years ago? Stephen, if you love me, you must ask him to go away. It isn't fair of you to expect me to allow him to ruin our social life. After all, I put up with him at family dinners, like tonight. I can't believe you'd allow him to countermand my orders for Davies's dismissal."

"Zoe, do I have to remind you again who the real master of Glendower is? My God, sometimes I think you've been playing the part of the lady of the manor for so long that you actually believe it."

"Isn't possession nine-tenths of the law? Haven't you spent most of your life here? Haven't you been master of Glendower in practically every sense of the word since your father died?"

From the set of his mouth, she realized she would have to try other tactics. "All right, darling, I won't nag. Come on, let's have our glass of port and I'll massage your neck. You look so tired. You've been working much too hard. Did you finish the picture of the pretty child?"

"Yes. Didn't I mention that I'm painting her mother, too? You must come up to the studio and see it."

"Tomorrow, darling. Then you must clean your brushes and put them away. We're going to be busy with social events." She went to the bedside table and poured port wine from a decanter into the two waiting glasses, then sat on the bed. Extending one leg from the folds of red silk kimono, she patted the satin eiderdown beside her in invitation.

He took a sip of his wine, then sat down on the bed, and she slipped the smoking jacket from his shoulders. Her fingers massaged his shoulders, then kneaded the bare flesh of his back until he sighed and stretched out beside her. There was magic in her touch and she knew it. He fell into an almost hypnotic trance, not dozing, fully aware of her hands and of her long hair brushing his skin as she bent over him, of the subtle whisper of her perfume and the low murmur of her voice.

This was the Zoe he'd fallen madly, passionately, in love with when he'd met her in New Orleans, that first time he'd visited America. He'd been dazzled by her beauty, astonished by her uninhibited lovemaking, stimulated by her witty conversation and quick laughter. She seemed possessed of extraordinary energy, able to do several things at once, while her mind leapt ahead to plan other endeavors. A week after he met her, he asked her to marry him. For six months his life with her had been breathlessly heady, all champagne and hot kisses in the tropical moonlight, music and dancing and the frenzied fusion of two bodies that clamored for one another constantly.

The first ominous signs came on the passage from New Orleans to England. First there were her sleepless nights, when she exhausted him with hours of conversation, pinching him if he drifted off to sleep. Then came her harridan's shriek when a steward displeased her. One evening when Stephen tried to make love to her, she suddenly bit him, drawing blood. She laughed until she became hysterical. The following day he came upon her berating a crewman in gutter French and had to restrain her physically from striking the man. By the time they reached England, she had sunk into a deep depression, refusing to speak at all.

Stephen had put the episode down to homesickness and the change of climate. Oddly enough, after her exhausting manic phase, the sullen depression was such a relief that Stephen found he was artistically inspired as never before. He was able to spend hours at his easel while Zoe posed, somewhat listlessly but without complaint.

A pattern was thus established. They lived at a breathless pace for weeks, months, going everywhere, doing everything—theater, opera, balls, parties, travel, new people, new places, new things; trying to cram every minute with all that life could offer. Then when Zoe's hysterical outbursts, increasingly irrational demands, and sexual appetite that both excited and appalled Stephen—since he feared it was also directed at other men—heralded another plunge into depression and withdrawal, they would retreat to Glendower. Never knowing how long the silent phase would last, Stephen painted with a sense of urgency that created pure lines, clear light, intense shade, and an economy of detail, resulting in a freshness born of swift execution that contrasted with the heavily overworked portraits of his day. Zoe was his taskmaster, his inspiration, his delight, and his torment. Before she came into his life he was a wealthy aristocrat who "dabbled in oils." After he married Zoe, he became an artist.

She suddenly leaned closer and nipped his ear with her sharp teeth. "Don't you dare doze off. I want you to make love to me."

He rolled over onto his back, looked up at her, and feigned a yawn. She picked up a down pillow and beat him with it. He caught her and they wrestled, kissing and laughing, until they were both too aroused to delay making love.

Zoe writhed and thrust her body toward him, moaning and giving sharp little cries of pleasure. Her fingernails clawed his back and her eyes were wide, gleaming. Often she talked while they made love, murmuring words of encouragement and praise, filthy words that no lady should know. Sometimes she even planned their activities, a picnic, a guest list, while still in the heat of passion—as if it were impossible for her to be content with one thing at a time, even the most intimate human bonding. Her body was all his, but he never knew where her mind was.

She was nearing her zenith, convulsive shudders rippling through her body, when she said, "The child Eleanor is not Mrs. Danforth's daughter. I'm sure of it. That woman has never borne a child. I looked at them both very carefully today. I've decided we should adopt the little girl ourselves. I want a daughter of my own. A beautiful, spirited one. I want Eleanor."

6

Owain Davies strode into the grange kitchen, his riding boots tracking mud. "Why is Ellie over at the house again?" he demanded. "She went to church with them yesterday, and her ladyship took her to the village Friday. Why?"

Charlotte had been checking the vegetables brought in from the kitchen garden and she looked up, pointedly fixing her gaze on Owain's cap. He pulled it from his unruly mop of black, curly hair and waited for a reply.

"Not that it's any of your business," Charlotte answered. "But her ladyship is very taken with my daughter. I'm grateful that she deigns to spend so much time with the child, as my duties leave little time for anything other than Eleanor's lessons."

Owain placed his hands on the scrubbed wood table and leaned forward. "Have you no sense at all then? Don't you know Lady Athmore is mad as a hatter? She might harm Ellie."

"*Eleanor,*" Charlotte corrected. "I'm well aware that Lady Athmore is, at times . . . highly strung, but no harm is going to come to Eleanor, not while Lord Athmore is also present."

"There's a fool that you are, Mrs. Danforth. Don't you see what's happening? They want a child of their own, which the good Lord in his wisdom has denied them. So they're after Ellie."

"What nonsense! One might also suspect *your* interest in the child, Davies. It surely goes beyond the bounds of mere regard for the daughter of a fellow servant."

57

Owain flushed slightly. "I know what it means to be small and helpless." He turned and left, slamming the door.

Frowning, Charlotte slipped off her apron and glanced at the clock on the kitchen wall. She was due over at the main house in half an hour for another session in Stephen's studio. She, too, was concerned about Lady Athmore's intense interest in Eleanor, but Stephen had assured Charlotte that he would be present on any excursions. Still, Charlotte couldn't put the spectacle of the screaming, naked Zoe aboard ship out of her mind.

Charlotte went up to her room to change into one of her newly delivered dresses. There were three. A russet-colored bombazine, a pale gray taffeta, and an evening gown of gold satin. She had tried them on the previous evening, parading shyly across their sitting room for Eleanor, who clapped her hands and exclaimed, "Oh, Charlotte, you look *pretty!*"

The surprise in the child's voice was understandable. Charlotte herself couldn't believe how different she looked. She'd had no idea what to expect, since Mrs. Carmichael's dressmaker had merely taken her measurements. Certainly not such fine quality material, nor the fashionable cut. But it was more than that; it was what each dress seemed to accomplish. The russet bombazine cast a warm glow on her brown hair, burnishing it with chestnut highlights. The gray taffeta almost exactly matched her eyes; not only did they seem larger, but also, mysteriously, her cheekbones now seemed more pronounced. But it was the evening gown that wrought the greatest transformation. It was cut to reveal every curve of her slender body in front, drawn back to a flounced bustle which owed its shape to a wire cage beneath the skirt. The décolletage was daringly low, emphasized by an embroidered bodice and nipped-in waist. The weight of the bustle caused Charlotte to stand and walk erect, with her shoulders back, and the narrow skirt shortened her strides, causing her hips, so cleverly outlined by the shape of the dress, to sway slightly as she moved. The effect was quite bewitching, making her feel more feminine than she had ever imagined possible. Further, the gold satin lit up both her hair and her eyes with an inner glow and gilded her rather pale complexion. It was as if she had stepped from the shadows into the sunshine.

There was no doubt in Charlotte's mind that Stephen must have selected patterns, material and, especially, the colors. Only his artist's eye could have foreseen how they would transform her.

That he'd also ordered an evening gown could only mean that she would be invited to one of the forthcoming *Gymanfa Ganu* parties. Her heart sang in the knowledge that he had such high regard for her, although a tiny voice warned that she was probably reading too much into the selection, and in any event, Zoe had said the cost of the dresses would be deducted from her salary.

For this morning's posing session, Charlotte selected the gray taffeta, and, five minutes before she was expected, she stood in Stephen's studio amid the canvases. Neither Stephen nor Eleanor had arrived, so Charlotte went to the long dormer windows to drink in the magnificent view of mountains and lake.

One of the windows was open, admitting a warm summer breeze. Feeling new and different and just a trifle reckless in her rustling taffeta gown, Charlotte impulsively stepped out of the window onto the parapet. It was about four feet wide, with no handrail, but Charlotte had always had a good head for heights.

She enjoyed the way the breeze plucked at her skirts and hair, the feel of the mellow sunshine on her face, and the scent of newly mown grass drifting up from the lawns below. Closing her eyes, she breathed deeply of the fresh mountain air and, almost instantly, heard Stephen's voice.

At first she thought he was speaking from the room behind her, but turning, saw the studio was still empty. Then, distinctly, she heard Zoe's laughter, which had an unnerving, brittle quality, like shattering glass.

They were on the terrace below her, out of sight, but their voices carried clearly up to the roof parapet. "Go then," Zoe said. "You mustn't keep your little model waiting." There was a pause, and then she added scornfully, "You're moved by that virginal look of hers, aren't you, my darling? It is a look I never wore."

Stephen's voice was so low that Charlotte barely heard his reply, "Zoe, my love, were you ever a virgin?"

Charlotte quickly stepped back inside the studio, the day suddenly spoiled. A few minutes later Stephen appeared, leading Eleanor by the hand, and Charlotte realized to her acute embarrassment that the child must have been with them during that enlightening exchange on the terrace.

Stephen's eyes lit up when he saw her. "Charlotte! You look marvelous. A new dress?"

As if he doesn't know, Charlotte thought, nodding and

lowering her eyes. Eleanor ran to her side and said, "Charlotte, guess what? Lady Athmore is going to have some dresses made for me, too, and I'm going to recite for the guests at the *Gymanfa* parties."

"How nice, dear," Charlotte murmured, her stomach lurching. In her headlong dash to save Eleanor from her grandfather and the awful Yarborough, had she unwittingly placed the child in even graver danger?

Charlotte went to her usual position on a velvet upholstered bench, and Eleanor sat beside her. Stephen donned his smock and picked up his palette.

Before he could begin to mix his colors, Zoe burst into the room. Her arrival was so sudden that Charlotte jumped, startled.

"What is it, Zoe?" Stephen asked quietly. Zoe's dark eyes whisked from Charlotte to Stephen and then back again, almost as if she expected to find them in some compromising situation, despite the presence of the child. Charlotte's uneasiness increased.

Unexpectedly, Zoe gave her a dazzling smile. "I just want to borrow Eleanor for a little while so that my dressmaker can take her measurements. The little darling has graciously agreed to recite for my guests next week, and she must have a suitable dress. You won't need Eleanor for an hour or so, will you, dear?"

"No . . ." Stephen said slowly, "I can get along without her for a little while." He gave Charlotte an apologetic, helpless glance, as if to say, "How can we refuse?"

Eleanor, delighted to avoid the chore of sitting for the portrait, scampered across the studio and trustingly placed her hand in Zoe's.

After the door closed behind them, Stephen said, "She'll be with the dressmaker . . . please don't worry."

Charlotte had risen, as though to go after them, and he stepped forward and caught her hands in his. "Zoe is enchanted by her. Please don't worry. She won't harm the child."

"Your wife . . . is she mentally unbalanced? Surely the incident aboard ship—"

"No! No, that was the absolute worst thing she ever did, and you have every right to be concerned about it. But I believe it occurred because of a combination of too much champagne, her *mal de mer*—she's a poor sailor—and her sorrow at leaving behind her beloved New Orleans. Zoe is subject to extremes of mood, but aren't we all, to varying degrees? We have our calm moments and our rages, our little excitements and deep disappointments. We're happy and then we're sad.''

Zoe's extremes, Charlotte thought, were surely too acute to be normal, but she reassured herself that there could be little harm in her taking Eleanor to her dressmaker. Charlotte herself was too much aware of Stephen's hands holding her own to offer any coherent argument.

Awkwardly, she withdrew her hands and sat down again. Stephen smiled. "Good girl. If Eleanor isn't back in a little while, I'll go and bring her. I really need to concentrate on you today, anyway, now that you're wearing something other than funeral black.''

He adjusted his easel, selected a brush, and studied her intently. Then he put down the brush and walked over to her. "Tilt your head a little more, hands . . . so. Your knees a little to the left.''

Why did his touch inflame her senses so? She clenched her teeth to keep from trembling when he touched her knees through the layers of skirts and petticoats.

Did it seem that today he touched her more frequently? A few strokes of the brush, then back to rearrange a hand, smooth her hair back from her forehead, press a tiny crease from her sleeve. Once he even brushed her upper lip lightly with his forefinger, feeling its shape and texture. She held her breath, not looking into his eyes. Did she hear the faint hint of a sigh before he returned to his easel, or was it the rushing of air as she painfully resumed breathing?

He worked in silence for a while, then stopped with an exasperated exclamation. "It's no good. I don't like it.'' Again his brush was dropped into a jar of turpentine and he came around the easel to where she sat. His expression was preoccupied as he stared at the demure lace collar of her dress.

Before she realized what he was about to do, he unfastened two buttons and pulled the lace collar away from her throat. "I thought so. A fine long column of a neck, and flesh like marble. This dress, pretty though it is, simply won't do. The high collar overwhelms the fragility of your face. We need distance—a frame within a frame, for those features. Do you have something more décolleté?''

Her cheeks burned. He meant the golden evening gown, of course, which he surely knew about, since he must have selected the pattern. Her neck felt curiously vulnerable and she swallowed, wanting desperately to close the buttons. She said stiffly, "Surely the presence of the child in the picture precludes the wearing of a low-cut gown?"

He chuckled and cupped her cheek with his hand. "Charlotte, oh, my sweet Charlotte. You're not afraid of me, are you?"

She shook her head, too confused to speak. Why did he keep touching her like this? He must be aware of the inner turbulence his nearness caused.

"Good. Then you will return tomorrow afternoon with a gown that doesn't smother your neck. If you can't bring yourself to wear it as you cross the courtyard, then carry it and you can change here."

Assuming he was ending the session for the day, and anxious to find Eleanor, Charlotte started to rise. Although his hand fell away from her face, he didn't step aside, and so, standing, she was close enough to feel his breath against her forehead.

"Despite the fact that you have had a husband and a daughter," Stephen said softly, "there is an incredible innocence about you. As if you had somehow managed to remain pure, untouched."

Her heart was hammering wildly. She felt herself leaning toward him, dizzy with longings that had no name, that overwhelmed her. The silence that had fallen between them lengthened, pulsating with energy.

Had not the studio door been flung open at that point, as Zoe returned with Eleanor, Charlotte didn't dare contemplate what might have happened. As it was, she and Stephen sprang guiltily apart. Zoe's dark eyes flashed with angry recognition.

Charlotte awakened to the sound of footsteps on the landing outside her bedroom. She sat up in bed and listened. The footfalls were heavy, and the room seemed to tremble uneasily from the sound.

It was pitch-dark and her first thought was fear for Eleanor, asleep in the next room. Charlotte slipped out of bed and opened her door.

The landing was illuminated by a wall lamp which was left burning all night, and in its faint yellow glow she saw Evan, about to go back down the staircase.

"Sir . . ." she said uncertainly. "Is there something you need?"

He turned, his huge face sinister, threatening, in the shadows. "Yes," he said shortly. "Will you join me down in the library?"

She went back into her room and lit the gas mantle. It was a little past midnight. Hastily she pulled one of her black dresses over her nightgown, slipped her feet into her shoes, and hurried downstairs.

He'd had a fire lit in the library and was filling two glasses with port wine. Jerking his head toward one of the fireside chairs, he said, "Sit down." She did so and he handed her a glass. "Here, this will ward off the chill of the night."

Knowing better than to argue, she took the glass but did not drink. "You wished to speak with me, Mr. Evan?"

He drew his chair closer to her. "You were over at the house today, posing for my nephew." It was a statement rather than a question, so she didn't respond. He went on, "You're no match for them, Charlotte. I'm worried that at least I may lose a good housekeeper and at worst you'll be destroyed by your infatuation. No, spare me your protests. You're blossoming, opening like a rose, a little more with each hour you spend in his company. Despite your travels, your marriage and your child, you are unworldly, sheltered, naive. As I said, no match for him. For either of them. They are sexual gourmands, and they delight in corrupting innocents like you."

Charlotte carefully placed her wineglass on a table beside her chair. "I'm unsure what it is you are attempting to tell me, sir, but let me hasten to say that the portrait Lord Athmore is painting is almost finished. After that there will be no need for me to visit his studio."

Evan leaned back in his chair, his face lost in shadow. As the flames in the fireplace began to die down, the room, lit only by a single lamp turned low, grew darker. "There were other innocents. Women like you who were swept away by his charm, his good looks, his talent, his apparent torment. They consistently misread his relationship with Zoe. I thought you were intelligent enough to realize that they really are well suited to one another. Her vitality is the necessary antidote to his lethargy. Without it, he would be unable to create. He'd wither and die. Don't you see, she *goads* him into being an artistic genius."

"Mr. Evan, I must protest your discussing Lord and Lady Athmore's private affairs with me. I also resent your innuendo concerning my posing for a portrait, with my daughter, I might add."

As though she hadn't spoken, he said, "Don't let him make love to you. For him it will be merely a conquest to enjoy for the moment and then forget. I've observed you carefully the short time you've been with me. For you it will be the surrender of your soul, as well as your body.''

Trembling, she rose to her feet. "Will that be all?"

"Not quite. I understand Zoe has asked your daughter to recite for her guests at the party on Saturday to launch the week of the singing festival in Llanrys.''

"That is so.''

"I'd like you to accompany me to the party.''

For an instant she was too surprised to respond. He said harshly, "Of course, if the idea of going as my guest is distasteful to you, forget about it.''

"I would be most honored to go with you, if you feel it would be proper for me to mingle with Lord and Lady Athmores' guests. I am only a housekeeper, after all.''

"As he is only a painter and she only a Creole courtesan.''

"I beg your pardon?''

"Nothing. I said I shall expect you to be ready to leave for the main house at eight.''

As the footman announced their names and they moved down the receiving line to be presented to the guests of honor—society friends of the Athmores who sponsored the *Gymanfa*—Charlotte was aware that conversation had died and everyone in the banquet hall at Glendower had turned to watch their progress. Angered at this display of bad manners, Charlotte held her head high, looked straight ahead, and kept her gloved hand resting firmly on Evan's forearm.

He looked splendid tonight, in perfectly tailored evening clothes: a god descended to earth, or Gulliver in the land of the midget Lilliputians. Why, oh why, did they stare at him so? He was not deformed, ugly, crippled in any way. He was simply larger than life. Charlotte wanted to leap onto the musicians' dais and soundly chastise the entire assembly.

When they reached the head of the receiving line, Charlotte realized that Stephen and Zoe were staring at her rather than at Evan. Zoe's eyes had narrowed to slits, and she let her gaze drift over Charlotte's gown in undisguised astonishment. Stephen's eyes flickered over the golden gown, and he gave her a smile of surprised approval.

As Evan led her across the marble floor, Charlotte wondered about both the enraged expression on Zoe's face and that surprised smile of Stephen's, which almost seemed to indicate her gown was new to both of them. Charlotte had not returned for another posing session in Stephen's studio, because he'd been called out of town for a few days. Otherwise he would have had a private showing of the gown, a prospect Charlotte had agonized over. It seemed that fate in the form of estate business had stepped in to ensure that he see her wearing the gown for the first time while surrounded by people.

Glancing about her, as this was her first view of the great hall at Glendower, Charlotte saw to her surprise that her golden gown echoed the gilt scrolls on ceiling and walls, the pale amber marble of the floor, and the gilded statues atop Roman columns that flanked the doors and the dais. Gold, amber, white and the silvery gray of the marble columns were the only colors used in the hall. Every sofa and chair faithfully duplicated the scheme, and the effect was almost as if the magnificent hall had been designed as a backdrop for Charlotte in her golden gown.

Evan smiled down at her as he saw her eyes drift to the gilded statues atop the marble columns. "You look like their queen, stepped down to join the mere mortals at their play. There isn't another woman present who moves with such feminine grace, nor captures the heart with such gentle countenance. The others look like overdressed butterflies, gaudy but inconsequential."

Too astonished to respond to such flattery, especially from a man noted more for his diatribes, Charlotte felt herself blush. In her embarrassment she blurted out, "Can those possibly be genuine Roman columns?"

"Oh yes. They were found in the bed of the Tiber. One of the early Athmores brought them to Glendower in the seventeenth century."

Evan selected one of the more substantial sofas lining the walls for Charlotte and himself to sit on, and they sipped champagne as the other guests were seated.

One of the choral groups who would be performing in Llanrys at the *Gymanfa* had been invited to sing for the Glendower guests this evening and, shortly after Evan and Charlotte arrived, the choir took their places on the dais.

"We can leave after the singing, if you like," Evan said. "That's all I really came for."

"I should like to stay and hear Eleanor recite, if you don't mind."

"Of course."

A footman, resplendent in white and gold livery, was passing out beribboned dance cards and programs. Waving aside the dance cards, Evan took a program and studied it, nodding in approval as he read the names of the songs to be performed. "How much do you know about the Welsh singing festivals, Mrs. Danforth?"

Charlotte replied, "I've heard of the Eisteddfods, of course. I understood this year's was to be held in South Wales."

He nodded. "Choirs travel to the Eisteddfod from all over Wales. Our local *Gymanfa Ganu* began originally as a week of rehearsal before the choir went to the Eisteddfod. But as time went by, other choral groups learned of our natural amphitheater in the valley of Llanrys where the chapel choir could raise the roof of heaven itself with their singing, and our little local *Gymanfa* assumed importance in its own right. Nowadays we get choirs traveling considerable distances for our festival."

He paused, his mouth twisting into one of the studiedly sardonic smiles he liked to give. "Naturally, much of the passion of Welsh music has to do with the desire to be free of the yoke of the English. I feel an ancient stirring of the blood myself when they sing *Men of Harlech,* despite the fact that I have little sympathy for the weaklings of the earth who give the English their power."

"You speak as a Welshman yourself, then?" Charlotte asked. It seemed that she was constantly being surprised by this man.

"Born of a Welsh mother in this very house, which stands on a Welsh mountain. I'm more Celtic than English."

"But I thought—"

"That I was born abroad. Most people do, except for those who think I came up from hell itself. My mother died giving birth, and the midwife informed my father that my abnormally large head was the cause of her death, that it indicated I would probably die in infancy of water on the brain. She said that if I lived I'd be an idiot. My father promptly sent me to an institution."

"You were brought up in an orphanage?" Charlotte whispered, aghast.

"Hush. The choir is about to begin singing."

The singing was more inspired, more moving than anything Charlotte had ever heard, despite the fact that she could not understand the Welsh words. Surely such an assemblage of voices, so clear and true, could never have been found in one tiny country like Wales—and this was only one of many choral groups of equal excellence. But Charlotte was unable to lose herself in the music and found herself reflecting more upon the enigmatic giant of a man who sat beside her. He seemed to rein over Glendower like some feudal lord, yet his position in the family was that of a prior generation's younger son with no claim to title or lands.

When the choir departed, Zoe led Eleanor to the center of the dais. Zoe wore a black gown that was a perfect foil for her diamonds, and she had dressed Eleanor in white. They were a study in contrasts: black and white, dark hair and golden curls. Charlotte then added in her mind, *decadence and innocence*. But perhaps that was merely an echo of what Evan had said about Zoe and Stephen. Charlotte was also troubled by Zoe's possessive attitude toward the child, whom she introduced as her "protégée."

Eleanor appeared unaffected by the large audience, and gave a lively rendition of Longfellow's *The Children's Hour*. Afterwards, Zoe again swooped down on the child, something like a voluptuous black vulture, Charlotte thought somewhat uncharitably, and dragged the little girl around the room to present her to the Athmores' friends.

One young man, apparently too impatient to wait for Zoe to reach him, rose, walked over to Eleanor and spoke to her. Charlotte saw the child's eyes light up and she smiled happily.

Evan said, "That's the Drury Lane actor, Tristan Cressey, reputedly the bastard son of a duke. It may or may not have been a coincidence that a certain duke made a substantial gift to the theater when it was in grave financial trouble. According to Zoe, young Tristan is the greatest romantic actor of our age. He doesn't usually perform in the provinces, so it's quite a feather in Zoe's cap to have him come all the way from London. He seems very taken with your daughter."

Charlotte watched the young actor chatting with Zoe and Eleanor. He was an imposing figure, with classically handsome features and moody, dark eyes. An older couple joined the group, a tall, silver-haired gentleman and a younger woman with vivacious features and pretty auburn curls. "Lord and Lady Ramsey," Evan murmured. "He's the third son of the old duke who made the gift to the theater. She's his second wife, Delia. They have a daughter about Eleanor's age, I believe. They're passionately fond of the theater and love to surround themselves with actors. I expect Tristan came with them."

"They could be brothers, then?" Charlotte asked. "Lord Ramsey and Tristan Cressey?"

Evan gave a somewhat ironic smile. "If the rumors are correct, yes. You sound surprised."

"It's just the difference in their ages. Lord Ramsey looks old enough to be Mr. Cressey's father, rather than his brother."

Evan gave her a quick sideways glance. "Some men sire children quite late in life. The old duke was no doubt one of them." A moment later he said, "They'll start the dancing now, and then there'll be a late supper. Shall I retrieve your daughter so we can leave?"

Charlotte was about to agree to this suggestion when Stephen appeared in front of her. He bowed formally. "Where is your dance card, Mrs. Danforth? I must get my name down quickly, before all of your waltzes are taken."

Blushing, she said, "Why, I—"

Evan said dryly, "Mrs. Danforth is saving all of her dances for me. But we can spare you a waltz. The second one."

Smiling, possibly to try to hide the fact that he was dumbfounded, Stephen nodded and moved on to converse with other guests. Charlotte turned to Evan. "I thought we were leaving."

He gave her a sidelong glance. "But how could I possibly deprive you of a dance with your beloved? Even if etiquette demands that you must first dance with me, since I am your escort."

"He's *not* my beloved," Charlotte said, wanting to run. But the musicians were already tuning up and the strains of a Strauss waltz filled the air. Evan rose and bowed to her. "May I?"

She placed her gloved hand in his, held up her skirt with her other hand, and he guided her out onto the floor. Her moment of embarrassment at the disparity in their height was instantly forgotten when it became evident that he was just as accomplished at waltzing as any shorter man, and considerably lighter on his feet than many of the other women's partners.

Long, long ago when she was a very young girl, Charlotte had learned to waltz, practicing alone in her room with a mop. She had never danced with a real live partner, but Evan's lead was so firm, his ear for the music so precise, that it was easy for her to follow him. She realized she was looking up at him, smiling, enjoying herself immensely, as he whirled her around the floor.

If the other couples were staring, Charlotte was unaware of it.

All she could think was, *Why have I waited so long to do something this pleasurable?*

The waltz ended too soon. Evan politely thanked her and led her back to her seat. Almost instantly, Stephen came over to claim his dance. She was still in a state of joyous abandon, and Stephen laughed at her delight and told her that her eyes were sparkling and her cheeks flushed and he wished he could whisk her away to his studio to paint that delightful smile.

When he returned her to where she had been sitting, Evan was no longer there. Stephen said, "Oh, Lord, I hope he hasn't gone to ask anyone else to dance." His eyes searched the room.

"But why? He's a wonderful dancer," Charlotte said.

Stephen looked at her quizzically. "You didn't mind . . . dancing with him?"

"I loved dancing with him," Charlotte declared, truthfully.

"Most women are afraid he'll trample them to death, or crush them with his brute strength. Or, worse, that they'll look ridiculous."

"One isn't aware of his height because of his grace, and his touch is firm but gentle. If other women have refused to dance with him, then it is their loss. Will you excuse me, please?"

Not recognizing that she was angry, Stephen stared at her blankly as she walked away from him. There was no sign of Evan in the banquet hall, so she crossed the room to the doors opening onto the terrace, thinking perhaps he had stepped outside for a breath of air.

A cool breeze fanned some of the heat from her face, and she walked slowly past great stone urns trailing flowers. Two figures detached themselves from the shadows. The first was one of the male guests, who nodded to her and went back into the house. The second, her hair in disarray, was Lady Athmore.

Zoe glared at Charlotte. "What are you doing out here?"

"I'm sorry. I didn't mean . . . I was looking for Mr. Evan."

Zoe looked her slowly up and down. "Since you are here and alone, I'd like to know where that gown came from."

"Why, from Mrs. Carmichael's dressmaker . . . if you will recall, you sent me to her—"

"Don't insult my intelligence! My housekeeper's dressmaker is incapable of making such a gown. Mrs. Carmichael ordered three plain day dresses for you, in brown, charcoal and navy blue."

"Then perhaps Lord Athmore . . ." Charlotte faltered.

A resonant voice behind her said, "*I* ordered the evening gown. I selected the material and patterns for several gowns for Mrs. Danforth. Her measurements were sent to *your* dressmaker, Zoe."

Charlotte looked around in astonishment as Evan emerged from the shadows. He offered her his arm. "Perhaps I could persuade you to dance with me again?"

Zoe lingered on the terrace, knowing that if she went back indoors immediately she would probably claw out the eyes of that sly little minx of a housekeeper.

Through the open doors she could see the great beast Evan dancing again with the Danforth woman. She'd never seen him dance before, and was amazed that somehow he managed to move so lightly on his feet and not look terribly strange . . . something like an adult dancing with a child, of course, but Zoe could see that the other female guests were watching with interest rather than revulsion.

This scene was very different from the one two years ago when a young woman had hysterically refused to dance with Evan and he'd rampaged out of the ball like a wounded bull.

Tonight's turn of events was probably a dangerous one. If ever Evan was accepted by society—or even, perish the thought, if he were to marry and have children—would he then reclaim his inheritance, putting Stephen and herself out in the cold? They certainly couldn't maintain their present life of luxury on what Stephen received in commissions for his portraits. Besides, Zoe had no intention of living as the wife of a mere artist.

Damn that Danforth woman. She was the cause of this. She was also the obstacle that stood in the way of Zoe adopting dear little golden-haired Eleanor. Never mind that Stephen had been adamant that Zoe shouldn't even consider the possibility. "This is just another of your passing fancies," he'd told her. "You'd soon become bored with motherhood. And our way of life certainly doesn't lend itself to spending much time with a child. Besides, Eleanor has a mother. The child obviously adores Mrs. Danforth."

Pacing back and forth on the terrace, Zoe saw with sudden brilliant clarity the solution to all of her problems. She must get rid of Charlotte Danforth.

7

ELEANOR CURTSIED TO signal the end of her performance, and Zoe clapped her hands. "Bravo! Wonderful, *magnifique!* Come here, *cherie,* and have another bonbon."

Somewhat reluctantly, the child approached the window seat in the room Lady Athmore called her "retreat." Although Zoe had showered her with clothes and gifts, Eleanor sometimes got a prickly, not-quite-right feeling when she was summoned to the main house. Owain had warned her to be careful because Lady Athmore was "highly strung" and Eleanor was beginning to understand what that meant. Charlotte always looked worried, too, but reassured her that it was all right when Lord Athmore was present. Today, however, he was not.

To be polite, she took another chocolate truffle from the box Zoe held, although no other adult would have offered so many, and Charlotte wouldn't be pleased when Eleanor couldn't eat her dinner. She sat down beside Lady Athmore, hoping the chocolate on her fingers wouldn't transfer itself to the delicate pastel chintz of the cushions piled into the window seat.

Zoe said, "You'll be marvelous at my party tonight. You didn't tell Charlotte, or Mr. Evan, or anyone about it, did you? It's to be a surprise for all of them. You know, dear, I only told you so that you'd be prepared to recite for the guests."

"I didn't tell anyone," Eleanor said. The sticky sweetness of the chocolate that tasted so good in her mouth didn't feel so nice in her stomach. There was something about the way Lady

71

Athmore's eyes glittered and darted about, in frantic accompaniment to the nervous fluttering of her hands, that worried Eleanor.

After a moment, as though unable to sit still, Zoe rose and began to pace about the room. She paused at her writing desk and slipped an envelope from a drawer. Eleanor could see that the envelope was crumpled, even a little soiled, and Zoe passed it from one hand to the other as if unsure what to do with it. "Darling . . . tell me again about your dear departed father."

Eleanor hated it when Zoe called him dear and departed, because that was a grown-up way of saying "dead," but Charlotte had explained why they had to pretend. Eleanor was afraid that in pretending something, she might cause it to really happen. She missed her father terribly, almost as much as she longed for her mother. "What do you want to know?" she asked cautiously.

Like a sinuous black cat, Zoe suddenly was back in the window alcove, curled up on the seat beside her. Her voice was very soft. "How did he die?"

"He was lost out west," Eleanor said in a small voice, parroting what Charlotte had told her to say.

But today it wasn't sufficient for Zoe. "Did he die from an illness or accident, or was he killed? Or perhaps he killed himself, to escape from the boredom of his marriage to your mother? Any man chained to such a drab little woman must surely feel despair . . ."

Jumping to her feet, Eleanor cried, "My father didn't kill himself! My mother isn't drab, she's beautiful! She's more beautiful than you are. She has lovely golden hair and sparkly blue eyes and—"

Too late, Eleanor realized she had been tricked. She clapped her hand to her mouth, but the words were already out. Zoe leaned back, smiling smugly. "Now, my dear child, you can tell me just who Charlotte Danforth is, and what the relationship is between you."

Eleanor tried to run, but Lady Athmore grabbed her wrist and held it in a painful grip. "Charlotte is my mother," Eleanor whispered.

"No, darling, she isn't. You just told me your mother has golden hair and blue eyes, just like you." Zoe leaned forward and placed a kiss on Eleanor's cheek. "Don't be afraid, it's all right, really. I know everything." She paused, then added in a dramatic undertone, "I even know about . . . the *Hathaways*."

Eleanor gasped. She tried to tug her wrist free, but Lady Athmore held on even more tightly.

"Aha! That name is familiar to you. Who are Mr. and Mrs. Hugh Hathaway, and why did Charlotte write to them?"

There was only one thing to do to bring this conversation to an abrupt close, and Eleanor had no trouble doing it—especially with all those sickly sweet chocolate truffles lying so heavily in her stomach. She vomited, all over Lady Athmore and her pastel chintz-covered window seat.

The letter had been returned from the main post office in Liverpool because it had been damaged somewhere between Llanrys and that city. The envelope bore enough postage stamps to take it to America, and the addressees' names were still legible, as well as the name and address of the sender, written in Charlotte's copperplate script on the flap of the envelope. But the name of the town, and American state, as well as most of the letter, had been water-damaged.

Zoe congratulated herself on her cleverness in instructing Whitcombe to bring all letters to her before taking them over to the grange. If only she knew who the Hathaways were and why Charlotte had written to ask their forgiveness. The decipherable parts of the letter read:

"Due to intolerable situation . . . please forgive, and know only that my first concern is . . . knowing your fears about the Indian situation, I could not bring her . . ." The middle portion of the letter was too blurred to read, then, "Eleanor and I will remain here at Glendower until . . ." There was something about instructions, then more blanks. "Or should you decide to come in person, directions to reach the estate are . . . take the train to Llanrys . . ."

Until what? Forgive what? Why would the Hathaways come here? Zoe had been beside herself with excitement. The Danforth woman was running away from someone, or something she'd done, Zoe was certain. She'd almost gotten it out of the child, if only the little wretch hadn't been sick all over the place. But she had given away that the Danforth woman was not her mother, that was the main thing. There'd be another opportunity to get the rest of the story out of her. Ah, but wait a minute . . . from what the child had said, her parents weren't dead . . . then why was she here and they somewhere in America?

My father was lost out west, Eleanor had said. Zoe was familiar with the dangers of the Western frontier. If the child's parents were out west, that might explain why she wasn't with them. *But not why Charlotte and she were so secretive about the whole situation.*

Zoe sank into the hip bath prepared for her and dismissed her personal maid, who carried away Zoe's soiled gown. "Be sure to tell the parlor maid to destroy all of the cushions and covers of the window seat."

Lying back in the scented water, Zoe was aware of a familiar pinprick of light behind her right eye and a dull throbbing pain in her temple. Ignoring both, her mind worked feverishly on her plans. If only there weren't so many things to do . . . But the most important things must take precedence. As soon as she finished bathing, she would burn the letter to the Hathaways. Evidently Charlotte had written to let them know where she and the child were immediately upon their arrival here, because Whitcombe's monitoring of her mail had begun a few days later and had not revealed any other personal correspondence. Therefore, it seemed likely that no one else knew of their whereabouts.

It was imperative she act quickly with regard to Charlotte Danforth. Once she was out of the way, it would be easy to tell the child that her friends the Hathaways had also perished. Wait . . . was it possible the Hathaways were Eleanor's *parents?* Had they left the child in Charlotte Danforth's care and she had run off with her, only to repent after they arrived in Wales?

Zoe's head buzzed with theories and possibilities. She studied the letter again, convinced now that no one but the Danforth woman knew that Eleanor was here at Glendower. Once Zoe informed her the Hathaways were dead . . .

Alone in the world, wouldn't she gladly be adopted by the wealthy Athmores? Zoe was determined the pretty and clever little girl would be her daughter. Despite Stephen's fear that Zoe would soon lose interest in Eleanor, Zoe was convinced that her childlessness was an affront to her femininity. All of her friends had children, and she wasn't going to be deprived of the prestige of motherhood, no matter what Stephen said.

Besides, there was an even more urgent reason to get rid of Charlotte. The situation over at the grange was becoming more alarming. Ever since the first *Gymanfa* party a week ago, it had been reported by the gossipy Lizzie to Zoe's maid that Evan no longer spent most of his time alone in his library or riding by himself on that great black horse he'd imported from Arabia. Instead, he wandered about the house, often in conversation with Mrs. Danforth. Lizzie had even heard him laugh once or twice, and remarked to Zoe's maid that he had sounded almost human.

It had, therefore, been necessary for Zoe to visit the village, on the pretense of calling upon some ill and recently bereaved relatives of Glendower employees, to fan the fires of fear of the giant. Periodically it was necessary to revive the rumors of his evil deeds among staff and villagers, as justification for toppling him from his position of power when the time was right.

So Zoe had clenched her nostrils and entered dismal cottages to dispense gifts and sympathy, to pat the tangled heads of filthy children and shake the hands of disgusting old men, assuring them that she understood the cross they had to bear, since she and her dear husband silently bore one of their own.

One of the scullery maids at Glendower had carelessly spilled a pot of boiling stew on herself, severely burning her hands and arms. Zoe had the girl accompany her to the village, her partially healed scalds in full view. Zoe made a fuss over the girl and took her to the inn for tea, confiding to the innkeeper in a stage whisper so that other patrons might hear, that tea with her mistress was only one of the little treats Zoe offered to try to make it up to the girl for what she had suffered at the hands of . . . there Zoe had broken off, apparently aghast, wiped a tear from her eye and returned solicitously to the scullery maid, who seemed too overcome by the presence of her ladyship to enjoy the pastries she was offered.

The message was clear. That fiend Evan Athmore had probably flown into one of his rages and caused the girl to be scalded. The great, sadistic brute ought to be locked up, and he would be if it wasn't for Lord Stephen Athmore's compassion and the tolerance of her ladyship. Such a kind and beautiful woman . . . Why, most scullery maids never even met the mistress of the house, let alone took tea with her.

The episode took care of the villagers' opinion of the giant, and Zoe had also insinuated to several friends of her own class that Evan had only appeared to be normal the night of the party because a clever doctor had given him a potion. Unfortunately, the effects wore off later, and he had plunged into a murderous rage that was so uncontrollable they had decided not to use the potion again for fear it had triggered the episode. Her friends responded that she was indeed a saint to put up with her husband's uncle, but she must take care that the strain did not affect her own health.

"Zoë—are you in there?" Stephen's voice came from her bedroom.

She called, "Yes, darling. Come and wash my back. I'm in the bath."

He appeared at the door, his face grave. "Zoe, Mrs. Carmichael tells me you ordered dinner for fifty people tonight, and Whitcombe says you instructed him to hire musicians."

"Yes, I did. We're having a party. I'm sure I told you."

He continued to stand in the doorway. "Did you also tell me that you'd accepted invitations to three other dinner parties this evening? Or that you had all of my canvases and paints removed from my studio and ordered the masons to brick in the windows? Zoe, for God's sake, what are you doing to me?"

She smiled. "I'm going to make a brand-new studio for you. An artist of your stature deserves something better than an old attic room. I'm going to tear down the west wing of the house, too. It's time we started renovating. This house is far too ugly for a couple as handsome as us. And regarding the parties tonight, we can go to all of them, darling, with a little planning. We must have fun tonight, because tomorrow we leave for the south of France."

"Zoe, I told you I don't want to go abroad again for a while. Nor do I intend to renovate the house. And I'm perfectly happy in my present studio."

"Ssh! We'll talk about it later." Extending her hand to him, she allowed him to help her out of the bath and wrap a towel around her. She turned and put her arms around him. "Could we make a baby now, please?"

His face looked stricken. "Oh, God! Please don't start that again, Zoe. You know why we can never have a child."

She pulled away from him, her expression contorted with hatred. "*Evan*. Always Evan."

Stephen turned away and went back into the bedroom, so she wouldn't see his face. He'd told her that he didn't want to risk having a child who might be afflicted with gigantism, like Evan. Actually, several doctors had assured Stephen that gigantism was more likely to be a random happenstance than due to hereditary factors, and that it was unlikely to reappear again in his family.

The truth was that Stephen feared Zoe's own malady, whatever it was, could be passed on to her child. Besides, he felt it was time, once and for all, to end the deception about the Athmore lineage. If there were no issue to his union, then the line would end and no one ever need know the truth, about him or about Evan.

"Don't walk away from me!" Zoe screamed. She followed him into the bedroom and hurled her silver-backed hairbrush at him. It caught him a glancing blow on the shoulder. She began to curse him in French, and, dodging her blows, he tried to take her into his arms to calm her.

Capturing her at last, he held her until she stopped struggling. She looked up at him from beneath a fringe of dark, silky eyelashes. "I don't need you to make a baby."

"We've been over this before, Zoe, but hear me again. If you become *enciente*, I shall know that the child is not mine, and I will divorce you."

Inexplicably, she began to shriek with laughter.

Stephen slapped her, a hard stinging blow to the cheek.

Her laughter stopped instantly and she flopped back on the bed, looking up at him with an expression so intensely sexual that he felt a ripple pass slowly up his spine. But instead of a provocative smile or a whispered invitation coming from her sensuous mouth, she spat at him.

His hand reached for her, grazed her cheek, then slid to her neck. His long fingers encircled her throat, digging into the flesh. "There will be no child, Zoe."

"Very well," she whispered, suddenly gentled. She shrugged off her dressing gown and lay naked before him, arms stretched over her head, black hair hanging over the edge of the bed to the floor. "But make love to me anyway."

He had seen those voluptuous curves a thousand times, painted her in every conceivable pose, knew her body as well as his own, yet the sight of her flesh, the skin flawless, almost incandescent, never failed to stop his breath in his throat.

He was too aroused to resist, despite his fear that she was hovering on the brink of another manic spiral. Tearing off his clothes, he fell on her like a ravening beast, hating himself and her for awakening those dark gods of the loins. In their coupling there was anger and reprisal, punishment with the pleasure, taunts rather than words of endearment. Their lovemaking was their battleground, and each claimed a victory of sorts.

When they were spent they lay side by side, not touching. At length Zoe said, "Tell me, my darling, do you think your virginal little housekeeper could love you like that?"

Stephen sprang from the bed and began to gather up his clothes. Zoe rolled over, trailing her fingers on the rug beside the bed. "Has it ever occurred to you that most men seek out mistresses because their madonna wives cannot satisfy them sexually . . . while you, *cherie*, are considering taking a madonna mistress!" She laughed suddenly. "Fornicate with her, Stephen. I dare you to. I shall so enjoy the disappointment you'll feel afterwards."

8

OWAIN HAD MOVED into the grange, but at Evan's suggestion after a few days he resumed his duties as head groom for the estate. No one, from the stablemaster to Lord and Lady Athmore, commented on his reappearance in the stables. It was as if by inviting him to live at the grange, Mr. Evan was making the statement that Owain would be given the sack by nobody but the man who had hired him.

One consequence of Lady Athmore's dismissing him, however, had been Owain's realization that a man could never be secure anywhere, unless he owned his own land. He had begun to think more and more how he could free himself from servitude to others, especially now that Lady Athmore refused to allow him to handle her favorite horses, or drive her to the village. He knew she was merely waiting for another opportunity to get rid of him.

On this particular afternoon, Owain was keeping an eye on the mass of purplish black clouds hugging the top of the mountain. The air was heavy with the threat of rain and, when the storm broke, the resulting thunder and lightning could be a problem with high-spirited thoroughbred horses, several of which were presently being exercised. He decided to bring them in; taking the most placid mare still in her stall, he rode out to the meadow where they were being exercised.

He had covered half the distance to the open fields when one of the grooms came riding pell-mell toward him. Reining his mount, he said, "It's the little girl, Owain. She came running up and wanted to ride Dreamer. I told her the mare was lame and still in her stall. But she said she had to go somewhere right away. Terrified, she looked, and she'd been crying. Before I knew what Miss Eleanor was about, she was up on the back of Scalliwag and riding—bareback—off toward the lake.''

"What? Why didn't you stop her, or go after her?"

The groom looked frightened. "I couldn't stop her, look you, I was surrounded by horses. And afraid I was to go after her, in case Scalliwag bolted with her when he heard me coming after him. You know how nervous he is.''

Owain swore and dug his heels in his horse's flanks to ride after her, yelling over his shoulder that the horses should be returned to the stables before the storm broke.

Ellie had been over at the main house this afternoon, he knew, and a little while later Lord Athmore had left to go to Llanrys, which meant Ellie had been alone with Zoe. God only knew what that black witch might have done to frighten the child.

He saw her as he came over the top of the hill, a small figure with flying gold hair, clinging to the mane of a stallion far too spirited for her to be riding. Oh, God, Owain prayed silently, don't let there be thunder or lightning until I get to her. At almost the same instant, the first fierce gust of wind hit him. The heavens opened and raindrops as big as florins whirled in the wind, striking the trees with such force that the leaves shuddered.

Lying close to the back of his horse, he urged her down the slope at reckless speed, speaking soothingly into the mare's ear to calm her as lightning flashed and thunder rumbled in the hills. As he closed the distance between them, he saw that Eleanor had no control over the stallion, who was bolting directly toward the thickest grove of trees near the lake. *Try to steer him away from the trees,* Owain willed her, but saw that there was nothing the child could do.

At least the dense copse of trees slowed Scalliwag's mad dash, enabling Owain to catch up with them. When he was close enough for her to hear, Owain shouted, "Hold on tight, Ellie, *bach,* I'm coming."

She gave him one frightened look over her shoulder as a thunderbolt shattered their eardrums and another flash of lightning rent the sky, stabbing the earth like a great scimitar.

Owain tightened the reins and by sheer strength of will forced the mare to ride in close to the stallion. When they were side by side, he reached over and grabbed Eleanor around the waist.

Scalliwag galloped off, whinnying in terror. Owain turned his mount to get away from the dangerous trees as quickly as possible.

They had reached the last of the great oaks when there was a flash, followed by a sizzling hiss, and a simultaneous deafening clap of thunder. Owain heard the wrenching sound of breaking wood over their heads, smelled the strong odor of sulphur, but had time only to fling Eleanor clear before the tree toppled.

He and the mare went down in a confusion of branches and excruciating pain. He had a moment's awareness of the smell of singed hair and burned flesh, of his leg twisting twice in the wrong direction, snapping the bone like tinder, of the scream of the mare. Then a great weight fell over his lower body, followed by oblivion.

Charlotte stood at the drawing room window of the grange, watching Lizzie dash across the courtyard seconds ahead of a deluge of rain. Lightning split the blackened sky and thunder roared down the mountains, growing louder as the storm moved directly toward them. Charlotte was at the front door before Lizzie reached it. "Where is she? Why didn't you bring her with you?"

Breathless, Lizzie pulled her shawl from her head and slammed the door against the driving rain. "She's not there."

"What do you mean, not there? Of course she's there. Lady Athmore sent for her before lunch."

"Eleanor ate too much chocolate and she was sick. Made a right mess all over her ladyship's window seat."

"Oh, dear, the poor child," Charlotte murmured. "But where is she?"

"Lady Athmore's maid said she cleaned her up and put on a fresh pinafore and sent her back an hour ago."

Charlotte's hand drifted anxiously to her throat. "She must be hiding somewhere. I expect she's afraid she'll be punished. Lizzie, Mr. Evan is already in the dining room. Would you serve high tea while I look for my daughter?"

Running up the stairs, Charlotte checked their rooms, then the box rooms, and then pulled down the ladder reaching to the attic. The undisturbed dust on the attic floor stopped her from going any further. Perplexed, she started back downstairs, thinking perhaps the child had gone into one of the pantries. Charlotte's heart thudded with fear. Eleanor hid only when she thought she was in desperate trouble. What else could have happened over at the house today?

The dining room door opened and Evan came out into the hall as Charlotte reached the bottom stair. "What's this about your daughter?"

"I think she's hiding because of an incident over at the main house this afternoon. I'm sorry, I didn't mean to delay your tea. Didn't Lizzie . . ."

"Never mind tea. We'd better find the child." He turned and addressed Lizzie, who was in the dining room. "I want every one of the servants to search the house. Except Davies—tell him to put on oilskins and come with me. We'll look outside."

"Davies hasn't come in from the stables yet, Mr. Evan," Lizzie answered.

"Very well, I'll go alone." He turned to Charlotte. "Don't worry, we'll find her. She can't have gone far."

But an hour later the storm raged even more violently, and a thorough search of the main house, the grange, and the gardens had not yielded a sign of the child. Evan returned to tell Charlotte he was going to the stables and would organize a mounted search party of the entire estate.

Charlotte waited, pacing up and down the hall in an agony of fear for Eleanor's safety, at the same time castigating herself for not taking better care of her.

The front door opened and a drenched, cloaked figure stepped into the hall. Zoe pulled back the hood of her cloak and said, "Ah, there you are, Mrs. Danforth. Come with me, I know where Eleanor is hiding."

Charlotte ran into the kitchen and pulled a rain cape from the stand, then dashed back into the hall. She followed Zoe out into wind-driven rain so fierce they had to turn their backs and lean into it in order to cross the courtyard.

It was only when they were in the hall of the main house that Charlotte noticed that Lady Athmore's eyes were very wide and bright and her movements somewhat rapid and convulsive. Charlotte had assumed that Eleanor must be ill and Lady Athmore had put her to bed, but now she recalled Zoe's exact words: *I know where Eleanor is hiding.* If that were so, then why leave her there? But there was no time to ask questions. Zoe was running along the vaulted corridor and Charlotte could barely keep up with her.

She led the way to Stephen's studio and flung open the doors. A blast of wind came at them out of the darkness. Someone must have left the windows open, Charlotte thought, surely not Stephen? His canvases might be damaged if the rain blew in. Since Stephen only worked during the daylight hours, there was no gaslight up here, but she knew he kept an oil lamp on one of the wall shelves. As she felt along the wall, she stumbled over something cold and hard and, bending over, her hand connected with what felt like a pile of bricks.

A flash of lightning briefly illuminated the room, revealing the fact that all of the window glass had been removed, exposing the entire sloping side of the studio. In that split second, Charlotte also saw that the room was bare, cleared of easels, canvases and everything but several piles of bricks.

Zoe clutched her arm and hissed in her ear. "She's out there on the parapet."

Charlotte's heart turned over. She called, "Eleanor? Eleanor, are you there? It's Charlotte—oh, my darling child, please answer me."

Between the thunder claps, the only sound was that of the wind howling in the chimneys and the steady dripping of rain from the eaves. In rising panic, Charlotte said, "We must find a lamp, I can't see a thing."

"Go out on the parapet and get her," Zoe said. "She's at the corner of the house. I'll hold on to your hand and you can pass her inside to me."

Zoe pushed her through the inexplicably gutted room toward the glassless window. Was there a small shape out there, or was it merely a shadow? Charlotte called Eleanor's name again, and clutched the wooden window frame as she stepped out onto the parapet.

The wind caught her skirts immediately, and the stone parapet under her feet was wet and slippery. "There," Zoe said, "at the corner—go on!"

Charlotte felt Zoe's fingers pluck at her hand, trying to pry her grip from the window frame. Another flash of lightning lit up the entire roof and Charlotte saw that lying on the parapet at the corner of the house was, not a child, but a dressmaker's dummy.

Now Zoe's hands were in the middle of her back, trying to push her forward, and Charlotte realized to her horror that the woman's intent was to push her off the parapet. There was nothing between her and the stone-flagged terrace, some forty feet below.

She clung for dear life to the window frame, as her feet slid out from under her. Zoe was screaming at her now in unintelligible

French, and beating her about her face and head with her fists. Charlotte took the blows rather than release her hold on the frame in order to protect herself.

This had to be a nightmare, but she could not awaken. She felt herself growing faint and feared she was about to fall; indeed, she would have fallen had it not been for her overpowering need to find Eleanor and protect her from this madwoman.

Suddenly the studio was flooded with light. There was a sharp command, and Zoe's blows ceased as she was wrenched away. Stephen's voice, sharp with fear, came through the window. "Charlotte—give me your hand! Careful . . . good, now the other one. It's all right, I've got you."

She was wrapped in his arms, clinging to him as a moment before she had clung to the window frame. His body was hard and warm, and he comforted and aroused her at the same time. She was oblivious to the presence of anyone else in the studio, although Zoe was still there, screaming hysterically, and evidently held by someone else to keep her from fulfilling her repeated threats to kill Charlotte.

At the stables, a groom had told Evan that the child had ridden off on Scalliwag, and that Owain had gone after her. They had all assumed that by now both of them would be back at the grange.

Evan saddled his own horse swiftly, and galloped toward the lake. He could hear the others coming after him, but he was the first to see Eleanor stumbling along on foot, her hair plastered to her head and her sodden dress torn to ribbons. Seeing him, she started to cry and pointed back toward the woods beside the lake. "Owain—oh, I think he's dead!"

The first of the grooms galloped up and Evan shouted, "Take care of the child. Then he urged his own mount forward again. The storm had now passed out of the immediate vicinity, the wind diminishing with longer periods between the lightning and the thunder, but it was still raining heavily.

The whinnying of Owain's terrified horse guided Evan to the fallen tree. The lightning bolt had split it cleanly in two, and Owain lay pinned beneath part of the trunk as well as the fallen horse. He was unconscious, the rain beating on his burned face and singed hair.

Dismounting, Evan snapped off branches in order to reach the injured man. Bracing himself, he shoved his shoulder under the tree trunk and began slowly to inch it upward.

The stablemaster and one of the grooms arrived and rushed to help. Much later, when the groom retold the story, he related in absolute awe that the giant of Glendower had not needed their help, that his incredible strength had lifted both tree and horse from Owain Davies.

Charlotte remained at Eleanor's bedside long after she had fallen asleep. The rain still beat a steady tattoo against the windows and the room acquired a damp chill. Charlotte fought another urge to take Eleanor and run. But there was no train out of Llanrys tonight, even if she could obtain a carriage to take them to the station.

She went over the facts again, trying to fill in missing pieces. Eleanor had said that Lady Athmore mentioned her real name, but had said "*the* Hathaways," as if unaware Eleanor was one of them. She had also tricked the child into admitting that Charlotte was not her mother. Eleanor had been so afraid that she would get Charlotte into trouble that the child had decided she would simply have to run away by herself. If she were not present, then Charlotte could not be accused of posing as her mother. Eleanor wasn't aware of all the ramifications of Charlotte's actions in taking her away from her grandfather, but evidently sensed that what she had done could bring severe punishment.

But it was Lady Athmore's behavior that puzzled Charlotte the most. Having learned the truth, why did she then lure Charlotte to Stephen's studio and try to kill her? Was it because the child was missing? Had she simply taken advantage of the fact that everyone was searching for her in order to get Charlotte alone? The chilling thought hovered at the back of Charlotte's mind that Lady Athmore had possibly been planning her death before today. The gutted studio, the removal of the window glass . . . But why? Was it true what Owain had said, that she wanted Eleanor? Or was it possible she'd become aware of the unspoken feelings between her husband and Charlotte? Could any rational person understand what went on in the mind of someone as unbalanced as Zoe?

There was a tap on the bedroom door, and she rose and went swiftly to open it. Lizzie stood outside, her face stupid with sleep. "They want you down in Mr. Evan's library."

"What about Owain Davies? Is he all right?"

"The doctor from Llanrys said it's a compound fracture of his leg. And Owain was burned from the lightning. He might be hurt inside, too, the doctor doesn't know yet. There's lucky to be alive, he is.''

"Indeed, yes."

"Excuse me, mum, but they're waiting for you."

Charlotte's heart had begun to hammer against her ribs again. This was the summons she had expected and dreaded. She drew a deep breath and followed Lizzie downstairs.

Evan was seated in his usual chair beside the fireplace, and Stephen stood with his hands on the mantelpiece, apparently staring at the ashes in the grate. He turned when Charlotte entered the room, a defeated look on his face, his eyes shattered with despair.

There was an interminable silence, as though each of them was waiting for the other to speak. At length, Charlotte cleared her throat and said, "I understand Davies will be all right. I'm so glad."

"The doctor isn't too hopeful about how well his leg will mend," Evan said. "It was a bad break. He's going to be laid up for a long time."

"I shall pray for his complete recovery. I am very grateful to him for saving Eleanor. If he hadn't arrived, I dread to think what might have happened."

There, she had mentioned Eleanor. Now they would accuse her of not being the child's mother and she would know where she stood.

But Evan said, "Tell me, Mrs. Danforth, what exactly happened tonight between you and Lady Athmore?"

She glanced at Stephen questioningly. Surely he must have explained? Evan said, "No, don't look at him for answers. I want to hear your version of the incident in his studio."

How could she possibly relate the horror of what had happened there? She began hesitantly, "Lady Athmore told me that Eleanor had gone out onto the parapet."

"Yes. Go on."

Charlotte looked imploringly at Stephen, but he merely ran his hand distractedly through his hair, staring at her with those shattered eyes. She continued in a low voice, "Lady Athmore . . . tried to push me from the parapet."

"No!" Stephen said, as though waking from a trance. "Zoe told me that she was holding you and you slipped—it was wet—that she was trying to pull you back inside."

Charlotte was stunned. "But . . . you heard her . . . the threats she was making. She was speaking in French, but she threatened to kill me."

"You misunderstood," Stephen said brokenly. "It's only natural, you'd been under tremendous strain, worrying about Eleanor. Zoe was hysterical with fear and what she was saying was that she'd been afraid you'd kill yourself, out there on the parapet in the storm."

Afraid her knees might give way, Charlotte collapsed into a chair, shaking her head in numb disbelief.

Evan said quietly, "You speak French, Mrs. Danforth?"

"Yes, fairly fluently."

"Zoe was very upset," Stephen said desperately. "She was almost incoherent . . . she was in the midst of one of her spells. But I really don't believe she meant Charlotte—Mrs. Danforth—any harm."

"Is it true," Evan asked, his voice resonating around the room, "that she ordered your studio to be stripped, the windows removed and bricked in?"

"Well, yes . . ."

"And that the servants were ordered to cook dinner for fifty guests tonight, that musicians were hired, but no guests arrived since everyone for miles around was attending other parties— invitations to which Zoe had also accepted?"

"Evan, I really don't think this is the time—"

Charlotte found her voice at last. "Mr. Evan, please. I must speak. I feel that Eleanor and I are perhaps the cause of the present difficulties here at Glendower and that the best solution would be for us to leave as soon as possible."

Evan rose slowly, towering over Stephen, dominating the room. "No, damn it all, it is Zoe who will leave. Stephen, you will either find a doctor able to treat whatever ails Zoe, or you will have her committed. She's getting worse and you can't go on hiding it indefinitely."

A small cry escaped Charlotte's lips. Stephen had turned very pale. She whispered, "Oh, please—"

Evan said, "You may go to bed, Mrs. Danforth. I'm sure you'll find everything to your liking here in the morning."

She turned to Stephen. "Is Lady Athmore calm now? Perhaps we could discuss—"

"My wife has lapsed into total silence," Stephen said. "It

usually occurs after one of these episodes and can last for weeks or even longer. I don't expect she will speak to anyone, not even me, for a long while.''

Charlotte nodded, murmured, "Good night," and left the library. Halfway up the stairs, it occurred to her that nothing had been said about her not being Eleanor's mother. Evidently Zoe had not told anyone yet. Perhaps by the time she emerged from her silence, or from the treatment Evan insisted that Stephen find for her, Charlotte would have received a reply and instructions from Eleanor's parents in New Mexico.

9

THE FOLLOWING MORNING, Glendower lay bathed in gentle sunlight and rain-freshened air. As Charlotte entered the breakfast room carrying a silver platter of thick slices of ham, the events of the previous evening lay heavily upon her mind. Her thoughts raced back and forth, from Owain Davies with his smashed leg and seared head, to Eleanor, mercifully unhurt, who refused breakfast and cried for her friend. But what had happened with Zoe in the ravaged studio was even more chilling. The whispered excitement among the grange servants added to Charlotte's tension.

"Mr. Evan was over at the main house at the crack of dawn, look you," Lizzie had told her. "And they say the doctor went from Owain to Lady Athmore and stayed all night." Charlotte sharply ordered the woman to stop gossiping and attend to her duties.

In contrast to the rest of the grange, the breakfast room was light and airy, with a wall of windows overlooking a pleasing array of shrubs and a bank of lupins and delphiniums. Unlike the dining room, with its massive carved mahogany furniture, here the table was an unpretentious natural oak, of a size to accommodate no more than four people, with a matching Welsh sideboard that held blue and white Wedgwood china. The effect, despite the higher than normal table and large chairs, was almost cozy.

"Good morning, Mr. Evan," Charlotte said, placing the ham platter on the sideboard.

"Put the food on the table and join me."

He had not asked her to eat with him again since that first disastrous dinner, although she often stayed and conversed with him while he ate. Charlotte removed the platter to the table and he pulled out a chair for her. He watched as she piled ham on his plate next to a mammoth omelet. "I'm not sure that either Stephen or I apologized to you for Lady Athmore's actions yesterday."

Charlotte picked up a silver teapot to fill his cup and he said, "Never mind that. I want to know if you will stay."

When she hesitated, he added, "I *want* you to stay. I can assure you that there will be no repetition of Zoe's behavior of last night. She is ill, as you know, and any blame must lie with her husband, who has ignored that fact for too long now. Mrs. Danforth, we all speak sometimes in the heat of anger and I should tell you that when I ordered Stephen to have her committed, it was simply the cry of a man who by threatening the worst enforces the least of what has to be done. I wouldn't really insist that Zoe be put in an asylum, but neither can she be allowed to disrupt lives around her."

Silently Charlotte contemplated that, in her own case, Zoe's intent had been more deadly than mere disruption.

Evan went on, as though reading her mind. "Everyone was in an extreme state of agitation last night, with the storm and the child running away, and it was very dark in the studio. Perhaps the truth of what happened there rests somewhere between your version and that of Stephen and Mrs. Carmichael."

Zoe's housekeeper had been the third person present, who had held Zoe as she screamed incoherently, while Stephen comforted Charlotte. It had been dark in the studio, and Stephen could have misunderstood Zoe's actions and words. Perhaps the housekeeper didn't understand French, although Charlotte had overheard Lizzie warning a new maid that both Whitcombe and Mrs. Carmichael had been brought to Glendower by her ladyship and would do anything for her. In the warm morning sunshine it was difficult even for Charlotte to accept that Zoe had tried to kill her. Perhaps she wanted to believe she had been wrong about Zoe, in order to justify Stephen's account of what had taken place.

"Nevertheless," Evan went on, "Stephen is going to take his wife back to London to a doctor there who felt he could help her, given several months in which to treat her. Unfortunately, while Lady Athmore refuses to talk to anyone, there's little point in taking her to the doctor. Therefore, today Stephen is going to hire a nurse who will watch over his wife constantly until she is fit enough to travel." He paused. "Will this arrangement be acceptable to you, as an inducement to remain at Glendower?"

I haven't anywhere else to go, Charlotte thought, and I've written to Eleanor's parents telling them we're here. Any day they could arrive, looking for their child. But the strongest urge to remain came from her aching longing to be where she might occasionally catch a glimpse of Stephen. Oh, dear God in heaven, why could Thou not have left me in ignorance of romantic love? To feel briefly the magic touching of two souls, and then to be denied the fulfillment of that most desperate of all human yearnings was surely too terrible a torture to bear.

"There'll be no need for either you or Eleanor to go to the main house, so you needn't be apprehensive about further encounters with Lady Athmore. I've already told Stephen that he'll have to finish his damned portrait from memory."

"Oh, but—" Charlotte faltered. "The portrait is so near to completion, I—" She broke off under the onslaught of his fierce gaze, which seemed to cut right through her unspoken longing to be with Stephen. A veil immediately descended over his eyes, shutting out her brief glimpse of his anger. He said calmly, "Very well. Since the studio is out of commission, he can come over here to finish the picture. He'll have to get it done quickly in any event, as he'll soon be leaving for London with his wife."

She passed his plate to him and drank a cup of tea while he ate. He inquired about Owain Davies and said he'd go and see the young groom, then abruptly asked if she'd learned what Zoe had said to cause Eleanor to run away. Charlotte tried to keep her voice level. "No, not really. But I think perhaps Lady Athmore's state of agitation . . ."

As she rose to leave, he said, "Stay awhile. I'd like to have a conversation with you that doesn't concern my nephew and his wife. Tell me more about America. It is a country that interests me greatly. Perhaps if I'd accompanied Stephen when he went there on his grand tour, we could have avoided a great deal of our present trouble."

Charlotte approached the main house with a feeling of both trepidation and joy that she would at last see Stephen again. Two weeks had elapsed since the night of the storm, and all of the horrors of that evening were beginning to lose their sharp edges in her memory. This morning Evan had asked, "How would you feel about going over to the main house to sit for the portrait one last time?"

"Why, I—"

"Stephen insists that the grange rooms are all too dark for him to paint in. I suppose I have allowed the oaks to shade the house too densely. They seemed a barricade against intrusion. He asks me to tell you that he's had his studio windows reglazed and there's a nurse to watch over Lady Athmore." Evan paused, frowning. "But I strongly urge you to refuse."

"Does he want Eleanor to accompany me?" Charlotte had already decided that, no matter what, Eleanor was not to be forced to return to the main house, since the child had become terribly afraid of seeing Zoe again.

"No. He says the portrait of the child is finished. He just wants you." Evan's eyes burned into her. She could feel him willing her to refuse. Lowering her eyes, she'd said, "I feel both artist and models have invested too much time in the picture not to see it properly completed."

Now as she went in through the tradesmen's entrance and along the corridor to the staircase leading to the attic, she carefully held up the hem of the gold satin evening gown she wore under a full-length cape Stephen had sent over to the grange, with a note suggesting the cape would conceal what she wore under it. The cape seemed new, made of soft black velvet, and by the time Charlotte reached the studio, between the cool sensuality of the satin and the gentle warmth of the velvet, her skin was aflame with sensation. She had tried to disregard the messages her body sent her, but could not. She thought perhaps she was more aware of her body because Stephen studied her so intently for the painting.

Stephen was waiting for her. He had not put on his smock and wore a loose linen shirt, unbuttoned except for a couple of lower buttons, the sleeves rolled up. She could see the shading of dark hair on his chest and forearms and, as he greeted her and helped her to remove the cape, his casually unbuttoned shirt and the décolletage of her gown created a feeling of intimacy between them that brought a flush to her cheeks.

"Thank you, dear Charlotte, for coming." He gestured about the restored studio. "I hope the memory of the night of the storm doesn't haunt this room for you. As you can see, it's just my studio again. But to be sure we shan't be disturbed, I'm going to slip the bolt on the door. Then you can relax.''

He went to the door and she looked around. Everything was as before, except that, in addition to the upholstered bench where she and Eleanor had posed, there was now a chaise longue in the center of the room, draped with a shimmering satin cloth.

She didn't speak, not knowing quite what to say. She knew from conversations with Evan that Lady Athmore's depression continued. When Stephen returned, he said, ''I want you to recline on the chaise.''

''But you have already almost finished painting us seated on the bench.''

''And that's how the portrait will be completed—in a moment. But if this is to be the last time you pose for me, I want to also sketch you in a reclining position. For a possible future picture. Charlotte, how can I explain to you how you move me? In a world of jaded beings you are truth and innocence and all that the rest of us have lost, or perhaps never had. Yet within that almost childlike purity, there is a hint of untapped femininity, of tethered passion. If I can capture on canvas that combination of innocence and sensuality . . . then, my dear, I shall make us both immortal.''

Placing his hands on her gloved arms, he moved his fingers lightly upward until he came to bare flesh. Charlotte felt faint as he gently urged her down on the draped chaise, pushed her backward, then lifted her feet from the ground. He smiled at her. ''Forgive the liberties, but I must arrange you just so . . .''

As he moved her arm, the back of his hand, apparently accidentally, brushed across her satin-encased breasts. Something very strange occurred instantly. It was as if he'd touched some secret lever that set in motion a chain of sensations . . . a tingling in her breasts, a drumming of her heartbeat, a breathlessness in her throat, a tightness in her lower body. Her cheeks felt flushed, her eyes glazed, her entire body coiled like a spring waiting . . .

His hand dropped slowly to her ankle. ''What a slender ankle you have,'' he murmured. ''Such tiny feet. Oh, how I'd love to paint you nude—'' Hearing her gasp, he chuckled, ''I'm sorry. I didn't mean to shock you. It's just that you are so delicately made, it would be a challenge to try to duplicate those skin tones, to hint of the fine bones beneath the flesh.''

Those skin tones, *the* flesh. Charlotte tried to tell herself that he saw her not as a woman, but as a means to express his art. Nevertheless, she couldn't stop the thudding of her heart.

He stood up, studying her with that faraway look he wore when working, which she attributed to his measuring light and shade, considering perspective and harmony of color and line. He bent suddenly and slipped the tiny puffed sleeve of her gown even further off one shoulder. His hand remained briefly in an almost imperceptible caress. Then he turned his back on her, leaving her feeling curiously abandoned, and walked across the studio to the shelves lining one wall. Picking up a sketch pad and piece of charcoal, he said, "Bear with me, Charlotte. I'll do a quick sketch and then we'll get back to the oils."

He stood in front of her, glancing at her frequently between rapid strokes on the pad. He knit his brows in concentration, and his eyes moved slowly down the length of her body. To Charlotte, it felt as if he were peeling away the gold satin gown and savoring what he saw beneath. But he gave an exasperated sigh and flung sketch pad and charcoal to the floor.

"It's no use. I am seeing only the gown." He came back to her, dropped to his knees and seized her hands, the look in his eyes so passionate that Charlotte's breath stopped somewhere between her heart and her throat. "Please don't misunderstand me, Charlotte. The gown is lovely, perfect for the portrait. But I must know my subject intensely—intimately, if you will—before I can capture her essence on canvas. If I paint the gown without ever having seen the body beneath it, then I shall have done an illustration of the dress, not a picture of you."

He kneaded her hands, his eyes liquid, imploring.

Charlotte could hardly breathe. "Are you . . . asking me to disrobe?"

"Yes. I'm asking that you reveal all of your loveliness to me. That you forget for a few minutes that I'm a man, and regard me only as an artist. No, please don't refuse. Think about it for a moment. Too often our response to an unusual or unexpected request is to quickly say no because we feel it's the proper thing . . . without ever considering what we want to do."

She was suspended between fear of the consequences and desire to please him. Eleanor's grandfather had called her a dried-up old maid and, at thirty, that was how she saw herself. She chided herself that she was prudish, foolish, ignorant . . . hadn't artists painted the naked female form since the beginning of time? Stephen hadn't asked to paint her in the nude, but merely that he see her body in order to know her.

Stephen took her face gently in his hands. "Charlotte, my dear, there could never be embarrassment or shame between you and me. We both knew, from the moment we met, that our lives had touched—our secret hearts had touched—for a reason. We also knew that our meeting had come too late for us to be everything that we want to be to one another. But, my dearest, accepting that, surely we can still let down our guard and be natural with one another? Can we not seek the truth of what we are and why we met?"

"Stephen, I . . ."

"You are not Eleanor's mother. I know. Zoe told me. Actually, I guessed it some time ago. You have never been married, have you?"

She had not been about to mention that, but shook her head. "How did Lady Athmore find out?"

"Eleanor told her. Probably Zoe tricked the child into doing so. It doesn't matter. You need have no fear it will make any difference to your status here."

"Does your uncle know?"

"No. I saw no reason to tell him. Is the child related to you in any way, or did you adopt her?"

"I adopted her," Charlotte said in a small voice, hating to lie to him but not wanting to confess the truth. Kidnapping was, after all, a serious crime.

"My dear, let's not discuss other people. We have so little time to be alone together."

He rose suddenly, ripping off his shirt as he did so. Before she realized what he was about to do, he had also discarded his trousers and underwear. "There. You see me as God made me. I feel close enough to you to reveal myself. Can you deny me the same privilege?"

Although her eyes were wide open, she did not see him clearly. The room revolved dizzily around him, and he appeared to her as a beautiful statue viewed through a misty veil. She realized that tears were sliding down her cheeks. All of her life she had denied her very existence, her womanhood. She had connected to others only to serve them, never to be ministered to in return. She had thought to grow old without ever knowing what it would be like to be naked and vulnerable with a man, and now fate had thrust Stephen into her life, and she felt humbly grateful.

She hadn't moved or spoken, but he must have sensed her acquiescence, for he bent and slid her gown down her body, then swiftly removed her camisole and petticoats, and finally her pantalets.

It was as if she were watching Stephen undress someone else. Her body no longer belonged to her. It was his, the instrument he would use for his art, for his pleasure, for whatever he wanted of her trembling flesh. First he drank in her body with his eyes, murmuring about the perfection of fragile bones and delicate curves, of the luminous quality of her skin; then his fingertip traveled lightly from throat to breast, as if sketching her living flesh.

"Lovely, so lovely. Your waist is so tiny, your rib cage small as a child's and my God, I've never seen more beautiful thighs. They are the color and texture of lily petals."

His sketching finger became a hand that caressed her. At the same instant he bent closer and slipped his other hand under her neck to raise her face toward his. He whispered, "I want to pay homage to you with more than brush and color. I need to be closer to you than that. Charlotte, I love you for your quietness, your serenity. I feel a great peace when I'm with you. I've been in such torment, such despair. All of my senses cry out for you. For the contentment only you could bring to the disarray of my life."

His mouth was so close to hers that she could feel his breath. Their lips touched, tentatively, then more urgently. She was drawn into the vortex of his mouth, and when she closed her eyes a curtain came down on all thought, all conscience. She was now a creature of the senses, of flesh without mind. All the long years of denial fell away like a cocoon. She returned his kiss, thrilled to his caresses, gloried in her own abandon as she greedily reached for his body. She who had never touched a clothed man now explored his naked maleness, feeling the life force that pulsed within him and demanded an answering chord in her.

He murmured endearments. His breath became heavy, ragged as her own, and still the frenzy within them built. Scarcely aware of what she was doing, she slid lower on the chaise and pulled him down on top of her.

Their kisses became even more feverish, a blending of lips and tongues that had a rhythm they had orchestrated long ago, before they ever touched. That rhythm rippled down the length of their bodies and every part of them that could connect did so. She was aware of only a second of pain and welcomed it as he pushed inside her. She lifted her body to meet each driving thrust, impaled on a sensual ecstasy so acute that she knew if she died in that moment she would carry this memory into eternity with her.

The cauldron boiled over and he spilled into her, and in the searing void there was a beauty and truth she knew would later elude her. She clung to him, reveling in the sensation of falling, floating in liquid silk, drifting down to a bower of earthly blossoms, through a universe irrevocably altered, more magnificent than she had ever dreamed.

The tremors began to subside and the room came back into dim focus, alien and starkly impersonal with its silent canvases and watching easels. The room was filled with bright sunshine, yet she thought she saw starlight reflected in his eyes, but perhaps her vision was blurred by the tears on her lashes.

"My darling love," she murmured. She raised her hand and traced the dear lines of his brow, his cheekbones, the oddly vulnerable cleft in his chin. He was a dark young prince and she was a witch who had transformed herself from a plain woman into a mysteriously beautiful siren, all tumbled hair and slender, twining limbs.

"Why are you crying?" he asked. "Don't. Please. I can't bear it." He stroked her forehead and pressed a kiss to her eyelids to absorb her tears.

"They are tears of joy," she answered. She concentrated on his caressing hands so that her feelings were there on the surface of her skin, and not on some dark journey of her mind.

He said, "How glad I am that I could make love to you in sunlight rather than darkness. You lie in a pool of amber light and your hair is capturing stray beams of the sun. If I could paint you as you look now, at this moment, it would be a masterpiece."

"Oh, Stephen, I love you. But I know what we've done is sinful and I'm afraid of our punishment."

"This is your punishment," he murmured, just before his mouth closed over hers again and he drew her back to sweet surrender. He was still inside her and, after a moment, he began to grow again. They swayed slightly, side to side, savoring the anticipation.

His hands glided over her breasts, then he raised himself so that he could look down and see how he had vanished into her in their secret joining. She felt a great wave of tenderness for him, as though she were entrusted with the essence of him. For one insane second she wished they could make a child. A black-haired son, with Stephen's beauty and poetry and genius, or a gentle daughter to love and cherish.

Rational thought faded as the fever came rushing back over her. They rode the waves of passion, conscious only of yielding flesh and sensory magic, and reached a crescendo in unison.

She lay in his arms, languorous, satiated; her fingertip traced small loving maps on the taut flesh of his back. She wanted to know his body in a way she did not even know her own. Their thoughts, she knew, were already closely tuned, as if one mind had occupied two bodies, one soul, too, perhaps. Maybe she would be able to remember that, so that she might bear all of the hours she could not be with him sharing his triumphs and defeats, his elation and his despair.

"I must sketch you," he said suddenly, and pushed her away in order to rise and find his sketch pad. She felt bereft without his warmth and wanted to ask him to return, but he walked around her in rapid circles, sketching with frantic haste. His eyes were alight with an almost metallic glow, as though he were in the throes of a violent fever. With rapid strokes, he covered several sheets of his sketch pad. Then went to his easel and placed a fresh canvas upon it and began to work in oils.

Hours passed, and Charlotte ached in every inch of her body, but he didn't appear to hear her gentle protests. When at last, unable to remain naked and still any longer, she started to rise, he threw a cover over the easel and returned to her.

They came together again like clashing titans, without preliminaries, a frenzied battering of flesh against flesh that left them exhausted. When it was over, he slept. She lay beside him as the sunlight faded and rain clouds again crept over the rim of mountains in grim formation, like an armada of attacking ships. The studio grew damp and chill, and she shivered and drew closer to Stephen, suddenly afraid.

Owain felt like a trapped hare, confined to his bed, but the doctor insisted he must remain there. The hours dragged by so slowly, he thought he would go mad. The blinding headaches and pain of his burns were almost a welcome relief to the monotony of lying still, his useless, numbed leg encased in plaster.

The grange servants now regarded him with superstitious awe. A man who had been struck by lightning yet had survived was surely touched by either the saints or the devil. In either case, he was no longer an ordinary mortal.

Ellie came to see him every day and valiantly pretended she wasn't frightened by his blackened face and scorched hair. One day she said to him, "When I'm ill in bed, Charlotte always reads to me. She says it's too wearying to read for oneself when one is weak. Would you like me to read to you?"

"I can read for myself," Owain said angrily. Then when a tear trembled on her golden lashes, he quickly said, "I'm sorry, Ellie, *bach,* I didn't mean to cast your kindness back in your face. If it would please you to read to me, then I'll not object."

She scampered away and returned with a book. "This is brand new, I haven't even read it myself. Charlotte said it was only recently published and she was lucky to find it in Llanrys. It was written by a lady named Anna Sewell."

"Well, I'd prefer a book written by a man," Owain said.

"Ah, but this is . . . what did Charlotte say the word was . . . an autobiography, that's someone's very own story." She paused, her eyes gleaming with an about-to-be-told secret. "This story is told by a horse! That's why I thought you'd like it. It's called *Black Beauty, His Grooms and Companions.*"

"A horse couldn't write a story."

"Silly! Of course not. I told you, a lady wrote it."

Eleanor began to read, and before long Owain was entranced by the story of Black Beauty, which was written with simplicity and restraint and, he quickly realized, was really a tract on the proper treatment of horses. Ellie was a natural performer, and seemed to change her voice to suit the needs of each character who spoke, while somehow conveying the narrative as if it were indeed told by Black Beauty, the horse.

Owain, who had never learned to read, although he would never have admitted it to the child, was astonished to find that he looked forward with keen pleasure to hearing the next chapter, and even thought about Black Beauty and his friends when Ellie had to leave. She left the book in his room and he looked longingly at it, wishing he could pick it up and while away the empty hours in the magic of make-believe.

Lizzie, who brought his food, no longer gossiped with him. She avoided meeting his eye, perhaps fearing the lightning bolt had imbued him with supernatural powers, and spent as little time as possible with him. Owain had only a vague idea of what was happening outside the confines of his room, filtered through the eyes and mind of the child. Eleanor was reluctant to talk about what Lady Athmore had said or done to cause her to run away, but she said she no longer had to go to the main house. She'd also heard Lizzie say that Lady Athmore was in one of her no-talking spells. From past experience, Owain knew that there were two possibilities when Zoe emerged from her withdrawn period. She would either be quite normal for a time, or she might immediately begin that mad spiral into unpredictable and irrational behavior. But then Ellie confided that Charlotte had said Lady Athmore was going away for treatment. Owain heaved a sigh of relief. Perhaps he and Ellie would both be safe for a while.

After a fortnight or so, Ellie began to appear in his room more often, for longer periods. When he questioned whether she'd get into trouble for spending so much time with him, she answered, "Charlotte said I should read my books for a while. She didn't *exactly* say I had to stay in the schoolroom."

Then, one afternoon, lost in Black Beauty's troubles, Owain realized with a start that Ellie had been with him for hours. "Ellie, *bach,* look at the time! They'll be tearing up the house searching for you if you don't go."

She turned away, but not before he'd seen a downcast turn to her lip. "What is it, Ellie, *bach?*"

"Charlotte won't miss me. She begins a lesson, then she tells me to read and she goes off by herself. She's gone for ages. I'm so lonely, Owain. Please let me stay with you."

Charlotte dreaded facing Evan each time she served a meal or encountered him in the hall. She was certain her expression, her every word and gesture gave away her state of mind.

She must look different, she knew, because she felt so different. During those precious days when she slipped away to meet Stephen, she didn't recognize herself. She was like a woman possessed. She could think of nothing but Stephen, his smile, his touch, the rapture of his lovemaking. She resented everything that prevented her from being with him and was even impatient with dear little Eleanor.

Perhaps, Charlotte rationalized, her sense of urgency was because she knew, deep down, that their love would be fleeting. Zoe would start speaking again and Stephen would have to take her to London. Or else word would come from America that the Hathaways were coming, and heaven only knew what would happen to her then.

Still, knowing that she and Stephen must part, she was not prepared for the afternoon when Stephen held her in his arms and told her that Zoe had arisen that morning, insisted that her maid dress her, and appeared at breakfast in a talkative mood. They were leaving for London the following day.

"I want you to come up to the studio with me," Stephen said. They had been meeting in different places: the gazebo, the woods, a rocky hollow on the mountainside, the summer house down by the lake. Secret, concealing places, away from prying eyes. "Just one more time, Charlotte, please. It's all right. Zoe's nurse is with her and they're packing. We shan't be disturbed, and there's something you must see."

It would be her finished portrait. She had almost forgotten about it. She nodded, still numb from the news that they would part so soon.

In the studio, the portrait of Eleanor and herself aboard ship stood on an easel near the window. Charlotte's golden gown matched Eleanor's golden hair, and their eyes were wide and seeking. They looked serene, but in the background the endless sea churned restlessly, hinting of turbulence to come. Despite the flattering way in which he had rendered her, Charlotte found herself disturbed by the picture, but unsure why.

"It's beautiful," she said uncertainly.

"Charlotte," Stephen spoke from behind her. "Look."

Turning, she gasped as she saw a second easel bearing another finished picture. In it she was alone, reclining on a satin-draped chaise longue. She was nude.

"Oh, Stephen, no! How could you?"

His anticipatory smile vanished. "How could I? Why, you little fool—it's the best thing I've ever done. It's you as you looked that first day I made love to you. It is the awakening of passion. The virgin in the moment she becomes a wanton. It is a woman in love and willing to sacrifice everything for an unattainable man, a forbidden love."

Charlotte reeled backward, as though he had struck her with his words. "You speak of *it* . . . as though I were an inanimate object, instead of a living, breathing person. As if your art were more important than my life."

"My art *is* more important than life, yours, mine, anyone's. Don't you understand? Art has the power to remake life."

"Stephen . . . I believed we came together in love. That we shared something more than the creation of a work of art. That we shared . . . a small portion of our lives with one another."

"Charlotte, I thought that you, of all women, would understand that life and art cannot be separated. To paint a picture that did not show an aspect of the world, or an insight into the human condition, would be like writing a novel without a theme. Can't you see what this picture reveals? That the flame of desire is the essence of life, consumes life, and is itself consumed by it.''

She could only back away from him, stumbling over her skirts. He made no attempt to follow or touch her. He stared at her with empty eyes, as though she had already disappeared from his life. She thought, in fascinated horror, he's disappointed because I'm not stammering praise for his work. Because his paintings are not as important to me as they are to him. He isn't grieving because we must part tomorrow. What he has rendered on canvas is finished. Now he can move on to the next subject . . .

She didn't say good-bye. She turned and fled.

The following morning, Charlotte lay in bed after a sleepless night, reluctant to rise and face the day. The past weeks of awakening to the anticipation of seeing Stephen were over, and she now saw in horrid clarity the truth of their affair. She had thought what she was feeling was a fleeting radiance, as if for a little while all the joy in the universe belonged to her alone, and that even when the brilliance was extinguished by the mundane matters of daily living, the memory of euphoria would sustain her forever. But the sordid reality she faced this morning made her hate herself.

Several times she threw back the covers to rise, but a terrible lethargy seemed to have overtaken her. More than the fatigue due to lack of sleep, this was a leaden-limbed, bleary-eyed hopelessness that seemed to drench her soul, causing the world to fade into bleak monotones.

When at last Lizzie knocked frantically on her bedroom door and implored her please to come because Mr. Evan was demanding his breakfast, Charlotte got out of bed. Instantly, a wave of dizziness and nausea assailed her.

She sat down again, waiting for the squeezing sensation in her head to cease.

Somehow she was able to dress and go down to the kitchen. Carrying Evan's kippers to the breakfast room made her so sick to her stomach, she was afraid she would be unable to serve them. Clenching her teeth, she willed herself not to retch as she placed the food on the sideboard.

"You look pale," Evan said. "Are you ill?"

"A little tired, that's all."

His eyes searched her face. "You know they're leaving for London today?" She nodded. He seemed about to say more but changed his mind and dismissed her.

The nausea she had felt on rising persisted all day, and as soon as she had served Evan's dinner, she was forced to tell Eleanor she was too tired for their customary hour together before bed.

That night Charlotte retired early and slept like the dead, but awakened more tired than before and couldn't keep her breakfast down. Her breasts felt strangely heavy and misshapen, as though filled with little wooden blocks.

She spent the following days battling the sickness and counting the minutes until she could crawl back into bed, at the same time insisting when Evan questioned her that she was not ill. She became obsessed with sleep; it was all she seemed able to think or care about. She was surprised that it took precedence over her feelings about Stephen leaving Glendower.

Three weeks later, it occurred to her that she had missed her monthly cycle, and she realized the enormity of her dilemma. She was carrying Stephen's child.

10

ELEANOR PIROUETTED AROUND her make-believe stage, turned to face an audience of lilac bushes and, arms akimbo, declared in ringing tones, "Why, Sir Giles, I could not possibly marry you. I am in love with Sir Owain—"

She broke off, listening. This part of the garden was a long way from the houses on the estate, and no one had ever found her here. Lately she'd been able to spend lots of time pretending to be a famous actress, because Owain still couldn't walk, and the stablemaster would not allow her to take out a horse by herself. Charlotte seemed to have forgotten she was supposed to be pretending to be Eleanor's mother. Her beloved nanny floated around the grange like a gray wraith, silent and frighteningly distant. Eleanor had several times come upon her retching into the china bowl on her washstand, or lying on the couch with a cloth over her eyes. Charlotte said she wasn't ill, yet she was so pale, and there were dark smudges under her eyes. Eleanor wished her mother and father would hurry up and come so they could take care of Charlotte.

A bird that had been singing in a nearby willow stopped abruptly. The sound that had intruded was louder now, a heavy footfall, the snapping of branches as he came through the copse of trees. Eleanor knew it would be Mr. Evan, even before he reached the clearing where she stood.

Although she had become accustomed to his great size and he had never said or done anything to frighten her, the mere fact that he was coming to her secret place was reason enough to be upset. She hadn't even told Owain about her little "theater."

One of the lilacs trembled, as if in fright, and the giant appeared. He wore riding clothes, and Eleanor stared at his shiny black boots. She had often seen him riding his enormous black horse, who had a long black mane and a hide as sleek and shiny as the boots his master wore. "Hello, Eleanor," he said in his deep voice. "I want you to come back to the grange with me now."

She walked beside him, silently worrying about the possible reasons why Charlotte would summon her from play on a Saturday morning, and why Mr. Evan would interrupt his ride to fetch her. Something was very wrong with Charlotte, and Eleanor didn't dare imagine what it might be.

Halfway across the lawn, to the rear of the grange, Mr. Evan said, "Do you remember the first of the *Gymanfa Ganu* parties?"

"Oh, yes. I recited *The Children's Hour*."

"Do you remember meeting the actor, Tristan Cressey?"

"Yes, sir." The actor had been very handsome and had told Eleanor she was enchanting.

"And Lord and Lady Ramsey, do you remember them?"

"Yes. Lady Ramsey said she had a little girl at home."

Eleanor waited for him to make some further comment, but he didn't. They entered the grange through the front door and he led her to the drawing room.

The reason for mentioning Lord and Lady Ramsey immediately became clear. They were seated in the drawing room, along with a plump auburn-haired little girl with a very freckled face. Charlotte was not present, which worried Eleanor.

Lady Ramsey smiled and said, "Ah, here's dear Eleanor. How are you my little love? We're so pleased to see you again. We would like to present our daughter, Veronica. Say hello, dear."

The red-haired little girl scowled as Eleanor said, "Good morning, Lord and Lady Ramsey. Hello, Veronica, I'm happy to meet you."

"We saw the picture that Stephen painted of you," Lady Ramsey said. "It's quite breathtaking, but not as pretty as you are in the flesh."

The scowl on the red-haired girl's face deepened, and Eleanor, recognizing unbridled jealousy when she saw it, wished Lady Ramsey would not gush at her so. Lord Ramsey, who with his silver hair and wrinkles seemed very, very old compared to his pretty young wife, merely smiled benignly.

Mr. Evan, who was now seated in his massive fireside chair, said, "Eleanor, before we send for your mother, we wanted to explain to you what we have been considering."

Surprised that grown-ups would deign to do such a thing, and not entirely comfortable with the situation, Eleanor waited expectantly. Evan went on, "Lord and Lady Ramsey have very kindly invited you to stay with them at their London house during the coming season."

Lady Ramsey interjected, "You could share Veronica's tutors, and attend the theater with us. I understand you're ten years old. I feel you're quite grown-up enough to sit in our box at Drury Lane and Covent Garden. Veronica has no playmates her own age, and we have been seeking a suitable companion for her for some time. Someone like you, dear, who is not only pretty and well-behaved, but also clever and talented."

Behind her mother's back, Veronica stuck out her tongue at Eleanor, who was still digesting the magic words: *theater, Drury Lane, Covent Garden*. "Charlotte . . . my mother would come, too?"

They all exchanged glances. Evan said, "No, Eleanor. Your mother would remain here. You would come back to spend Christmas with her, of course. This is an exceptional opportunity for you, but there is another reason I would like you to accept this invitation. Your mother is not well. I fear that caring for you while she is ill is too taxing for her. She has been neglecting your lessons of late, and then wearing herself out worrying that she has done so. If she were assured you were well cared for and properly tutored, she could then perhaps recover her strength."

"Darling," Lady Ramsey said. "If, when we send for her, you tell her you'd love to come, we think she might agree."

Eleanor didn't know what to say. She wished she could discuss the offer privately with Charlotte. As it was, she'd have to accept or decline without her advice. It was certainly true that Charlotte hadn't been her normal self lately, and there'd been no lessons at all. Charlotte could barely drag herself through her household duties. The prospect of going to the real theater was tempting, but what if Mother and Father arrived while she was away? Eleanor supposed Charlotte would send them to London. She'd miss Owain, of course, but he'd told her a secret. As soon as he could walk and ride again, he was leaving Glendower to seek his fortune.

They were all looking at her expectantly, except for Veronica, who glowered menacingly and twisted her gloves as though wringing the neck of a chicken.

Charlotte felt as if she had turned completely inward. Nothing mattered beyond her constantly churning stomach, her heavy, tingling breasts, and the endless fatigue that no amount of sleep could cure. She felt as if she were a prisoner in her own body, and her physical miseries prevented her from thinking about anything other than how to get through each wearying day.

Having to serve Evan's meals was the worst ordeal. The mere smell of most food sent her racing to lose her own meager last meal. She was losing weight, and her pretty new gowns hung loosely on her gaunt frame. She was concerned that there'd been no reply to the letter she'd sent to Eleanor's parents and thought perhaps she should send another, but she could never find the strength to write it.

She was sitting at the kitchen table, bracing herself to serve Evan's lunch, a savory beef pasty and pickled cabbage, when a footman came into the room. "Mr. Evan wants you in the drawing room. Better take off your apron; he's got company. Lord and Lady Ramsey."

"Thank you," Charlotte said. He hadn't mentioned he was expecting guests, and, in fact, never entertained. In any event, the Ramseys were Stephen and Zoe's friends. She stood up slowly, having felt faint when she rose too quickly, and started for the drawing room. Evan had watched her closely lately, and inquired frequently if she were feeling well enough to work, but he couldn't possibly suspect the true nature of her malady. She knew she would soon have to make plans for when her pregnancy became obvious, but now she simply didn't have the strength.

In the drawing room, she listened as Lady Ramsey told her of their plans for Eleanor, adding, "Your daughter is in the same position here at Glendower that Veronica is in London. That is, neither of them have children their own age to play with. You see, except for the theater season, we spend most of our time at our estate in Surrey, while Veronica is away at boarding school. We've already talked to Eleanor, and if you'll give your permission, she would like to come."

Their daughter looked to be a rather spoiled and disagreeable child, but Eleanor's eyes lit up when Lady Ramsey said "theater season," although she looked at Charlotte questioningly. The child wanted to go, but only with her blessing. How could she know what a relief it would be not to have to worry about her for a while? She'd have excellent tutors, the opportunity to see London, and visits to the theater—a dream come true for her. "You certainly have my permission, Eleanor, if you would like to go," Charlotte said.

Evan watched from his study window as Charlotte snipped the last of the roses and placed them in a basket over her arm. She moved slowly, every line of her slender body expressing a weariness that worried him greatly. He knew little or nothing about women's ailments, but it was obvious that she was in a decline, and he felt helpless and angry. Charlotte's poor health had begun when Stephen and Zoe left for London. The connection was obvious. She was pining for Stephen.

Several times Evan started for the door to go to her. But what could he say to ease such pain? She would be embarrassed to know that he was even aware of it. He wasn't sure what it was about this frail little woman that awakened in him feelings he thought he had long since stifled.

Once, in his youth, he had fallen madly in love with a young woman and confessed his love. Her rejection was still too painful to recall.

Years later, when he came to Glendower a wealthy man, he thought that perhaps his new position in life might persuade a woman to accept his height, and in his loneliness he recklessly proposed to a young widow without means. He had been humiliated beyond endurance when she had gasped in horror. She'd screamed at him that he was not to think of her so, that it was disgraceful and degrading and how dare he imagine she would want to hear she was loved by a monstrous freak?

It wasn't long before rumors started to fly that no decent woman was safe near him, and he found himself shunned by most men as well.

After that he confined his advances to women who accepted remuneration for the pleasure of their company, and despised them and himself for it. When several of Stephen's conquests left Glendower abruptly, blame was always placed on the giant. Even servants on the estate believed it—he supposed because people expected such deeds of a man so different from other men. He told himself he disliked women, their vanities, their weakness, their empty-headed chatter, and since he had no men friends, he became a near recluse.

Until Charlotte arrived at Glendower. She was not like other women. The casing of ice around Evan's heart melted before her quiet dignity, her fearlessness. A frail little woman who stood up to him when strong men would not was surely a rare and precious find. Yet there was also a soothing tranquility about her that calmed his nerves. When he danced with her at the *Gymanfa* party, she had felt like gossamer in his arms, and he had felt such tenderness toward her that he could scarcely speak. He was falling in love again, and didn't know how to stop.

But she loved Stephen. All women loved Stephen, while he only sought in them the qualities he couldn't find in Zoe. Evan turned away from the window so he wouldn't have to see what Stephen had done to Charlotte.

Moments later there was a knock on his study door and he was surprised when Owain Davies hobbled into the room, a crutch under his arm. "Could I have a word with you please, sir?"

"I thought the doctor told you to stay in bed. Here, sit down."

"I was getting bed sores, sir. And weak from lying about."

"What did you want to talk to me about?"

The young groom looked him directly in the eye. "Miss Eleanor, sir. She told me she's going to London with Lord and Lady Ramsey."

Evan was amused. "And you don't want her to go? I don't blame you. I understand she's been reading to you."

"It's not that, sir. I'm worried, look you. Lady Athmore is in London and she had it in her mind she wanted Ellie—Miss Eleanor."

Evan liked young Davies, but he was going too far now. A groom had no business even thinking about his employer's affairs. Still, it had been Owain Davies who saved the child's life, at considerable cost to himself. He deserved an answer. "Lady Athmore is under a doctor's care in London, which is a very large city. There is no possibility she and the child will meet."

Davies didn't look convinced, but he raised himself awkwardly on his crutch and started to leave. Evan said, "Wait a minute. I recall that you told me you went to work down in the pit when you were ten. Did you ever go to school? Learn to read?"

Owain mumbled, "Went to school for a bit, but I never learned to read English properly. Just a bit of Welsh."

"Would you like to?"

"Beg your pardon, sir?"

"You're not much use to me as a groom at present, although

you're the best man on the estate when it comes to horses, and even the stablemaster heeds your advice. Therefore I don't want to lose you. There's a retired schoolmaster in Llanrys who tutors students. I could arrange for you to move in with him.''

Owain was so flabbergasted, he almost fell off his crutch.

Charlotte finished arranging the vase of roses for the table and, seeing that Cook had dinner well under way, went up to see how Eleanor was proceeding with her selection of the clothes she wanted to take to London. Thanks to Lady Athmore, Eleanor had more than enough clothes to impress the Ramseys.

When Charlotte entered Eleanor's room, however, she found the child lying facedown on her bed, sobbing uncontrollably.

"Why, my dear, whatever is wrong?" Charlotte asked, sitting down beside Eleanor and drawing her into her arms. "Darling child, if you've changed your mind about going to the Ramseys, you certainly don't have to go."

Raising a tearstained face, Eleanor said, "It's not that . . . it's . . . oh, Charlotte, Mother and Father are dead! They're really dead and it's because we pretended they were.''

"What are talking about? Darling, they're not dead. Just because we haven't heard from them—"

Eleanor struggled free and reached down beside the bed. She picked up two crumpled magazines and thrust them into Charlotte's hands. "Lizzie found these in Llanrys and bought them for me because they're from America.''

There was an ancient copy of *Harper's Weekly*, and a more recent *Leslie's*. Both carried long, featured articles about Indian warfare in the southwestern states, Arizona and New Mexico in particular.

Charlotte flipped rapidly through the pages of pictures, captions and headlines:

RANKING SECOND IN REPUTATION FOR CRUELTY AND ATROCITIES ONLY TO THE COMANCHES, THE APACHES MURDER WOMEN AND TORTURE CHILDREN . . .

PIMA VALLEY OVERRUN AND DESOLATED BY RED DEVILS . . .

THE WORD APACHE IS SYNONYMOUS WITH MURDER.

COUNTLESS RANCHERS AND SHEEPHERDERS SLAIN BY RENEGADE APACHES.

ARIZONA SCOUTS ON THE GILA DISPLAY THE TROPHIES

OF THEIR HUNTING, WHICH IS DEVOTED TO MAKING LIVE
INDIANS INTO GOOD INDIANS.

NEW MEXICAN RANCHER IS COOKED TO DEATH BY
BRAVES OVER HIS OWN STOVE.

But worse than the lurid text were the pictures—sketches of
depraved looking Indians butchering and scalping settlers, heart-
rending illustrations of homesteads ablaze, children being carried
off by Apaches, a stagecoach with a dead driver, and a passenger
riddled with arrows. If the magazines had carried only hand-
drawn sketches, Charlotte could have explained that sensationalism sold magazines, but there were a few grim photographs, too.
There were photos of a murdered sheepherder who appeared to be
Mexican and a dead soldier. The articles indicated that an
undeclared war of a particularly deadly sort was sweeping the
entire southwestern United States, and that the settlers and
soldiers were losing to the Indians.

"They're dead," Eleanor sobbed, resisting Charlotte's efforts
to enfold her in her arms. "We've been here ages and ages. If
Mother was alive, she would have answered your letter."

Charlotte pressed her hand to the continual ache in her back.
"Eleanor, you must stop imagining the worst. There are many
reasons why we haven't had a response to my letter. Perhaps my
letter never reached them."

The nagging thought at the back of Charlotte's mind was the
fact that, in order to leave Boston, she had contrived to make
Eleanor's grandfather believe they had drowned. Charlotte was
beginning to fear that Stansfield Hathaway had sent word of their
demise to Eleanor's parents before her letter from England
reached them, and that they had returned to Boston. But if she
were now to write to Stansfield's home in Boston and disclose
what she had done, she had no doubt he would press kidnapping
charges against her.

Or else, as these dreadful magazine articles suggested, Amy
and Hugh Hathaway might indeed have perished at the hands of
the savage Indians.

The possibilities were simply too much to consider in her
present physical and mental state. Anxious to console the child,
she said, "If we haven't heard from your parents by the end of the
month, then I'll take you home to your grandfather."

Eleanor's tears stopped instantly. "No! No, please, Charlotte,
I don't want to go back there. Grandfather hates me, and that

terrible, old Mr. Yarborough will touch me and squeeze me . . .''

"Then you must be patient, at least for a little while longer. If there is no letter from New Mexico by the end of the month, I'll find a way to ascertain where your parents are.''

"But I'll be in London with Lord and Lady Ramsey at the end of the month.'' She dissolved into tears again. "They're dead, I know they are. They've been killed by murdering redskins, like the magazines say.''

Charlotte felt her stomach churning again, and had to end the conversation. She picked up the magazines and tucked them under her arm. "Promise me you won't say that, or even think it. And I promise I'll find out where they are.''

She struggled against the inexorable pull of quicksand, thrashing, sinking, in the horrid muck. Somewhere over her head she saw the silhouette of a man feverishly flinging paint onto a canvas. He glanced down at her and her soundless scream echoed across the sinister marsh. He merely held his brush at arm's length, measuring perspective, and returned to his easel. She thought, in absolute horror, *he's painting a portrait of death . . . of my death! I no longer exist for him . . . perhaps I never existed.*

Children must be seen and not heard, Charlotte. Don't pester me, dear, I must write my sermon. Do be quiet, Charlotte, I'm expecting the ladies of the Charity League for tea . . . go to your room and stay there until teatime.

Stephen . . . oh, Stephen please look at me. See me. I would do anything for you . . . anything. Let me serve you, let me love you . . .

The quicksand was closing over her head, sucking her down.

Just before the blackness engulfed her, she awakened, sitting bolt upright. Pale moonlight fell in a single beam from window to bed, like a silver path to heaven. For a minute she fought to catch her breath, her hand clutching her breast to still the pounding of her heart. Bending over the bowl she had placed beside her bed, she retched up a foul-tasting fluid.

Trembling, Charlotte lay back on her pillow, cold perspiration clinging to brow, breasts and hands, her entire body ravaged by aches and pains. During the day she bound a length of flannel sheeting around her abdomen, in addition to her stays, to disguise the swelling, and usually it was a relief to take it off at night. But tonight the faint fluttering she had felt inside her was curiously absent. Had she killed the child within her by binding herself too tightly? The thought should have struck terror into her, because then she, too, was surely doomed, yet the idea that she might cease to exist was somehow comforting. Not to have to force her exhausted limbs to move. Not to be faced with Eleanor's tears for her parents, or with the fear of the consequences of so many rash actions. Most of all, to be able to let go of the longing for Stephen's arms around her again.

For a moment she savored the idea. How easy it would be . . . Zoe had shown her the way. The roof parapet outside Stephen's studio . . . she could step from it into merciful oblivion. But wait, if she were dead, then there was no one to restore Eleanor to her parents. She would write another letter then, this time to Mr. and Mrs. Hugh Hathaway in care of Stansfield Hathaway of Boston. That way, a member of Eleanor's family would be sure to receive word of where she had taken the child.

Relief flooded over Charlotte. She rose and went to her writing table and wrote the letter, addressed and sealed the envelope. Next she wrote a letter to Eleanor, in care of Lord and Lady Ramsey in London, explaining that she had to go away on a long journey, but that her parents would shortly come for her. In the morning, both letters would be delivered to Whitcombe so that the butler could give them to the postman.

After that, Charlotte could slip up to Stephen's now deserted studio, step out onto the parapet, and . . .

She went back to bed and fell into a dreamless sleep.

Whitcombe watched as Mrs. Carmichael held first one and then the other letter to the spout of a steaming kettle. Peeling open the envelopes, the housekeeper read Charlotte's words with obvious excitement.

"Well?" Whitcombe asked.

Mrs. Carmichael looked up at him with crafty-eyed satisfaction. "Isn't it fortunate," she asked archly, "that today I take the train to London to be with my mistress? These letters will be in my lady's hands by nightfall."

The butler snatched the letters from her and read them himself. He gave her a stern look. "You be sure to tell her ladyship I was the one who sent them to her. When she reads this, I'm sure she'll be more than generous to both of us."

"You just be careful what you say to him over at the grange, look you. If he finds out my precious Zoe is no longer under that doctor's care . . ."

"I know where my loyalties lie," Whitcombe said coldly. "And speaking of letters . . . you'd better burn the one inviting you to London. I'll tell Mr. Evan you've gone to look after your sister in Cardiff."

The housekeeper pulled a sheet of paper from her apron pocket and read it once again.

> MY DEAR MRS. CARMICHAEL:
> STEPHEN AND I HAVE LEFT THAT DREADFUL CLINIC AND NOW HAVE A FASHIONABLE ADDRESS IN THE HEART OF THE CITY. I NEED YOU TO RUN MY HOUSEHOLD FOR ME. ENCLOSED IS YOUR FARE TO LONDON. TELL WHITCOMBE THAT HE IS TO REMAIN AND WATCH OUT FOR OUR INTERESTS AT GLENDOWER. I WISH HIM TO REPORT TO ME EVERYTHING THAT EVAN DOES, AND ESPECIALLY ANY NEWS IN REGARD TO MRS. DANFORTH AND ELEANOR.
> NEEDLESS TO SAY, WE DO NOT WISH THE GIANT TO KNOW ABOUT OUR RELOCATION. YOU WILL ALSO FIND ENCLOSED A BANK DRAFT FOR YOU AND ONE FOR WHITCOMBE, TOKENS OF MY APPRECIATION TO GOOD AND FAITHFUL SERVANTS.

Mrs. Carmichael dropped the letter into the flames of the kitchen fire. "Wait till my lady finds out that little Eleanor is with the Ramseys and living in the city so close to her."

There had been no opportunity to slip away to Stephen's studio. All day long Charlotte had found her footsteps dogged either by one or other of the grange servants, or by Evan himself. During the afternoon Owain Davies had come in from Llanrys, where he was now living with a retired schoolmaster.

Although still needing crutches, Owain looked stronger and his burns had healed, leaving only slight scars that spider-webbed his brow and disappeared into his curly, black hair. "I wondered if you'd give me Ellie's address," he said gruffly, avoiding her eyes. "I'd like to send her a book for Christmas."

There seemed no gracious way to refuse, so Charlotte wrote the address of Lord and Lady Ramsey on a slip of paper and handed it to him. She saw his lips move slightly as he carefully read what she had written. He smiled, his eyes lighting up and transforming his fierce expression into a gentler countenance.

He's learned to read, Charlotte thought, and probably to write, too, and he's awed by the power it's given him. Or perhaps that smile was one of contemplation, at the prospect of sending a present to Eleanor.

Feeling already removed from worldly cares, Charlotte suddenly wanted these last hours on earth to be generous ones, so she said, "I'm sure Eleanor misses you, Owain. You were her only true friend here."

"I miss her, too," he answered softly. "It was a pleasure just to watch her walk across the garden. She brightened every corner of the earth just by being there, look you." He looked embarrassed all at once, and abruptly thanked her and left.

That evening as she served Evan's dinner she found she was more aware of him than she had been for weeks. The look of concern in his eyes, the way his great hand hovered near her as she placed a plate before him, as though ready to catch her if she should stumble. When she brought in a heavy silver dish containing lamb stew, he immediately leaped to his feet and hurried to take it from her. It struck her again how graceful he was, considering his enormous size, and she wondered how many other evenings he had acted with such consideration for her and, lost in her misery, she had been unaware.

"Are you feeling better, Mrs. Danforth? You seem perhaps a little less pale this evening."

"Yes, thank you. Much better."

"I wish you would speak with the doctor. Perhaps a tonic of some kind . . ." He gestured helplessly, as someone of superior physical strength may do when faced with the frailty of others.

"I'm all right, really."

"I trust you are not missing your daughter too much. She'll be returning for a visit soon."

"Yes . . ." Charlotte looked away, blinking a tear from her lashes.

As she was leaving she turned and looked at him, smiling her gratitude for his concern. "You have been very kind to me, Mr. Evan, and patient with my recent poor health. Thank you." She paused, then added, "Good night, and may God bless you."

Now why did I say that? she wondered as she went up to her own room. Did it sound final? Did I, in fact, say good-bye, or good night? Well, no matter.

In her own room she put on clean underwear and then, for no reason she could fathom, slipped the gold evening dress over her head. It was very tight over her bosom and especially her abdomen. The child moved inside her, a little bump protruding from her, clearly visible through the satin. A foot, a tiny fist? So, he was awake. Forgive me, my darling, but there is no place in this world for you and me. We go to a much better, safer place, where we'll always be together. We won't bring grief or shame to ourselves, or to others.

She brushed her hair, then slipped the cape Stephen had given her over her shoulders, her fingers caressing the cool, impersonal softness of the velvet.

No one saw her as she left the grange and crossed the courtyard. It was a moonless autumn evening, with a chill in the air that spoke of winter. She breathed deeply, feeling a blessed calmness creep through her.

The tradesmen's door of the main house was never locked, and at this hour most of the servants would be at their evening meal. She went unobserved up to Stephen's studio and lit the lamp. Most of his canvases had been removed. She supposed they'd been sent to him in London. His empty easels seemed abandoned, lonely and forlorn. She trailed her fingers over the worn wood, conjuring a vision of Stephen in her mind. He was not to be judged or condemned, as other men might be. His genius exempted him from society's rules and conventions.

She moved toward the wall of windows as if in a trance.

As she opened the window a gust of cold air momentarily startled her, and for an instant she was afraid she would not be able to step from the parapet. Wasn't it always thus? That the toothache disappeared at the dentist's door. Her nausea had vanished today, and she'd awakened with a sense of well-being, despite her disturbed sleep. She told herself she was feeling better simply because she had made the decision to end it all, and she stepped out onto the parapet.

Are you watching, Mama and Papa? Soon I shall neither be seen nor heard. Will that please you?

Below on the terrace, the great stone urns, empty of flowers now, regarded her like the sightless sockets of a skull. The bare branches of the trees beckoned, urging her to jump. She closed her eyes and murmured a prayer for forgiveness.

She wasn't aware of sound or movement behind her, only of

massive arms surrounding her. Fighting like a demon, she felt one foot dance in the air, and she screamed for him to let her go.

Zoe bestowed one of her radiant smiles upon Mrs. Carmichael, who was enjoying a cup of tea in the kitchen of the mews house near Hyde Park that Stephen had rented.

"You are such a treasure, how glad I am to have you here," Zoe said, placing Charlotte's two letters on the table in front of her. "What an interesting story unfolds here."

"Well, of course, madam, I never read the letters myself, so I wouldn't know," Mrs. Carmichael said primly. "But I decided right away they should be brought to you. If I may say so, my lady, it's a treat to see you looking so well."

Zoe read the letters a second time, then folded them up. "After you're settled in, we'll discuss hiring a staff. Lord Athmore also needs a carpenter to convert one of the bedrooms into a studio."

"You won't be returning to Glendower then, Lady Athmore?"

"We shan't go back in the near future. My husband will return to take care of estate business from time to time. Of course, we'll take up residence there again one day." She paused, her dark eyes narrowing to slits. "When certain obstacles have been removed."

Leaving her housekeeper to finish her tea, Zoe returned to her study, feeling particularly pleased with herself. Not only had she convinced the doctor that she was perfectly sane and normal and that the stories of her "derangement" were nothing more than Stephen's uncle's attempt to depose them from the estate, but now she had in her hands the means to make Eleanor her very own daughter.

These letters told the complete story, including Charlotte's confession of the ruse to make the Hathaways believe their child had drowned. Now all Zoe had to do was turn Charlotte's deception against her. She would send a letter from America—easy for Zoe to accomplish by writing to her old nurse in New Orleans—informing Mrs. Danforth that Eleanor's entire family had perished. Perhaps a fire had destroyed their home in Boston? Zoe giggled. She loved imagining such disasters and inflicting them upon people who had angered her.

But wait . . . apparently Eleanor's parents had gone west, leaving her with her grandfather in Boston who had terrorized the child and whose friend had molested her . . . at least in the Danforth woman's opinion. Her letter stated that she had brought Eleanor to England because the situation was intolerable in Boston, and she feared exposing the child to the dangers of the Western frontier by taking her to her parents. Charlotte had written:

"While I realize the seriousness of what I have done, and am aware of the charges that could be brought against me, I do beg of you not to return Eleanor to her grandfather's care. I fear if you do, either great harm will come to her, or she will run away."

That man, Stansfield Hathaway, seemed to have inspired great fear in Mrs. Danforth. Therefore a better plan would be to make her, and Eleanor, believe that Eleanor's parents were dead but that he was still alive . . . it might be convenient at some time to use his existence, and the threat of Eleanor being returned to him, to her own advantage.

She glanced at Charlotte's letter to Eleanor again and the last paragraph leaped from the page, suddenly taking on new significance.

". . . and my dear child, although I will never see you again, in a way I'll always be with you. Do you remember when we sailed from New York, how we watched America vanish beyond the horizon? We could no longer see the land, but we knew it was still there. I shall always be there for you, so that even when you can't see me, if you need me, all you'll have to do is think of me and I shall be the little voice in your mind guiding you . . ."

Why, the words sounded like those of one who knew they were going to die, and the only people who knew that were suicides . . .

Charlotte felt as if she were floating up a long dark chimney, rising toward light and sound, yet thinking she would prefer to remain in the peaceful void below.

A deep voice addressed her, urging her to wake up. "Charlotte, do you hear me? Please, open your eyes."

Her eyelids were heavy, but she obeyed. Evan's face, worry written in every line, hovered over her. He said, using her given name again, "You fainted, Charlotte. I carried you back to your room in the grange. No one knows you were in the studio tonight. Forgive my taking the liberty, but I removed your gown as it seemed to be restricting your breathing."

Beneath the blanket her traveling fingers learned that she wore only her chemise. He had not only removed her gown, but also her stays. That knowledge was the least of her problems. She stared up at him. "You should have let me go. You had no right—"

"No, my poor, dear love, you do not have the right. You have no right to deprive us of your gentleness and wisdom, of the beauty of your soul. Don't you see, it was but a temporary madness that overcame you tonight? In the morning you will remember that there are always solutions to seemingly insurmountable problems."

"You don't understand—"

"You're carrying Stephen's child. I know that now and curse myself for a fool that I didn't realize it before."

Charlotte turned her face from him. "Oh, dear God in heaven . . ."

Gently taking her by the shoulders, Evan turned her to face him. "Listen to me carefully. I own a villa in Italy. I haven't been there for years. You will spend the next few months there, until your child is born. Eleanor can stay with the Ramseys, and we'll tell her you're abroad for your health."

Charlotte was too overcome to speak. Evan asked, "Does Stephen know?" She shook her head. He said, "Good. I'll make the arrangements first thing tomorrow. You must rest now."

Incredibly, as he tucked the blanket around her, he bent and kissed her forehead, as though comforting a child.

How very kind he is, Charlotte thought, as sleep began to take her. Tomorrow I shall tell him the truth about Eleanor and me. He will know what to do to reunite the child and her parents.

How could she have known that Zoe's letter was already on the way to Glendower containing the dreadful news that Hugh and Amy Hathaway had both been killed by Apaches? The letter was supposedly written by an anonymous servant of Stansfield Hathaway, advising Charlotte that he had intercepted her letter to Hugh and Amy Hathaway, and, being aware of his master's vindictiveness, suggested that she not take the chance of communicating with him again.

Charlotte traveled to London to break the news to Eleanor that she was an orphan, then continued on to Italy to await the birth of Stephen's child.

11

CHARLOTTE LEANED FORWARD eagerly to drink in the winter-bare beauty of the countryside as the carriage rolled toward Glendower. Stripped of foliage and flowers, the gaunt ridges and jagged peaks of the mountains and the tracery of tree branches etched against the sky provided a landscape of unadorned grandeur that was breathtaking in its sheer simplicity.

Spring came late here in North Wales, but there was already a certain quality to the air that promised an end to winter.

How comforting it was to see that the earth remained un-changed. Its inhabitants came and went, growing older, always in a state of flux, marked by passing time that did not seem to touch the mountains and streams. She had spent far more time in Italy than she planned, well over a year, due to the fact that she had been ill for a time and slow to recover, yet the journey from Llanrys might have followed her last trip by only a day. Until she reached the Glendower estate.

The carriage had been traveling on the estate for several miles when it occurred to her that there was a curiously empty aspect to the land that had nothing to do with winter dormancy—an eerie quietness broken only by the sound of wheels on gravel and the occasional chirping of a bird.

After awhile, she realized that they hadn't passed a living soul, no laborers or gardeners preparing for spring planting, no plows, horses, carts, or tradesmen's vehicles.

Drawing closer to the house, she saw that there was also a

neglected appearance to the trees and shrubs, while weeds had sprouted and died in the gravel of the drive. Surely at this time of day the grooms should be exercising the horses? Servants would be coming and going to the kitchen gardens and sheds. But the entire estate seemed deserted.

The sleeping child in her arms stirred and murmured. She looked down at her son and felt a familiar thrill of pride, overlaid with acute anxiety. There were times when she still could not believe the handsome little boy was truly hers. Had she not endured a two-day labor and delivery that had almost killed her, she might have worried that she had fantasized giving birth and that in reality she had stolen one of her employer's babies, just as once she had run off with Eleanor Hathaway. Charlotte's love for her son was so overwhelming that she also lived with the constant fear that she would not be able to take care of him properly or protect him. A penniless, unmarried woman and an illegitimate child had few options in a world that condemned them equally for breaking society's rules.

Charlotte had given her son a Welsh name, Gwynfor, and as was the case with a beloved child, used a diminutive, Gwyn. He had a sweet disposition, and it was already obvious that he had inherited his father's good looks, further adding to Charlotte's feeling of astonishment that he was also part of her flesh. There was absolutely nothing she would not do for Gwyn. She would, quite literally, have died for him. According to her doctor in Florence, she almost had. But Gwyn's need for her had saved her, and she now felt quite well, and more alive than ever before.

The house was now in sight, and she saw the familiar, towering figure standing on the front lawn, watching the carriage approach. Evan must have watched for their arrival from the main house, since from the grange he could not see the lane winding over the hill.

His huge face broke into a wide smile as he helped her down from the carriage. "Welcome home, Charlotte. Come, you must be exhausted after your journey."

She noticed immediately his use of her first name, the fact that he referred to Glendower as her home, and also the quick, anxious glance he gave to the sleeping baby in her arms.

A very young girl with pink cheeks and apprehensive eyes hovered awkwardly a few feet behind Evan, and he beckoned for her to approach. She gave Evan a terrified glance as she passed him. He said, "This is Moira. She's the eldest of a large family and has had plenty of experience with babies. She is to be your son's nursemaid."

Charlotte allowed the girl to take the sleeping baby, having no fear that if Gwyn awakened he would be frightened, as he was such a trusting baby. She walked toward the house at Evan's side, feeling a mixture of emotions—gratitude to him for providing his villa in Florence all these months and for his asking her to return as his housekeeper, curiousity about what had become of Stephen and Zoe, and speculation regarding Evan's reasons for being so kind to her. She felt him looking at her out of the corner of his eye, and she said, "How shall I ever be able to repay you for all you've done for me?"

"There is no need," he answered gruffly. "I'm happy to have a competent housekeeper once again."

He glanced at the main house as they entered the inner courtyard leading to the grange. "The main house is closed. Whitcombe takes care of the place, no doubt in the vain hope that Stephen and Zoe will one day return. The whole place is run-down, you'll find. It seems everyone in the village feels I drove off Stephen and Zoe with my wickedness. The stories of my supposed excesses would be amusing, were they not so vicious. It seems that Stephen's charm and Zoe's beauty were all that was needed to align everyone for miles around on their side. Would you believe that rumor has it I was responsible for Zoe's irrational spells? But I mustn't trouble you with village gossip. Perhaps now you're back, you can persuade some of the former staff to return."

Charlotte was silent, afraid if she replied she would reveal how angry she was at the superstitious bigotry of men and women who were small both in stature and mind when compared with Evan. As for blaming Evan for Zoe's madness, why, that was unconscionable.

In the entry hall at the grange, the present staff stood in line waiting to greet her. Lizzie, the parlor maid, was the only familiar face. A pair of frightened-looking scullery maids, a cook long past her prime, and a footman who looked no more than fourteen years old regarded her expectantly, as if they had been promised she would magically put everything in order.

Charlotte waited until Evan departed, then sent Moira to take the baby to the nursery. Turning to Lizzie, Charlotte said, "Come into the office for a moment."

In the housekeeper's office adjacent to the kitchen, Charlotte asked, "What on earth happened to the staff?"

Lizzie sighed, although her eyes lit up with the prospect of passing along news and gossip. "No one wants to work for him, look you. Right after Lord and Lady Athmore left we started to lose the staff. I thought at first it was old Whitcombe, dismissing everybody just to make things bad for Mr. Evan, because Whitcombe always hated him and didn't like it when Lord Athmore brought him here. But after you went . . . well, Mr. Evan was so hard on everybody. Ranting and raving, and no patience at all. Then there were the nasty rumors . . ."

She paused, her eyes darting about as though afraid Evan might jump out and reprimand her. "Some said Mr. Evan was trying to steal his nephew's inheritance. There was stories about him rampaging about the estate looking for Lord Athmore . . . thinking he was hiding here somewhere. And some said there were bodies buried on the estate . . . women who'd worked here and the giant—I mean, Mr. Evan—had done away with. I'll tell you the truth, I nearly left, myself, look you. There's scared of him I was. He's never kept a housekeeper, and after you left I thought if I stayed I'd get the job, but . . ."

Charlotte's apprehension grew. "I didn't see any laborers, or grooms, or outside staff."

"Gone, all of them. Mr. Evan sold all the horses except that big black one, Emperor, that he rides, and a mare to pull the carriage. Whole estate is going to wrack and ruin, look you. Worst thing he ever did was to send Lord Athmore away. Now even tradesmen from the village don't want to come to Glendower. Why, I was in town last month and the postmistress there said even in Llanrys they've been hearing of the dreadful things done by the mad giant of Glendower."

"Thank you, Lizzie," Charlotte said quickly. "That will be all."

The poor man, she thought, feeling guilty that her affair with Stephen had caused such repercussions for Evan. His reclusive life had left him ill-equipped to run the estate without Stephen. But why hadn't Stephen returned? Was it possible that he had refused to do so without Zoe? And, most perplexing, why had Stephen simply walked away from his inheritance?

At breakfast on the third day after her return Evan asked if she would like to send for Eleanor. "I'm not sure she would wish to leave London just now," Charlotte replied. "I visited her before I came north."

"I trust she and the Ramseys were well," Evan murmured.

"Quite well, thank you. Although Eleanor still has a great fear of having to return to her grandfather's house in Boston. She is going to appear on stage with Tristan Cressey next autumn." Charlotte smiled proudly. "She will be the youngest actress ever to appear with Tristan's troupe. With your permission, I'd like to invite her here for the summer."

"You don't need my permission," Evan said. "Please consider this to be your home."

"How very kind you are."

Their eyes met and held, then she began to serve his breakfast and the delicate thread that had connected them for an instant was broken.

"The Welsh winter must be a shock to your system after living in Italy," Evan commented.

"I'm rather enjoying it. Besides, spring is almost here."

"You've acquired a certain . . . serenity, since I last saw you. I suppose motherhood . . . ?"

She smiled. "And being back at Glendower. I was a little homesick in Italy."

"You don't mind the neglected appearance of the place?"

"I think of it as the countryside reclaiming the land."

"It will be lonely here, I warn you. I've become a hermit, I suppose. No one comes to visit. There will be no parties, no entertaining."

"I shall not be lonely. I have my son and . . ." She broke off, confused. She had been about to say, "And you for company."

"Charlotte—"

"Yes?"

Different emotions claimed his face, flitting by too rapidly for her to read. He seemed about to speak, then said, "Nothing. I'll see you at dinner. I must go into Llanrys today on business. Since Stephen departed more of the estate business falls on my reluctant shoulders."

"Ah, but very capable and strong shoulders they are." Charlotte was surprised by the long, quizzical look he gave her, as if wondering if she were taunting him.

Evan stood at the dining room window, his back to her. She placed the vegetable dish on the sideboard and the lid rattled slightly, no doubt alerting him to her presence. Usually he was seated when she arrived, and tonight there was something forbidding about that great back turned to her.

She cleared her throat. "Good evening, Mr. Evan. I trust you had a pleasant day in Llanrys?"

"You went to his studio today," Evan said, in a curiously flat tone. He turned and looked down at her, like some phantom judge.

Charlotte flushed. "I . . . he painted a picture of me. I wondered if it was still there."

"He took all of his canvases with him to London. There was some talk of an exhibition of his work, but that was before he was forced to commit Zoe."

Charlotte digested this news in silence, glad that Stephen had at last realized he must protect others from his wife. "That must have been a difficult decision for him," she said quietly.

"It's a private institution," Evan said. "Quite pleasant surroundings, from what I hear."

Charlotte studied the succulent pink slices of ham, growing cold on the silver platter. "Where is he now?"

"Abroad somewhere. I haven't heard from him since he left. I thought after he placed Zoe in the asylum he'd turn up in Florence while you were there. Tell me, would you have been glad to see him? Do you wish you could see him now?"

Her heart fluttered like a caged bird. She must take care not to say anything that might jeopardize her position here, or cause her son to lose his comfortable home. "I only wondered about the picture."

A great sigh escaped from Evan. He sank slowly into his chair and gestured for her to be seated. "Charlotte, it's time I told you the truth about Stephen and myself. Including the fact that he won't be returning to Glendower . . . not without my permission, which I doubt I'll be inclined to give. So if you came back here in the hope of seeing him again, it is a futile quest."

He gazed at her thoughtfully for a moment. "I wanted to tell you the truth when you confided in me about your real relationship to Eleanor. But I wasn't sure then you'd ever agree to come back to Glendower."

She waited with some trepidation. Often the revelation of a secret was made in the hope of a similar exchange of confidences. She was unsure if what he was about to say was in reciprocation for her confession about Eleanor, or if it would precede a request for her to tell him about her affair with Stephen. She desperately wanted to regain Evan's former high regard for her, to let him know that her fall from grace had been temporary. Evan had provided for her and Gwyn all these months, and even invited her to return to Glendower, but she feared he had done so only out of a sense of responsibility for his nephew's actions. Sponsorship reluctantly given might easily be withdrawn.

"Stephen is not my nephew. He has no claim to the estate, the title, or even the Athmore name," Evan announced abruptly.

Charlotte waited, not fully comprehending.

"His name really is Stephen Meadows, the name he uses in his artistic endeavors. He took the surname of the English artist who was his mother. He and I had the same father, who did not see fit to marry Stephen's mother. Or perhaps it was she who refused to marry him. She was a bohemian-type woman, with little time to devote to husband or family."

"You are *brothers?*"

"Half brothers, actually. As I told you once, my father married a Welsh woman, my mother, who died when I was born. They blamed my size for her death, and the midwife and doctor warned my father that his wife had given birth to a monstrously large idiot. I was placed in an English orphanage, the story was circulated that I'd died with my mother, and my father went abroad. He met Stephen's mother a few years later, in Paris. She was then an art student. My father doted on Stephen and, when his mother eventually left them, brought him to Glendower. Stephen grew up unaware of the fact that he was a bastard, so you can imagine his shock when our father died suddenly and the family records turned up the fact that the true heir to the title and lands was still living—and by this time running the orphanage. To give Stephen his due, I must admit he immediately came to see me."

Evan paused, staring into space for a moment. "I wasn't very gracious to him. Nor had I much interest in taking over the responsibilities of the title and estate. Eventually, we reached what we thought was an acceptable compromise. He would masquerade as Lord Athmore, and I would return to my ancestral home. A special house—the grange—would be built, with ceilings and doors to accommodate my height. Servants and others would be told that I was Stephen's father's younger brother."

He smiled bitterly. "We were so secretive about my origins and where I'd been lurking all those years, that I suppose it was inevitable that stories of my evil deeds would be concocted by servants and villagers. Anyway, I became Stephen's uncle. It worked fairly well, until he went on his world tour and found himself in New Orleans, bewitched by Zoe."

There was a long silence when he finished speaking. As Charlotte digested all that he had told her, many things became clear to her.

"Charlotte," Evan said at last, "I must know . . . did you come back in the hope of seeing him again?"

She looked into his eyes and saw the shadow of anger, and something else she couldn't define. She said, "No. I hope never to see Stephen again." Lowering her eyes, she hoped he had not recognized the lie.

The moment she entered the kitchen, Charlotte became aware of the excitement of the servants. Their whispering ceased and they all made a great show of attending to their tasks. They had been told that Charlotte had married an Italian gentleman who died shortly after the birth of their son, and she had decided to use her first husband's name, Danforth, instead of a difficult-to-pronounce foreign one. She wondered if the staff believed the story, in view of their surreptitious glances and whispers, which seemed even more pronounced today.

Ignoring them, she went over the day's menu with Cook, checked the provisions in the pantry, gave instructions to the maids, then went back up to her room for her customary hour with Gwyn before tackling the household accounts.

The nursemaid, Moira, had just finished bathing Gwyn. He gurgled happily as he saw his mother, and stretched out his arms to be picked up. Charlotte held her son, walking to the window with him. "Moira, something seems to have caught the fancy of the staff this morning. Do you have any idea what?"

Moira shook her head. "Why no, Mrs. Danforth. There's very little that they tell me about what's going on, look you."

The words were scarcely out of her mouth than there was a loud knock on the door. "Charlotte!" Evan's voice called. "May I see you please?"

The only time he had ever visited her room had been to carry her back there after she had attempted to kill herself. Charlotte hastily handed the baby to Moira and hurried to open the door, fearing that he was bringing news of a calamitous nature. He strode into the room and said to Moira, "Take the child and leave."

Moira lost no time in obeying, as she was terrified of Evan, and it was clear from his expression that he was in a terrible rage. Even Charlotte, who felt she had grown to know him, shrank from his anger. He held a newspaper in one hand and his other fist was clenched, as though ready to strike someone.

He said, "Zoe left the nursing home where, contrary to what he told me, Stephen had placed her. I warned him that she needed to be locked up, that she'd leave otherwise. Apparently those in charge kept it quiet, hoping she'd return. Eventually they notified Stephen, and he returned to London and found her."

Charlotte let out her breath. "Then all is now well? She is back under a doctor's care?"

Evan slapped the newspaper against his hand. "I've been footing the bill for expensive round-the-clock care at the best private asylum in the country. It hasn't cost him a penny. He receives a generous allowance from the estate, in addition to the commissions he is paid for his portraits. There was no need for him to resort to sensationalism in order to sell his work."

"Sensationalism?"

He waved the newspaper. "All of London, not just the art world, is agog at rumors that at a forthcoming exhibition he will unveil the most erotically beautiful picture of a woman ever painted." He paused, his eyes boring into her. "A nude he calls *The Passionate Virgin*. Everyone is speculating as to the identity of the unknown woman in the picture. Wagers are being made in men's clubs and rewards offered for information as to who posed for the picture."

Charlotte's heart had begun to thud. She prayed silently, please, please, please, don't let it be . . .

"Is it you, Charlotte? Is the picture they are talking about the one of yourself that you were looking for in his studio?"

She turned away from him, her cheeks scarlet with shame, unable to speak.

His great hand closed gently around her shoulder. "I shall go to London and stop the exhibition."

"How is that possible? At Glendower you can command him, but in his art he is his own master."

He turned her to face him and she cowered before the expression on his face. "Charlotte, don't you understand—you are the latest victim in a long history of the male artists' unjust punishment of women for their sexual appeal. Walk through any gallery or museum and what do you see? Paintings of women posed in ways to fulfill the artists' sexual fantasies . . . not all of which are harmlessly erotic. How many pictures are there of women being tortured and raped? Have you ever studied Rubens' *Rape of the Daughters of Leucippus?* If you do, you'll see that the artist's skill has made a despicably ugly act beautiful. For hundreds of years male artists have painted pictures of madonnas and virgins, and the message is that all women must fit into those categories or be portrayed as sinners and man-eating wantons. In portraying you as "the passionate virgin" who tempted him, he absolves himself from guilt."

"But we are so remote here at Glendower. Perhaps no one will find out I posed for the picture."

"Damn it, Charlotte, you're missing the point. He has to be held accountable. All artists must be held accountable. They cannot place form over content. They cannot be excused from moral outrage simply because they are talented. Humane values can't be tossed aside . . . Lord, sometimes I wonder why our civilization produces such so-called art, and worse, reveres it."

"What do you suggest I do?" Charlotte asked, frightened by the impassioned intensity of his voice. "It's too late to undo what's already done. If you're afraid I'll bring disgrace to your household—"

He groaned. "For God's sake, stop blaming yourself! Don't you see, the picture is simply the last stage of his betrayal of you. He can't be allowed to profit from the exhibition of your most private moments together. He must be stopped. I won't have your name bandied about men's clubs. He seduced you, abandoned you, and drove you to thoughts of self-destruction. Now he would exploit you by boasting of his conquest to the whole world. Yet other than my banishing him from Glendower, he got off scot-free."

Charlotte placed her hand on his arm and was surprised to feel him tremble slightly, like a great oak touched by a powerful wind, yet her fingers barely grazed his sleeve. "Please, I beg of you, do nothing. If we try to stop the exhibition, we shall only add fuel to what is surely a temporary ripple of excitement in the art world. Let's ignore it and people will soon forget. Besides, how can anyone find me here? Even if the servants know, they won't dare speak of it." She thought, but didn't say, that no one ever came near Glendower, anyway; they were as isolated as if they lived on the moon.

Evan gave an exasperated sigh. "For your sake, Charlotte, I'll do as you wish. But I believe we'll all live to regret it. Give Stephen the proverbial inch, and he'll take a mile."

Certain sections of newspapers and periodicals were missing, Charlotte noted, and some magazines disappeared entirely. She was grateful, because she had no wish to know what was happening in London. She even opened letters from Eleanor nervously, in case there was some mention of Stephen's exhibition. But Eleanor wrote about rehearsing with Tristan and his friends, and said that Lady Ramsey had found a voice tutor for her who recommended singing lessons and that everyone said she had a very sweet singing voice. Everything was wonderful, except that it appeared Veronica Ramsey was still Eleanor's nemesis. For one so young, a certain sophistication had crept into the tone of Eleanor's letters, and Charlotte hoped that in spending so much time with the theatrical crowd, the child was not growing up too fast.

Charlotte avoided going to the main house, not only because she didn't want Evan to believe she was pining for Stephen, but also because she disliked the sullen butler, Whitcombe, whose former status had been diminished by the closing of the house and who was now little more than a caretaker. The crafty-eyed housekeeper, Mrs. Carmichael, had left Glendower some time ago.

It was a pity that Owain Davies had been the first to leave, hoping to better himself. She thought that if Owain had been aware of Evan's difficulties he might have remained, since he had seemed grateful for all Evan had done for him after the accident.

Lizzie told Charlotte, "There's a fool, young Owain is, look you. He thinks he'll get taken on as stablemaster at some big estate, but no master will give him a chance when he goes to apply, not with that limp of his. Oh, he's all right in the saddle, and rides as well as ever, but his leg never mended properly."

It was soon evident to Charlotte that a large segment of the estate had been parceled out to tenant farmers, and the rest allowed to grow wild. As Evan had warned, no visitors called. Their isolation was complete. They were master and a handful of servants, camped on a vast estate, like the last defenders of some abandoned planet. It was little wonder that strange stories circulated about Evan, since he rarely left Glendower unless forced to attend to estate business that could not be conducted by letter. He was content to spend his hours reading in his study, or riding his big black stallion.

Deeply concerned by his lack of contact with people, Charlotte found herself lingering in the dining room while he ate; it seemed natural that after a time he suggested she join him each evening for dinner, rather than eat with the servants.

They talked easily, and Charlotte was surprised that for the first time in her life she seemed able to contribute to a conversation. She didn't just listen, but commented on what Evan said, and even brought up subjects herself. She found he was a deeply sensitive man and, considering how shamefully he was shunned by society, concerned with his fellow man and what was happening in the world.

Then suddenly, without warning, Charlotte responded to the doorbell one afternoon and came face to face with Stephen.

She stared into his beautiful, haunted eyes, allowed her gaze to drift to the vulnerable cleft in his chin, and forgot every moment of misery he'd caused her. He smiled easily, that endearing smile that had surely broken stronger hearts than hers. "Hello, Charlotte. How are you?"

Her throat was too constricted to allow her to speak. He stepped into the hall and as he passed her he squeezed her shoulder in a familiar manner. "You look very well, indeed. Italy must have agreed with you. There's a new softness to your face, and something in your eyes that makes me want to get out my sketch pad."

The Passionate Virgin. How could she have forgotten? She said stiffly, "Mr. Evan is out riding. He should return shortly. May I offer you tea, or would you prefer to go straight to the main house?"

"I didn't come to see Evan."

"Then—"

"I came to see my son."

12

Tight-lipped, Charlotte led the way into the drawing room and closed the door. She wished Evan were present, or at least that she didn't feel so defenseless against Stephen. She no longer loved him with the consuming passion she had once felt, yet she feared his power over her, for was she not connected to him forever through the child they had created?

Stephen leaned forward, smiling, and tried to kiss her on the lips. She drew back and said with as much conviction as she could muster, "What was between us is over. Why did you come back?"

His expression hardened. "This is my home, despite what Evan might have told you to the contrary. Besides, I want to see my son. Where is he?"

"How . . . how did you know about him?"

"Why do you think I was banished from Glendower? Evan told me, of course. Right after he threatened to horsewhip me if I ever touched you again." His gaze flickered over her. "What is it about you, Charlotte, that arouses such passion in men? I've never seen Evan so furious, or so fiercely protective."

Charlotte reached for the doorknob. "You will wait here, please, until he returns. I have nothing to discuss with you."

His hand closed around her wrist. "Where is the baby?"

"No! You shan't see him. I won't let you."

"If you don't take me to him at once, I'll inform the newspapers that you posed for *The Passionate Virgin*.".

Charlotte gave a mirthless laugh. "What difference do you

132

suppose that will make to us here in the Welsh mountains? We live in complete isolation.''

He leaned closer, his breath fanning her cheek. ''Are you forgetting your other little secret? Supposing I were to inform a certain Mr. Hathaway of Boston, Massachusetts, U.S.A. as to the whereabouts of his granddaughter, as well as that of her kidnapper . . . her former nanny?''

Charlotte felt all of the color drain from her face. She leaned back against the door. ''How . . . how did you know?''

''My clever wife unearthed the whole story. Zoe tells me that although Eleanor's parents are dead, apparently her grandfather is still very much alive.''

''Oh, dear God, please don't tell him where Eleanor is! If she's forced to return she'll not only be at the mercy of a tyrannical old man, but also of a pedophile . . .''

''My son, Charlotte. Where is he?''

Charlotte had a sudden vision of Eleanor, sitting in the Ramseys' box at Drury Lane, eyes fixed on the stage, studying every inflection in Tristan Cressey's voice . . . lost in the magic world that only born performers seemed to understand. At the same instant, Charlotte saw the grim house in Boston and an embittered, old man determined to punish every woman who crossed his path for his wife's desertion. There was no need to recall the monstrous thing Yarborough had done, there were enough other reasons not to allow anyone to send Eleanor back to Boston. Besides, of even greater concern to Charlotte was how her son would be affected by any possible repercussions to her actions.

Silently, she opened the door and led the way up to her suite of rooms. Moira sat in a rocking chair in the nursery, a basket at her side, folding the baby's napkins. Gwynfor slept contentedly in his cot.

Placing her fingers to her lips to signify silence, Charlotte gestured for Moira to leave. Before the girl had picked up the laundry basket and departed, Stephen had crossed the room and stood looking down at his son.

Charlotte watched Stephen's face as his expression changed to one of delight and pride. ''Why, he's the image of me!''

Before she could protest, he picked up the sleeping child and swung him into the air. ''Wake up, my son, and let me see your eyes. So, you got your mother's eyes. Good, her best feature. Ah, but those other features are mine, you handsome little devil.''

Despite the rude awakening, Gwyn smiled down at his father and gurgled happily to find himself the object of so much attention. Stephen clasped his son to his chest and kissed the top of his head, surveying Charlotte over the baby's silken hair.

"I am more moved than I can express. I had never thought fatherhood would affect me so. I long ago resigned myself to remaining childless because of my wife's malady. When Evan told me you were carrying my child, I felt only anger that I'd sired another bastard generation. But now . . . seeing him . . . what do you call him?"

"Gwynfor," Charlotte answered, her own feelings too fragmented to bring into focus. She knew she ought to feel shame for having borne an illegitimate child, and she did, but she also felt pride. And seeing Gwyn in his father's arms seemed to obscure the bitter memories of Stephen's treatment of her. She had to steel herself against melting before that paternal tenderness, since she worried constantly about Gwyn being fatherless.

"Hmm . . . Gwynfor . . ." Stephen frowned. "Why handicap him with a Celtic name? I would prefer an English one."

"You were not available to offer an alternative when he was born," Charlotte pointed out.

"You never told me you were *enciente*."

"But you knew, you just said that Evan informed you. You also knew I went to Italy, you mentioned it when you arrived. Yet you made no attempt to come to see either your son or me."

He shrugged and gave his old disarming smile. "Ah, but I have a plan whereby we can all be together in future."

He walked across the room and sat down in the rocking chair recently vacated by Moira, the baby on his lap. Gwyn reached up to play with a button on his jacket.

Charlotte remained standing. "What plan is this?"

"As you're no doubt aware, Zoe has been in a nursing home. Her doctors informed me her treatment might be quite lengthy, so I went abroad. To my great consternation, I recently learned she managed to get out and roam around London for a while. She's quite rational between episodes, as you know, and clever enough to evade pursuers. She'd been out for several weeks before they notified me and I came back and found her. I know her well enough to think almost as she does, and I was able to trace her path from the home. I felt guilty that she thought I'd abandoned her, and in future I must never be far away from her. I've taken a house in London, and Zoe will live with me during her rational periods.''

He paused, giving Charlotte one of his sadly yearning looks, and she asked, ''Where is all this leading?''

''I want you to come to London and be my housekeeper.''

She gasped, too shocked to speak, and he went on rapidly, ''Think of all the advantages . . . our son will have both of his parents, we'll have one another, and you can see Eleanor whenever you wish.''

''You'd expose Gwyn—and Eleanor—to your wife's danger-ously irrational behavior?''

''Zoe would only join us when she was in her calm periods.''

''But her violent episodes come on without warning.''

''Not really. I've learned to watch for certain signs. Besides, she would never harm a child. She has desperately wanted one of her own for years. The worst she would do is spoil him with too many extravagant gifts. One doctor felt that Zoe's depressions are caused by her childlessness. He also felt that it is only when she is frustrated or opposed in some way that she behaves irrationally.''

''And what would you tell her about Gwyn? Or, for that matter, about me?''

Stephen picked up one of the baby's hands and held it in his palm. ''Just like a little star . . . tiny fingers so perfect. I can't wait to paint him.'' He looked up at Charlotte. ''I couldn't tell her the truth, of course. We'd use the lie you're using here—that you were married and widowed. I'd say that I hired you as our housekeeper so that there'd be a baby in the house. Perhaps I'll paint a portrait of Zoe holding him.''

Charlotte was trembling with anger, but kept her voice as calm as she could. ''Please put Gwyn back into his cot. We can discuss the situation downstairs.''

Stephen ruffled his son's hair and the child laughed happily. ''I'm not sure I want to relinquish him yet. What do you think of my plan, Charlotte?''

''I would prefer to discuss it downstairs.''

As if she hadn't spoken, he went on, ''Evan will undoubtedly cut off my allowance, but I shall be very much in demand as an artist after my exhibition.'' He glanced at her slyly. ''Perhaps we'll keep the identity of *The Passionate Virgin* a secret for a while, to keep the art world's curiosity piqued, and then spring you on London society when the time is right. We'll invent an

Italian count to be your late lamented husband, and perhaps a mythical lover for you, too, who is willing to pay any amount for the portrait. We'll have him challenge me to a duel . . . oh, yes, I can see it all happening. Every dowager and debutante in the country will be begging me to paint their portrait after they see you in the flesh and compare my rendition of you on canvas.''

Charlotte was speechless for a moment. ''You actually think I would agree to this? To live with you and your wife in some obscene ménage?''

His gray eyes turned to flint. ''I have not painted since Zoe was put away. I need her. I need the anger, the rage, the desire, the blind, unreasoning jealousy she arouses in me. I've often been so incensed I've wanted to kill her, but instead I drain my emotions onto my canvases. Perhaps her sheer intensity is a flame that must consume itself from time to time . . . then when she's gone from me, I can lose myself in my art. Come with me, Charlotte, I need you for the quiet times. I need my son. I had thought my art guaranteed my immortality . . . but here it is in my arms. I want my son; I must have him with me.''

''I shall never agree to such an arrangement. Have you forgotten that your wife tried to kill me?''

''Then you can remain here with Evan,'' Stephen said coldly. ''I shall take my son with me, by one means or another. It's your choice, Charlotte, either let me have him or I'll have you charged with kidnapping Eleanor Hathaway.''

''How can you treat me so—'' Charlotte began, then stopped as heavy footsteps pounded up the stairs and along the landing. Stephen froze, holding Gwyn as if he were a shield.

The doors to the rooms on the upper floors of the grange were of normal size, and Evan had to duck his head in order to enter. His anger was evident in his expression and his huge clenched fists. His towering presence seemed to fill the small room.

Evan glanced briefly at Stephen, then looked at Charlotte. ''Do you want him here? Do you want your son in his arms?''

She shook her head, but said quickly, ''Please . . . the baby . . .''

''Put the child back into his cot, Stephen,'' Evan said.

''And have you break my bones as you throw me out? I think not. I'll hold the boy while we talk.''

''Damn you, there's nothing to talk about. I warned you what would happen if you came back here.''

"I want my son. I'm taking him back to London with me . . . Charlotte, too, if she'll come, but if not, no matter."

A cry of rage came from Evan's lips as he stepped toward Stephen. Charlotte sprang between them and clutched Evan's arm. "Please, you'll hurt the baby . . ." Turning to Stephen she said, "Will you give him to me, please, if Evan promises not to touch you?"

"I'll give no such promise," Evan growled. "He can't hide behind the child forever. I'll wait until he tires of this game and then I'm going to beat him within an inch of his life. Damn you for a scoundrel, Stephen, you've caused this woman all the pain and indignity that I'll allow. Now I'm going to see to it that you never trouble her again . . ."

He stepped around Charlotte and picked up the rocking chair with Stephen still seated in it, the child in his arms. Evan held the chair off the ground as if it were a feather pillow. "Charlotte, take the child."

She hesitated, fearful that Stephen would drop the baby, and in that instant they heard a terrified shriek. Spinning around, Charlotte saw Moira standing in the doorway, staring at Evan, her eyes wide with fright. Then, still screaming, she turned and ran.

"You great fool," Stephen said. "Put me down before she causes the entire household to panic."

The chair hit the floor with a thud, partially dislodging Stephen, and as he began to slip, Charlotte snatched the baby from his arms. They could hear footsteps thundering up the stairs and a babble of voices as all of the grange servants except Lizzie, and half a dozen former Glendower laborers, led by Whitcombe, burst into the room.

Charlotte had only an instant to wonder why Stephen's butler was here in the grange, rather than the main house, and how he had managed to muster the laborers, before the startled baby began to cry. She pushed through the group to the door, and heard Stephen shout, "Seize him, quickly, before he kills me."

There was the sound of scuffling and breaking furniture in the room behind her as, terrified for her son's safety, Charlotte fled.

Owain spread the newsletter on the back of the horse he was grooming and read it slowly for the tenth time.

". . . Emigrants are assured that they will be their own master within a few months of their arrival in the American West.

Millions of acres of prime farmland are theirs for the taking, along with magnificent forests abounding in game and beneficial streams. The land is practically given away, and even the poorest tenant now sweating on his master's land in Europe can easily buy eighty acres or more.''

Owain brushed the mare's hide, still holding the news sheet with one hand. It was one of many such brochures flooding the country, and despite the fact that some legitimate newspapers warned that the American railroad barons had to find something to do with the excess acres granted them by their government and therefore immigration agencies were paid by the head for settlers lured west, the appeal of the agencies' brochures was irresistible to men who had no hope of owning their own land in Europe.

He put the mare back into her stall and limped out of the stable into the brisk morning air. It had been a mistake to leave Glendower; he now worked as a groom on an estate in Cheshire for less pay. His leg had mended crookedly, an inch shorter than the other, and although he could sometimes conceal the pain it gave him, he could not walk without that damned limp.

What grand plans he'd had when he'd set off, a letter of recommendation from Mr. Evan in his pocket and such self-confidence now that he could read and write! A stablemaster's position, he thought, was his for the asking. But all a prospective employer saw was his limp.

Taking the crust of bread and wedge of cheese that served as his breakfast, he wandered into a meadow, sat down on the ground, and laid the brochure beside him. He pulled a letter from his pocket, written weeks earlier. He supposed Eleanor had been too busy to respond to the two letters he'd written her since then, begging her to be careful and to please write Charlotte or Mr. Evan and tell them what had happened. He read her letter again.

DEAR OWAIN, MY GOOD AND TRUE FRIEND,
    SOMETHING VERY FRIGHTENING HAPPENED, BUT YOU MUST PROMISE NOT TO TELL ANYONE IF YOU VISIT GLENDOWER, BECAUSE I DON'T WANT TO BE SENT AWAY FROM HERE. I COULDN'T BEAR NOT TO WORK WITH TRISTAN. HE'S THE BEST ACTOR ON EARTH, AND HE SAYS ONE DAY SOON I SHALL BE READY TO PLAY THE CHILD OPHELIA, ALTHOUGH NOT WITH HIM, OF COURSE, AS HE DOESN'T DO SHAKESPEARE. SO I MUST STAY, NO MATTER

WHAT. I SHALL BE THE YOUNGEST ACTRESS EVER TO PLAY THE PART!

I'LL START AT THE BEGINNING. VERONICA AND I WERE BOWLING OUR HOOPS IN THE LITTLE PARK ACROSS FROM THE MEWS HOUSE WHERE WE LIVE WHEN A CARRIAGE WENT SLOWLY BY WITH THE CURTAINS DRAWN. THEN A VEILED WOMAN PEERED OUT, RIGHT AT ME.

I DIDN'T SAY ANYTHING TO VERONICA BECAUSE SHE WOULD HAVE GLEEFULLY TOLD HER MOTHER I WAS SEEING THINGS AGAIN. (SOMETIMES I HAVE BAD DREAMS AND THINK SOMEONE IS LOOMING OVER MY BED. I SHARE A ROOM WITH VERONICA SO SHE KNOWS IF I WAKE UP CRYING.) VERONICA DOESN'T LIKE ME, AS YOU KNOW. TRISTAN SAYS SHE'S LAZY AND EXPECTS EVERYTHING TO COME EASILY, AND WHEN IT DOESN'T SHE WHINES AND STUFFS HER FACE WITH CREAM BUNS. SHE'S TURNING INTO A BUTTERBALL. SHE PINCHES AND PUMMELS ME IF I SHOW HER UP, AS SHE CALLS IT, BY GETTING BETTER MARKS FOR LESSONS. SOMETIMES I MAKE MISTAKES IN ARITHMETIC ON PURPOSE, JUST SO SHE'LL STOP.

ANYWAY, THAT NIGHT I REALLY DID WAKE UP TO FIND A DARK SHAPE LOOMING OVER MY BED, CLUTCHING AT ME. I SCREAMED AND WOKE VERONICA AND THE VEILED WOMAN RAN AWAY. OWAIN, I WASN'T DREAMING, I SWEAR IT. THE VEIL SLIPPED, AND I SAW IT WAS LADY ZOE ATHMORE!

OH, OWAIN, SHE WAS SO WILD LOOKING! SHE WHISPERED IN MY EAR THAT I WAS GOING TO LIVE WITH HER AND BE HER LITTLE GIRL!

LADY RAMSEY CAME AND SHE HAD A FOOTMAN SEARCH THE HOUSE, BUT HE FOUND NO ONE. THEY SAID IT WAS ONLY A NIGHTMARE. THEN LADY RAMSEY TOLD ME THAT I MUSTN'T BELIEVE THE STORIES ABOUT LADY ZOE ATHMORE BEING MAD, BECAUSE THEY WEREN'T TRUE. THAT HORRIBLE GIANT EVAN MADE THEM UP, SHE SAID, BECAUSE HE'S TRYING TO STEAL HIS NEPHEW'S ESTATE. ZOE SUFFERS FROM MALARIA, LADY RAMSEY SAID, THAT SHE CAUGHT IN HER NATIVE LOUISIANA, AND MUST SOMETIMES GO INTO A NURSING HOME TO RECOVER. BESIDES, THE ATHMORES WERE ABROAD, SO I COULDN'T HAVE SEEN ZOE EITHER IN THE PARK OR IN MY ROOM.

BUT OWAIN, I DID. I SUPPOSE I SHOULD BE GLAD I
SHARE A ROOM WITH OLD FAT VERONICA, EVEN IF I DO
HAVE TO BUTTON HER SHOES FOR HER.

I SHAN'T WRITE AND TELL CHARLOTTE, BECAUSE I
DON'T WANT HER TO SAY I CAN'T STAY HERE ANYMORE.
SO THIS WILL BE OUR SECRET, MY GOOD AND TRUE
FRIEND.

ARE YOU SAVING EVERY FARTHING SO THAT YOU'LL
SOON BE YOUR OWN MASTER? I THINK OF YOU OFTEN.

LOVE AND KISSES, ELEANOR

Owain finished his bread and cheese and stared moodily at the
letter. So they hadn't committed Zoe, after all. Well, who'd
believe she was mad if they met her between spells? And Stephen
usually took care that no one outside the family saw her in a mad
fit; if they did, they pretended she'd had too much champagne.

He believed Eleanor and was uneasy about the situation, but
what could he do? He wasn't even a relative of the child.

Nor did he care for the way Eleanor talked about the actor
Tristan Cressey—like he was a prince, or something. Still, she
had the Ramseys to take care of her, and Zoe had undoubtedly
been scared away after she was nearly caught.

Perhaps it would be a good idea to go to Glendower and tell
Mr. Evan about Eleanor's letter. At least he could look into the
matter of Zoe stalking Eleanor in London. If he took a train into
North Wales as soon as he finished his work on the day before his
day off, he could be in Llanrys by nightfall and have all of the
following day before he had to return.

His eye fell on the newsletter telling of the unlimited opportunities in the American West, and he recalled that when he left
Glendower Mr. Evan had said, "Don't be too proud to come
back, Davies, if you don't find what you're seeking. I shall never
forget that you saved my life once, as well as that of the little girl.
I'll always be in your debt."

In retrospect, Owain realized how seriously he had misjudged
the giant of Glendower. After he saved Owain from being sacked
by Zoe Athmore and allowed him to move into the grange, it had
quickly become evident that Mr. Evan was far from being the
monster of the stories whispered among the servants and in the
village. Then after the accident, he had been kindness itself.
Would any other master have paid for his lodgings and tutor's fees

so he might learn to read and write? Owain often felt ashamed that he had believed all the ugly rumors about Mr. Evan and regretted leaving Glendower. He was no closer to his goal of being his own master. But he couldn't go back, either, because if he did he'd be a groom for the rest of his life.

Turning the brochure over in his hand, Owain reached a decision. Only a young, new country offered the opportunities he was seeking. After he'd been to Glendower and made sure Mr. Evan would watch out for Eleanor, he would emigrate to America.

Charlotte rocked Gwyn back and forth, singing softly to calm him. She was in her own room and the sounds of the commotion had faded, so perhaps Stephen had left.

She had rung for Moira, but there had been no response. It seemed that Stephen had come prepared for an altercation with Evan, since he'd evidently had Whitcombe and some of his former employees waiting nearby. Charlotte held her baby and thought about Stephen's demands and threats. Had he really meant all that he said?

As soon as Evan calmed down she would have to talk to him. He'd know what to do. Oh, thank God for Evan! Without him, she certainly would have been forced to turn Gwyn over to his father. Even with Zoe's illness, Gwyn would have fared better in a wealthy household than in the workhouse that would have been the only place for a woman with an illegitimate child.

At last, Gwyn fell asleep against her shoulder, and she gently laid him down on her bed, with a pillow beside him to keep him from rolling out, then went out onto the landing.

The grange seemed very quiet as she went down the stairs and entered the kitchen. Lizzie sat at the table, nervously gulping down a mug of tea. She was alone.

"Oh, Mrs. Danforth! There's glad I am to see you."

"Where is everyone, Lizzie?"

"Gone—dismissed. Mr. Evan was so angry. He sacked everyone except me. Thank God I had enough sense not to listen to Whitcombe. I stayed down here when they all went upstairs. Whitcombe said Lord Athmore had come back but he feared for his life, and he'd instructed Whitcombe to keep watch in case Mr. Evan came back from his morning ride before he'd finished talking to you. Well back he came, and Whitcombe brought those rough laborers in and said they were all to follow him and overpower Mr. Evan . . . What happened up there, Mrs. Danforth?''

"I don't know. I left the room. What did you see?''

"Mr. Evan came down the stairs, dragging Lord Athmore by the scruff of his neck, look you. Whitcombe and all the others were on his heels like a pack of dogs, but when one of them dared lay hands on him, he batted them away like they were flies. He threw Lord Athmore out the front door and down he went, sprawling on the ground. Mr. Evan bellows at everyone that he is the true Lord Athmore and Glendower is his. Then he comes back and dismisses everyone but me.''

"Moira, too?''

"Oh, yes. She was screaming that everyone in the village knew the giant was wicked and violent and hadn't she seen it with her own eyes? And hadn't she just heard with her own ears the giant saying he'd kill Lord Athmore? She was wailing that if her father hadn't been laid up and her mother poorly and in need of her wages, she'd never have gone into his service. And Whitcombe was shouting that Mr. Evan had now gone completely mad. 'Get over to the main house and pack your belongings, then lock up the place. I don't need it or you,' Mr. Evan shouts back. 'Go on,' he says, 'all of you, be off. I don't need any of you.' ''

"Where is Mr. Evan now?''

"In his study, I think.''

Charlotte glanced at the kitchen clock. "You'll have to prepare his lunch. There's soup left from dinner and plenty of cold lamb. Then I want you to see if you can find anyone in the village willing to work at the grange. I'm going to him now. Ring the bell as soon as his lunch is ready.''

She went to the study, knocked on the door, and entered. Evan stood at the window, gazing across the inner courtyard toward the main house. He turned and immediately sat down when he saw her, gesturing for her to take a chair.

"I'm sorry if I frightened the baby, Charlotte.''

"He's all right. He's asleep.''

"You'd better tell me everything Stephen said to you.''

Charlotte regarded him with growing concern. How could she possibly repeat Stephen's threats? Evan was angry enough already at his half brother. Evading his eye, she answered, "He wanted me to be his housekeeper in London, and to take Gwyn with me.''

"And I burst in upon you before you had a chance to respond. I suppose you want to go?"

"Merciful heaven, no, I don't!"

He gave a sigh of relief. "Good. I shall make sure he never troubles you again."

She bit her lip. She couldn't let Evan deal with his half brother without knowing all of the facts. "He made certain threats. To make public that I was the model for the nude he calls "The Passionate Virgin." Also . . . to notify Eleanor's grandfather that I kidnapped her. He has also removed his wife from the nursing home."

Thunderclouds appeared in Evan's eyes, and she saw his fists clench on the table in front of him. "When I think of all the mischief perpetrated by those two . . . particularly Stephen, since Zoe probably can't help herself, I could cheerfully strangle him."

Charlotte bit her lip. "Please, you mustn't enrage yourself so. I am as guilty as he, perhaps more so."

"For what?" Evan roared, the table shaking under the pressure of his hands. "For saving a child from a pedophile? For being sweet and kind and gentle and so pure of thought and deed that a sinner like Stephen couldn't bear it because the contrast to him and his slut of a wife was so great? Isn't it always thus? That the most depraved among us try to drag everyone down into the slime with them, so they can say, look, this is the way of all flesh."

"Oh, please don't distress yourself so!" Charlotte cried. "Surely we all participate in our own fate? I must take responsibility for giving in to him . . . I'd never known anyone like him, so handsome, so talented, so tormented . . . oh, God forgive me, it was as if the accumulated passion of my whole lifetime burst forth from me and I became a creature possessed . . ."

She watched the tight lines of anger on his face change to a desperate emotion she could not define. Was it pity? It seemed almost to be a longing, perhaps a desire to heal her hurt. "Ah, Charlotte, if only he could have been worthy of you . . . How I wish . . ."

He fell silent, but several times seemed on the verge of speaking. She waited, but each time he held back.

After a few minutes the lunch bell rang and Charlotte said, "If you will excuse me, I must go to my son. Lizzie will serve your lunch."

"Charlotte . . ."

"Yes?"

"Don't worry about Stephen's threats. I'll speak with him. There are always alternatives. I don't want to lose you again. Damn it, I won't, not on account of that womanizing swine." He paused. "I'm going out. I'll be back for dinner, and we'll talk then."

Charlotte went to feed the baby and have her own lunch. That afternoon after Lizzie had departed to try to find someone willing to work at Glendower, Charlotte took Gwyn down to the kitchen and put him to play on the floor with a collection of pots and pans. She then turned her attention to preparing dinner.

Without help, she was busy until evening and, when Lizzie still hadn't returned as the dinner hour approached, Charlotte had to bathe and feed the baby and put him to bed, then change her gown and hurry down to put the finishing touches to Evan's dinner.

Long shadows now filled the grange, and without the footsteps and voices of servants, or Evan's presence, the house was eerily silent and empty. Charlotte lit the lamps in the dining room, set the table, and returned to the kitchen to take a shepherd's pie from the oven.

An hour later, she was still alone and beginning to worry that neither Evan nor Lizzie had returned. It was as if she were the last person left alive on earth, so acute was her isolation. This vast estate, she thought, and Gwyn and I are its only inhabitants.

She went back to the dining room to wait. After a time she sat in one of the gigantic chairs. The minutes ticked by. What could possibly have happened to prevent the return of at least one of them?

At last she decided to go back upstairs to see if Gwyn was all right. Entering the nursery, which was in darkness, she saw a flicker of orange light on the window curtains.

She swiftly crossed the room and lifted the curtain. Her breath caught in her throat as she looked across the courtyard to see a scarlet flame leap from the roof of the main house. Even as she watched, a portion of the roof collapsed to reveal the rooms beneath engulfed in fire.

13

OWAIN SAW THE flames long before he reached Glendower. He was on foot, limping as fast as he could toward the house, and realized instantly that the mountain would block the view of the fire from the village. Still, there were enough people on the estate to fight the blaze as long as the wind didn't rise and transfer sparks from one building to another. He decided to go on rather than return to the village to call out the fire brigade.

Judging by the height of the flames, a large structure must be afire, and his first thought was to hope it wasn't the stables.

His progress seemed painfully slow and he wished he were astride a horse, but he didn't own one. He'd taken a train to Llanrys and had been offered a ride on a coal cart to the village so had decided to walk the rest of the way tonight rather than waiting to call on Mr. Evan the following morning.

He came to the stables and carriage house first, and was relieved to see they were not burning. Then it occurred to him that the buildings were unusually silent. A quick look in the stables confirmed that there were no horses, grooms, or boys. The hay smelled stale and it was evident that, except for the first stall where Mr. Evan kept Emperor, the stable had been unused for some time. The big black stallion was gone, but fresh water and feed indicated that he had been there recently.

Owain's apprehension grew as he hurried to the stablemaster's cottage. Dreamer, the gentle mare on which he had taught Eleanor to ride, was harnessed to a carriage in front, but the cottage was dark and empty. There was a deserted air to the entire estate, he thought, as Dreamer nuzzled his hand anxiously, glad to see a human being, and frightened by the smell of smoke.

The breeze shifted, and the acrid stench became stronger. Owain broke into an awkward run, dragging his bad leg like a restraining anchor.

He could hear the crackle of the flames now, and suspected from the direction of the sound that the main house was afire.

Emerging from the woods in front of the house, he came upon a terrifying scene. The upper part of the main house was engulfed in flames, a gigantic bonfire of brilliant red and orange lit with gold and bronze sparks that danced in the inferno like fireflies. A great billowing cloud of smoke rose against the night sky, whirling and eddying like a monstrous genie emerging from a burning lamp.

For an instant Owain stood still, staring in fascinated horror. There was no sign of men fighting the fire. It might have been burning on some uninhabited island.

Then he saw that there was one man, astride a huge black horse, silhouetted against the orange glare. Evan observed the blaze for an instant and then turned his mount and galloped away, disappearing into the shadows.

Where were all the servants, the gardeners? Were there living souls inside the house? Why was nothing being done to fight the fire? There was little one lame man could do on his own, so Owain turned back and ran to the stablemaster's cottage to unharness Dreamer. He didn't wait to find a saddle, but flung himself on her back and rode for the village as if all the hounds of hell were on his heels.

He met the column of carriages, carts and men on horseback on the lane approaching the Glendower estate, and was astonished that Mr. Evan could have ridden swiftly enough to mobilize the village. Then, recognizing one of the Glendower laborers at the reins of the first farm cart, he yelled, "Where's the fire brigade? Let them through."

The man looked blank. "Fire? What are you talking about? We're off to capture a madman, look you."

The cart rolled by before Owain could question him further. Behind the vehicles came men on bicycles and on foot. He guided Dreamer to the side of the lane as an open carriage approached, bearing a figure in a floating white cape. Like Bodicea in a chariot riding out to challenge the Romans, the tall and regal figure, black hair flying loose, was on her feet using a whip on the horses. Owain drew back beside the hedgerow, as the carriage carrying Zoe Athmore passed him.

Behind her it seemed that every servant and laborer who had ever worked on the Glendower estate, as well as the villagers, followed.

Among those on foot, Owain recognized Lizzie and called to her. She pushed through the crowd and came to him, grabbing the reins of his horse. In the light of a rising moon, he could see her eyes were wide with trepidation. "Owain, *bach!*" she exclaimed. "There's glad I am to see you! Help me up, man, and I'll ride back with you."

He dismounted and lifted her onto the mare's back. When he didn't join her she said, "Come on, Owain, we'll miss all the excitement."

"There's plenty of men, look you, they don't need me. I shan't frighten the mare by riding her in that crowd. Besides, I think it's too late to save the house. I'll take you back when the crowd's gone."

Exasperated, Lizzie looked at the villagers surging along the lane, then down at the ground, obviously wondering whether to try to ride alone, or to jump down and walk. Owain said, "You stay where you are for a minute and tell me what Zoe Athmore is doing back here."

"What do you mean, save the house?" Lizzie asked.

"It's on fire. I thought they were going to put it out."

"Oh, no! I didn't think he'd go that far."

"Who?"

"The giant, of course, who else? There's mad he's gone. Sent everyone away except Mrs. Danforth and her baby—and thank God she sent me to the village, or I'd be back there no doubt roasting to death along with her."

Owain felt a chill. "She was in the grange, though? Not the main house?"

Lizzie nodded.

"What happened?"

She told him in rapid and often colorful Welsh of the events of that afternoon. "Then I came to the village. Lady Athmore was standing on the inn balcony and telling everyone that her husband had gone to Glendower early that day and not come back as he promised. That some of the men he took with him had returned and told her that the giant had lost his mind. She said she feared for her husband's life. That the giant had driven them from their home and claimed Glendower was his. She said Mr. Evan tried to put her in an asylum to get rid of her, and had threatened to kill Lord Athmore."

"But Zoe is mad, who'd believe anything she said?" Owain asked.

"Well look you, *we* know about her fits, but who outside of Glendower does? Whitcombe and Mrs. Carmichael dealt harshly with any servant who carried gossip to the village. Besides, Zoe's well-liked because she's always handing out gifts to anyone who takes her fancy. And hasn't Stephen always been popular with them? He's lived at Glendower since he was a boy, after all, while the giant didn't come until after the old lord's death."

"An accusation of murder, though . . ."

"Ah, but the girl Moira confirms it. Said she heard the giant say Stephen would never bother anyone again. Then some of the Glendower laborers who were there this afternoon said that Stephen went to his house to get some of his belongings. And still there, he was, when the giant left the grange and went over to the main house. No one's seen Stephen since."

Owain reached up and lifted her off the mare. "What are you doing?" she asked. "You're not going to make me walk—"

But Owain had already mounted and was galloping back toward Glendower, heedless of who was in his path.

Minutes later he heard gunshots. The column of servants and villagers came to a jumbled halt. By the time he was able to make his way through the knot of shoving, shouting people, half a dozen of the brawniest laborers had lifted Evan's huge body onto a hay cart.

In the illumination of the cold moonlight, Owain could see one powerful arm dangling over the edge of the cart, a dark stain spreading down the sleeve, as blood dripped from the fingers to the ground below.

Charlotte wrapped the blanket more closely around the baby and wondered if the red glow in the sky above the woods was beginning to fade. Surely Evan, or someone, would come to her soon.

Only moments after she realized the main house was ablaze, Evan had returned to the grange. She had heard him come into the hall, and when she stepped out onto the landing he called, "Pack a bag for yourself and the baby. I'll gather some of my valuables in case the fire spreads to the grange, and it might, if the wind rises and the oaks catch fire.''

"Is there no one to help us?'' Charlotte cried.

"I'll ride to the village as soon as you and the child are safe.'' Evan strode into his study. Charlotte ran back into the nursery.

In less than five minutes, Evan was at her door. "Come now, or it will be too late to save anything of the main house.''

He left them in the summer house near the lake, then rode off on Emperor. Charlotte could no longer see the fire as the view was blocked by the woods, but the ominous glow in the sky deepened to an angrier red.

Not wishing to take the baby into the smoke, she could only wait and hope for Evan to return.

She had made a makeshift bed for the baby on a slatted bench in the summer house, and placed Evan's leather bag and her own valise beside the child. She wondered which of his possessions he valued enough to save.

The thunder of hooves sent her back to the wooden rail enclosing the summer house. Peering into the shadows, she saw a riderless horse. Emperor whinnied in fright and pawed the ground.

Although she was a little afraid of the huge animal, Charlotte ran down the steps to him and caught his dangling reins. "There, there, boy . . . it's all right . . .''

She reached up to stroke his neck to try to calm him, and her hand encountered sticky wetness. She stared at her fingers. Blood . . . There was blood on the saddle, too, but the horse didn't appear to be hurt, merely frightened.

"Oh, dear God!'' she exclaimed aloud. "Evan . . .''

14

OWAIN FELT RAGE such as he'd never known at the sight of the fallen giant. They had tossed Evan up on the cart as if he were nothing more than the carcass of an animal. It had taken six of the brawniest villagers to lift him, and there he lay, his face upturned in the moonlight and one arm dangling like a felled tree trunk, fingers dripping blood into the dirt.

They backed away from him then, perhaps awed by what they had done. The man who had shot Evan leaned the gun against the wheel of the cart and rubbed his hands together, as if trying to wash away the deed.

Owain caught a flutter of white in the periphery of his vision, and Zoe Athmore pushed through the suddenly silent knot of men. "Is he dead?" she asked calmly.

The men looked at one another, but no one answered.

"It's all right, you've done well," Zoe cried. She went to the cart and seized a handful of Evan's hair in order to turn his face toward her.

Afterwards, Owain was never sure what happened in that instant. He found himself propelled by a tremendous surge of energy. He shoved men out of his way, grabbed Zoe by the shoulder and spun her away from Evan, then picked up the gun and leaped up onto the cart.

"Get back, all of you," he shouted. "You bloody cowards—look at how many of you it took to bring down one man."

A voice in the crowd mumbled that the Glendower giant was no ordinary man. Owain shook the rifle at them. "Damn you to hell, you didn't have to shoot him."

"If he isn't dead," Zoe shrieked, "then he'll hang. He murdered my husband. Stephen never came back from Glendower." She turned to the watching circle of men and, pointing at Evan's inert body, shouted, "If that monster is still alive, he must be taken to prison. Seize him at once!"

Owain vaulted into the driver's seat and snatched the whip from the hands of the startled owner of the cart, then pushed the man to the ground. He grabbed the reins and, for the first time in his life, laid the whip on the back of a horse.

The cart lurched off down the lane, men jumping out of his path as the frightened horse broke into a gallop.

Someone shouted, "Stop him!" and a chorus of voices responded, "He's got the gun, look you."

The cart picked up speed on the downhill run and Owain hoped Evan's body would not be dislodged from the open bed. He threw away the whip and slackened the reins, but was glad of the fast pace as the shouting voices behind him receded into the distance.

Then the cart was on Glendower land and the horse smelled the stench of smoke and panicked. Owain used all of his skill to turn the terrified animal toward the lake. Perhaps if he could reach the thickly wooded area along the lakeshore, he would at least be able to determine if Evan were dead or alive, and they'd have a place to spend what was left of the night. He didn't believe the villagers would dare trespass on Athmore land, no matter what Zoe told them.

He wasn't sure why he had plunged so recklessly into the fray, nor why he had been so enraged at the injustice of so many attacking one man. God knew he had been as superstitious as any of them when it came to believing stories about the giant. Yet despite it all, Mr. Evan had kept him on and no one could have been kinder following his accident, even paying room and board for him so he could live with the schoolmaster and learn to read and write. He owed Mr. Evan a debt of gratitude, but what if he really had killed his nephew, as Zoe claimed? Owain decided to put his faith in Evan, rather than the mad Zoe.

Just before they reached the lake, they came to the Athmore summer house, and Owain saw the big, black stallion tied to the wooden fence. Emperor raised his head and whinnied as they approached. At the same time a woman emerged from the shadows of the summer house. Thank God, Mrs. Danforth had escaped the flames.

She ran lightly down the steps and was at Evan's side before Owain could jump down from the cart. "Is he . . ."

Cradling the great head to her breast, she looked up at Owain with eyes filled with sorrow. "Oh, dear heaven, who did this?"

Owain frantically searched for a pulse beat, feeling Evan's wrist and then his neck. There was so much blood, he was unsure where he'd been shot.

Charlotte bent her ear to Evan's lips and listened. "He's alive," she said. "But he needs a doctor at once. Why did you bring him here? You could have killed him. You should have taken him to the village."

Owain gave a short, mirthless laugh. "If I'd left him there he'd be dead, look you. Can you take care of him while I ride to Llanrys and fetch a doctor?"

"*Llanrys?* That's too far. There's a doctor in the village."

Owain was already unfastening Emperor's reins from the rail. "Listen to me . . . Zoe Athmore has the whole village in an uproar. She convinced them Mr. Evan has gone mad and murdered her husband. Mr. Evan was shot by one of the Glendower laborers. From the mood of the men, I'd say he's going to have to lie low for a while until things quiet down. Can you take the horse and cart down to the trees by the lake? It will be out of sight, just in case any of them come this way. I'll get a doctor and be back as fast as I can. See if you can stop his bleeding."

He was gone in a thunder of hooves and flying turf before Charlotte could question him further. Turning her attention to Evan, she gently felt his chest and then the arm that hung over the side of the cart. Her searching fingers found the source of the bleeding and felt bone protruding from his shattered elbow.

She pulled a leather lace from his boot to make a tourniquet, using a twig to tighten it, then tore a strip of material from her petticoat to bind around his arm.

The moon slid out from behind a cloud and now she saw that the side of his jacket was soaked with blood, and there was blood in his hair, trickling down his face. She felt a stab of fear. If he'd also been shot in the head . . .

A faint sound came from his lips, not quite a moan, nor yet a sigh, and it took her a moment to realize he had whispered her name.

"Yes, yes, I'm here . . ." She tore more of her petticoat and wiped the blood from his brow. Perhaps the bullet had only grazed his scalp . . . he surely wouldn't be able to speak otherwise. "Lie still," she begged as he tried to sit up. "I'm going to get the baby and then take the cart into the trees. When we're hidden from sight, I'll get some water and clean your wounds. Owain has gone for a doctor.''

"Owain . . .'' he murmured with something like satisfaction overlaying the pain in his voice. "Good man . . .''

Charlotte hurried into the summer house to get the suitcase and valise. When they were stowed on the cart, she went back for the baby. There was a lantern in the summer house, but she decided not to risk lighting it and alerting anyone to their presence. Besides, it would be dawn soon. She placed Gwyn at Evan's side, then went to lead the horse into the grove of trees.

About an hour later as she sat on the cart, pressing a compress to Evan's head to staunch the flow of blood as he drifted in and out of consciousness, she heard voices and hoofbeats. They were somewhere in the vicinity of the summer house. She picked up the baby and held him to her breast, terrified that he would cry and alert the searchers to their refuge. After a while, the voices faded.

A sullen dawn crept over the rim of the mountains, illuminating the angry red furrow that creased Evan's hair. She had loosened the tourniquet on his arm at regular intervals, covered him with all of the clothes she'd packed in her valise, and cleaned and bound his elbow as best she could. She hadn't dared remove his coat and shirt from the ominous patch of blood on his side. She wondered how long it would take the bullets embedded in his flesh to cause septicemia.

As the gray light of the new day spilled down the hills, he opened his eyes and looked up at her. "I cannot find the words to properly thank you . . .''

"Hush, save your strength. Owain should return any minute.''

"Charlotte . . . I am probably light-headed and speaking foolishly, but I must tell you . . .'' He broke off, trying to catch his breath, and she saw beads of perspiration on his brow despite the damp chill of the morning. "I have wanted . . . to tell you . . .''

Whatever it was he was about to say was forgotten as a carriage came rattling through the trees toward them, and Charlotte saw to her intense relief that Owain held the reins. He was accompanied by a man and a woman.

"How is he?'' Owain cried, throwing a medical bag to the ground.

"Alive, but please, Doctor, hurry . . .''

In the faint light she saw that the doctor was quite elderly, almost infirm, and even though Owain helped him down from the carriage the young woman hovered solicitously at his side, her arm around him.

"This is Dr. Thomas," Owain said. "His granddaughter insisted on coming, too."

"My name is Megan," she said quietly. "My grandfather is retired but cannot seem to resist pleas to minister to gunshot poachers, even though it means long and torturous rides through the chill of the night."

Poachers? But of course, Owain would have had to make up some story to explain the gunshots. "I'm so grateful you could come," Charlotte murmured.

Ignoring all of them, Dr. Thomas began to examine Evan as Owain held the lantern. To her dismay, Charlotte saw the doctor's hands shake and he swayed slightly on his feet, but Megan steadied him. In a low voice, he murmured to his granddaughter medical terms that she evidently understood.

Gwyn had begun to whimper with hunger, but Charlotte waited as the doctor examined Evan. Both the doctor and his granddaughter were calm, and showed no surprise at Evan's tremendous size, or the fact that he lay on a farm cart in the woods. In the dim light of the lantern, Charlotte saw that Megan was very young, probably little more than fourteen or fifteen, with pert features and wavy, auburn hair. She opened the medical bag and began to lay out instruments and bandages.

The doctor glanced up at Charlotte and said, "Madam, you'd better go and see to your infant."

"Doctor . . . forgive me, but are you capable of treating him?" Charlotte asked, as the man was now trembling noticeably.

"My palsy does not interfere with my knowledge of what must be done for the patient," he answered testily. "Megan will carry out my instructions."

Megan turned and looked at Charlotte. "I've helped my grandfather many times."

"Followed me around since she was five years old," Dr. Thomas said. "A proper little nuisance." There was pride in his voice, despite his words.

Owain put in, "No one else would come with me this far, Mrs. Danforth. We've no choice."

Gwyn's hunger cries were becoming more demanding. Charlotte nodded her agreement, then picked up the baby and said to Owain, "I'm going back to the grange . . . it's still standing I hope?"

"Main house is burned to the ground, but the grange is untouched," Owain confirmed. "Take the doctor's carriage and get some food and then come back here. No doubt Zoe Athmore and her bloodhounds will be searching the estate as soon as it's fully light. As soon as we can move Evan we'll have to leave."

As she climbed into the carriage, it occurred to Charlotte that Owain took it for granted that she would go with them. She had intended to leave Glendower in any event, but never dreamed Evan would be going with her.

She guided the doctor's horse through the silent estate. The acrid odor of smoke and burned debris hung everywhere, and even the birds were silent.

There was no sign of life in the courtyard. Charlotte stared at the smoking remains of the fine, old house. It had, as Owain indicated, quite literally burned to the ground. Apparently no attempt had been made to save it. She thought of the priceless art treasures and beautiful furnishings it had contained, all gone forever.

She hurried into the grange and went straight to the kitchen. The entire house smelled of smoke, and the windows were covered with a film of soot, but no stray sparks had blown that way and the grange had been spared.

The shepherd's pie she had made for dinner the previous evening, covered with a tea towel, was on the kitchen table. She went into the pantry, found a picnic hamper and placed the pie, bread and cheese and a cooked ham into it.

Only minutes had passed since her arrival, but she felt a frightening sense of urgency and was desperate to be gone. Still, she must be calm and think of what else she must take. Clothing for herself and Gwyn and Evan . . . they'd need more than what little they'd hurriedly packed last evening, and most of hers was stained with Evan's blood. And she mustn't forget her savings, and the household money in her office. Evan usually took the household funds from a cash box in his study, so she should take that, too. She was unsure how long it would be before Evan could return, and he'd need money to live on and, she feared, money for a legal battle to prove he was the true heir to the Athmore fortune. Charlotte didn't even consider the possibility that he would have to defend himself against Zoe's accusation that he'd murdered Stephen, since it was simply too outrageous.

Placing the baby in the wicker basket she sometimes used as a temporary cot, she darted about the grange, gathering whatever she felt might be useful. In addition to food and personal items, she collected as many small valuables as would fit into a pillowcase, feeling like a thief with his swag. When there was no room for anything else in the carriage, she gulped the remainder of a jug of milk and scooped up Gwyn.

It was a relief when the carriage rolled out of the courtyard and the gaunt and blackened skeleton of the main house was out of sight.

By the time she returned to the cart, the sun was rising. The doctor and Megan had finished ministering to Evan, who looked pale, but was fully conscious. His big face broke into a smile as Charlotte approached.

Dr. Thomas was angrily speaking to Owain. "I'm telling you that I shall not be responsible for what happens if you insist on moving him. He's lost too much blood. He should be taken to the hospital."

Owain's eyes met Charlotte's and sent the urgent message that they must leave. She said briskly, "How much do we owe you for your services, Doctor?"

Ignoring her, the doctor continued in his wavering voice, "Furthermore, it is my duty to report gunshot wounds to the police. If this man was shot while poaching—"

"Grandfather," Megan interrupted softly, her hand on the old man's arm. "He's no poacher, he's a gentleman. Look at his clothes, look at those boots."

Dr. Thomas glanced at Evan, who watched all of them silently, as though fascinated by the scene. "Nevertheless," the doctor insisted, "gunshot wounds . . ."

Turning to Charlotte, Megan said, "A bullet passed right through his elbow and lodged in his side. We removed it and set the elbow as best we could, considering the damage. He also has a head wound, but Grandfather doesn't think the bullet entered his skull. If it did, it will have to remain. Apart from everything else, he lost a great deal of blood. Even a man of his size cannot stand to lose so much. Where do you intend to take him? He's in no condition to travel."

"Thank you, but we must take him home," Charlotte answered, opening her handbag. She took out her purse, and looked at the doctor expectantly.

He frowned and muttered, "Very well, be it on your own heads. Two guineas, please. But I must warn you that you are endangering his life."

After the doctor was seated in the carriage, Megan ran back to Charlotte's side and whispered, "Don't worry, we won't tell anyone about your friend."

Owain was already unloading the contents of the carriage and placing them on the farmer's cart. Evan watched. His eyes were dull with pain, but a small smile of amusement plucked at his mouth.

As the doctor's carriage rattled off over the uneven ground, Evan asked, "Do you intend to steal the farmer's horse and cart?"

"Yes, and this rifle, too," Owain replied. "We might need both before we're safely out of here."

"Where shall we go?" Charlotte asked, the enormity of their dilemma striking her. A man of Evan's size, badly wounded, would surely not be easy to hide. But it would only be until Stephen reappeared, proving the lie of Zoe's wild accusations. After that the worst they could do was accuse Evan of deposing them from the estate, and Evan could inform the world that he was the rightful owner of Glendower.

"Away from Glendower, to start off with," Owain answered as he harnessed Emperor beside the stout farm horse. The spirited stallion snorted disdainfully and pawed the ground, as if warning the other horse who would set the pace. Owain tied the gentle mare, Dreamer, to the back of the cart.

Without realizing quite what she was doing, Charlotte picked up Evan's hand and held it. "Will you be all right? We'll travel as slowly as we dare. We'll take good care of you, we promise."

He looked at her and his gray-green eyes were luminous, almost as if tears lurked somewhere in their depths. He murmured, "I'll be all right . . . at this moment I feel happier than at any other time of my life . . ." His voice was choked and he bit his lip, shaking his head slightly.

The poor dear man, Charlotte thought, he is weak with pain and shock, and doesn't know what he is saying.

Owain helped her up beside Evan, put the baby in her arms,

and then climbed into the driver's seat. "There's a shepherd's cottage up near Lost Man's Peak. It's not used much this time of year, too high for the lambs. If we could get up there, I doubt anyone would find us. But we couldn't take the cart."

"I'll be able to walk," Evan said. "My legs aren't hurt."

"Oh, no, it would be much too strenuous!" Charlotte protested.

"Mrs. Danforth, the mood of the villagers was too ugly to risk letting them get their hands on Mr. Evan again," Owain said. "Better we stay out of sight for a while until we can get to Llanrys and bring a constable."

Evan looked at Charlotte. "Don't worry, we'll take our time, and you and Owain can help me."

When they reached the barren outcropping of rock that was known as Lost Man's Peak, Charlotte marveled at the superhuman strength Evan possessed. It was not she who helped him climb the craggy mountain, but he who offered his good arm to her while Owain carried the baby. But the effort cost him dearly, and he was deathly pale and breathing heavily by the time they reached the cottage.

The shepherd's cottage was built of stone and sod, and had not been used since the previous summer. The single iron bedsteads were without a mattress and far too short to accommodate Evan's height, so they made him a pallet on the floor. Owain knocked two holes in the wall so that Evan's feet could protrude, as the cottage was too small to accommodate him lying full-length.

Owain returned to the valley to bring up the food and other items she had packed. When he returned, Charlotte had gathered wood to light a fire but he quickly stopped her. "We can't risk someone seeing the smoke. There are shepherds in the valley east of us, and they may move their herds this way."

"Fortunately I have bread and cheese and ham," Charlotte said, reaching for the picnic hamper.

"I must go back and bring the horses up here now."

"What about the cart? Won't the shepherds see it if you leave it down there?"

"I'll shove it over the edge."

"I have turned you both into fugitives," Evan said, his voice slow, heavy. "Stealing, destroying property . . . what was I thinking of?" He tried to rise but was exhausted from the climb and fell back.

Charlotte rushed to his side. "You must not worry about such things. We can pay the farmer for his horse and cart when everything is back to normal.''

"Soon as we've had something to eat, I'll ride into the village and see if I can find out what's happening," Owain said.

"I think not," Charlotte said. "You'll be arrested for stealing the horse and cart, not to mention the gun. I shall go."

"You know how to ride?" Owain asked in surprise.

"No," Charlotte responded. "But you said Dreamer is a gentle mare. I shall learn."

"My God, Charlotte! Not in these mountains," Evan protested.

"I could take her down to the lane," Owain said, "and help her into the saddle. I think she could manage Dreamer then. It's not far to the village."

"If necessary, I shall walk," Charlotte said. "But we must know what mischief Zoe has done. We can't hide in this cottage indefinitely."

An hour later, she regretted her brave words when Owain lifted her up onto Dreamer's back and put the reins in her hands. The mare was not a large animal, but the ground looked frighteningly far away.

"Take your time, you'll be all right," Owain said, patting Dreamer to get her started.

Charlotte clutched the reins and gripped the mare's flanks with her knees, regardless of the fact that her skirt slid so high that most of her legs were on view. Still, she wouldn't see many people until she reached the village, and she intended to dismount before then. She called over her shoulder, "Hurry back to the cottage, Owain, and take good care of my son."

As soon as she was alone, she began to worry about leaving the baby. But Gwyn would probably sleep until her return.

Except for one stop along the way when Dreamer decided to nibble at some tender new shoots of spring grass at the side of the lane, the journey to the village was accomplished without difficulty. As the first of the outlying cottages came into view, Charlotte flung her arms around the neck of the mare and slid somewhat awkwardly to the ground. She took the reins and led Dreamer until she reached the village square.

A farmer with milk cans on his cart had just reached the square and several laborers on their way to neighboring farms were leaving their cottages. To a man they stopped and stared at Charlotte as if she were a ghost.

The innkeeper's wife came out of the inn, a broom in her hand ready to sweep the pavement in front of their establishment and, seeing Charlotte, she called out in Welsh.

Then it seemed that people converged on the square from every direction. They surrounded Charlotte, babbling in Welsh and apparently not hearing her when she told them she could not speak their language and please to speak English.

At length an English voice cut through the cacophony of guttural Welsh, and Charlotte recognized the voice of the Athmores' English housekeeper, Mrs. Carmichael. She pushed through the crowd and surveyed Charlotte with a faintly disappointed look on her face. "So you're safe, after all. Where is your child?"

"He's safe, too," Charlotte replied. "No thanks to any of you who did not come to put out the fire."

"Do you know where the giant is?" Mrs. Carmichael demanded.

"I have no idea where *Mr. Evan* is."

"Are you sure? When did you see him last?"

"I haven't seen him since he left to bring the fire brigade last evening," Charlotte said.

Small, cunning eyes examined every inch of her face, as if trying to probe her thoughts. "He was shot, he can't get far. That fool Owain Davies helped him escape."

"Shot? Escape? You make him sound like a fugitive. What has he done?"

"He killed his nephew . . . he killed Lord Athmore," Mrs. Carmichael said, her voice trembling either with outrage or perhaps excitement. "My poor lady is distraught."

"What nonsense," Charlotte said. "Mr. Evan would never harm anyone."

Mrs. Carmichael's deep-set eyes gleamed. "You fool . . . they found Lord Athmore's charred body in the ruins of the burned house this morning."

15

EVAN'S HEAD ROLLED slowly from side to side, his huge body twitched, and he muttered something in Welsh.

Charlotte mopped his brow and whispered, "What did he say?"

In the fitful light of a lantern burning low, Owain's expression was worried. "He's delirious. Burning with fever. He needs a doctor."

Evan's eyes opened suddenly, and he stared at them blankly. "It's all right," he said in English, his voice a feeble echo of his normally commanding tone. "Don't worry. I'll take the blame. You tell the headmaster I did it. I'm stronger than you. I can stand the caning. The last welts are almost healed."

"Oh, dear heaven, he thinks he's a boy again. I believe he's reliving the days he spent in an orphanage."

"Orphanage?"

"Where he spent his boyhood. Oh dear, he probably didn't want anyone else to know."

"Not the cupboard!" Evan cried, trying to sit up. Even in his weakened state, it took all of Owain and Charlotte's combined strength to force him to lie down again.

"I'm going for the doctor," Owain said. "I'll be back by morning."

"No! You can't. There's a warrant for your arrest for stealing the horse and cart." Charlotte caught his arm. "We need you, Owain. I can't take care of the baby and Evan all by myself. What if it becomes necessary to move him?"

"He's got to have a doctor. Look at him."

Charlotte looked down at Evan, twisting and turning on the makeshift pallet, his feet thrust through the holes Owain had knocked in the walls. Evan had lain there for two days and was becoming weaker. In the damp chill of the unheated cottage, he might easily contract pneumonia, but he would fare worse in the prison hospital where he would surely go if he were caught. Mrs. Carmichael had informed Charlotte, with a nasty smile of satisfaction, that her ladyship had two witnesses, former Glendower laborers, who had seen Evan running from the house carrying a flaming torch. No doubt Zoe had paid the men to lie.

A net of circumstantial evidence had closed rapidly around Evan. In the minds of the villagers, he had a plausible motive and sufficient opportunity, and now there were witnesses willing to perjure themselves. Zoe had cleverly built her case against Evan for years. It must have been she, or someone she paid, who started the fire. But surely Zoe would not have killed Stephen? Charlotte remembered what Evan had once said: *Think of them as climbers, roped together on the sheer face of a cliff . . . if one falls, they are both lost.*

But the possibility that Stephen had died in the fire haunted Charlotte. She told herself sternly that her fears merely reflected her concern for both of the half brothers, not that she still loved Stephen.

"Better arrested than dead," Owain said. "I have to fetch the doctor, or he'll die."

"You stay here," Charlotte said. "I'll go."

"All the way to Llanrys? In the dark?"

Evan had dislodged his blanket in his restless thrashing, and Charlotte covered him again. Owain was right, she could never handle a horse for that distance. She weighed the danger of Owain being arrested against Evan's need for medical attention.

"I'll talk to the doctor's granddaughter, look you. Megan did most of the work anyway. And she promised to keep the old man quiet about Mr. Evan."

"Yes," Charlotte said, relieved. "That's an excellent plan. But you must take care not to be seen. By now the news will have reached Llanrys."

Owain buttoned his coat. "Young Miss Megan Thomas is going to have an unexpected visitor at her bedroom window. I hope she doesn't scream."

Charlotte remembered the cool efficiency of the doctor's

granddaughter and doubted that Megan's reaction to any situation would be to scream.

The fever dream ended in an explosion of red and orange fire, and Evan drifted back up to the surface of consciousness. Charlotte sat beside him, wringing out a cloth in a bowl of water. There was no sign of Owain.

Evan closed his eyes, hoping that when he reopened them the stone walls of the cottage would have receded to a more comfortable distance. Instead, they seemed closer than ever. He suppressed a shudder, not wanting Charlotte to know how desperately trapped he felt by those walls.

He supposed claustrophobia was something that came with his size, but he still was ashamed of what he felt was a weakness. He'd always had a horror of closed-in places. His earliest recollection of mind-numbing panic had been of being locked in a cupboard at the orphanage. The standard punishment for misdeeds was several strokes with a bamboo cane across either palms or buttocks, but because no one could ever elicit a tear or a groan or even a grimace of distress from him, they decided that he was impervious to physical pain and other means of punishment must be devised.

The cupboard was not high enough to accommodate his height, nor wide enough to enable him to sit, so he spent miserable hours with hunched shoulders and bent knees, until cramped muscles and locked joints screamed in protest, and an inner rage built in him that one day erupted in a barrage of blows against the door. The wood splintered and he burst from the cupboard, wrenching the door off its hinges, smashing it to smithereens.

Even now, so many years later, he recalled the satisfaction he felt, as well as the looks on the faces of the wary circle of masters and monitors who surrounded him. He'd said, "I'm too big for that cupboard. I couldn't stand it any longer."

The headmaster, a sallow-skinned man with bagged eyes that resembled poached eggs, had cleared his throat nervously. "You are not too young to go to prison for this vandalism, Master Jones."

He had been placed in the home under the name of Evan Jones, his mother's maiden name, and had never heard the name Athmore until he met Stephen, years later.

The headmaster continued, "But out of the goodness of my heart, I shall instead allow you to work and pay for the damage." He turned to his chief monitor. "Young Master Jones has the strength of ten men, it seems. We must put it to good use. In addition to the chores he is required to perform here at the home, he will in future be offered for hire to any local merchant who has need of a strong back."

Because of his size, no one believed how young Evan was, and because of his physical strength he was constantly tested. Could Evan Jones carry still another crate, never mind that he already carried twice the number of anyone else? Could he work for longer without pause than ordinary mortals? Why hire three or four when one brute such as Jones would suffice? He was a child with the mind of a child inside a man's body, and, lacking mental maturity, was dubbed "backward" and "slow," for hadn't his own father admitted when he'd placed the baby in the orphanage that the boy was an idiot?

Years later when Evan himself ran the orphanage, he always tried to be especially kind to the boys whose own parents gave them up, feeling that their burden was perhaps harder to bear than the orphans who at least had the comfort of knowing their parents had been deceased and therefore unable to care for them.

By the time he was sixteen he was not only the chief handyman on the premises but was also a major source of income for the home. Despite a sketchy education it was clear he was far from mentally deficient. The headmaster was puzzled by Jones's intelligence and especially by his knowledge, and wondered how he'd acquired it. He never learned that one of Evan's employers, a wealthy carriage maker with an extensive library, had given the boy permission to read any book he chose as long as he finished his work ahead of time.

There had been a brief, disastrous escape from servitude, shortly after his sixteenth birthday.

On his way back to the home after a particularly grueling day of hauling mammoth rocks from a stone quarry, he was suddenly confronted with a wondrous sight. Coming down the lane toward him were six fully grown elephants.

Behind them came carts bearing caged lions and tigers, and prancing on foot were a troupe of clowns, lovely girls in spangled costumes, strutting men, a portly ringmaster in a brilliant orange and purple jacket, a sinewy lion tamer wearing bush clothes and a disdainful sneer, trapeze artists in tights, and a muscular bald-headed man wearing a leopard skin and necklace of animal teeth.

Evan stood at the roadside, entranced, and watched the circus enter a field and begin to set up tents. The quiet country lane and buttercup-strewn meadow were alive with raucous voices, barked orders, the sudden chilling deep-throated roar of a lion, and the nervous nickering of horses. There had been a light rain that morning, and the smell of trampled grass mingled with fetid animal odors in the humid air.

The circus had paraded through town and the performers were in costume and wore greasepaint, but Evan's gaze was drawn to a slender, young woman whose face was clean and whose pale gold hair shone like a halo. She seemed aloof, not part of the milling, sweating throng. She wore the tights and spangles of a trapeze artist, and he saw that two swarthy-skinned young men and an older man hovered protectively near her. She was as lovely and fragile as a flower, and Evan could not stop staring at her.

"You," a voice barked at his elbow, making him jump. "You look like a strong young fellow. I'll give you two tickets to the first performance if you'll help put up the big tent."

He looked for the lovely blond girl as she worked, but didn't see her again, nor the older man. The two swarthy younger men changed into work clothes and helped with the tent. From the circus posters Evan learned that the trapeze artists were called The Great Cordonis. The swarthy men were father and sons, and the blond girl was called Cella.

Just before Evan left, one of the stands holding the seats began to sway alarmingly seconds after it was set up. The men who had not secured it properly had already moved on to the next task, and only Evan saw the imminent collapse. He rushed over and grabbed the shaking stand, then put his shoulder under one end to hold it up until help came. The first person to join him was the bald-headed man with the bulging muscles. He no longer wore his leopard skin, and in ordinary clothes he looked much older and very tired. His eyes met Evan's in a glance of weary recognition, as though they had met before, or perhaps shared some secret. "I am Kasimir," the man said.

"My name is Evan," he responded, just before the others came to shore up the stand.

The headmaster of the orphanage refused to allow Evan to use the tickets he had been given. "No, you cannot go, young Master Jones. It wouldn't be fair to the other boys."

He lay awake that night thinking about the circus people, especially the lovely Cella. He thought of the tender curve of her mouth and wondered what it would be like to kiss her. Then he fell asleep and dreamed that the bald-headed Kasimir was beckoning him to follow into the dark cavern of a huge mountain.

That day Evan had to work again at the stone quarry, which meant he must pass the circus on his way back to the orphanage. He was now the oldest boy in the home, since at fourteen the others were found employment and sent out into the world. But Evan's earning capability and the fact that he single-handedly kept the tumbledown orphanage in a passable state of repair made the headmaster reluctant to lose him. Evan knew before he turned into the circus field that he intended to stay to see the performance. He didn't know then that he would not return to the orphanage, at least not for a while. But later he did wonder if he'd had a premonition of tragedy. Kasimir's and his own.

Occasionally, in later years, he dreamed he was back with them. The dreams were particularly vivid as he hung suspended between life and death in a drafty hovel, high in the Welsh mountains.

Evan seemed to be sleeping, but Charlotte worried that it was an unnatural sleep. A gray dawn had crept over the rim of the mountain, but still there was no sign of Owain. She told herself that perhaps he was having trouble persuading Megan to come, but as the hours passed her uneasiness increased.

She rose, her limbs stiff from the long night's vigil, as Gwyn began to stir in his wicker basket. As she fed the baby, questions hammered at her tired brain. What to do, what to do? Surely the preservation of life must take precedence over all else?

Evan's life hung by a thread, just as hers once had. He had quite literally saved her life, and more than that, her sanity. She couldn't let him die, no matter what. Besides, seeing him in his present helpless state had aroused in her feelings that both puzzled and intrigued her—as if in contemplating his possible death she focused on what he had meant to her in life. She recalled his many kindnesses to her, the companionable nature of their conversations, the startlingly uplifting quality of his sudden booming laugh, and most of all, the unspoken knowledge that they were kindred spirits, each an outcast in his and her own way. Oh yes, she cared more deeply about Evan Athmore than she had realized. Was it possible she even loved him? Had she been so beguiled by Stephen that she had not noticed how much more noble and compassionate Evan was?

Suddenly overwhelmed by her feelings, she regretted deeply

that she had never shown true gratitude to him for all he had done for her, including saving her life. Charlotte determined that she would save his, at any cost.

As the minutes ticked away and the sun rose high in the sky, it was evident that Owain must be in trouble. Evan was becoming weaker; there were no longer any periods of rationality. Just before noon, Charlotte decided to go and ask the shepherds tending their flocks in the valley below to carry Evan down the mountainside.

Quickly she changed the baby, then wrapped a shawl around both of them.

She was halfway down the steep path when she saw the sun glinting on the auburn hair of Megan Thomas. The young woman was running up the mountain, fleet-footed as a goat, hatless, her hair flying free.

When she reached Charlotte she was breathless and, from her dishabille, it was clear she had left home in a hurry.

Charlotte's heart sank to her feet. "Owain?" she began.

Megan shook her head despairingly. "We'd almost got through the village—we had to come that way, there's no other road for a carriage—when two men saw us and recognized Owain. Oh, God, they dragged him down from the carriage . . ."

Charlotte felt herself sway dizzily, and she clutched the baby tightly, afraid she would drop him.

Megan seized her arm to steady her. "They're coming. They're coming for Evan Athmore. I'm sorry . . . it's my fault, I led them here . . . but you had to know that Owain had been arrested—"

Charlotte could hear the sound of feet scrambling up the hillside, dislodging stones, breaking the boughs of small bushes, and soon the din included voices, shouts, even excited laughter. There would be no escape for Evan now.

In the wake of the fire and Evan's disappearance, Zoe and Mrs. Carmichael had moved immediately into the grange, along with several Glendower servants, including Lizzie. Mrs. Carmichael was a formidable buffer between her ladyship and the servants, but the housekeeper could not hide the fact that Zoe did not lose a minute in formulating grandiose plans for the rebuilding of the main house. Indeed, the very first day of her return, Zoe employed laborers to sift through and clear the debris left by the fire.

Lizzie, braver than the rest, remarked to Mrs. Carmichael that it was amazing how well her ladyship was bearing up after the death of her husband.

"Her husband isn't dead," Mrs. Carmichael answered calmly. "It was all a misunderstanding."

"But . . . the body they found—" Lizzie stammered.

"Whitcombe," Mrs. Carmichael said shortly, not looking up from a shopping list of provisions she was making. "I intended to call everyone belowstairs together this morning and explain the situation, but you might as well hear it now."

"You mean, Mr. Evan killed the butler?"

"The house burned to the ground and Whitcombe was inside," Mrs. Carmichael said. "It will be up to the courts to decide what happened."

"But, look you, her ladyship told everyone that it was Lord Athmore who was burned to death."

"As I said, a misunderstanding. My poor lady was beside herself with fear for her husband, knowing the threats that had been made against him by his uncle. Lord Athmore was called to London unexpectedly, in regard to an exhibition of his work. He decided to call on Mr. Evan before leaving, and then proceeded to Llanrys and caught the train. But her ladyship had expected him to return to the village inn before departing, which is why she raised a hue and cry."

"But . . . what were they doing, staying in the village?"

"They have a perfect right to stay wherever they choose. They love this part of the country, why wouldn't they come here?"

When Lizzie went into the village to buy the supplies, she found that the mood there was no less hostile toward Evan Athmore because the body had been identified as Whitcombe. Young Owain Davies was wanted also, and there were serious charges against him, as he'd used a gun during the theft of the horse and cart. Men were out scouring the countryside for the fugitives. Charlotte Danforth had also beat a hasty retreat, undoubtedly fearing she would be called upon as a witness.

The following day Lord Athmore arrived, was barely civil to the footman who opened the door to him, stormed into the kitchen where Mrs. Carmichael was supervising the preparation of dinner, and demanded to know where his wife was.

Zoe was in the massive bedroom that had been Evan's room. Except for an enormous four-poster bed, a carved trunk at the foot of the bed, a wardrobe and chest of drawers of heroic proportions, the room was bare. Zoe had removed all of Evan's clothes from the wardrobe, thrown them in a heap on the floor, and was going through the contents of the trunk.

"Darling!" she cried as Stephen came into the room, slamming the door behind him. "I wasn't expecting you until next week."

"Obviously," he said grimly, tossing his hat on the bed. "Oh, God, Zoe, what have you done now?"

She went to him and slipped her arms around him, smiling up at him in a tentative, little-girl way. "How . . . how did you know I was here? Did you go to the inn?"

"It wasn't necessary. A complete account of the fire, the discovery of the burned body, and Evan's disappearance appeared in the London papers last evening. I caught the first train north this morning. I knew you'd be here. Zoe, you promised me you'd wait at the inn. You swore you only wanted a rest in the country."

"I did, I did! But the men who went with you to Glendower came back and told me how he'd humiliated you."

"So that's how you knew I went there that day. I wondered about that."

"Tell me, my love, did you go to see the little housekeeper? I understand she came back from Italy with a mysterious baby in her arms. Surely motherhood destroyed her allure for you. How many times have you told me you can't bear the way childbirth ravages a woman's body?"

"You were the one who wanted to come back to North Wales," he pointed out quickly.

"Only after you expressed your homesickness for Glendower, dearest." She pulled his face down so that she could kiss his lips, but he pulled away.

"I want the whole story, Zoe. Everything."

"Evan set fire to the house. Whitcombe was inside and apparently couldn't get out in time."

"Damn you, tell me the truth! The first newspaper accounts said you told the police I was in the house."

"Darling, it *could* have been you. I thought they would be more conscientious about arresting Evan if they thought he'd burned up his nephew rather than the butler. I knew you were on the train to London so . . . After all, I was distraught. I became hysterical and imagined the worst. The constable was very understanding."

Stephen grabbed her by the wrists and pulled her roughly to her feet. "Did you set that fire? Was it you, Zoe?"

"Of course not!"

He shook her. "Don't lie to me!"

"I was in the village, at the inn. Ask anyone."

"Then you paid someone to do it." All the energy drained from him. He released her, his face ashen.

Her eyes narrowed to black slits. "He stole your inheritance. Glendower is yours, it's been yours since you were a boy. It's yours by right of possession. Someone had to get it back for you! You never would have done it for yourself."

"Don't you understand what you've done? Do you realize what will happen to Evan and the young groom who helped him? Have you no conscience at all?"

She shrugged. "Perhaps they won't be found."

"They've already been found, Zoe. I heard in the village on my way here. Both Evan and Davies are in custody."

Stephen and Zoe had just finished eating dinner when Mrs. Carmichael entered the room and said, "Begging your pardon, madam, but Mrs. Danforth is here."

"Charlotte?" Stephen said, half rising from his chair.

Zoe flashed him a warning glance. "Show her into the drawing room. We'll be along in a moment."

The housekeeper nodded and departed. Stephen started to follow and Zoe said, "Wait. Don't be so damned eager. What do you think she wants?"

"Why don't we go and find out?"

"Let her wait. And when we do see her, leave all of the talking to me. After all, *ma cherie*, you weren't here, so you can't possibly know what happened during these last eventful days, can you?"

After half an hour, Zoe leisurely rose from the table and proceeded to the drawing room, Stephen anxious at her side.

They both stopped in surprise as they saw that Charlotte had brought the baby with her. Zoe gave Stephen a quick sideways glance and said, "Good evening, Mrs. Danforth. I see you've brought the baby, how delightful. May I see him?"

Stephen silently marveled at Zoe's aplomb as she bent over the infant. He saw, too, the acute longing in his wife's dark eyes and wondered if he had perhaps misjudged her by dismissing her longing for a child of her own as merely one of her passing fancies. Perhaps her biological urges were unaffected by her mental imbalance.

Charlotte was very pale, her composure obviously costing considerable effort. Surprising him still further, she asked in a low voice, "Would you like to hold him, Lady Athmore?"

Zoe took the baby from her, smiling down at him in obvious joy. Stephen felt his heart lurch, despite the circumstances, because Zoe was more beautiful in that moment than he had ever seen her. He turned to Charlotte and asked, "Where are you staying?"

"At the inn. I . . . took a room there today."

"Please, let's sit down," Stephen said. "Charlotte, Mrs. Danforth, we realize that the fire, Evan's arrest . . . everything that occurred these past few days in fact, must have been a terrible shock to you . . . to all of us. If there's anything we can do for you and your son . . ."

Charlotte sank gratefully into a chair and gripped the arms, as if afraid she might fall from it. "Yes, there is. You can have Evan released from the prison hospital and brought home."

"I beg your pardon?"

"He was shot. He's very ill. I'm afraid the prison doctor may be too overworked to care for him properly. Besides, being confined like that . . . he suffers from claustrophobia."

Zoe snapped, "Of course he does. As large as he is, he must feel confined wherever he goes."

"Except here," Charlotte said quietly, "at the grange." She glanced about her, up at the high ceilings, across the uncluttered expanse of floor to the uncurtained bay windows that pushed the room outward, extending it into the garden.

Stephen said, "Naturally, we will do all we can for him. It was unfortunate, the villagers acting as they did, taking the law into their own hands. The police are conducting a full investigation—"

"Please," Charlotte interrupted. He realized then that she was shaking violently. Her lips were white and her eyes wide.

"What is it, Charlotte?" Stephen asked. "What are you trying to say?"

"He's dying. He needs the best possible medical care. You can save him. You have the power. The men who say they saw him set fire to the house are lying. You can make them tell the truth. You know Evan didn't do this monstrous thing. You *must* save him. He won't live long enough for the police to complete an investigation. Please, he must come home at once.'' Her voice rose higher in her desperation.

Oblivious, Zoe placed the baby on a chair and sank to her knees beside it. She slipped her emerald and diamond bracelet from her wrist and dangled it over him, then laughed as a tiny hand batted at the shiny stones.

Charlotte said quickly, all in one breath, ''You can take him, bring him up yourself, adopt him, whatever you wish, and all I ask is to be allowed to visit him occasionally.''

The silence that fell seemed to resound around the room. Stephen took her words apart in his mind and reassembled them. Zoe turned and stared from one to the other.

Charlotte went on, less hurriedly now that she was sure she would be able to continue. ''In return, you must bring Evan home immediately and have the charges against Owain Davies dropped. A good nanny must be found, and Gwyn placed in her care. I've given a great deal of thought to the situation and believe it would be best if we told Gwyn . . .'' she hesitated, close to tears, ''that I am his aunt.''

Stephen stared at her, finally comprehending, and incredulous. ''You would do this—make this sacrifice—to save *Evan?*''

She regarded him silently with eyes too drowned to read.

He thought, my God, she must love him. She must actually love that great, lumbering beast. Stephen felt a stab of acute jealousy.

Zoe gathered the baby up into her arms and cooed at him. ''Stephen, you fool, don't you realize that she's ensuring a place in the world for her son. Just as your mother gave you up so you could grow up at Glendower.''

For an instant Stephen froze, wondering if Zoe could possibly know that she was holding his son in her arms.

Zoe went on, ''Not that it matters why she's doing this. All that matters is that we have a son.''

''I insist upon interviewing nannies myself,'' Charlotte said. ''I shan't leave Gwyn with you until you have a nanny I can trust and Evan is home.''

''Where will you go?'' Stephen asked.

''Away from here. But I'll return to see my son as often as I can. Will you agree—to bring Evan home today?''

''What I have wrought . . .'' Zoe replied lightly, ''I can . . . unwrought. We'll begin rebuilding the house immediately. We can go away until the work is finished so we won't have to share the grange with Evan. I should think he will be properly chastened by his experiences lately. Our giant has been tamed, my darling, and won't give us any trouble in future. Now that he knows I can instantly summon help to deal with him.''

Charlotte's eyes were blazing, the only sign of life in her numbed features, as she rose and walked over to Zoe. "I'll take the baby now. We'll wait at the inn until Evan and Owain are free.''

The moment the door closed behind them, Zoe seized Stephen's hands and danced a jig. "Oh, it's all too wonderful! I can't believe how well it's all working out. Come on, let's go over to the stablemaster's cottage, I haven't been there since the night of the fire.''

"Stablemaster's cottage?'' Stephen repeated in bewilderment.

"That's where I had Whitcombe store most of our objets d'art and valuables, *cherie*. You didn't think I'd let them burn up in the fire? Whitcombe must have gone back inside for one more piece and couldn't get out in time.''

16

THERE WERE BRIEF interludes when Evan thought death beckoned, but he resisted; times when he thought he was running through a black fog. He ran until he was exhausted, and then forced himself to continue to run.

Once he thought he was back in his room at the grange, and Owain Davies was standing over him, telling him that he knew he would be all right now, and that he had come to say good-bye as he was going away. There were violent nightmares and then there were periods of nothingness, and Evan feared oblivion more than anything else because it signified death.

The curtain of awareness parted slightly. He saw a young girl in white, with bright auburn hair escaping from a white cap. An old man, very wrinkled, a dusty unused air about him, at her side giving instructions. Her hands, cool and efficient, obeying his commands. They blended and became one. An old man with a girl's hands. The curtain of consciousness closed again, and they vanished.

But it was all part of the nightmare, he realized, when Kasimir's bald head floated before him like a drifting moon.

Kasimir had been the circus strong man for nearly thirty years, and he was old and tired when Evan joined them, but it didn't stop him from defending his territory like a battle-scarred old bull taking on a brash, young challenger.

The ringmaster saw Evan arrive for their first performance and approached him immediately. "You're the young giant who single-handedly held up the stand yesterday. How tall are you, and how old?''

"Why do you ask?''

"Because if you've ever thought of running off with a circus, now's your chance. With your size and strength, we can easily think up an act for you.''

A surprisingly soft voice behind Evan said, "Run off to sea, emigrate to some raw, young land, apprentice yourself to a gravedigger. Do anything at all, but don't join this circus.'' It was Kasimir and his ferocious glare gave the softness of his tone a particularly chilling quality.

The ringmaster laughed. "Old Kasimir is afraid I'll give you his act. You see, a circus strong man is the highest paid performer. We can always find clowns and fliers and fools willing to step into a cage with tigers, but a strong man is born, not made. Back in your cage, Kasimir.''

At that moment Cella had walked by. She didn't look at them, although she could hardly have failed to notice Evan towering over the ringmaster and the strong man. Evan felt his heart turn over.

"Well?'' the ringmaster asked. "Will you join us?''

Evan thought of the years of misery and abuse he'd suffered at the orphanage, of the daily toil of working for wages he never saw. The headmaster had kept him long past the age when he should have been released, by the simple device of telling him that there was no place for him in the outside world. He was a giant, a freak of nature. No one would give him steady work, they'd be too afraid he might go on a rampage, as indeed he had at the orphanage, a fact the headmaster would be forced to divulge to prospective employers. Evan had thought he was trapped there for life, but the ringmaster was offering him not only a job, but a place to live where his size and strength would be advantages rather than handicaps.

Dismissing Kasimir's warning looks as envy for his youth and strength, Evan promptly told the ringmaster he would be glad to join them.

He worked with the elephants at first, an act pitting his strength against one of the huge animals in a tug-of-war. There were several clashes with Kasimir, none of a very serious nature. The strong man at first attempted to humiliate him for his lack of experience or knowledge of circus life, and when that didn't work, he deliberately tried to sabotage his act, one day even going so far as to insert a thorn in the ear of one of the elephants, making his behavior dangerously unpredictable. Only Evan's youth and quick reflexes saved him from being trampled. The animal trainer discovered the problem and wanted to accuse Kasimir, but Evan dissuaded him. The paradox was that in some strange way Evan felt a bond between Kasimir and himself, although he couldn't define it.

Weeks elapsed before Evan plucked up enough courage to speak to Cella. By then he had learned she was Cordoni's adopted daughter. Her mother, as well as the mother of Cordoni's two swarthy sons, had both been killed in their act, attempting a dangerous triple somersault. Cordoni had been their catcher, and now he caught Cella.

Evan couldn't watch as she flew through the air, fragile as a butterfly. He was sure that even if she didn't fall, she would disintegrate in Cordoni's powerful hands when he caught her. Evan always closed his eyes in that moment when Cella let go of her swing and hurtled toward her father. They worked without a net.

After their performance one afternoon, Evan smiled shyly at Cella and said, ''Watching you takes my breath away.''

''I'm part of a team, a family,'' she said quickly, a trifle coldly. ''Without my father and brothers, I would be nothing.''

''You could never be nothing,'' Evan replied. ''You are too beautiful.'' He was amazed at his own temerity and humbly grateful when Cella merely smiled enigmatically.

Oddly, it was Kasimir who first recognized that Evan had fallen achingly, agonizingly in love with Cella. ''So, young Goliath,'' Kasimir said one day, ''you hang around the Cordonis hoping for a smile or word from your beloved. Perhaps she will drop a glove and you can retrieve it, or perhaps some lout will make an inopportune remark in her presence and you can thrash him. Watch out, or Cordoni and his sons will have your hide.''

Evan felt himself flush. ''Why don't you mind your own business?''

''You are my business, Goliath. Don't you know that one day soon the ringmaster is going to say the king is dead, long live the king.''

''You make no sense, Kasimir.''

''The ringmaster is preparing you to take my place. But Kasimir is not yet ready to be put out to pasture. And when he is, there will not be a young Goliath waiting to step in. Oh no, the circus will mourn me and feel my loss before they find a replacement.'' Kasimir gave an evil chuckle. ''Funny that you're besotted by Cella Cordoni. Because her stepfather and I have a lot in common. Two old war-horses waiting to die in harness.''

''What do you mean by that?''

Kasimir scratched his bald head, his deep-set eyes glinting with pleasure that he had at last found the Achilles' heel of his rival. ''Cordoni works without a net. He never used to. There was a net when Cella's mother fell, but she hit the edge of it and bounced out. Ever since then, he's worked without one.''

Evan's blood froze as he thought of Cella, flying through the air as she let go of her swing and somersaulted toward her father's outstretched hands. ''Surely . . . surely you're not saying—''

The strong man started to walk away. Over his shoulder he muttered, ''Like I said, Cordoni wants to die in harness, like me. And he doesn't care who he takes with him.''

Evan knew then that he had to take Cella away from the circus. He didn't know how, but if he didn't, sooner or later there would be a ghastly accident. He had nightmares in which he saw the bloodied and broken body of Cella lying on the sawdust floor.

He began to seek her out more often, taking her small gifts, picking flowers for her, always eager to perform some small service. What did it matter that she treated him like an overgrown puppy that followed her about, or that her brothers openly ridiculed him, or that her father scowled at him but was too afraid of his size to drive him off.

Cordoni did approach him once and say, ''My daughter Cella is a child. Pure and innocent. I and my sons would kill any man who defiled her. *Any* man, no matter how big and strong. Even a giant has to sleep. You understand me?''

''I would never do anything to hurt her,'' Evan replied. ''I give you my word of honor, sir.''

''Then stay away from her.''

''I speak to her only in friendship.''

''No male ever seeks out a female only in friendship,'' Cordoni growled, turning his back and marching away.

On the days that Cella smiled at him, Evan's heart sang, and the exchange of even the most banal conversation with her was enough to send his hopes for the future soaring.

When she confessed to him that she did not like flying, that she was always afraid, and had taken her mother's place only because her stepfather insisted, Evan asked, "Would you leave, if you could?"

She gave a dreamy, faraway smile. Her eyes were the palest tint of blue, almost transparent, and her skin was so white that she appeared ethereal, a creature of spirit rather than flesh. "Oh, yes, in a flash! But I have no money of my own, no way to live if I leave."

"I would take care of you, Cella," Evan said shyly, first love in his sixteen-year-old heart overflowing, washing away all the obstacles.

She lowered golden eyelashes over her transparent eyes and murmured, "When you have saved twenty pounds, we'll speak of this again."

Twenty pounds! It was a fortune. He stammered, "But I only earn five shillings a week . . ."

"When you take Kasimir's place as strong man," Cella said softly, "you will earn much more. It's time you showed the ringmaster that you can do everything Kasimir does and more. You're far stronger than he is."

It was true. Evan knew he could lift the weights Kasimir lifted, break the chains he broke, and even outperform the climax of his act, when he stood tethered to two mounted horsemen who attempted to ride off in different directions while he restrained them.

For Evan, the days whirled by in a haze of anticipation. Hadn't Cella, by implication at least, promised to be his?

Secretly he practiced all of Kasimir's feats of strength. He became more at ease in front of an audience. He learned not to let Kasimir's smoldering resentment or the Cordoni brothers' taunts bother him. Cella came to watch him practice lifting barbells that weighed two hundred pounds, one in each hand. She flattered him and encouraged him and he was wildly happy, oblivious to the disaster in the making, until the evening he found old Cordoni himself barring his way. "Stay away from Cella, you hear me? I will give her to no man, least of all to a freak like you. You think I would let you have her when I denied my own son?"

Evan had wondered about the older of the Cordoni brothers, a swaggering twenty year old named Fredo. He had seen him watching Cella with more than brotherly interest. But what difference did it make? She cared for him and soon he'd have Kasimir's job and when he'd saved twenty pounds . . .

"Cella has a right to make up her own mind," Evan responded.

Cordoni's eyes burned into his skull. "I would let her fall before I'd let you or any other man have her."

Evan gasped as the trapeze artist walked away. Surely he didn't mean it? But hadn't Kasimir said that Cordoni had wanted to die ever since Cella's mother was killed?

Flinging caution to the winds, he ran to the Cordoni caravan, hoping to find Cella alone. At least he knew her father wasn't there. At first there was no response to his knock on the door. He pounded even louder and after a moment Cella appeared, looking flushed, the buttons of her dress undone and her usually smooth, gold hair tangled. "What do you want?" she asked, with no welcome in her voice.

"You must come away with me at once," Evan blurted out. "You must never get on a trapeze with your father again. He intends to let you fall, he just told me."

"What?"

"I love you, Cella. I'll take care of you, protect you with my life. We don't need twenty pounds. I'll get a job . . . another circus, a fair perhaps." He paused, his face scarlet. "I want to marry you."

At first he mistook her shocked expression for horror at the fate her stepfather intended for her, but then she gave a small scream. "*Marry* you? Are you mad? Let a great oaf like you touch me? How dare you think of me in such a way? Oh, no, oh God, I feel sick! Do you really believe any woman would ever marry you? Don't you know what you are? You're a freak of nature."

He reeled backward. "But . . . but you said if I saved twenty pounds . . ."

Fredo Cordoni appeared behind her then, casually buttoning his shirt. He grinned at Evan. "The twenty pounds was for her and me. We were going to leave the old man and start an act of our own."

Trembling with anger, Cella cried, "You asked if I would leave, and I said I would if I had the money. You were always giving me things. I thought you'd give me the money, too."

Fredo dropped a proprietary arm on Cella's shoulder, and his fingers played with her hair. Their passion for one another was obvious in the way they looked and touched one another. Evan turned and stumbled away, almost colliding with her father.

The old man's face was gray and there was a terrible, mad gleam in his eyes, but his gaze was directed not at Evan but at his son and adopted daughter. "So . . ." Cordoni said, "I follow the giant to see what he's up to and, instead, what do I find? Get inside, both of you."

As he walked away, Evan heard the caravan door slam and Cordoni shouting at his son.

Evan knew he would have to leave the circus. He wouldn't be able to bear being near her, knowing of her perfidy, knowing she and Fredo were lovers. He resolved that he would give his last performance that night. When he told the ringmaster of his decision, he also asked that the Cordonis not be allowed to fly until tempers had cooled.

The ringmaster laughed. "Cordoni has told you that he'd let her fall before he'd let any man have her. You must understand, it's all part of the drama. He doesn't mean it. Circus life is drama and danger. We all live on the thin edge. If we didn't dramatize ourselves, how could we impress an audience? Now, as for your leaving, forget that nonsense. You're almost ready to take Kasimir's place. I intend to tell him today."

No amount of argument on Evan's part could dissuade him. "No matter what you do, I'm leaving," Evan said. "After tonight's performance."

As he prepared to enter the ring for the last time, Kasimir materialized at his side and, with a particularly evil smirk, muttered, "I hear you made a fool of yourself over at the Cordonis' today. Now the fat's in the fire. The old man knows what everyone else has known for months about Fredo and Cella."

"Save your breath," Evan said. "I'm leaving tomorrow."

Kasimir looked at him strangely, almost with regret, but he said, "Good riddance to you, Goliath. Console yourself with the thought that you never could have filled Kasimir's shoes, anyway."

When he finished the tug-of-war with the elephant, Evan couldn't resist picking up Kasimir's two-hundred-pound weights and raising them over his head, then tossing them contemptuously at the strong man's feet. Kasimir's mouth dropped open, and he suddenly looked very, very old.

The trapeze artists were on next and Evan stayed to watch, although he knew it would tear his heart out to see her. There they were, high on a platform above the darkened tent, the Great

Cordonis, taking their bow. Then powdered hands grasped the trapeze bar, the band struck up a lively tune, and Cordoni swung out over their heads.

Evan had forgotten the presence of Kasimir, who still stood at his side, until one of the clowns suddenly rushed up to them. "Where's the ringmaster?" he asked in a loud whisper. "He's got to get them down. Cordoni found out that Fredo and Cella are going to run away together tonight. *He's going to let her fall!* He really means it."

"It's too late," Kasimir hissed back. "Look, she's ready for the somersault."

The drums rolled, and Evan's heartbeat sounded as loud. It seemed as if everything had slowed to a snail's pace, as if, for an instant, fate wondered how to deal with all of them. Then . . . confusion.

Kasimir running forward into the ring. Cella gaining momentum as she swung back and forth. Cordoni hanging by his heels . . .

Then the flash of white, screams and shouts, a sickening thud, and tangled bodies seeping blood into the sawdust. Evan was the first to reach them. Cordoni was already dead, but Kasimir, who had attempted to break his fall, lived another minute, long enough to look into Evan's eyes with that same wordless recognition he had given him the first time they met. And now Evan realized what that look meant. Pity. Kasimir felt sorry for him.

Over his head Cella still swung back and forth, but now she was sitting on the bar, looking down. She had never gone into the somersault. Was that what had caused her stepfather to falter and fall?

Evan awoke with a start, disoriented, at first not recognizing his surroundings. When he came fully to his senses, he realized he was back at the grange at Glendower, in his own bed.

His body felt strangely alien. His right arm was encased in plaster. Tentatively he ran his left hand over his chest and felt protruding ribs. Good God, could this gaunt frame be his? There was a rough, puckered area on his right side, a wound of some sort, but healed now.

Memory returned slowly, fragments, half-seen images. He recalled being shot, and the torturous walk up the mountainside. Charlotte had been with him then, and Owain.

The girl in white with pretty auburn hair came into the room carrying a vase filled with white roses. Could summer have come and he have been unaware? She smiled and said, "Ah, you're awake. How are you feeling today?"

"Better." His voice cracked horribly and she put down the roses and poured water into a glass, holding it to his lips. She looked vaguely familiar, but he couldn't remember where he had met her.

"Thank you. You're a nurse?"

A hint of a frown crossed her brow. How very young she was; her complexion was as flawless as the rose petals, her eyes clear and green as a forest. "No," she said shortly. "I'm not a nurse. I assist my grandfather. He's a doctor and he's been treating you. Well, actually he retired some years ago. You don't remember us? Dr. Thomas and Megan."

"How . . . how long have I been here?"

"Don't worry about it now. Just a few weeks."

Weeks? He was aghast that time could have vanished without a trace.

"Would you like something to eat?"

"Not yet. How did I get here?"

"Lord Athmore brought you. You . . ." She broke off.

"Were in a prison hospital," he finished for her. "I remember now. Who else is here in the house?"

"Just me and Grandfather and your servants."

"Mrs. Danforth?"

"No. She isn't here."

"Where is she?"

"I don't know, I'm sorry. I don't think she went with Lord and Lady Athmore. They went back to London I believe, while their house is being rebuilt."

He felt tired again and couldn't seem to take enough air into his lungs. "Later," he whispered, "I shall have a great many questions."

Over the course of the next few days, he learned that Stephen and Zoe and a nanny had taken a baby to London, and then on to Paris. What baby? Where had the baby come from?

Owain Davies had emigrated to America. Stonemasons, bricklayers and carpenters were building a house fit for a king on the site of the ruins. The exhibition of Stephen's paintings was successful beyond his or anyone else's wildest dreams. *The Passionate Virgin* had been sold to an unknown buyer for the largest sum ever paid for a portrait by a living artist. Stephen had been commissioned by several members of the royal family to paint their portraits.

Evan raged silently that all this had taken place while he lay in delirious oblivion, unable to do anything about it. So Stephen and Zoe had won, after all. He could, of course, go to court to prove his claim to the estate, but he was reluctant to do that because it would mean washing all the Athmore dirty linen in public. Besides, what did it matter if Stephen and Zoe lived at Glendower now that Charlotte was gone?

As he lay in bed, slowly recovering his strength, Evan realized why he had thought so much about his circus days and his hopeless first love lately—because in remembering Cella, he recognized the difference between infatuation and love. There had been little beneath Cella's surface perfection to admire or care about, while the depth of beauty in Charlotte's soul inspired in him a love that he knew would last through eternity. He didn't doubt that Charlotte had gone away because of Stephen. Perhaps when Stephen returned, he would know where she was.

17

CHARLOTTE HAD FLED to London. She took a room in a boardinghouse in the East End and although she intended to find a position as quickly as possible, for several weeks she found she was unable to do anything but sit in her dismal room in a state of utter despair. Her longing for her baby was a physical pain that twisted inside her like a knife.

She had placed Gwyn in the hands of a young nanny from Scotland, an eager, capable young woman named Lorna McDougan who reminded Charlotte of herself when she had first taken charge of Eleanor Hathaway. Charlotte knew from her own experience that the nanny would have almost total care of the infant, who would be brought out for the Athmore's friends to admire, or played with for an hour or so by Stephen and Zoe, then handed back to his nanny.

Her son was in good hands, she told herself. Lorna would watch over him and so would Stephen, who seemed genuinely thrilled to have his son live with him. Between them they offered the baby the kind of security impossible for Charlotte in her present circumstances to provide.

When she had hesitated, at the last moment, before handing Gwyn to the nanny, Stephen had drawn her aside and sworn that he would never allow Zoe near the infant if there was the slightest indication she might be in one of her spells. "He's my son, Charlotte, and I would die before I'd let any harm come to him."

Charlotte believed him. Gwyn would live in luxury, in a style she never could have managed on her own, even if she could have found an employer willing to hire her with a baby, which was doubtful. Leaving Glendower with a child in her arms could very well have sent both of them to the workhouse. Employers like Evan Athmore were rare, indeed. But reassuring herself of the logic of her decision did nothing to ease the ache of her empty arms.

At least Evan and Owain were safe. Her last glimpse of Evan had been as he was carried, unconscious, into the grange. Dr. Thomas and Megan accompanied him and Megan had whispered to Charlotte, "Don't worry, he's enormously strong. That strength, along with Grandfather's skill will save him."

Charlotte prayed that it would be so. She also wished Godspeed to Owain, who was leaving for America. He had looked at her with an inquiring gaze and said, "I don't know how you did it, but I've no doubt who we owe our freedom to and I'm grateful to you. Will you . . . will you tell Ellie that I'll write to her, as soon as I'm settled?"

"Yes, of course," she responded. Owain hadn't known that she was also going away. He thought that everyone would resume their places at Glendower: Zoe and Stephen in their grand new house and Evan and Charlotte in the grange. But of course, that could never be again.

During those first weeks in London, she didn't even visit Eleanor. Depression had her in its grip, and she sank ever deeper into despair, often remaining in bed all day. She had no idea what was happening beyond the four walls of her room, and no desire to know.

Eventually when her meager savings were exhausted and her landlord threatened eviction unless she paid her rent she was forced to go out and look for work.

It was midsummer again, and wealthy families had closed their town houses and repaired to their country estates. No one was seeking a housekeeper or a nanny. Charlotte lowered her expectations and looked for work as a maid. But since she did not wish to divulge that she had been employed by the Athmores and therefore could not offer prior references, she was turned away from even the most menial jobs.

Eventually, in desperation, she decided to go and see Eleanor. Perhaps Lady Ramsey would know of someone who would hire her. She sent a note to their London address and several days went

by before she received a response. There was no return address on
the stationery, which bore the Ramsey crest, but the postmark
showed that Delia Ramsey's letter had come from Surrey.

"Dear Mrs. Danforth," she read. "We have closed the London house for the summer, however, I will be in town next
Monday afternoon. I suggest we have tea together . . ."

There was no mention of Eleanor, but Charlotte assumed the
little girl would accompany Lady Ramsey.

The following Monday, Charlotte pawned the black velvet cape
Stephen had given her in order to buy a small gift for Eleanor, a
book on acting, and to pay for a hansom cab to the tea shop
specified. She was looking forward to seeing Eleanor again,
hoping that the sight of the little girl would help in some way to
assuage her loneliness.

But Lady Ramsey's table in the tea shop was set for only two.
Delia Ramsey greeted Charlotte in a slightly strained manner and
ordered tea and petit fours.

As soon as the waiter departed, Delia said, "Let's dispense
with formality, Mrs. Danforth, shall we? Lord and Lady
Athmore are dear friends of ours, and we know . . ." she paused
and lowered her voice, ". . . *everything.*"

"I beg your pardon?" Charlotte asked faintly. Surely they
couldn't know about Gwyn? The arrangement with the Athmores
had been that they would tell everyone he had been adopted from
an orphans' home.

"Your relationship to Eleanor, your taking her without permission from her grandfather's house. Lady Athmore wrote me at
length, informing me that she had thoroughly investigated
Eleanor's background. We have already taken the necessary steps
to rectify the situation, so if you have come to me with the
intention of blackmailing us . . ."

The room spun dizzily around Charlotte's head. "Blackmail? I
had no such intention . . . I merely wanted to visit Eleanor
and . . . and to ask if you knew of anyone who has need of my
services. Lady Ramsey, I assure you I know how happy Eleanor
is with you and would not do anything to cause an impediment to
her present security."

Delia Ramsey looked somewhat mollified, but she continued,
"As far as recommending you for employment to any of our
friends is concerned, well, we can hardly do that in view of the
fact that you were dismissed from your last post, can we?"

Charlotte had not eaten that day and she felt faint. The waiter brought the tea, and she quickly sipped some, trying to clear her fogged senses. "You must have misunderstood, Lady Ramsey. I was not dismissed from Glendower. I left of my own free will."

"Mrs. Danforth, we are well aware of what happened in North Wales. As I said, Lady Athmore wrote us. She told how Evan Athmore became temporarily insane and set fire to the house . . . causing the death of one of the servants. I'm not sure what part you personally played in what happened, but I do know that you and that dreadful man are extremely fortunate that Lord and Lady Athmore were able to hush up the whole unfortunate business and that no charges were brought against anyone."

Drawing a deep breath, Charlotte said, "If we could return to the situation regarding Eleanor. You said you had taken steps to . . . rectify the situation. What exactly does that mean?"

Delia played with her cake fork. "We have sent word to her grandfather of her whereabouts, of course. What else could we do?"

Charlotte caught her breath. "Then . . . he will insist she be sent home and I . . ."

"Might possibly have to face charges in her abduction," Delia finished for her. "If you think I feel sympathy for you, you are mistaken. My husband and I would never have taken her into our home, and allowed ourselves to become attached to her, had we known the truth."

"Lady Ramsey, if you will allow me to explain why I took Eleanor away—you see, a friend of her grandfather's . . . molested her . . ."

Delia's mouth opened in horror and she blushed. "Mrs. Danforth, please! I don't wish to hear any sordid flight of fancy to justify what you did. I've already questioned Eleanor at length and she said nothing about such an incident. She said you left because her parents went away and her grandfather dismissed you."

"She was probably afraid to tell you the whole story. Her grandfather refused to believe us at the time. If you would just allow me to speak with her—"

"No, Mrs. Danforth. I believe it would be better if she did not see you again, pending any decision her grandfather might make. By now the cable we sent to Boston should have arrived. I have the address where you're staying so, if necessary, the authorities will be able to find you."

Charlotte didn't remember leaving the tea shop. She found

herself out on the street, walking blindly. How cruel life could
be, piling one misfortune upon another. For her to be uprooted so
soon from Glendower, to lose Gwyn, to part from Evan, then to
find that Eleanor was lost to her, too. Now, in addition to the loss
of everyone she loved, she would have to face Stansfield Hathaway's wrath and probable imprisonment.

A news vendor was shouting the headlines of one of the more
lurid of the scandal sheets. At first his cockney whine registered
on her mind only as part of the din of the city, but as she drew
closer, she heard, "Artist's passionate model unmasked!"

Passionate model? Could he mean Stephen's *Passionate Virgin?* The boy certainly couldn't yell the word *virgin* on a public
street. He didn't look at her face as she handed him a penny for
the newspaper.

The story was on page one, along with a report of the
scandalous divorce proceedings of a prominent member of the
House of Commons.

NOTED ARTIST STEPHEN MEADOWS (LORD ATHMORE),
WHOSE RECENT EXHIBITION DREW WIDE ACCLAIM IN THE
ART WORLD AND WHOSE FLAGRANTLY EROTIC RENDER-
ING OF THE FULL-LENGTH NUDE HE CALLED *THE PAS-
SIONATE VIRGIN* SOLD FOR THE LARGEST SUM EVER PAID
TO A LIVING ARTIST, HAS REFUSED TO COMMENT ON
RUMORS THAT HIS MODEL'S IDENTITY HAS BEEN RE-
VEALED. IT HAS BEEN REPORTED BY A RELIABLE SOURCE
THAT THE MYSTERIOUS BUYER OF MEADOWS' PICTURE
HIRED A FIRM OF SOLICITORS TO TRACE THE MODEL. HER
NAME IS CHARLOTTE DANFORTH AND SHE WAS A SERVANT
ON THE ARTIST'S ESTATE IN NORTH WALES. AT THIS TIME
NO OTHER INFORMATION IS AVAILABLE, EXCEPT THAT THE
ANONYMOUS MILLIONAIRE WHO FELL IN LOVE WITH HER
PICTURE IS ANXIOUS TO MEET HER . . .

Charlotte stumbled along the hot pavement as she read,
keeping her head down, although there was no reproduction of
the picture in the paper because of its nudity, and certainly no one
who saw her now could possibly recognize her. She was thin as a
stick, eyes sunken and smudged with dark circles, and her head
seemed to hang permanently over her chest in an attitude of utter
defeat.

A wave of panic assailed her. Great God, how had it come

about that plain little Charlotte Briggs had become a notorious woman? Sought by a mysterious anonymous millionaire . . . and, as soon as Stansfield Hathaway arrived, undoubtedly the police would be on her trail, too.

She would have to leave the boardinghouse immediately. But where could she go? Oh, if only she could vanish into thin air! She walked for hours, until she felt so light-headed and faint that she was forced to pause and rest for a moment in the doorway of a modest building on an unfamiliar street.

Waves of dizziness passed over her and she leaned against the door, closing her eyes for a second.

When she opened her eyes she saw that the glass panel in the door was inscribed with peeling gilt paint proclaiming this to be the London office of the Missionary Society.

Visions of her childhood and her parents flashed through her mind. Surely some power wiser than herself must have directed her footsteps here?

Drawing a deep breath, she opened the door and went inside. A thin young man wearing pince-nez was seated at a desk in a Spartanly furnished room. He looked up and smiled nearsightedly.

"My name is Miss Briggs," Charlotte said. "My father was the vicar of a parish in Sussex for many years, and before that he was a missionary who served in India. That was before my birth, but I do have a Church of England education and a great desire to do God's work."

The young man jumped to his feet to pull out a chair for her. "We will discuss your background and qualifications thoroughly, Miss Briggs. But I can tell you right away we have need of teaching missionaries in Ceylon."

Charlotte sank wearily into the chair. Ceylon . . . so far away. She would be unable to visit Gwyn. But then, if she were wanted by the police, she wouldn't be able to visit him, anyway. Perhaps there was nothing for her to do but vanish into thin air, after all.

Evan was still too weak to leave his bed when Stephen and Zoe returned to Glendower to check on the progress of the building of their house. Evan supposed he should be grateful to his half brother for having brought him home and having had the arson and murder charges against him dropped, but it was difficult to feel gratitude when the perpetrator of the crime was clearly Stephen's wife and he refused to admit the fact.

Lizzie, who was acting as housekeeper at the grange in Charlotte's absence, informed Evan that Lord and Lady Athmore had adopted a baby son, whom they had named Geoffrey. The infant had remained at their London house with his nanny while Stephen and Zoe made the quick trip north to Glendower.

"Lord Athmore wanted to know if you're up to receiving visitors," Lizzie said. "He'd like to come over and see you."

"I'm anxious to talk to him, too," Evan responded.

An hour later there was a hesitant knock on his bedroom door and Stephen entered. He was alone. For a moment he stood looking at Evan from across the room.

"It's safe for you to approach the bed," Evan remarked dryly. "As you can see, my right arm is encased in plaster of paris, and I find that my legs are still quite unsteady when I attempt to walk."

Stephen took a few tentative steps toward him. "Look, Evan, we have to come to an understanding, you and I. Surely there's a way we can both live at Glendower in some sort of harmony?"

"Where is Charlotte?" Evan demanded.

"I don't know . . . exactly. But she will be visiting us from time to time."

"Visiting *us?*"

Stephen's haunted eyes refused to connect with his. He looked at his feet, at the canopy over Evan's bed, and finally his gaze drifted to the open windows where the branches of the great oaks stirred restlessly. "Evan, you might as well know the truth. I think perhaps it will influence how you feel about Zoe and me living at Glendower. And, of course, it will bring Charlotte here regularly . . . I think I can guess how you feel about her. Who knows, perhaps when she's had time to forget her lost love—"

"Damn you, what are you trying to say?" Evan shouted.

"The child Zoe and I adopted . . . is my son. Mine and Charlotte's. Zoe doesn't know that, of course."

Evan felt an unbearable pain rip through him. So that was what Charlotte had done to ensure his freedom. The extent of her sacrifice both thrilled and appalled him.

"STEPHEN . . ." EVAN WROTE.

IT'S FORTUNATE FOR YOU THAT WE ARE PRESENTLY SEPARATED BY OVER TWO HUNDRED MILES. I HAVE, OF COURSE, READ THE NEWSPAPERS. I WANT THE ANSWER TO TWO QUESTIONS IMMEDIATELY. FIRST, WHERE IS CHAR-

LOTTE? SECONDLY, I DEMAND THAT YOU WRITE AND
GIVE ME THE NAME OF THE MYSTERIOUS ANONYMOUS
MILLIONAIRE WHO PURCHASED THE PICTURE.

MY DEAR EVAN:
I CANNOT TELL YOU THE NAME OF THE PURCHASER OF
THE PASSIONATE VIRGIN FOR THE SIMPLE REASON I DO
NOT KNOW IT. THE PICTURE WAS SOLD AT AUCTION TO AN
AGENT ACTING FOR THE BUYER.
NOR CAN I TELL YOU WHERE CHARLOTTE IS. AS A
MATTER OF FACT, THE RAMSEYS ARE MAKING EVERY
EFFORT TO FIND HER BECAUSE ELEANOR BECAME HYSTER-
ICAL WHEN SHE LEARNED HER GRANDFATHER HAS BEEN
NOTIFIED OF HER WHEREABOUTS. NEITHER THE RAMSEYS
NOR TRISTAN CRESSEY HAVE BEEN ABLE TO CONSOLE THE
CHILD AND THEY FEAR SHE MAY BECOME ILL.
YOURS, STEPHEN

STEPHEN,
IF I DO NOT GET A RESPONSE TO MY SEVERAL LETTERS
WITHIN THE WEEK, I SHALL COME TO LONDON.

SORRY, EVAN, BUT I STILL DON'T KNOW WHO BOUGHT
THE PICTURE, OR WHERE CHARLOTTE DISAPPEARED TO.
THERE HAS BEEN ANOTHER DEVELOPMENT, HOWEVER.
THE RAMSEYS RECEIVED WORD THAT ELEANOR'S GRAND-
FATHER DIED SUDDENLY OF HEART FAILURE ABOARD THE
SHIP BRINGING HIM TO ENGLAND. SINCE HER PARENTS
WERE KILLED IN A TRAIN CRASH ABOUT THE TIME
CHARLOTTE BROUGHT HER TO ENGLAND, THE CHILD IS
NOW ALONE IN THE WORLD AND WILL NO DOUBT BECOME
A WARD OF THE RAMSEYS.
I DIDN'T TELL YOU THIS BEFORE, BUT IT SEEMS THAT
CHARLOTTE VISITED DELIA RAMSEY JUST BEFORE VANISH-
ING, AND DELIA WARNED HER THAT SHE'D CABLED
ELEANOR'S GRANDFATHER. IT SEEMS LIKELY THAT CHAR-
LOTTE DISAPPEARED TO AVOID PROSECUTION, WOULDN'T
YOU SAY? WHAT ABOUT THE VILLA IN FLORENCE? COULD
SHE HAVE GONE THERE? OR POSSIBLY BACK TO AMERICA,
WHO CAN TELL? EVAN, IT'S A VERY LARGE WORLD AND IF
SHE DOESN'T WANT TO BE FOUND . . .

MY DEAR EVAN:

IF THERE'S ONE REASON FOR CHARLOTTE TO EVER RETURN, IT'S GEOFFREY (SHE CALLED HIM GWYNFOR). THEREFORE, I WONDERED IF I MIGHT SEND THE BABY AND HIS NANNY TO GLENDOWER? I REALIZE THE HOUSE ISN'T FINISHED YET AND THEY WOULD HAVE TO MOVE INTO THE GRANGE WITH YOU . . . BUT, WELL, ZOE HASN'T BEEN WELL LATELY. SHE WANTS TO GO HOME TO NEW ORLEANS AND WE'RE LEAVING NEXT WEEK . . .

18

How very old... and small the villages and towns looked, Owain thought, as the train steamed southward toward London. The patchwork quilt of meadows, stitched together with hedgerows, was lushly green, but the fields were miniatures compared to the vast openness of America. Although the countryside was more beautiful than ever, during his seven years absence it seemed that England had shrunk in size. But perhaps it was just that his horizons had expanded.

Another tiny cluster of houses of age-darkened brick was coming into view, their steeply sloping slate roofs glistening with rain. A single beam of sunlight pierced the leaden clouds and found the stained-glass window of a church.

The steeple flashed by, then a bridge. A crocodile of blue-clad schoolgirls led by a nun wound its way over the bridge. They would be about ten or eleven years old, as Ellie had been the last time Owain saw her. Seven years ago . . .

With what high hopes he'd set off for America and how quickly he'd learned that the false promises of vast, affordable acres of land being practically given away were laughably false. He'd been swept up with the tide of immigrants moving westward with the railroads, a source of cheap labor not only for the railroads, but also for farms and ranches that were springing up in the newly opened territories.

Owain constantly had to prove that his limp did not prevent him from working as long and hard as any other hungry migrant. He left the railroad gangs and became that lowliest of hirelings, a cowboy. It was good to be in the saddle again, where his limp was of no consequence. He soon learned the finer points of rounding up cattle, branding, roping, how to extricate a thrashing steer from a clump of mesquite or a flood crested river, and, when lightning lit up the range and thunder roared, he faced the cowboy's ultimate test—turning a stampeding herd.

Those first years had been hard and lonely. He either rode the range alone, or found himself in a bunkhouse with slow-talking cowpokes who regarded him as a foreigner, and made fun of his singsong accent.

He had come close to despair many times, but looking back he saw that his final triumph probably wouldn't have been possible without the early toil and failures. The irony of it all was that his change of fortune was brought about by an Englishman.

Peter Maitland-Howard, fresh from Oxford, son of a wealthy English shipbuilder whose hobby was breeding racehorses, had originally gone west to hunt grizzlies and mountain lions. Instead he fell in love with the country and persuaded his father to invest in a cattle ranch. The rancher for whom Owain worked sold several horses to Maitland-Howard, and Peter first heard Owain's Welsh accent as he coaxed a spirited stallion into a corral.

"Well now, here's a man who knows horses," Peter drawled. "Hullo there, Taffy, you're a long way from home."

"My name is Davies," Owain snapped, irritated.

One of the Englishman's golden eyebrows went up in a quizzical arch. "I do beg your pardon, old man. Wasn't aware you Welshies were so sensitive about a harmless nickname."

"I am a Welsh*man*," Owain corrected. "And perhaps you've forgotten the rest of the old rhyme . . . 'Oh Taffy was a Welshman, Taffy was a thief . . . Taffy came to my house and stole a side of beef'?"

It could have been an inauspicious beginning to a friendship, but as it happened Peter laughed delightedly and assured Owain that he had been properly chastised and would never call him Taffy again. He did, of course, just as Owain returned the favor by occasionally addressing Peter as "Limey" in a good-natured way. But that was months later, after Peter had persuaded Owain to work for him.

"As your foreman?" Owain had asked. "I'm ready for more than cowpokin'."

"As a matter of fact, I have something more in keeping with

your previous experience in mind," Peter said mysteriously. "First, we're off to Kentucky . . ."

"I've heard they breed some fine horses there," Owain said, his interest caught.

"I've always had a sort of friendly rivalry with my pater. Now that the ranch is making money, it's no longer a challenge. I want to breed a racehorse capable of beating one of my father's. Tell me, have you heard of the newly instituted race called the Kentucky Derby?"

As the train taking Owain to London entered the outskirts of the city, he glanced across the compartment at Peter, who dozed, unconcerned about his forthcoming reunion with his father after his long absence in America. Owain wished he could feel as confident about meeting Ellie again.

Standing in the wings as Tristan began the soliloquy, Eleanor could feel the hostility of the audience wafting over the footlights.

Her head ached and her palms were clammy from the effort of willing those unseen people out there in the darkness to like him, or at least to accept his performance on its own merits rather than comparing it with his portrayals of less tragic heroes.

Tristan was certainly suffering the slings and arrows of outrageous fortune tonight. Seats banged and heavy footsteps fell as members of the audience got up and left. Someone cleared his throat loudly. There was a faint hiss.

She knew exactly what was wrong and had tried to warn Tristan. It wasn't that his rendering of Hamlet was unworthy; it was simply that his legion of adoring admirers wanted him to continue to play the brooding romantic heroes he'd played in the past. They were not a Shakespearean audience and had come only to see Tristan. Audiences didn't like it when their favorites changed styles. This particular audience probably didn't even understand the bard.

Someone touched her lightly on the shoulder, and she saw her dresser frantically pointing to the clock on the wall beside her. Eleanor nodded and reluctantly turned away.

At the stage door, a hansom cab waited to take them across town to the theater where Eleanor was performing.

Bundling her unceremoniously into the cab, her dresser said, "You won't have any more than five minutes to change. I told you not to go. I knew it would upset you. Nobody wants to see Tristan in a Shakespeare play. They want to see him flashing those eyes of his and kissing the heroine. Oh, Lord, look at the time! How am I ever going to get your hair done?''

Her dresser was young, only a year or two older than Eleanor, who had recently celebrated her seventeenth birthday. The girl's name was Maeve and she had taken over her mother's job. Over the years the two girls had become friends and, in fact, Maeve was Eleanor's only friend of her own sex. She had learned long ago that her looks alienated her from most other women. She would have had to be blind not to see the way wives clutched at husbands' arms when she entered a room; not to be able to recognize the hostility she generated in women of all ages. Maeve, sturdily built and plain of feature, seemed to be the only exception to this rule. Even Delia Ramsey had eventually distanced herself from Eleanor, when Delia's own admirers began to defect in favor of her ward.

Eleanor was appearing in a music hall variety show. She had not set out to become a singer, her ambition having always been to become a dramatic actress, but she had been either blessed or cursed with a haunting contralto voice that captivated everyone who heard it. Years ago Tristan had obtained parts for her in several plays, but her reviews were less than enthusiastic, dismissing her as yet another inexperienced pretty face. Then a stage director had heard her sing at a private party. After that, no one except Tristan gave serious consideration to a dramatic role for her. The fact that she had become a music hall singer had further alienated her from the Ramseys. They could accept acting as an art form, but a performer who appeared on stage with acrobats, trained animals, and other such acts, occasionally taking part in comic sketches, was déclassé.

She didn't miss her cue, despite Maeve's misgivings, and as usual at the end of the evening she returned to find her dressing room filled with flowers. Maeve had strict instructions not to allow any of the stage-door johnnies to enter the dressing room, but tonight Eleanor was annoyed to see that a man dressed in well-tailored evening clothes was seated at her dressing table. He rose as she entered and gave a slight bow. Off in a corner, Maeve was clearly beside herself with excitement.

''Forgive the intrusion,'' the man said. He had rather sinister features, and an expression that said he was privy to the weaknesses of others and despised them for it. It was a look of disdainful superiority that irritated Eleanor immediately. ''I am here as an emissary only. In your audience this evening was a man of considerable rank. Since there was no royal box, he was forced to sit inconspicuously in the stalls. He would like to meet you.''

''Oh?'' Eleanor said, thrilled that a member of the royal family had watched her perform. ''Who is he?''

He glanced in Maeve's direction. His eyes, a light blue, had the cold glitter of an arctic sea.

Eleanor decided on the spot that she disliked this man intensely, royal emissary or not. ''Maeve is my friend. You can speak freely in front of her. I take it from your earlier remark that your . . .'' she paused, choosing a word to which he might react with the same irritation she felt, ''. . . master . . . is a member of the royal family?''

One well-sculpted eyebrow rose slightly in what could have been interpreted as either acknowledgment of her taunt or agreement with her assumption. His hat, gloves and an ebony cane with a silver knob lay on her dressing table, and he picked them up. ''Are you coming with me, or not? HRH doesn't like to be kept waiting.''

Unable to contain herself any longer, Maeve burst out, *''His Royal Highness!''*

''You'll have to wait while I change,'' Eleanor said. ''And even if you don't wish to use *his* name, I think it's extremely rude of you not to introduce yourself.''

''I am Thane. He wants you to come just as you are. There's a closed carriage waiting.''

His eyes flickered over her and she knew the glance was meant to be insulting. She thought, why, he wants me to refuse. Damn him, I'll go in spite of him. She said to Maeve, ''Get my hooded cape, would you please?''

She had never gone out wearing a stage costume and greasepaint before, but as this impossibly arrogant man had stated, there was a closed carriage waiting at the stage door. She was disappointed to see there was no royal crest on the door, but then Thane had said HRH preferred to remain incognito.

Thane—was that his first or last name?—opened the door for her and helped her climb inside.

Even in the dimness of the interior of the carriage she recognized her companion instantly and understood the need for discretion. A thrill of excitement raced through her that he had sought her out, but then she felt strangely letdown because her royal visitor was older and less attractive than his pictures portrayed him. Still, that aura of impeccable breeding was unmistakable. She was actually sitting in a carriage with a man who would one day be king of England.

The instant she was aboard, the carriage began to move at a brisk pace. Since she could hardly curtsy in a moving carriage, she inclined her head and said, "Good evening, Your Highness."

"Thank you for coming, my dear. I enjoyed your performance tonight. You have a lovely voice."

"You're very kind," Eleanor murmured, wondering exactly what he had in mind, and how one said no to a future king.

As if in answer to her unspoken question, he said, "How very young you are. You seem older on stage."

"I'm seventeen," she said, a little defensively.

He smiled. She could see the gleam of even teeth in the darkness. "An old lady. Tell me, am I keeping you from . . . an appointment with someone else?"

Eleanor began to relax. So . . . like everyone else, he thought she and Tristan . . . how funny! But that rumor about the two of them had protected her in similar circumstances. She replied, "I'm honored that you wanted to meet me, sir. I'm sure . . . my friend . . . will understand if I get home late."

"Tell me about yourself. When did you begin your career? Did you always want to be on the stage?"

She began to tell him about coming to London to live with Lord and Lady Ramsey, of the hours she had spent watching Tristan and his friends rehearse, studying every inflection of tone and change of expression, every motion and every step they took.

"I appeared in a couple of Tristan Cressey's plays under the name of Eleanor Ramsey."

"And now you are Eleanor Hathaway. Tell me, did you adopt that name because of the Bard of Avon's Anne Hathaway?"

She smiled. "Hathaway is my real name."

He seemed fascinated by her conversation and she was astonished at how much time had passed when the carriage came to a stop and he lifted the window curtain and glanced out. "Good gracious! It's almost dawn. I know you have a matinee today and you must get some sleep. Fortunately, Thane keeps an eye on such things and he has brought you to your doorstep."

Still floating in a cloud of disbelief, Eleanor found herself being helped down from the carriage by the sinister Thane, who had evidently ridden with the driver.

They had almost reached the door of Tristan's flat before she realized where they were, and she quickly decided she didn't want to divulge to this taciturn man that he and HRH had made the wrong assumption in regard to her living arrangements. Eleanor had her own flat, fortunately not far away. She could walk over there as soon as they left.

"It would be better not to mention the name of the gentleman you were with tonight," Thane said. "His mother . . ."

"Yes, I think I understand."

"If you'll give me your key," Thane went on, "I'll open the door for you."

Foolishly, she fumbled in her purse as though searching for it. "There's no need," she mumbled, afraid of disturbing Tristan.

"My instructions are to see you safely inside."

"And I'm telling you to go." Her voice rose to an indignant squeak.

Almost instantly the door opened, and Tristan, looking slightly ridiculous in his nightshirt, peered out at them. "Eleanor? What on earth—"

She shoved him back inside and followed, slamming the door in Thane's face.

Tristan turned up the lamp and stared incredulously at the clock. "Good God! It's after four!"

"You won't believe who I was with," Eleanor began.

"I don't want to know," Tristan replied coldly. "Where were you when I needed you? Do you know or care what the critics said about my opening? I sat in that damn cafe surrounded by Philistines all evening, watching the door for you." His voice dripped with self-pity. "Now, of course, the rumors will start that you've deserted me because I flopped so horribly as Hamlet."

Eleanor hugged him. "Dear Tristan! You were wonderful as Hamlet. I stayed as long as I could—and I would have come straight to the cafe, honestly, but I was whisked away by a perfectly fearsome man, and guess who was waiting to meet me?"

"I don't care if it was the Prince of Wales," Tristan sneered. Eleanor's eyes widened, but she had no chance to comment as Tristan continued. "And if you came to my flat at this ungodly hour to apologize, I'm sorry, but I can't forgive you."

"Then I'll leave. Perhaps you'll be more reasonable tomorrow, and we can talk then."

"I may not be here tomorrow," Tristan said darkly. "My career is in ashes and my life may be over."

"Now you're becoming maudlin." She sniffed suspiciously. "Oh, Tristan, you haven't been drinking, have you?"

"No," he lied. "But perhaps I'll forgive you just a little and we can have a nightcap together. I'll get the brandy."

"You know that I'm even sillier than you when I drink. Good night, Tristan," Eleanor said firmly.

She opened the door and slipped outside. The closed carriage was gone. As Eleanor walked through the deserted, dawn-silvered streets, she wondered if she had perhaps imagined HRH and the sinister Thane.

19

EVAN'S LONELINESS HAD never been harder to bear than in the third year following Charlotte's disappearance. The first year he still hoped she would return, and the second he had hired several different people to try to find her. He kept in touch with Eleanor, in case she heard from her former nanny, but Eleanor was as baffled as he was by Charlotte's disappearance. Hope slowly began to fade that third year.

But as is often the case, after the door figuratively closed behind Charlotte, another unexpected door opened for Evan.

Right from the start, Stephen and Zoe had deposited the infant Geoffrey and his nanny at the grange whenever they went off on one of their jaunts, which was fairly frequently.

At first Evan ignored the presence of the baby, and in fact did not even see him. The grange was certainly large enough and the servants quarters' isolated from his own. The nanny, Lorna McDougan, was a competent young woman, well aware of the fact that she and her charge were there on sufferance, and she took care to keep the child out of his way.

The main house was at last finished, in all its dreadful splendor. Zoe had insisted upon adorning the exterior of the enormous three-story house with wrought iron balconies, painted white to match the facade of the house, looking delicate as lace. The result was a vague imitation of the Creole mansions of her native New Orleans, hideously out of place in the rugged mountains of North Wales.

"Your house looks like a gigantic wedding cake," Evan informed Stephen when it was completed. "I'm going to plant more oaks between us, to shield that monstrosity from my view."

Stephen shrugged. "Suit yourself. Fill the whole courtyard with oaks if you wish. Personally, I like the new house. It's different. Foreign and exotic. Ideal surroundings for an artist."

If they loved their house so much, Evan thought, why didn't they spend any time in it? They were always either in London, presiding over another exhibition of Stephen's paintings, or traveling abroad. The baby and his nanny didn't accompany them. Periodically Zoe would disappear for a while, presumably to a private hospital for the duration of one of her manic spells, the onset of which Stephen had apparently become expert in detecting. When they were in residence at Glendower there was a continual round of parties to which Evan was never invited. Not that he cared. His recovery from his wounds had been long and slow, and after he was well again he found he had little interest in anything beyond the walls of the grange. He withdrew into himself, lonely, missing Charlotte, and content to let Stephen and Zoe take over. He simply lacked the will to fight them.

Geoffrey Stephen Phillip Athmore was four years old when Evan looked through his study window and saw the little boy clinging precariously to a high branch of one of the oaks, peering through the glass at him.

For a moment they regarded one another with intense interest. Charlotte's son had inherited his father's smooth, dark hair and well-shaped head. His features were Stephen's also, handsomely chiseled. But the eyes . . . oh, those true gray eyes blazing with honesty, surprisingly knowing in a child so young . . . they had come from Charlotte. Evan's heart turned over.

Very carefully, Evan slid the window open and extended his hand to the little boy. "Won't you come in? It's time we met formally, don't you think?"

When the child was safely standing in the study, Evan said, "So, young Master Athmore. Do you know who I am?"

"You're my Uncle Evan. How do you do, sir. Lorna said you were a giant, but I didn't believe her. You never come out of your house."

"Oh, yes I do. I often go riding."

"I've never seen you."

"Well, I daresay you were taking your nap or your bath or whatever it is small boys do in the early morning. Besides, you cannot see my house from yours, not with all the oaks between us.''

The child solemnly surveyed Evan from head to toe. "You *are* a giant, aren't you?"

"Yes, I am.''

"What does it feel like?''

"Sometimes not too jolly.''

"But you can pick apples from the top of the tree.''

"Oh, yes.''

"And reach things from high shelves.''

"Of course.''

"Well, that should make you feel jolly.''

"I'm sure your nanny must be looking for you. I'll take you back now.''

"Uncle Evan—''

Evan was inexplicably touched by the child's calling him by his name. "Yes, Gwyn?''

"My name isn't Gwyn. It's Geoffrey.''

"I'm sorry. I forgot.''

"Would you carry me across the courtyard on your shoulder? I should like to know what it's like to be so high in the air.''

They went downstairs together and, once outside, Evan hoisted the little boy to his shoulder and walked toward the main house.

A small hand went around Evan's neck, then crept tentatively into the hair on the back of his head. "It's awfully high up here, Uncle Evan. The ground is *very* far away.''

"It only seems so to you. My legs go all the way down to the ground, you see.'' Evan blinked, wondering if he was really having this conversation.

The small fingers wandered curiously through his hair, feeling its texture. "Oh! Yes, I see.''

After a moment he asked, "Uncle Evan, can I come and see you pick an apple off the top of the tree?''

"The apples won't be ripe for months.''

"But when they are . . . ?''

"We'll see.''

When they were halfway across the courtyard, his nanny came running, her face pink with embarrassment. "Oh, Geoffrey! You naughty boy. Where have you been?''

Placing the little boy carefully on the ground, Evan said, "Please don't be cross with him. He came to visit his uncle. It's quite all right.''

Geoffrey turned to his nanny. "I wish I could grow so tall. It's just like being a king, up there. I think my Uncle Evan *is* a king." He laughed delightedly at the thought. "He's king of the whole world."

He extended his small hand to Evan for a handshake. "May I come to see you again soon?"

Evan smothered a smile. "By all means."

Such a funny, solemn, thoughtful little boy. Evan wondered if Charlotte had been so appealingly serious and imaginative as a child. He decided she had.

As time went by and Geoffrey's visits to the grange became more frequent, Evan saw many endearing traits in the child that he attributed to Charlotte rather than Stephen, despite the fact that, except for his eyes, Geoffrey looked more like his father than his mother.

During Stephen and Zoe's long sojourns away from Glendower, Evan became acquainted with Charlotte's son. Only when Geoffrey spoke of "Mother and Father" did Evan feel a pang of acute sadness. He wanted to say, "Zoe isn't your mother. Your mother is a kind, compassionate, brave, sincere woman. She is quiet, even-tempered, gentle, and wise. A lovely feminine woman with the heart of a gladiator." But a little boy of five would not have understood.

Evan reluctantly began to accept the fact that Charlotte must be dead. Surely if she still lived, she would have returned to see her son?

Zoe had quickly lost interest in the boy once all of her friends had seen him and complimented her on achieving the state of motherhood. Stephen was an erratic father, smothering the boy with attention and gifts when it occurred to him to do so, and virtually ignoring the child when the creative urge was upon him and he felt compelled to spend long hours in his studio. It was left to Evan and Lorna McDougan to fill in the gaps in Geoffrey's upbringing.

Evan found himself conferring with the nanny about the boy's welfare. "Don't protect him to the extent that you smother him," he cautioned her. "He must be allowed to explore new territory and fall down occasionally. He needs to play with children of his own age, too. I want you to take him to the village at least twice a week. Have you started teaching him to read? Good. Bring him to the south lawn this afternoon after his riding lesson, I'm going to teach him to play cricket."

On Geoffrey's sixth birthday a circus came to Llanrys. Evan overheard the servants discussing it, and his first thought was that every child should see a circus. His second thought was that the circus ghosts that still haunted his memory prevented him from taking Geoffrey himself. Stephen and Zoe were in Paris.

But on the last day of the circus, Evan told Lorna to prepare herself and the boy for an outing. When their carriage drew closer to the big tent, Geoffrey's eyes widened and he clutched Evan's arm. "It's a circus! Look, look, *elephants!* Oh, Uncle Evan, it's just like in my picture book."

Evan had never been near a circus since the night Kasimir and Cordoni died, but the smell of sawdust and animals and trampled grass, the sight of the colorful clowns and the spangled costumes of the fliers, made the years fall away. Several of the performers who were circulating in the crowd outside the big top saluted him as he went by.

"They know you," Geoffrey whispered in awe.

They didn't, of course, but perhaps they thought he was one of them, because of his size. Even after all these years, perhaps they recognized he had been one of them.

The crowd converging on the circus stepped respectfully aside as he approached and took care not to stare. He felt different, less conscious of his great height, when he was with Geoffrey. The little boy marched along at his side, looking up at him with such trust and pride that it was impossible for passersby not to feel the love that existed between them. The presence of the child miraculously changed him from outcast to respected member of society; the guardian, however temporarily, of the next generation. Geoffrey gave him a place in the grand design of life.

Although Geoffrey was thrilled by the performance, Evan saw beyond the glitter to the tawdry underpinnings of what was a small, second-rate circus. The strong man was obviously drunk, the clowns were jaded, the animals weary, the ringmaster indifferent. Evan had worried when the trapeze artists appeared that the old wound inflicted by Cella might tear open, and he was surprised to find that it had healed completely. Perhaps the greater pain of losing Charlotte simply overwhelmed it.

As the trapeze artists whirled through the air and Lorna and Geoffrey watched, spellbound, Evan asked himself for the hundredth time why he had let those early rejections by women, particularly Cella, stop him from asking Charlotte to marry him. He had come so close to declaring his feelings to her. The first time had been when he dragged her back from the brink of self-destruction and learned she was carrying Stephen's child. But he realized she was too emotionally vulnerable then. She would have accepted perhaps, but only to give her child a name. Perversely, he didn't want her on those terms.

Then when she returned to Glendower from Italy, he had decided to proceed very slowly, to attempt gently to court her, to show her with actions rather than words how much he loved her. He thought there would be plenty of time. Was that the worst of human failings? To blithely convince oneself that there is no need to act today because there will be time tomorrow. He closed his eyes, giving in to sadness. *Oh, Charlotte, how I miss you.* I try to tell myself I've lost you forever, yet some stubborn thread of hope persists, tormenting me.

Geoffrey tugged at his sleeve anxiously. "Uncle Evan? Are you tired?"

He blinked, then smiled down at the boy. "No. The lights were too bright, that's all."

"This is the best birthday I ever had," Geoffrey said happily. "Oh, look! The man is lifting the donkey up in the air."

"He's the circus strong man," Evan said.

"He's not as strong as you. You could lift up a elephant."

Evan laughed. "A very small elephant, perhaps. What would you say if I told you I once worked in a circus?"

The boy's eyes grew even larger. "Goodness! I'd say you're the bestest uncle in the whole world."

That night after Geoffrey was tucked into bed, Evan went back to the grange and tore Kasimir's moth-eaten leopard skin down from the wall paneling, knowing he was no longer the boy who had failed to earn the right to wear it.

Soon Evan's life revolved almost entirely around Geoffrey. His first thought upon awaking and last thought at night were of the boy. They spent more and more time together, Evan pouring out all the love he had never been able to express to anyone else. He loved the boy so much that he began to fear what the consequences of his attachment would be. He'd loved Charlotte, too, and she had vanished. Would her son also be taken away from him?

Evan decided he cared enough about the boy to take that risk. Being with Geoffrey was like having a second chance at his own childhood, to do and see and feel all the wonders and joys of life through the eyes of a child.

What a magic world spread out for them, a banquet of hitherto unimagined delights. They visited the ancient castles of North Wales, explored the mountains, and fished in the lakes. They took a train to Liverpool and visited the zoo, the museums, the botanical gardens. They rode the ferry across the river to the seaside resorts of the Wirral peninsula, and paddled in the sea, and played in the sand. They dined in cafes, went to a comic opera, fed the pigeons in the park, and watched a puppet show. They listened to the soapbox orators advocating the overthrow of the government, and they took a steamship for a visit to the Isle of Man.

And never for a moment did Evan give a second thought to his physical size, or dwell on the fact that he was different from other men. With Geoffrey at his side, he was what the boy saw him to be, king of the world, a godlike being who could do no wrong, who was strong and good and protective and wise.

Nor did Evan worry particularly about Zoe's influence on Geoffrey, since she so rarely saw him. Besides, Lorna was a diligent young woman who watched over her charge with such hawklike intensity that Evan realized how determined Geoffrey must have been to meet his uncle the day he managed to elude her. Days drifted into weeks, then months, and Evan refused to hear that distant voice warning him that Geoffrey was Stephen's son, not his.

When Stephen and Zoe returned unexpectedly one day and whisked Geoffrey away for a week at the seaside, Evan was devastated. It was as if the sun had been extinguished and his whole world plunged into darkness.

Upon their return he sent word to the main house that he wished to meet with Stephen, who responded that he would come to the grange that evening. Evan had never set foot in the new house, although he knew from the gossipy Lizzie that, mysteriously, much of the Athmore art collection had been saved from the original house.

He had avoided contact with either Stephen or Zoe, and, except for signing documents pertaining to the estate and authorizing the payment of bills, he left the running of Glendower to Stephen, as he had in the past. But now there was an urgent reason for him to be more actively involved. He instructed Stephen to bring all of the ledgers and bank statements with him.

Stephen arrived promptly at eight, as promised, carrying a bulging valise. He exuded his customary savoir faire and remarked casually, "You look well, Evan. How fortunate you were not to be left with any scars as a result of your run in with the law."

Evan gestured for them to go into his study. "I was shot by one of our own laborers. But I didn't send for you to hold a postmortem on that miserable episode."

Stephen dropped the valise on Evan's desk and poured himself a drink. "You want to go over the accounts. Fair enough. Here they are. But I warn you, I can't make head nor tail of them. The bookkeeper will be here for his usual monthly visit soon. Why don't you have him explain them to you?"

"I'll look at them later. Mainly to reassure myself that your wife is not frittering away everything of value. My main concern for now is Geoffrey. I want to make him heir to Glendower. I thought I should discuss it with you first, before sending for my solicitor to draw up a new will."

Stephen sat down abruptly. "Well, now . . . this is a surprise. Or is it? I'd heard you spent a great deal of time with him while we were away. And, of course, when he looks at you in a certain way . . . well, that's Charlotte's look, isn't it? Tell me, are you still nurturing your hopeless love for her?"

"Don't try to bait me, Stephen. I'm not in the mood. I should think you would be delighted to hear that your son will inherit Glendower."

"Oh, I am, I am. There's just one small problem. Officially, he isn't my son."

"But you formally adopted him."

"Actually, no. I didn't." Stephen waved his hand vaguely. "I meant to . . . but, well, I wasn't sure what sort of questions would be asked by the authorities. Where he'd come from and so on. I didn't know if we needed Charlotte's permission. And I'm damn sure I didn't want Zoe to find out that Geoffrey really is my flesh-and-blood son."

"Then you will institute adoption proceedings at once."

Stephen studied his hands, flexing his fingers. "I can't do that, old man. You see . . . well, Zoe was locked up in the asylum when Charlotte went to Italy and had the baby. It was fairly easy for us to tell people that Zoe had a difficult pregnancy and remained in bed in a nursing home while she carried Geoffrey . . ."

"You mean everyone believes you and *Zoe* are his real parents?" Evan asked incredulously.

"I thought you knew."

"I assumed you put out the story that you were his adoptive parents. Besides, how did you explain the fact that Zoe turned up here just before the fire and didn't have a baby then, while Charlotte did."

"We said we kept Zoe's confinement a secret because the boy was sickly at birth and not expected to survive, so he remained in the hospital and we didn't make the announcement until he was fit to come home. As far as Charlotte having a baby was concerned, well, not many people saw him and, anyway, babies change so much in the first months of life.

"You didn't devise such a plan, Stephen, so it must have been Zoe's idea. Doesn't it ever worry you that, in addition to her mental illness, she is so damned clever at concocting stories to justify everything she does?"

Stephen's silence was more eloquent than a reply. Evan fingered the estate ledgers on his desk. "We'd better have our solicitors come out as soon as possible and discuss the matter with them."

"Is it really necessary for anyone else to know Geoffrey isn't our son, Zoe's and mine, born in wedlock? I thought you were fond of the boy. Would you brand him as illegitimate? Can you even imagine what it's like, finding out you are a bastard? If not, allow me to enlighten you."

The bitterness in Stephen's voice and the pain in his eyes distracted Evan for a split second only, until he recalled that it had been Stephen who caused another bastard to be born. "Better to accept a parent who flouted society's rules than to believe one is the son of a madwoman," Evan snapped, but in his heart he wanted to spare Geoffrey all pain.

"Zoe isn't—" Stephen began.

"Oh, for God's sake, spare me! She burned down your house, killed your butler, damn near had me killed. Looking back, I see now that she probably tried to kill Charlotte. What's next, Stephen? What will happen the next time Zoe wants something and someone is standing in her way?"

Stephen drummed his fingers nervously on his empty glass. "Look, Evan, don't you think you might be creating a problem where none exists? In your last will you named me as your heir. Geoffrey will, of course, be my heir. He will eventually inherit, anyway."

"But you see, I had in mind bypassing you in favor of the boy.

I want to be sure there is an estate to leave Geoffrey, and there might not be if Zoe continues in her extravagant way. I realize I've been lax in keeping an eye on things in the past, but that is going to change immediately. Zoe is no longer going to pour money into that white elephant of a house, nor is she to spend the Athmore fortune on gems and furs. As of today, I am taking over the administration of the estate and all its holdings. This will necessitate my assuming my true identity as Lord Athmore.''

Stephen had gone very pale. ''You can't . . . it will mean disclosing our real relationship. Do you have any conception of the duties of Lord Athmore? Business to attend to, a seat in the House, a thousand things that have to be done *in public*. Do you want to put yourself on display? Do you actually want to wash all the Athmore dirty linen in public? Above all, would you expose Geoffrey to the resulting scandal?''

Evan looked down at his half brother with a strangely serene expression. ''I believe the truth will set us all free.''

Stephen faced Zoe in her elegantly appointed bedroom, which was an exact replica of Marie Antoinette's boudoir. Zoe wore a floating, Grecian-style robe that was almost transparent, and her black hair streamed about her shoulders. Her sensuously full lips curled back from feral white teeth in that expression Stephen dreaded more than any other. *''What?* What do you mean, he intends to assume his rightful place? What rightful place?''

''He intends to announce to the world that he is Lord Athmore. He demanded that I turn over all the estate accounts and said he will be taking care of everything from now on.''

Hoping it might soften the blow, Stephen added hastily, ''He wants to make Geoffrey his heir.''

''He can't do this to us,'' Zoe said. In her anger she held on to the end of *this* and *us,* and the resulting hiss reminded Stephen of an aggressive reptile he'd once encountered. ''Promises were made . . .''

''Not by Evan,'' Stephen said. ''Charlotte was the one who made the promises, on condition we save Evan's skin.''

''Charlotte,'' Zoe said suddenly and her black eyes gleamed. ''Of course!''

Stephen caught her wrist. ''What about Charlotte? Good God, I wondered why she never came back . . . Zoe, you didn't . . .''

She looked at him contemptuously. ''Do you care? No, don't pull away from me. I want to know. Did you really care for that little gray dove of a woman? Do you miss her? What a sly minx she proved to be . . . pretending to be so pure and then having a child out of wedlock.''

Stephen tried to assume an expression of mild interest. "Out of wedlock? But I thought she married an Italian—''

Zoe cut him short. "There wasn't time for her to meet someone, marry, and have a child after she left Glendower. I realized that when she brought Geoffrey to us, so I wrote to the caretakers of the villa in Florence.''

"What made you do that?''

"Darling! How naive you are! Didn't it occur to you what a coincidence it was that your father left Evan a villa in Florence, and lo and behold Evan's housekeeper disappears to Italy, then returns supposedly a widow, with an infant? Why, it's the oldest subterfuge in the world.''

Stephen squirmed inwardly, afraid to speak. Had Zoe guessed the truth? And if so, what would she do?

"Now, of course, we know for certain,'' she said, watching him with eyes as black as midnight. "Consider the situation. The giant has started going out in public with Geoffrey. He wants to take control of the estate. He wants to cut you out of his will and name Geoffrey his direct heir.''

"What are you insinuating?'' Stephen asked faintly.

"That Charlotte Danforth was pregnant *before* she ever left Glendower,'' Zoe said coolly. "I might have suspected you, my darling, but you've never been able to impregnate me, despite the fact that I never used any preventive measures, and I tampered with all of yours. Therefore, there was only one other answer to the riddle.'' She turned suddenly and began to pace the floor.

"Zoe . . . you aren't thinking that . . .'' He couldn't bring himself to give voice to the thought.

"We can't let him take over,'' she said, talking to herself. "If he finds out how much in debt we are . . . no, we have to think of ourselves first. We have the answer now, of course. We just have to be strong enough to use it to protect ourselves.''

She stopped abruptly and whirled around. "Besides, Geoffrey is already tall for his age. What if he suddenly starts to grow excessively . . . and turns into another giant? Would you want to claim him as your son if he looked like Evan? I wouldn't.''

"Zoe!'' Stephen gasped. "You think *Evan* is Geoffrey's father?''

"I know he is. Why, you can see the family likeness in the boy's face; it becomes more pronounced with every birthday.''

Stunned, Stephen started toward the door. Dear God, surely

she wouldn't harm the child? He felt sick. If Zoe had wondered if Geoffrey was Evan's son before, now that Evan wanted to make him his heir, she would be convinced. That was certainly enough to put Geoffrey in jeopardy.

Zoe called sharply, "Where are you going?"

"I need a drink."

"Don't you want to hear what I plan to do?"

"No. Not until I've had a drink."

Zoe lowered her voice to a seductive whisper that was far more compelling than any strident command, "But *cherie,* aren't you even a little bit curious about what happened to Charlotte Danforth?"

20

MAEVE REGARDED ELEANOR'S reflection in her dressing table mirror. "Has he . . . taken any liberties with you yet?"

Eleanor laughed. "He kissed me good night last night."

"What was it like?"

"It was like four lips coming together. Nothing very alarming. Could have been commoner lips as easily as royal ones."

"Did you feel . . . *you know*," Maeve persisted, brushing Eleanor's hair so hard in her excitement that Eleanor winced. "Oh, sorry! It's just that I thought after so many secret trysts with HRH . . ."

"That we'd be making mad, passionate love at his royal retreat? Sorry to disappoint you, but he's been a perfect gentleman. He's awfully sweet, really. He loves to talk about the theater, and hear all the latest backstage gossip." Eleanor frowned suddenly. "I'm much more afraid of that sinister Thane. He looks at me like a hungry wolf. I dread to think what might happen if ever HRH bowed out of the picture."

"You think Thane might . . . try to have his way with you?"

For once Eleanor didn't giggle at her dresser's melodramatic turn of phrase, because that was exactly what Eleanor feared. Thane looked at her with the practiced eye of a man who could see right through her clothes. When he helped her into the royal carriage his hard fingers would grip her hand, or insinuate themselves into the soft flesh of her upper arm, then linger there. At the conclusion of one evening, instead of merely taking her hand to help her down to the pavement, Thane placed both hands on her waist and lifted her bodily from the carriage. He held her in midair and said, "There is a puddle of muddy water here. I'll carry you across it."

At Tristan's door, Thane suddenly muttered, "Why the hell don't you tell him you don't live here?"

"W—what? I don't know what you . . ." Her voice trailed off. Even in the dim lamplight, she could see the derision and scorn on his face. "How did you know?" she whispered, one eye on the waiting carriage.

"I make it my business to find out all there is to know about the women who catch HRH's eye. You have a flat of your own several streets away. You have never had an affair with Tristan Cressey. I thought at first that he preferred men to women, but apparently he does not. He is one of those not-so-terribly-rare individuals who are truly asexual."

Eleanor was glad it was too dark for him to see the blush that stained her cheeks. No man alive had ever spoken so frankly to her. "Knowing that I don't live with Tristan," she asked, "why didn't you inform HRH of that fact?"

He shrugged. "I have my reasons. Good night, Miss Hathaway."

Before he left he gave her one of those unnerving glances that swiftly undressed her. Remembering that glance, Eleanor shivered involuntarily.

Maeve said, "I knew it! You're trembling just thinking about being with HRH tonight. Don't tell me you don't want him to make love to you. Who wouldn't want to go to a royal bed?"

"Actually, I'm thinking about Thane. He's the one who is really in charge of my evenings with HRH. It's Thane who decides where we go and how long we'll stay. He's always there, hovering somewhere nearby, like a great vulture."

"He does have a hawkish face, but it's an exciting one," Maeve said. "Not handsome, but . . . different. If he were an actor wouldn't he make a wonderful villain?"

"He would, indeed," Eleanor replied. "He's arrogant, overbearing . . . you know, even though he always comes to take me to HRH, I have the feeling that he's looking for a way to get me out of the picture. He's rude to me every chance he gets and makes terrible remarks about actresses, implying that we have no morals at all."

"I think it's because you're so pretty, Eleanor. A man who knew he couldn't have you might be inclined to belittle you. By calling you nasty names, he's convincing himself you aren't worthy of him.''

Eleanor looked at her dresser's reflection in the mirror. Maeve's intelligent hazel eyes set in her earnest, well-scrubbed face, looked back at her without envy or resentment or any of the other emotions Eleanor saw in other women's eyes. ''How did you become so wise, Maeve?'' she asked softly. ''And what did I ever do to deserve a friend like you?''

Maeve flushed with pleasure. ''You took good care of my mum while she was ill, and I'll never forget how good you were to me after she died. Look, your tea's getting cold. Drink it up and I'll give your tea leaves a quick read.''

''There isn't time, I'm on in a minute,'' Eleanor protested, but she drained her teacup to humor her friend. For all Maeve's innate intelligence, she was even more superstitious than most actors and actresses, and Lord knew how superstitious they were.

Twirling the cup three times, Maeve dumped the last drops of tea into the saucer and studied the patterns made by the remaining tea leaves. Usually she told of forthcoming meetings with handsome strangers, wonderful audiences, letters and gifts and unknown admirers, or else mysterious events occurring in a three, five, seven . . . hours, weeks, years? Today she tried to stifle a gasp. She said hurriedly, ''Oh, it's all too jumbled up to read.'' But Eleanor saw the worried frown.

''What is it, Maeve? What did you see? Tell me, or I'll miss my cue.''

''Trouble, I'm afraid. But I can't tell what kind. You must be careful. There's a powerful enemy in your cup.''

Eleanor relaxed. Naturally there'd be an enemy . . . Thane.

''I see two men,'' Maeve continued. ''They're both going to cause you a lot of grief. And HRH isn't one of them. These two are both young. But please be careful . . . there's a cloud over every part of your life. Health, career, romance.'' Maeve shoved her toward the door. ''But we'll worry about it later. Right now, ducks, you're on.''

Eleanor walked quickly from her dressing room to the wings, immediately forgetting the warning of the tea leaves. Maeve's predictions sometimes came true, probably because she knew so much about Eleanor's life, but more often than not it was just a game.

Then she was onstage and the orchestra was playing her introduction. The footlights danced in front of her eyes as she hung her head for a moment, waiting for her cue, and then she lifted her face to the audience and began to sing. When she finished, a collective sigh whispered around the theater just before the applause began, but for once it didn't lift her spirits.

She was on again in the last act before the final curtain, a musical sketch. She went through the motions, the repartee with her stage lover, the few lines she had to speak between songs; but she felt restless, unsatisfied with either her own performance or the audience's reception. She hadn't thought about serious acting for a while, but all at once she wanted desperately to be playing a dramatic role.

Tristan was right, she was wasting her talents. "You have a nice voice," he said. "But it's nothing compared to your possibilities as a serious actress. The only real drama a singer can aspire to is grand opera . . . and let's face it, love, your voice isn't *that* good. In fact, in a few years when your looks begin to fade, I daresay your singing voice won't be considered quite so arresting, either. But in the legitimate theater, you can grow old gracefully."

It was a disturbing thought, and one she feared was only too accurate. She knew that much of her appeal lay in her beauty, yet she was too unsure of her acting talent to disagree with those who told her she would be foolish to aspire to the serious stage.

After her final bow she walked offstage and almost collided with Thane. She gasped. "You startled me! What are you doing here? I wasn't expecting HRH until later."

He took her elbow in a proprietary grip and ushered her toward her dressing room. "He isn't coming to pick you up tonight."

"Very well. You've told me. You may leave."

Pushing open the door, he said to Maeve, "Lay out the plainest dress she owns, nothing gaudy. And no jewelry." He turned to Eleanor. "Hurry up and get that muck off your face."

"I thought you said he wasn't coming."

Thane dragged her screen around her to give her privacy while she changed, which seemed to her somewhat ludicrous, in view of the way his eyes ripped off her clothes. He said, "He isn't coming to the theater. I'm taking you to a rendezvous with him."

Wordlessly, Maeve came to help as Eleanor fumbled with the hooks on her dress, her heart thudding uncomfortably. So tonight was to be the night. Well, what had she expected? That HRH would be content to ride her around the park in his carriage, or take her to ill-lit private clubs, making polite conversation? That wasn't why aristocrats sought out actresses. But what he didn't know, was that she was still a virgin. She told herself that, actress or not, she had hoped that when she first made love it would be with someone of her own choice. Someone she cared about. But the truth was that she was deathly afraid of physical intimacy with a man. She had heard enough snippets of information on the subject from other actresses to be revolted by the idea. This, of course, was one of the less attractive features of going on the stage. Everyone believed all theater people were "loose." Even Maeve seemed to assume that every man who asked Eleanor out ended up in her bed, to say nothing of misinterpreting her relationship with Tristan.

There, she had finished dressing. Ignoring the simple but elegant gown Maeve had laid out, Eleanor had deliberately chosen a navy blue dress with a demure lace jabot at the throat. She hated this particular dress as it was ill-fitting and matronly, made her feel dowdy and prudish. Somewhere at the back of her mind a little devilish voice whispered that perhaps HRH would not find her alluring enough tonight to make unwanted advances.

Thane tapped the silver knob of his ebony cane against his palm impatiently while he waited. She put on her hat and slid the long hatpins through the felt to secure it to her hair. Nodding to Thane that she was ready, she bade Maeve good night and went out into a moonless night.

Preoccupied with the coming ordeal, she hardly noticed where the carriage was taking her, although she saw that tonight Thane had a different carriage, with a crest on the door. Since HRH was not in it, Thane sat inside with her instead of taking his customary place beside the driver, but she ignored him.

Inexplicably, she thought of Charlotte. How she wished Charlotte could be there, to advise her what to do. But Charlotte had vanished from the face of the earth. Not even a letter from her in all these years . . . Eleanor still thought affectionately of her former nanny, despite the fact that her perfidy had come to light after the death of Eleanor's grandfather. She had then learned that the story Charlotte told of her parents being killed by Apaches was untrue. In actual fact, they had perished in a train wreck before ever reaching Silver City. They had been dead before she and Charlotte left America. No matter how urgent the reasons, it had been cruel of Charlotte not to tell her, to let her go on hoping they would come for her.

Memories of her mother sent a tear coursing down Eleanor's cheek.

"Are you crying?" Thane asked harshly. "It's a little late for that, isn't it? You knew what he had in mind the first time he sent me to bring you to his carriage. You didn't have to go.''

"Yes, I did," Eleanor exclaimed. "How could I refuse to meet . . . His Royal Highness?"

"The same way you would refuse any other man, had you so chosen. You're not a serf. Haven't you ever heard of the Magna Charta?"

"It was all your fault. You . . . goaded me into meeting him."

"An interesting interpretation. In fact, I did everything possible to dissuade you from going to him."

She fumbled in her handbag for a handkerchief and dabbed her eyes. It was a mistake to engage this terrible man in conversation. The yellow glow of a lamplight briefly lit the dark interior of the carriage as they paused before turning a corner, illuminating Thane's face. He looked decadent, and at the same time savage. Was it possible for him to be both? On the one hand, he was worldly and sophisticated beyond the ken of most men, and on the other primitive as a man just out of the cave.

"Tell me, Miss Hathaway, are you having serious second thoughts?"

"Shut up and leave me alone."

Thane was right, of course—that was what made him so maddening. She should never have allowed herself to get into this fix. She never had with any other man. She had been so flattered that a member of the royal family had shown an interest in her, she simply hadn't thought the situation through to its logical conclusion. Tristan had warned her many times that she had to curb her impulsiveness.

"Learn to be a little more cold-blooded, love," Tristan had told her. "Don't rush in first and then decide if you really want to be there or not. What do the sages say? Be careful what you want, you might get it? I'd paraphrase that in your case and say be careful what you show a casual interest in . . . because you, my beautiful Eleanor, are certain to get it."

She thought of Charlotte again, and wondered what her advice would be if she could suddenly pop into the carriage at this moment. Almost at once, as if Charlotte were answering, Eleanor thought, why, I can still say no! I can tell him the truth. I was honored and flattered by his attention, but I don't want to sleep with him!

The relief that swept over her was exhilarating. She wanted to laugh out loud. Perhaps she had, since Thane immediately said,

"So you intend to plead an indisposition," his voice was heavy with sarcasm. "A headache? The onset of a cold? Or perhaps that old reliable standby, the vapors? A dizzy spell, faintness? I'm disappointed in you, Miss Hathaway. I'd have expected a woman of your considerable talent to deal more cleverly with the situation."

"You're quite wrong about me," Eleanor responded coldly. "I shan't pretend to be ill."

The carriage came to a halt in front of a fashionable restaurant, and as they went into the well-lit interior, Eleanor glanced up at Thane and whispered, "Isn't this a bit . . . public?"

"He won't be dining with you. After dinner I'll take you to a more private place."

They were given the best table and excellent service. Waiters scurried to respond to the slightest movement of Thane's hand or turn of his head, while used dishes vanished instantly.

Halfway through the meal Eleanor felt his eyes on her and, looking up, saw he was studying the bodice of her dress. Uncomfortable under his scrutiny, which seemed even more insolent under the bright lights, she said, "I see now why you wanted me to dress conservatively. It was because you had been ordered to dine with me. Tell me, would it embarrass you to be seen with an actress if anyone recognizes me? Not that I think they will, not in this dress."

His eyes flickered over her again. "You don't need to gild the lily, Miss Hathaway. You're beautiful no matter what you wear. But you're right that I asked you to tone down your usual somewhat flamboyant mode of dressing because I wanted to bring you here, where I'm known."

"Did it occur to you that *I* might see someone I know? Or that I wouldn't want them to see me out with you?"

"No, it didn't. And if it had, I wouldn't have cared." He concentrated on his food and wine, obviously relishing both, and ignored her for the rest of the meal.

Eleanor drank more wine than she was accustomed to, hoping it would drive away the specter of HRH waiting for her in some secluded love nest.

They left the restaurant and rode in silence until the carriage stopped in a quiet, tree-lined square in front of an ordinary-looking terraced house.

Thane climbed down and offered her his hand. Ignoring it, she jumped down to the pavement unaided and cried out as her narrow skirt hampered her, causing her to twist her ankle. Instantly, Thane's arms went around her, steadying her. His body felt like a pillar of iron and his arms steel tentacles. For a second she felt utterly helpless, the proverbial rabbit in the snare, then she shook free and tried to walk, only to find her ankle refused to bear her weight. In her frustration, she uttered Tristan's favorite oath, "Oh . . . buckets of turds!"

Unexpectedly, Thane laughed. In contrast to his harsh, almost guttural voice, his laugh was light, airy, quite musical, and certainly infectious. In spite of herself, Eleanor grinned, too. It seemed the more she tried to be disdainfully worldly, the younger she managed to act.

"Allow me," he said, and swept her up into his arms to carry her up the steps to the front door. She held her breath, feeling threatened, almost violated, by his nearness. She didn't dare look up at him, but she could feel his breath against her forehead; it seemed to scorch her skin.

The front door must have been unlocked, as he kicked it open and walked into a long, narrow hall. At the end of the hall was a room illuminated by the flickering glow of a coal fire. He placed her on a sofa, then lit a gas mantle.

She looked around, surprised. She was in the most spartan, masculine room she had encountered since leaving Glendower's grange, where Evan Athmore's taste also ran to the antithesis of Victorian clutter.

Dark oak paneling, unadorned, covered three walls, surrounding shuttered windows and a plain marble fireplace. The fourth wall was lined with books. Besides the leather sofa upon which she reclined, there was a leather wing chair, a plain oak desk, and a matching cabinet. The bare floor was polished oak.

It was not at all the kind of room she expected HRH to be comfortable in. He surely loved the opulent, the extravagant, the luxurious. Thick carpets, tapestries, brocade furniture, priceless bric-a-brac. There was about HRH an almost feminine love of beautiful surroundings; he had often discussed furnishings, draperies and pictures with as much interest as any woman. He always commented on her costumes, and on the stage backdrops. She supposed this feminine streak in HRH was inevitable, since his upbringing had been mainly matriarchal, due to his father's early death. Oh, there was no doubt that he loved women, his reputation had not been unearned, but she felt his rank alone made it easy for him to persuade women to surrender to him. He would never have to seduce a woman in the virile, active way of a more forceful man.

Thane was unbuttoning his coat. She cleared her throat. "Is he here? We're not alone, are we? Someone put coal on the fire not long ago."

"There's a manservant," he answered shortly.

"Is this . . . does HRH own this house?"

"No. I do."

Eleanor stared into the leaping flames in the fireplace. "Is he coming here to meet me? Did you allow him to use your house for . . ." She broke off, embarrassed.

He crossed the room and stood looking down at her. "For immoral purposes? Come now, don't look away in outraged innocence. To answer your question, I have never before brought any of HRH's lady friends here."

Before she realized what he was about to do, he dropped to one knee and picked up her foot. "We'd better take off your shoe and have a look at your ankle."

"Let go of me. My ankle will be all right. I don't know what game you're playing with me, but I'm quite sure whatever it is HRH won't like it. And I certainly intend to tell him. Where is he?"

Ignoring her, he unbuttoned her shoe and removed it, then raised her foot so that her leg rested on the sofa. He stood up, walked over to the wing chair, and sat down. "He isn't coming. I brought you here to explain to you that it would be better for all concerned if you refused HRH's next invitation to be alone with him."

"Really? Tell me, who decided this . . . HRH or you?"

The door opened silently and a man came into the room carrying a tray containing a decanter and glasses. "Put it down," Thane said. "I'll pour myself."

After the servant had left, Thane said, "For one who has been on the boards since childhood, you're surprisingly naive, Miss Hathaway, so let me tell you the facts of life as simply as I can. HRH has a wife, family, and obligations of state that ordinary men never have to consider. His . . . friendships with various women are usually transitory and therefore fairly harmless. But once in a great while a woman comes along who is dangerous . . . a woman who could cause an upheaval in the ship of state that could rock the country. Do I have to remind you of such women as Nell Gwynn, or Emma Hamilton? Perhaps you are unaware—you're young, after all—that you possess the same deadly allure of such women. In short, Miss Hathaway, you have that Helen of Troy type of beauty that spells trouble for any man. A man in the position of HRH has to be protected from you.''

Trembling with anger, Eleanor inquired, ''And pray tell me, who has determined I'm such a femme fatale? You? Is that why you've been so rude to me? Is that why you look at me in that . . . that way you have?'' She stopped to take a breath, feeling strangled by her high-necked gown.

''What way is that?'' he asked softly. ''With lust, you mean?''

''Oh, it's impossible to talk to you,'' Eleanor fumed. ''Take me home at once.''

''Not until I'm sure you understand the situation. I want you to sit at that desk and write HRH a note, telling him you regret that you will be unable to see him again, as you are leaving the country.''

''Are you ordering me to leave the country so he will be safe from me?'' Eleanor asked incredulously.

''Yes, I am. Your career won't suffer, however, as I have the power to arrange a tour of foreign bookings for you in any country you choose.''

Eleanor realized that she had tensed every muscle in her body. Her ankle had begun to swell and throbbed horribly. ''Just who are you, Thane?'' she asked, all at once overwhelmed with both the power and the menace this man exuded.

''Oh, you could say I was with the diplomatic corps,'' he said, his voice faintly sarcastic. ''I see to it that people in high places are protected from themselves, as well as from others. My assignment now is to get you out of HRH's life. I can assure you that I shall successfully achieve this, by whatever means necessary.''

He rose suddenly and crossed the room, then dropped down beside her on the sofa. One arm snaked around her and he pulled her to him, bent back her head and kissed her. His mouth was a pulsing demon that attacked rather than caressed, his tongue forcing its way between her teeth, his lips smothering her. At the same time his hands were on her body, finding her most intimate places. It was a demonstration of power, not affection, and she felt more frightened than ever before in her life.

''Since you were so sure you would be the object of a man's carnal appetite tonight,'' he said, his mouth still grazing hers, ''I hated to disappoint you. Shall I go on? Do you want more?

Frankly, I find copulation without affection a vastly overrated pastime, but if you wish . . .''

Summoning her last ounce of strength, Eleanor raised her hand and slapped him across the face as hard as she could. He slapped her back. They glared at one another for a second. She felt faint, helpless, yet enraged beyond endurance. She wanted to smash her fist into his mocking face, but reason prevailed. She had to get away from here, away from this man. "Will you take me home?" she asked icily. "Or at least send for a cab for me?"

"*After* you've written the note to HRH, I'll take you anywhere you please."

Halfway through the writing of the note, the truth of the matter dawned on Eleanor. She looked up at him. "You're employed by his wife, aren't you? She's the one who wants to get rid of me. I should have realized it before now. Or could it be his mother who sent you to spy on him? That fierce old dragon . . ."

"Sign your name," he instructed.

They didn't speak on the journey back to her flat. Her ankle was now so swollen and painful that she didn't protest when he lifted her from the carriage.

In the shadows nearby, where Owain had waited for her return, he watched with a heavy heart as the tall, muscular man carried Eleanor inside. The man had a long-legged, confident stride. He carried himself with authority.

The carriage that waited for him at the curb bore a crest and was pulled by the finest horses Owain had ever seen. But surely that was the kind of man Ellie deserved? How could he have imagined otherwise? Night after night, Owain had sat in the darkened theater watching her, listening to her sing, so awed by the woman she had become that he hadn't been able to gather enough courage to go around to the stage door to see her. Tonight he had waited patiently for her to come home to the address she had given him in her last letter. But how could he possibly compete with a man such as the one who had just carried her inside?

Owain limped off into the night, feeling betrayed and chiding himself for being a fool, because Ellie didn't even know he was back in the country. He had wanted to surprise her.

21

WATCHING ZOE AS she put the finishing touches to an elaborate upswept coiffure, Stephen wondered how she could be so unaffected by conscience or remorse, no matter how terrible the consequence of her deeds. Behind that beautiful face was a mind so warped that it could plot the destruction of innocents as if it were merely planning a menu.

He had a dark vision of what it might be like to journey through Zoe's mind, picturing blood-red clouds swirling over jagged peaks and into the blackest valleys, drifting over pools of slime, around burned branches dripping gray moss, and roots infested with fungi. He found himself painting this imagined horror, hoping that if he transferred it to canvas it would cease to haunt his nightmares. He took it out of its hiding place occasionally, hoping too that if he studied it he would be able to break his addiction to Zoe. But the simple truth was that he didn't know how to live without her.

Sitting on her bed, his arms tightly folded, feeling chilled all the way to the marrow, he forced himself to face the fact that she was conscienceless. He had always rationalized that her sometimes dreadful behavior was a manifestation of her mental illness, due perhaps to her extreme swings of mood. But now he wondered if perhaps in addition to that malady she was afflicted with another, more deadly flaw. Could she be one of those evil few, a true sociopath?

He hadn't wanted to believe that. For if it were true, then she could never be cured and they were both doomed. Always he'd hoped that doctors would find a reason for her mood changes, a brain lesion perhaps, that could be excised. Or that a miraculous cure, some potion to regulate the upward and downward swings, would be discovered. So he had endured, perhaps even aided and abetted some of her schemes, especially when it was to his advantage to do so. It was as if in some strange way she were his own darker side, the shadow that lurked within him that was capable of complete selfishness, fascinated by deviousness and venality. But that ruthlessness in her that he had vicariously shared had escalated dangerously the night Glendower burned. He could no longer excuse her by finding reasons for her behavior—that Evan stood between him and his rightful inheritance, or that the butler had died because of his own carelessness . . . Because now it was Geoffrey, his beloved son, who might be in danger.

Zoe was convinced that Geoffrey was Evan's son and that surely put the child in jeopardy. Stephen steeled himself to hear all of Zoe's plans before deciding what to do. He also waited with dread for her to explain just how she had "Taken care of Charlotte Danforth."

After a moment, he prompted her. "When did the letter come from Ceylon?"

Zoe tapped her lip with her forefinger, considering. "Oh, about six months after Charlotte called on Delia Ramsey. We'd almost finished the lower floor of the house and I came to look at the plans for the second story. You were in London getting ready for an exhibition."

"And Charlotte said she had gone to Ceylon as a missionary?"

She giggled. "Penance, perhaps?"

"What else did she write?"

"Well, of course, she wanted to know how Geoffrey was. She said she'd agreed to spend at least two years in Ceylon but would return to England then, and would we show her picture to the boy to keep her alive in his mind, and tell him she loved him. She reminded us of our promise to tell him she was his aunt."

"But she didn't return to England at the end of two years," Stephen said. "Did you hear from her again?"

Zoe sprayed perfume onto her hair, fingered her diamond earrings, then swiveled slowly on her dressing table stool to look at him. "Not after I wrote and told her that her son was dead."

Stephen felt a numbness begin somewhere in the pit of his stomach and gradually envelop his entire body. How could she be so oblivious to the pain and suffering she caused, and worse, take pleasure in it?

"Diphtheria," Zoe said, rising and stretching like a cat.

"What?"

"I told her he'd died of diphtheria. Many infants do, you know. I was very sympathetic, and said we'd buried him in the family plot and I took flowers to him every day and I cried every night and prayed for his soul. I was so convincing, but then I always am."

"Oh, God, Zoe, how could you be so cruel?"

"Darling, I was being kind, not cruel. I was freeing her from the burden of an unwanted, illegitimate child. Besides, we couldn't have her turning up at Glendower masquerading as his aunt, could we? No, it was a tidy solution and I thought it was very obliging of her to go to far-off Ceylon."

At least, he told himself in rising desperation, Charlotte was still alive. For a moment he'd been afraid when Zoe said she'd taken care of her, that she meant she had killed her. The memory of Charlotte on the roof parapet that stormy night, struggling with Zoe, had flashed through his mind.

"Zoe . . . you're sure, that she's in Ceylon? I mean . . . well, she's never written to Eleanor, either, and they were very close."

"Oh, yes, she wrote to Eleanor several times. Delia and I decided it was not in Eleanor's best interests to receive the letters. After all, Charlotte Danforth had kidnapped her from her home and really caused the death of the child's grandfather. He did die en route to this country to prosecute her, didn't he? So Delia and I decided that Charlotte should be out of sight and out of mind. While Eleanor lived with the Ramseys, Delia intercepted the letters and burned them."

Stephen put down his brandy glass, fearing that the blurred images he was seeing were partly due to a few too many drinks this evening. "Tell me, what did you mean when you said earlier that it's because of Geoffrey that Evan shows all this interest in taking over the title and estate . . . that the only way to regain the upper hand is to remove the cause. Zoe, you weren't . . . you didn't mean . . . I thought . . . I thought you cared about the boy."

"Frankly, darling, I would have preferred a girl. Seven years ago Eleanor would have been more suitable. She was past that annoying age. But between Evan and my dear friend Delia and yourself, well, you all put paid to that idea, didn't you?"

"You wouldn't have been able to pass Eleanor off as your own daughter, however. At the time, you were delighted to pretend you had given birth to the boy. Zoe, you *do* care about Geoffrey, don't you?" He hoped his desperate fear for his son was not evident in his voice. Thank God for Lorna McDougan, who protected the child with that fierce, lioness-for-her-cub vigilance of the good nanny.

"Stephen, *cherie*, Geoffrey is a very appealing child, that is the whole problem, don't you see? He even appealed to your monstrous half brother. Don't you see, Evan sent Charlotte away to bear his child, so this change of heart toward the boy is a recent one. Dearest Stephen, I love you, but you are sometimes so simple about such things. Evan and Charlotte formed an attachment for one another, but then they somehow couldn't get in step with it. When she wanted him—when she was pregnant—he sent her away. Then when he brought her back, she didn't want him. Now, belatedly, Evan has discovered Geoffrey. Because of that he wants to take your place as Lord Athmore. The next step would be to bring Charlotte back, to complete this happy family. *If* he knew where she was. We know where she is. Ergo, we can use this knowledge to our advantage."

"Zoe, please . . . the dinner gong is going to ring any second and Evan will be arriving. Tell me, quickly, why did you ask him to come to dinner? What did you say to him that made him accept?"

She laughed, and pirouetted in front of him to show off her gown of vivid scarlet. "I told him we wanted to discuss Geoffrey's future with him. But what I intend to tell him is . . . where he can find Charlotte Danforth. Oh, not an address that he could write to, just a vague description of a remote mission in the jungles of Ceylon. I fully expect he'll go there himself and will be out of the way for months. While he's gone we'll send Geoffrey away to a boardingschool, it's almost time, anyway. You know how children are, he'll become wrapped up in new friends and new activities and forget all about his Uncle Evan. If and when Evan returns, he'll find a disinterested schoolboy far less appealing as a prospective heir."

"What do you mean, *if* Evan returns?"

She shrugged. "Perhaps he'll decide to stay and work with the missionaries, especially if Charlotte wants to. We can tell him that we'll send Geoffrey to them if they wish. But by the same token, we won't give up the boy if Evan brings Charlotte back to

Glendower. That should be an inducement for them to stay out of the country.''

He stared into those fathomless eyes, trying to read her mind to see if there was more there than she disclosed. For once it seemed she had a workable plan to solve all of their problems. But there was one major flaw in her reasoning. Stephen said quietly, ''I love Geoffrey too much to send him so far away. I might never see him again.''

''You could visit him then. Spend months at sea if you must.'' Her black eyes narrowed to slits. ''Or must I devise some other method of taking care of our problem? While Evan wants to make Geoffrey his heir, you and I, *cherie*, and everything we have, are at risk.''

''Don't go downstairs, Zoe,'' Stephen said heavily. ''I'll talk with Evan. He'll be more receptive to me.''

Evan stood in the center of a drawing room that he felt would have been more appropriate in a New Orleans bordello than any English aristocrat's country estate. The scarlet and gold brocaded walls had begun to close in on him when at last Stephen appeared, followed by his housekeeper, Mrs. Carmichael, and a pair of burly young footmen. Stephen looked paler than usual, and his eyes were more haunted and tragic than ever.

''Sorry to keep you waiting,'' he said. Mrs. Carmichael and the footmen stationed themselves at the door, like sentinels.

''A drink before dinner, old man?'' There was a false note of affability in Stephen's voice that Evan detected immediately. That and the hovering servants indicated that unpleasant news was about to be imparted, and Stephen wanted witnesses present.

''Is your wife joining us?'' Evan asked.

''No . . . she isn't feeling very well.''

''Why don't you dismiss the servants, Stephen, and tell me what it is Zoe wanted me to know? I assure you I will keep my temper, no matter what.''

''Wouldn't you like to have dinner first?''

Evan shook his head. He sat down carefully in the most substantial looking chair he could find. Stephen gestured for the footmen to leave but said, ''I'd prefer Mrs. Carmichael to stay. She is fully aware of all our secrets, and well . . . frankly, I don't care to be alone with you when I tell you what I have to tell you.''

''Very well. What is it you want from me?''

''That . . . in return for certain information, you postpone all of your plans to assume control of the title and estate for a period of at least six months." Stephen gave a forced smile. "Actually, Evan, I think perhaps when I tell you what I've just learned, you may want to spend the next several months traveling abroad."

"That's extremely unlikely. For God's sake, stop beating about the bush and tell me what Zoe's done now."

Stephen had been pacing nervously around the room and now he stopped at the spirits cabinet and poured himself a large brandy. He drained the glass and then drew a deep breath. "I suppose you wondered why Charlotte never returned to see the boy?"

"You know damn well I had people search the length and breadth of England and Wales for her."

"We know where she is. Zoe . . . heard from her. It was some time ago, but we think there's a good chance Charlotte is still in the same place."

Evan caught his breath. "Where? Where is she? You say she's abroad, which country? America?"

Stephen moved behind a chair, as if to barricade himself in, and said, "Not so fast, old man. We need a breathing space to put our affairs in order before you start washing all the dirty Athmore linen in public."

"If I decide to go and look for Charlotte, will you allow me to take Geoffrey with me? I would be uneasy leaving him to Zoe's tender mercies, now that she knows I want him to be my heir."

"What if instead I promised to place him in the best boarding school we can find, one of your choosing? Perhaps after you've found Charlotte, I might consider sending him to you. You surely don't want to be burdened with the care of a child while you're traveling, anyway. There is also the danger to him of tropical diseases."

"She's in the tropics?"

Stephen nodded. "She's a missionary. They tend to work among the lowest castes in stinking jungles and expose themselves to filthy illnesses. After you find her you can take a decent bungalow and hire servants, and I'll put him on a ship to you. But whatever you decide, before I tell you where she is, I want your word that you won't depose me for six months."

"You have it," Evan said. "Now tell me where I can find Charlotte."

22

ELEANOR WAS SURPRISED to receive an invitation from the Ramseys to spend the weekend at their country estate. It came in the form of a gushing note from Delia promising that some very special guests would be present, whom she was sure Eleanor would want to meet. Tristan could travel down from London with her, since his play had closed.

The variety show Eleanor had been appearing in would also be closing. The announcement had been made abruptly and mysteriously, the day after her last meeting with Thane.

"I haven't heard from Lady Ramsey in ages," Eleanor said to Maeve. "Funny that she would want me to go down to the country the first weekend after we close. Shall I go?"

"Yes," Maeve said firmly. "It will take your mind off closing, and get you out of the city before that awful Thane comes looking for you again. Do you really think he'll send you abroad?"

"He can't make me go anywhere I don't want to go," Eleanor replied, but there was little conviction in her voice. It hadn't been mentioned, but she was not a British subject. She was an American citizen, a foreigner, and therefore subject to deportation if Thane so ordained. But he would surely have to have grounds? She hadn't done anything, but could he trump up some charge against her? She had a feeling Thane could accomplish anything he chose to do, by legal or illegal means. Wasn't there a law about clandestine meetings with a married man? They called it "alienation of affections." Would that be reason enough for deportation?

"Tristan is in the front-row stalls," Maeve offered. "With a face like a wet week."

"He's very depressed. He never should have attempted Hamlet. You know, for Tristan's sake, I think I will go down to the Ramseys'. He needs to get away more than I do."

On the night of her final performance, Eleanor felt the usual emotional turmoil and sadness at leaving the company of people she had seen every day for weeks, as well as the uncertainty of what the future would hold. There was always the worry of getting another booking, but now there was added concern about what her association with HRH might precipitate.

As she took her last bow, amid a storm of flowers and blossoms that pelted the stage, tears sprang to her eyes as the waves of applause washed over her. She looked at the front-row stalls to where Tristan had been sitting, but he had gone. Undoubtedly he was waiting in her dressing room. Instead of connecting with his mournful gaze, her eyes met a pair of fierce dark ones set in a swarthy, tanned face.

Slowly the flowers she had picked up slid from her fingers. She stared, blinked, looked again. The craggy face broke into a slow smile as he rose to his feet, clapping his hands furiously. Surely . . . it couldn't be?

It was! She found herself running down into the orchestra pit, along the first row, stumbling over feet, laughing and crying, until she reached him and flung herself into his arms. "Owain! Oh, my sweet Owain! My good and true friend! Why didn't you let me know you were coming?"

They had piled coal in the fireplace of Eleanor's flat, placed a jug of cider on the hearth, and sat on her sheepskin rug in front of the roaring fire, talking into the small hours of the morning.

With the lateness of the hour, the exhaustion of closing night, and the strongly alcoholic cider Eleanor had consumed to ward off a slight sore throat, she found herself becoming tearfully emotional when she related to Owain the trials and tribulations of seven years past.

"You left and Charlotte vanished and I felt so alone. Then Delia—Lady Ramsey—told me my grandfather was coming for me. I didn't know where to turn . . . I even asked Delia if I might go back to Glendower. I had some wild idea that Mr. Evan would protect me. But, of course, at that time he was still under the doctor's care and very ill. You know, when we heard that my grandfather had died of a heart attack on the ship on the way over . . . I was convinced I'd caused his death. I had nightmares for ages and was sure I'd be struck dead myself for wishing something would happen so I wouldn't have to go back to Boston with him. Tristan was hopeless, of course. He's useless unless someone else writes his lines for him. He goes all to pieces in a crisis.'' She sniffed. "Your letters were very . . . *brief*. And I still don't know why you didn't let me know you were coming."

"My letters were brief because I'm not an educated man. I can't put into writing all I feel. Writing a letter is a chore to me. I'm ashamed to say I never wrote to Mr. Evan."

Eleanor cocked her head to one side and studied him carefully. "Your voice is different . . . I've just noticed. Your accent has changed. You've lost a lot of that Welsh singsong quality and, my goodness! You're beginning to sound like an American."

Owain smiled. "I spent time in the Arizona and New Mexico territories, and several years in Kentucky. I'm not sure where I belong anymore. Over there, they still ask where I'm from. You know, Ellie, *bach,* when I traveled across America I used to try to imagine you there, as a very little girl. I nearly visited Boston before we sailed from New York, just to see where you came from, but there wasn't time."

"We? Who is we? Didn't you come alone?"

"Maitland-Howard came with me. Peter decided it was time he visited his family here. He's in Kent. I was supposed to join him there, but I hung around London instead."

"Goodness! I've just remembered. I'm supposed to go to the Ramseys' country place tomorrow . . . today! Tristan will be coming for me at the crack of dawn."

"I must be off then, and you've got to get some sleep. Could I . . . see you when you get back?"

"I'll be shattered if you don't. Owain . . ."

"Yes?"

"Would you say, *look you*, just once, so I can be sure it's really you?"

"There's a ninny you are, Ellie, *bach,* look you," Owain responded laughingly. He stood up and extended his hand to her to help her to her feet.

Swaying slightly, she held on to his hand. "You never mentioned what made you suddenly decide to come home."

"Have you heard of a horse race called the Kentucky Derby?" She shook her head.

"Well, I trained a horse to race in it, and Peter mortgaged

everything he owned to bet on it. It won, and he insisted on sharing the winnings with me. It was a tidy sum.''

"But how wonderful! He must be a good friend.''

"He's not a bad sort,'' Owain said, "for an Englishman.''

There was an air of suppressed excitement at the Ramseys' country estate. Eleanor felt it the moment she arrived. Tristan had told her that Delia would not even reveal to him the identity of their guest of honor at the planned party that evening.

Someone important, Eleanor decided, noting that the servants were in a high state of anxiety. It was evident that the house had been scrubbed from roof to ceiling; oil paintings had been restored and carpets cleaned. Brasses gleamed, mirrors and chandeliers shone. Outside, the grounds had been groomed within an inch of their lives, each blade of grass clipped, each bush trimmed.

Eleanor had slept late that morning, and she and Tristan had missed their train, so they did not arrive until quite late in the afternoon. Eleanor was still battling her sore throat, and wanted to excuse herself to go and lie down before dinner, but good manners demanded that she first spend some time with the Ramseys.

They were receiving in the drawing room, and Eleanor's old, familiar sinking feeling assailed her when she saw that Veronica, nemesis of her childhood, was present. But, of course, she would be home for the summer from her Swiss finishing school.

Veronica had grown from a pudgy, discontented child to an obese, sharp-tongued young woman. Her small eyes were almost lost in a plump face, and they darted over Eleanor's slender body with undisguised hostility. "Ah, here comes our little nightingale at last. Late, as usual.''

An enamored theater critic had once called Eleanor a nightingale, but Veronica managed to make it sound more like an insult than a compliment.

"Sorry,'' Eleanor murmured, kissing Delia's cheek. "We missed our train.''

Veronica's gaze was fixed on Eleanor's apple-green dress. "That color is totally unsuitable for day wear,'' she said, "I do wish when you come to visit Mother and Father that you'd leave the music halls behind and dress like a lady.''

"Oh, come now, Veronica,'' her father said mildly, offering his hand to Tristan. "Eleanor looks very nice, as always.''

"The color is a trifle gaudy,'' Delia said, siding with her

daughter as usual. Eleanor wondered sometimes if things would have been different if Veronica had displayed the hoped-for acting talent. Looking back, it was clear that the Ramseys had taken her to live with them in the hope that her love of drama would be caught by Veronica. But even if she hadn't been so lazy, Veronica's obsessive overeating would surely have limited her to comedy roles rather than the Shakespeare her mother had in mind. Eleanor was certain that it had been Delia who persuaded Tristan to attempt his ill-fated Hamlet.

"Are you listening, Eleanor?" Veronica asked sharply, and Eleanor realized that the conversation had proceeded without her. Lord Ramsey and Tristan were discussing the work of a new playwright, and Delia and Veronica were looking at her.

"I'm sorry . . ." Eleanor said. She was beginning to feel disassociated from her body; only her raw throat and throbbing head kept her from floating away.

Delia said, "I said I hoped you'd brought a ball gown. Tonight is a very special occasion."

"Yes, you told me that in your note," Eleanor replied.

"Don't try to guess who's coming," Veronica remarked. "Mother won't even tell me. It's to be a surprise."

"Darling," her mother put in anxiously. "Perhaps you shouldn't eat any more of that Turkish Delight? Your new gown is rather skimpily cut. In fact, why don't you lie down for a while, so you'll be fresh for tonight."

"Oh, what a good idea," Eleanor exclaimed, relieved. "I should certainly like to take a nap."

She escaped from the drawing room as fast as her somewhat unsteady legs would carry her.

There was a bottle of wine in her room, and she quickly drank some to relieve the scratchiness of her throat. Then she took off her gown and stays, lay down on the bed, and pulled the eiderdown quilt over her.

Being with Tristan all day had not given her a chance to be alone and think about Owain's return. She was fascinated with the changes the last seven years had wrought in her friend. There was a hard, reckless gleam in his eyes and, despite his limp, he had acquired a somewhat belligerent way of walking, as if defying anyone to get in his way. He stood with squared shoulders, head held high, in a challenging manner that was a far cry from the deferential, touching-the-forelock stance he'd been forced to adopt as a groom at Glendower. He'd had those fierce, dark eyes then, too, but had usually kept them averted. Last evening he'd taken her out for a late supper before they went to her flat; she'd observed him, noting how very masculine he seemed in comparison to Tristan and the other actors with whom she spent most of her time. The difference between an indoor and a vigorous outdoor way of life, she supposed.

Yet she'd been disappointed in Owain, too; because that bold authoritative manner had vanished the moment they were alone. In her presence he was shy, almost hesitant, and he looked at her with such an adoring gaze that it was obvious he had fallen in love with the Eleanor-beyond-the-footlights during those evenings he had spent as an anonymous face in her audience. She knew that look only too well, and hated seeing it on Owain's face, because it meant he was dazzled by the actress with the sweet singing voice, just like everyone else. Didn't they realize that was not truly Eleanor?

She'd pretended not to notice and tried to treat him as her good and true friend of old, hoping that he was simply overwhelmed by their first meeting and would soon revert back to the Owain she remembered—or, better still, show her that masterful side of himself he'd apparently acquired in America.

Her throat now hurt so much that she had two more glasses of wine, hoping to numb the pain. She drifted off to sleep and dreamed she and Owain were back at Glendower, riding together down the steep slope of a hill with the wind in their faces and the sun glinting on the lake below. They were laughing and so happy; then all at once, she looked back and saw storm clouds menacing the mountain behind them.

"Miss Hathaway," a voice yanked her abruptly back to consciousness and she looked into the anxious face of a young maid. "Please, miss, wake up. Lady Ramsey says everyone must be downstairs before the guest of honor arrives."

Eleanor felt worse for her nap rather than better. Her head ached, she felt feverish, and her throat was more sore than ever. She was scarcely aware of dressing, and when she started down the wide, twice-turning staircase of the Ramseys' rambling country house, a wave of dizziness caused her to stop and clutch the banister for support. In the hall below she could hear the excited murmuring of guests but, afraid to move in case she fell, stayed where she was.

After a moment Tristan materialized beside her. "Are you all right, love?" he asked solicitously. "Come on, I'll help you.

Lord, you reek of wine! And you talk about me nipping in secret. Here, pop this peppermint in your mouth, just in case Delia's guest of honor is the dowager duchess.''

Eleanor felt curiously removed from it all. She was aware of Tristan helping her down the staircase, of Veronica looming up, bulging in a too-tight pink satin gown, lavish with seed pearls, of Delia's disapproving glance as she swept by to attend to last minute details.

There seemed to be legions of guests. The cream of society, liberally laced with enough young bachelors to stock a regiment. Eleanor recognized several who had hung around the stage door, and saw Veronica simpering at a wary-looking guardsman.

"Tristan," Eleanor whispered, "I've got to sit down. I feel so . . . strange."

He was able to half-carry, half-drag her to a chair by the wall, just as Delia organized the receiving line. A moment later the doors opened and a deferential silence fell.

"Oh, no," Tristan muttered. "Brace yourself, love. It's HRH."

Eleanor blinked, but nothing came into focus. "Is there a sinister-looking man with him? Dark hair, cold blue eyes?"

"You don't have to describe the frightful Thane to me, love. I've seen him bring you to my door, remember? Lord, you are in a state. Don't see him. Actually, I can't see much of anything from back here. Will you be all right while I go and pay my respects?"

She nodded, wanting nothing more than to crawl back into bed and sleep. What did it matter if HRH and she found themselves at the same party? Thane couldn't blame her for such a coincidence. After all, Lord Ramsey's father had been a duke—and, if rumor were true, Tristan was his bastard son. Since she had lived with the Ramseys for several years, it wasn't surprising that they would all move in the same social circles. Thane had to see that. Oh, damn Thane, why was she worrying about him?

Besides, even in her wine-induced disorientation, Eleanor realized that Delia would never have invited her tonight—she was too much competition for Veronica when there were so many eligible males present—unless she had been requested to do so. Which meant HRH had asked Delia to arrange tonight's party. How on earth would she explain this turn of events to Thane?

Moments later she was formally presented to HRH by Lord

Ramsey. She rose unsteadily to her feet and managed a small curtsy. Out of the corner of her eye, she saw Delia glaring at her.

Then, mercifully, the dinner gong sounded.

Time passed in a hazy blur. Her appetite had fled, but her sore throat begged for surcease and water didn't help, so she drank wine. After dinner the men remained in the dining room with their cigars and brandy, while the women moved to the drawing room.

Halfway across the hall, Eleanor collided with Veronica, who drew her aside and hissed in her ear, "You're tipsy! How absolutely disgusting. How could you do this to Mother?"

"I may be tipsy tonight," Eleanor said, mustering all of her dignity but spoiling it with a small hiccup. "However, tomorrow I'll be sober. But you'll still be fat."

Veronica's mouth popped open. "Oh!"

Eleanor tried to walk away with her head high, but she tripped over her own feet and had to clutch a passing footman in order to keep from falling. Oh, God, had she really said that to Veronica? She stumbled into the nearest room, which proved to be a solarium, filled with plants and ferns.

Gratefully she sank down into a rattan chair and pressed her fingers to her throbbing head. Several peaceful minutes passed.

"Your note disappointed me greatly," a voice said.

She blinked and looked up to see HRH standing beside her. The solarium was lit only by the moonlight spilling in through a wall of windows, and in the dim light she could see that he regarded her with a sorrowful expression.

"Tell me, my dear, was any pressure brought to bear in order to persuade you to write that rather terse note of good-bye?"

She was at a loss for words. The dizziness she had felt earlier was now worse than ever and her brain refused to function.

"I suppose you already know that this whole gathering was arranged only to give me an opportunity to hear from your own lips that you do not wish to spend any more time with me."

"I explained in my note," she said in a hoarse whisper.

"But was it written under duress?" he persisted. "Eleanor, about Thane . . . he was formerly an army officer, decorated for bravery many times, the son of a dear friend . . . and I regret, a dismal failure as a diplomat when my father was persuaded to give him an embassy position. Now I seem to have inherited his services while he is between assignments. But I'm well aware that he is not a domesticated animal. The point I'm trying to make is that he sometimes takes it upon himself to overstep the boundaries of his duties."

Little explosions of light were now flashing in Eleanor's eyes. She had only the vaguest awareness of what he was saying and was sure at any moment she would slide to the floor in a dead faint. "I . . . I'm sorry . . . I don't feel very well."

In the semidarkness his hand touched her cheek and he exclaimed, "Oh, my poor, dear girl, you are very feverish. Stay here. I'll return in a moment."

Around her the ferns cast grotesque shadows. She felt as if she were floating above them. The moon vanished behind a cloud and the darkness closed in, suffocating her.

"Influenza," a voice somewhere said. "Let her sleep. Best thing for her. Keep using the poultice and have her gargle with salt water when she wakes up."

She felt cold, shivery. Her eyelids were too heavy to raise. She slipped away again to oblivion.

The next time she awoke, she saw that she was still in the guest room at the Ramseys' country estate and she remembered Owain, waiting for her back in London, but she fell asleep again before she summoned the strength to pull the bell cord.

Faces drifted in and out of her vision. Delia, looking worried. Veronica, briefly, keeping her handkerchief clamped to her mouth. Lord Ramsey, kindly and concerned. Tristan, helpless and solicitous. There was daylight, and darkness. Sunlight. Twilight. Rain pattering gently on the windowpane.

She sat up in bed and exclaimed, "Owain! He'll wonder what on earth happened to me."

"Miss?" A young parlor maid was arranging roses in a silver bowl on her bedside table.

"Would you bring paper and a pen, quickly? And don't let me fall asleep again until I've written a note."

She lay back on her pillow, weaker than any kitten. The maid returned with a writing case, and Eleanor managed to scribble a few lines to Owain. "Is Tristan still here?" she asked, thinking he could take the note back to London with him.

"Oh, no, miss. He left on Monday."

"What day is this?"

"Wednesday, miss."

Shocked that she had lost three whole days, Eleanor handed

the note to the maid and asked, "Where did all of the flowers come from?"

"The cards are still with them, miss," the maid said. "I was just going to start taking them out of your room for the night, 'cause the doctor said they'd use up all your oxygen. But I can leave them another minute, if you like."

"Yes, please . . . take the note downstairs first."

Eleanor was asleep again long before the maid returned.

She spent the next two weeks with the Ramseys, too weak to even consider returning to London. If Delia was curious about her relationship with HRH, she was too well-bred to inquire about it, and Eleanor was not about to bring up the subject.

The first day she felt strong enough to get out of bed, she discovered that the largest bouquet of roses bore no card. They were undoubtedly from HRH. What had she told him? She couldn't remember.

There was a note from Owain, expressing concern for her health, hoping for a speedy recovery, and telling her that he would like to see her again as soon as she felt well enough to receive him. He had not sent flowers, choosing instead to send her a complete set of the issues of *Household Words* containing Dickens's novel, *Bleak House*.

As much as she loved to read, however, she simply didn't have the energy. She felt utterly lethargic, disinterested in everything around her, as her body attempted to heal itself.

Then one afternoon Delia came into her room and said, "I've sent for a maid to help you dress. You have a visitor. You can receive him in the solarium."

"Him?" Eleanor asked. "Oh, good . . . it's Owain."

"No," Delia said, her expression rather strange. "It's a Colonel Thane."

It was the first time she had seen him in the daylight, Eleanor realized, as she went into the solarium and he turned to face her. She was aware of his eyes first. Pale blue, clear, penetrating. The kind of eyes that connected and wouldn't let go. Dark eyebrows and high cheekbones seemed designed to emphasize those eyes. The mouth was hard, the facial expression cynical. He stood rigidly erect, she supposed that was a legacy of his former military career, and he tapped the silver knob of his ever-present ebony cane against his palm, indicating his impatience at having had to wait for her.

She had already decided that she wasn't going to let him bully her, so she wobbled across the solarium to the nearest chair, sat down and looked at him defiantly. "If you're here to chastise me about the Ramseys' party for HRH . . . I had no idea he was coming."

"He's convinced himself that your impending illness was the reason for your note."

"Well, then . . ."

Thane pulled a chair close to hers and sat down. "Tell me about Owain Davies."

"How do you know about Owain? Oh, I see. You've been spying on me."

"I know all there is to know about you. I've just completed an investigation into your background."

"On whose orders?"

"I'm not at liberty to say. I can tell you that, so far, I have not disclosed anything I've learned about you to anyone else."

"How dare you come marching in here . . . intimidating me like this. I haven't done anything. I haven't broken any laws."

"Intimidating you? My dear Miss Hathaway, I merely asked about a man with whom you have kept in touch for years. A man recently returned to England to see you. The only man in your extensive circle of admirers you chose to notify of your illness. Let me be more specific. Is Owain Davies a man you care about?"

"He's an old and dear friend. Where is this conversation leading?"

"Will he be returning to America soon?"

"I suppose so."

"You could marry him. Go with him."

"*Marry* Owain? That's ridiculous. He's a friend, nothing more. I haven't even seen him for seven years. Besides, he hasn't asked me."

"He will, with a little encouragement from you. Think about it for a moment. A woman with your looks is better off married; you need a husband for protection. Davies has apparently done quite well for himself in America—he's been talking to investment brokers in London. It's far better for you to return to America as Mrs. Owain Davies than to go as an actress on tour. You're not well-known; the best you could hope for would be second-class theaters in dreary little towns. I've been to America, and I can tell you that entertainers are looked upon there in exactly the same way they are here, perhaps with even more disdain since they don't have the equivalent yet of our theatrical elite.''

"But I wasn't planning to go on an American tour."

"Oh yes, one way or another you are going back to America, where you came from. The third alternative is deportation. Shall I elaborate?''

"No," Eleanor answered in a small voice. The weakness that had gripped her since the onset of the influenza returned with a vengeance. She leaned back, closing her eyes. "Why do you hate me so much?"

"You flatter yourself, Miss Hathaway. I don't care enough about you, one way or the other, to hate you. I've been instructed to get you out of HRH's life. I intend to do just that. You can cooperate and it will be easy for you, or you can resist and learn just how much influence I wield.''

He rose abruptly and started for the door. Pausing, he looked back at her. "By the way, I strongly advise you not to communicate with HRH in any way. The consequences for you will be exceedingly grave if you do. I'll be in touch with you after you return to London.''

23

ZOE STOOD AT at the window of her boudoir, looking out across the courtyard. The oaks stood between the main house and the grange like a protective army, the mature trees near the grange permitting only a glimpse of chimneys and roof between their dense branches, while the younger trees planted after construction of the new house were already turning the courtyard into a forest.

As the door opened, she turned and asked, "Has he gone?"

Stephen replied, "Yes. I saw the ship sail from Liverpool yesterday. He's on his way to Ceylon. You won't have to worry about him for several months."

Her eyes glittered and her lips curved into a smile, or was it, he wondered, a grimace of satisfaction? She hummed softly under her breath as she went to the bed and sat down, pointing to a bottle of champagne on the bedside table. "Open it, *cherie*, we will celebrate. Then we will make love."

Stephen tried to ignore the knot of tension in his brow. He picked up the champagne and looked at her, searching for telltale signs. Apart from that glitter in her eyes, which could have been anticipation of sex since he'd been gone for several days, she seemed calm.

"Did you take care of all of your other business in Liverpool?" she asked, swinging her legs up onto the bed.

"Yes. I think Evan was surprised when I turned up at the docks to see him off." He glanced sideways at her. "Tell me, why did you insist that I be in Liverpool when he sailed?"

She shrugged, allowing her nightgown to slide from one

shoulder. "I wanted to be absolutely sure he was aboard that ship. I didn't want him to change his mind at the last moment, or perhaps miss the sailing time."

"He sailed aboard the s.s. *Southern Star*. Yesterday, at noon." Stephen handed her a glass of champagne. "But Zoe, he won't stay away forever. We're going to have to make some plans for when he returns, and he will, sooner or later. I can't see him staying indefinitely in Ceylon. We have to face the fact that we can never go back to the way things were."

Raising her glass, she said, "Let's not talk about it now, my dearest. Let's toast our reunion, then make love."

They didn't finish their first glass of champagne. The sexual magnetism that existed between them flared swiftly, and he undressed and lay beside her, pulling her hungrily into his arms.

Within seconds all thoughts of Evan fled from his mind as he lost himself in her silken embrace. But in that last instant of ecstasy, as he crashed over the edge of the abyss, some rational portion of his mind again asked how much longer he could pretend he was in control of Zoe's actions. He wondered whether he would be able to prevent her from hurting anyone else, if he could continue to ignore her madness . . . simply because she held him in sexual thrall. Then, exhausted, he fell asleep almost immediately.

Zoe watched him for a moment, then rose from the bed and slipped on her robe. She picked up the champagne bottle and tiptoed from the room, filled with the need to tell someone of her triumph. The one person she had always confided in, whom she could trust with any secret, had surely also remained awake awaiting Stephen's return.

When Zoe entered her housekeeper's room, Mrs. Carmichael's cunning eyes lit up. Zoe gave a small dance of victory. "It's done," she exclaimed. "He's aboard the *Southern Star*." She poured champagne and handed a glass to Mrs. Carmichael. Then, raising her own, she said, "To the end of the tyrant."

"Are you sure, my lady? He won't be back?"

"I'm certain; he's gone forever. This time my dear husband can't stop it. You see, aboard the *Southern Star* there is a man who will see to it that Evan Athmore never troubles us, or anyone else, again."

Mrs. Carmichael leaned forward, eager for details. "Does your man know how big he is? Wouldn't be easy to toss him overboard, would it now?"

"Oh, he won't do anything while they're at sea. He'll study Evan carefully during the voyage, gain his confidence. I daresay nothing will happen until they reach Ceylon. Life is cheap in such places. No doubt the man I hired will hire others. I paid him only a small retainer, with the promise of a great deal more when he returns to England with proof of Evan's death."

A radiant dawn was breaking over a flawless opal sea as Evan stood in the bow of the ship and searched the horizon for his first glimpse of the island some said was paradise.

That he was bound for a fairytale island had been confirmed not only by virtually all of his fellow passengers who were returning to Lanka, as many of them called Ceylon, but also by the very quality of the air as landfall drew close. The air was a gossamer veil, fragrant with the perfume of exotic spices and mysterious blossoms. It was little wonder that Charlotte had remained here all these years.

According to the tea planters who were returning after spending their leave in England, Ceylon was hot in summer and subject to drenching monsoons, but the climate at the higher elevations of the island, where the tea plantations were situated, was pleasantly balmy. Evan leaned on the ship's rail and breathed deeply, hoping that Charlotte was doing her missionary work at some village high in the mountains. Zoe had conveniently forgotten where in Ceylon Charlotte's letter had originated, and it was a very large island.

A voice at his elbow remarked, "So, Lord Athmore, we've left behind the barren and parched shores of Suez and Aden. We've toasted our captain's seamanship for bringing us safely to this dream harbor, and we've listened to tall tales about this island Eden. Are we now ready for the sweltering reality of Colombo?"

The man was diminutive, even by ordinary standards, and beside Evan he seemed like a dwarf. Small, bright eyes peered out of a round pink face and a sparse sprinkling of white hair did little to protect his pink scalp from the sun. His straw hat was in his hand, as if defying the tropical sun to do its worst. He had been friendly to the point of being intrusive, the entire voyage. Evan had lived too much alone to wish to spend much time with a man with whom he had little in common, but he had suffered Drackleby's company out of politeness. Besides, he evidently knew Ceylon and its peoples very well.

Still, there was something in Drackleby's attitude toward him that was not quite right. Evan couldn't determine what it was, but it was disconcerting—a certain veiled hostility that was at odds with the surface friendliness. He was also reticent in regard to talking about himself, giving no information other than that he had a government position in Colombo. Customs and Excise, Evan guessed, from the way Drackleby scrutinized everything and everyone.

"Good morning, Mr. Drackleby," Evan said. "I shan't be staying in Colombo. At least, not for long."

"For long enough to take a rickshaw ride and visit the gaudy, hideous Buddhist temples, I expect. Also the equally hideous Christian churches. The latter are grim and uncompromising, and the former beset by beggars and no less irritating guides and acolytes who will harass you at every turn, demanding fees. On my travels I'm constantly appalled by the mischief done in the name of religion."

It was obvious, from the sardonic gleam in Drackleby's eyes that he hoped Evan would rise to the bait. Evan had been open in telling fellow passengers that he was traveling to Ceylon to try to find a missionary friend who had gone there years before, in the hope that one of them may have heard of her.

Evan said shortly, "I've no wish to argue religious issues with you. It's too perfect a morning."

"Let me tell you, Lord Athmore, what the missionaries have accomplished in India and Ceylon. You see, for every Christian they made, they also made a hundred drunkards."

"I beg your pardon?"

"They were total abstainers before the missionaries arrived. Strong drink was forbidden to Hindus, Mohammedans and Buddhists. Before we white men appeared on the scene it was difficult to obtain and very expensive. We made it available to them, in the interests of revenue, and the missionaries gave them permission to drink it by telling them that their religions were false, thus breaking down their taboos."

Charlotte's missionary status made it impossible for Evan to let the taunts go unchallenged. "But our religion is very much opposed to drunkenness also. You can hardly blame the missionaries for the availability of strong drink. Blame the merchants, blame the Raj."

"But it is the missionaries who break down the native cultures.

I've seen it all over the world. You strike me as being a fair and open-minded man, and it was a disappointment to me to learn you are associated with one of Lanka's enemies.''

He paused as one of the younger passengers strolled by. Tall and burly of build, with a somewhat unkempt mop of mahogany colored hair and a relaxed manner that had endeared him to nearly everyone aboard, including Evan, the man had played shuffleboard and deck quoits with him, and Evan found him to be jovial. He was undemanding in his conversation and apparently oblivious to Evan's size.

Drackleby nodded in the young man's direction as he went by. ''And there's another type the island could well do without. Young Fenmore is too charming to be true. I also noticed he drinks too much and has a gambler's gleam in his eye. He's probably one of those misguided Englishmen who come here with the idea that being a planter is a gentleman's avocation, and all they'll have to do is pocket the profits. This island is crawling with broken-down gentlemen, mostly planters, who couldn't stand the loneliness and sheer monotony of life on the estates. Even the richest planters can only hope to go home every three or four years.''

''Fenmore's plans are none of our business, are they?'' Evan said, wondering if Drackleby counted on his diminutive size and elderly appearance to protect him from repercussions to his outrageous remarks.

At that moment the mountains of Ceylon appeared, rising cool and blue above mists that lay like petrified surf in the valleys.

In silent awe, Evan's gaze moved slowly to the palm-fringed shores of the island. He was not religiously inclined, but there was a spiritual beauty to the mountains that conveyed a sense of serenity. Spellbound, he remained on deck as the island drew closer.

The ship entered the harbor, steaming past a formidable breakwater. Other passengers now crowded the rail to watch an armada of outrigger canoes that skimmed over the surface of the water toward them.

Drackleby remained at his side. ''The canoes bring traders who will offer unwary passengers precious stones at inflated prices, or trips ashore after we drop anchor. The dusky-skinned ones are Tamils, the lighter-complexioned are Sinhalese—see how they twist their long hair into a thick knot surmounted by a tortoiseshell comb? Gives them a curiously feminine appearance, doesn't it? The gents in the first canoe wearing the colorful costumes and brimless hats on their shaved heads are Indo-Arab traders."

"Excuse me," Evan said. "I must go to my cabin and finish packing."

A red haze seemed to hang over the port city of Colombo, but Evan thought perhaps he imagined it, because of the fiery heat. He was aware of broad streets lined with shops, and barrackslike buildings that were out of place in the exotic East. A large hotel of fiercely western architecture faced the harbor. Pairs of Indian humped bulls were drawing chests of tea down to where dusky Tamils and Sinhalese took it into boats for delivery to waiting steamers. A constant barrage of jabbering voices hung in the torrid air, unintelligible, musical.

On the quay he paused, unsure if the waiting rickshaw drivers would refuse to take him to his hotel because of his size.

"Don't be deterred by the apparent fragility of the coolies," a voice behind him said. "They're a lot stronger than they look, and the rickshaw is constructed in such a way that they can pull several times their weight. Where are you staying? I'll negotiate a price for you."

Fenmore, the affable young man Drackleby had taken a dislike to, stepped forward.

"Thank you. I'm going to the Grand Orient Hotel," Evan replied.

A wide smile appeared on Fenmore's face. "What a coincidence, so am I!" He approached the nearest rickshaw and started what appeared to be a heated discussion in pidgin English.

A second voice from the rear remarked, "You're putting your faith in the wrong guide, Lord Athmore. Fenmore doesn't know what he's doing. If you will allow me to be of assistance . . ."

Evan glanced back at Drackleby, glad he wouldn't have to deal with the man again. At the same instant Fenmore waved for him to come to the rickshaw. "Thank you, but that won't be necessary. Good-bye, Mr. Drackleby."

A moment later, he and his baggage were in the fragile-looking cart, and Fenmore boarded a second rickshaw. The drivers picked up the long shafts and sprinted away at an incredibly fast pace, considering their skinny bodies. They whirled along the street, took a corner at perilous speed, and were at the doors of the hotel before Evan could catch his breath.

Only then did he realize that he had been whisked around the very same hotel he had seen facing the harbor when he disembarked. Looking up he saw the giant letters G O H above the roof of the hotel. The Grand Orient Hotel. Of course, how stupid he'd been. He could have walked across the street if he'd taken the time to inquire. The rickshaw driver had simply taken him on a short detour to justify his fee. So much for the helpful Mr. Fenmore, whose following rickshaw was now in sight.

The coolie placed Evan's luggage on the pavement and waited. It was then Evan realized he had not yet converted his pounds to rupees.

In the periphery of his vision, a hand appeared, flipping a coin in the direction of the rickshaw driver. *"Palyan!"* a familiar voice commanded. Rickshaw and driver were gone before Evan turned to face Drackleby, who wore a mocking grin.

Feeling foolish, Evan asked, "How much do I owe you?"

"Don't insult me."

Fenmore arrived, gave him a rueful smile and gestured helplessly. "Cheeky buggers got a rise out of us, sorry, my fault."

Drackleby said quickly, "Have a drink on the verandah with me, Lord Athmore. I know I can be of assistance to you."

"Excuse me, but I have business to attend to," Evan said. "Good-bye, Mr. Drackleby."

An hour later, he had unpacked a few essentials and inquired at the hotel desk about the location of missions and trains into the mountains. Returning to his room, he was about to bathe to wash away some of the sticky heat when there was a knock on his door.

Fenmore stood outside, two tall glasses in his hand. "Guaranteed to drop the body temperature several degrees. Stand aside my friend and let me in. I have good news for you."

Evan took the glass and gestured for Fenmore to enter. The young man glanced at the bed. "That must be a problem for you."

"Not as much as the sleeping accommodations at sea were," Evan replied, and they both laughed.

"Remarkable coincidence just occurred," Fenmore went on. "I wanted to see some of the night life in the native quarter before I leave Colombo for the tea plantation, and I just talked with a guide willing to take a gentleman sahib to one of the more notorious clubs. Now, during the course of our conversation, what do you suppose he mentions? That he was recently con-

verted by the missionaries, but that his heathen sister dances at
the club . . . and knows of a missionary lady here in Colombo
who helps girls in trouble. Evan, old chap, even if that missionary
lady isn't the friend you're looking for, she will no doubt know
where she is."

"What time are we leaving for the club?" Evan asked.

They met their guide in the hotel lobby, a slightly built youth
with huge, brown, velvet eyes, immaculate in a white suit.
Flashing brilliantly white teeth in a smile, he salaamed as
Fenmore introduced him.

"This is Keribunda, and he has a rickshaw wallah waiting."

"This place we go not good for gentleman-sahib without
guide," Keribunda put in. "You never go there without
Keribunda, understand, sahib? We go to club where my sister is
heathen dancer. Not good Christian, like me." He paused and
added piously, "Judge not, lest ye be judged."

Evan and Fenmore exchanged glances, smothering their grins.

A couple of hours later, curry and rice had burned a fiery path
to Evan's stomach, already slightly uneasy from the assault of so
many pungent odors and the press of perspiring humanity in the
tiny club.

There were a number of white men wedged among the
olive-skinned Sinhalese seated elbow to elbow at the tiny tables,
and every eye peered through spirals of tobacco smoke that stung
the eyes to a heavy, embroidered curtain at the back of a small
space where evidently the dancers were to perform. A trio of
musicians were barely visible through the smoke after the lights
were dimmed. The sounds they made on their unfamiliar instruments were oddly disturbing, high-pitched melodies that seemed
to insinuate themselves into Evan's nerve endings.

A sudden thrill of excitement electrified the watchers as a
slender arm, wearing a number of gold bangles, slowly emerged
from behind the embroidered curtain. The arm moved in circles,
snakelike, and light flashed on the jewels of several rings worn on
long, tapered fingers. A moment later a tiny foot appeared, with
bejeweled toes, and a dainty ankle encircled with bracelets.

When Keribunda's sister was revealed in all of her stunning
beauty, a long, collective sigh whispered around the room. The
watchers stared, mesmerized, at a vision of female sensuality.
She wore a diaphanous purple gown, embroidered in gold, that
both clung to her slender body and moved with it, so that the

sheer material appeared to be a magical mist that made love to her, while with her hands, feet, and swaying hips, she in turn seduced her audience. Long ropes of pearls, rubies and sapphires hung about her neck, and her tiny waist was encircled by a gold sash. Unlike the other Sinhalese women who wore their hair in fat buns on the napes of their necks, her hair fell loosely almost to her hips, and a single ruby hung suspended in the center of her forehead.

Her movements were languid, almost as if she were hypnotized by her own body, oblivious of her audience, lost in some private fantasy. Yet she ignited passion in every man watching her, a palpable force Evan could feel all around him.

The men seated adjacent to where she danced waved money at her and when she moved close enough, they would tuck it into her sash, or even into the décolletage of her dress.

Keribunda muttered angrily, "They defile her. Treat her as a dancing whore. I hate all of them."

He started to rise, and instantly a hand closed around his wrist, forcing him back. "Don't make a bigger fool of yourself than nature's already done for you."

Evan knew before he turned to peer at the man who had somehow contrived to place a chair next to his in the smoky darkness, who that man would be.

"Damn you, sir," Fenmore said, before Evan could speak. "Are you following us?"

"Since I frequently come here when I'm in Colombo," Drackleby replied, "I might accuse you two of getting under my feet."

The dance ended and the lights came on again. Drackleby snapped his fingers to summon a white-clad, red-turbaned waiter, and, ignoring their protests, ordered another round of drinks.

Keribunda rose, giving Drackleby a wary glance, and said he was going to ask his sister about the missionary lady.

After he disappeared through a beaded curtain, Drackleby said, "The dancer's name is Rhani. No doubt a contraction of "maharani" coined to hint of royal blood," Drackleby went on. "She is actually Keribunda's half sister. His mother was a victim of the old Roman Dutch law that still prevailed after Ceylon became a British Crown Colony. According to that antique specimen of the balance of justice, at the caprice of her husband, a wife could be left completely unprovided for at either her husband's demise, or by his transferring his affections else-where.''

The man had a knack for capturing Evan's attention. He turned to listen as Drackleby continued, ''After Keribunda's father deserted his mother, she took up with a down-and-out English planter. The dancing girl was the result of that union. She is Eurasian. Did you notice how much fairer her complexion is?''

Keribunda returned, smiling broadly, but Evan noticed sweat glistening on his upper lip. ''Rhani says she know where is missionary lady. I get rickshaw wallah.'' He scurried for the door.

Evan started to rise. Drackleby said, ''Don't be a fool. Make them tell you where she is. Don't go anywhere else with them. Rhani is little better than a prostitute with a number of unsavory friends, and I'm not at all sure Keribunda's conversion to Christianity has really taken. Even a man of your considerable strength is vulnerable to a knife in the back in some dark alley.''

The close heat and highly spiced food had given Evan a terrible thirst, and he had finished his drink and drained the one ordered by Drackleby. Now his stomach was a rumbling volcano. He seemed to have trouble breathing the smoke-laden air. The faces around him had become sinister, threatening. All of the other white men had left, vanishing into the night the minute the dance ended. He felt like an intruder now, despite the presence of Drackleby and Fenmore.

He said, ''At this moment I'd rather take my chances in an alley than remain here. The food or drink has disagreed with me, and I feel ill.''

''Sit down. You do look green,'' Drackleby said. ''I'll order something to settle your stomach.''

The room revolved slowly before Evan's gaze. His knees felt unsteady and he sat down again. Drackleby's eyes were alert, watching him in a knowing way.

Fenmore said, ''I say, you do look ill. I'll get a rickshaw. Follow me outside in a couple of minutes. We can come back some other time and see Keribunda's sister.''

Drackleby commented, ''Now there are two gentlemen obtaining rickshaws for you. I suggest we leave by the back door and I'll take you to a doctor I know nearby.''

Evan asked, ''Just who the hell are you? And why have you insinuated yourself into my life?''

Drackleby's face broke into a cherubic smile. "I am your most humble servant, Lord Athmore."

Some sixth sense warned of danger. Evan forced himself to his feet. "Stay where you are," he snapped as Drackleby rose also. "I'm leaving . . . alone." He stumbled through the crowd to the door.

The air outside was free of smoke, but too hot and humid to revive him. There was no sign of either Fenmore or Keribunda, or any rickshaws. Evan started to walk, aware of the smothering darkness, of shadows that moved silently, of whispering menace all around him.

He had taken only a few steps when a prickling sensation on the nape of his neck caused him to look backward. His assailant lunged by, missing him by inches. The silver flash of a knife registered briefly, then a weight descended on his shoulders, and he realized that a second man had jumped on him from above. At the same time, two others hurled themselves out of the shadows.

Evan flung the man from his back and spun around to face four attackers, at least one of whom was armed with a knife. But his worst enemy was the increasing pain in his stomach and an uncontrollable lethargy that seemed to sap all of his strength. He thought, as he prepared defend himself, *I've been poisoned*.

24

UPON HER RETURN to London, Eleanor found every theatrical door closed to her. No one, it appeared, had a part for her, in any stage production. She tried clubs and music halls in less desirable parts of the city, without success.

Tristan was sympathetic and tried to be helpful. "Perhaps you need a longer convalescence, love. You still look a little pale and puny, and you know in our business one has to convey a sense of energy and stamina."

"They've always wanted me to sing, at least," Eleanor said. "But now you'd think I have the plague . . ."

She sat down abruptly on Tristan's chaise longue, forgetting that he hated people to sit on it as he used it solely for learning his lines. "Oh, Lord, Tristan . . . you don't think that awful Colonel Thane has forbidden anyone to give me a part?"

"Of course not. He doesn't have that kind of power. I told you, you don't look strong enough for the rigors of even a short run yet," Tristan said, frowning. "Be a dear and find somewhere else to sit. Do you want to stay to tea? I've got boiled bacon and watercress. Oh yes, and Banbury tarts."

"No, thank you. I'm meeting Owain."

"Ah, your fierce Celt."

"He isn't fierce," Eleanor replied, sighing.

Tristan placed a finger under her chin and raised her face. "What was the sigh for?"

"Nothing. I just wish he could have stayed my good and true friend, like you, Tristan."

"I see. Oh, Eleanor, have I spoiled you for all other men? Do you keep hoping they won't gaze upon you with lust and then find yourself constantly disappointed? How many times have I explained to you that I am the *only* exception to the rule that men and women can't be just friends?"

Eleanor merely smiled and rose to leave. There was no need for Tristan, or anyone else, to know about her nightmares—the recurring dream of the dark figure menacing her in her bed. Long ago, Franklyn Yarborough had bestowed upon her a legacy of fear of physical intimacy. Even though she told herself that sooner or later she would make love with a man she cared about, and then she would be able to separate the woman she was from the little girl she'd been, she still shrank from a man's embrace. Any man. Even dear Owain.

He was waiting outside her flat, holding a wilting bunch of violets when she returned. "I'm far too early, Ellie, *bach*," he said. "But there's anxious I was to see you. I've got a surprise for you." His Welsh accent returned when he was excited, she'd noticed.

"Good, I need cheering up," Eleanor said. "I didn't have any luck today finding a part."

They went to a small cafe that was a favorite of hers, and Owain self-consciously ordered a bottle of wine.

"When are you going to tell me your surprise? I can't wait another minute," she declared as soon as they had toasted one another.

"You know I've always wanted to own my own land? Well, now I do. I bought a farm," Owain said proudly. "With Peter's help."

"Oh . . . that's wonderful news," Eleanor said, all at once feeling sad that he would be going away. She would miss him terribly, but it was clear she couldn't hope to maintain their friendship while he was falling in love with her, so he might just as well go back to America. "When will you be leaving?"

"Right away . . . that is . . ." he hesitated, flushing. He stared at his menu for a moment. "Do you remember when you were a little girl and you asked me if you could come and live with me when I had my own place?"

"Yes. But I didn't think your place would be in America. I don't want to go back, Owain, at least not now. I want a career on the stage here. That's what I've been working for. I can't give up that dream."

"I'm not going back to America," Owain said. "The farm is in the north of England."

"What? But . . ."

"I told you that Peter and I made a great deal of money on the Kentucky Derby? I'm going to breed racehorses. Peter will be my silent partner. He'll go back to America and . . . well, between us we hope to have entries in the big races on both sides of the Atlantic."

He reached across the table and picked up her hand. "I know I'm only your good and true friend, Ellie, *bach*, but I love you so much it hurts. Perhaps you would come to love me in time, if we could be together. Will you marry me? Let me take care of you?"

Eleanor had anticipated the proposal, and had rehearsed how she would let him down gently, pointing out that she had to remain in England to pursue her career. But he wasn't leaving after all, and now what could she say?

"I think I've loved you since you were a little girl," Owain said softly. "Now . . . seeing you as a woman . . . I know I don't deserve you. You're the most beautiful woman I've ever seen and you could have any man on earth. But I swear that not one of them could love you the way I love you. All I want is to spend my days trying to make you happy."

She barely heard him as her thoughts raced around in several different directions. "Can you do that?" she asked. "Just come back here to live? After living in America for seven years?"

"I'm still a British subject. I didn't take out American citizenship. Yes, of course, I can just come back." He laughed. "Just like you could have gone back to America any time you wished."

Suddenly Eleanor had a vision of Thane's cynical face. He had actually suggested she marry Owain, in order to get rid of her. What a joke on him if she were indeed to marry Owain . . . and stay in England. Thane couldn't have the wife of a British subject deported.

The more she thought about it, the more the idea appealed to her. Owain was a dear, and they got along together so well because they'd known each other so long. Once she had a husband, she wouldn't have to worry about the advances of other men. She could remain here and continue acting.

He was watching her with eager eyes, his fingertip gently stroking the back of her hand, and it occurred to her then that as his wife she would have to submit to the ordeal of the physical side of marriage. But perhaps after she had borne a child for him, he wouldn't trouble her again in that regard? Surely she could steel herself to submit once or twice? Eleanor's knowledge of conjugal rights was extremely limited. She knew there were "good" women and "bad" women, and the latter actually enjoyed such disgusting intimacy while the former put up with it in order to produce children. Even among the theatrical people she had associated with, these rules applied, despite the fact that everyone believed all actresses were "loose."

"Ellie, *bach?*" Owain asked, "what are you thinking? Please, you can tell me, no matter what it is."

"I was thinking," Eleanor replied, smiling, "about all the different names I've been called. I was Eleanor Hathaway, then Eleanor Danforth . . . some people even called me Eleanor Ramsey when I lived with the Ramseys. Then I was Eleanor Hathaway again. Now I'm going to be Mrs. Owain Davies."

"Will you come with us, Maeve?" Eleanor asked. "I can't bear the thought of moving up north and not having you to confide in."

Maeve's expression was troubled. "Are you sure, Eleanor? That you're doing the right thing? If Owain were an actor, perhaps it would be easier. He'd understand . . . but—"

They were in Eleanor's bedroom, and she was sorting through her possessions, deciding what would go north with her. "I shan't be giving up the stage," Eleanor responded firmly. "As soon as the honeymoon's over, you and I will make the rounds. There are lots of theaters in northern cities. In fact, it will probably be easier for me to get a booking there. Perhaps even a part in a play. Lord knows I've not had much luck in London lately. Before you can say 'curtain's up' you'll be getting me ready to go on stage again, I promise."

"You're sure you're not just marrying Owain to spite Thane?"

"Why, Maeve, what an odd thing to say!"

"Let's make a pot of tea and I'll read your tea leaves."

"No! I'm not sure I want to know my future just now."

"There, you see what I mean? Please don't rush into it. Marry in haste, repent at leisure."

"It's not in haste. I've known Owain since I was ten."

"Then a few more months won't matter. Wait a bit and see."

Her doorbell rang, and Eleanor glanced at the clock on her mantelpiece. "That surely isn't Owain already? He said he wouldn't be here until six."

"I'll go and see who it is," Maeve said. "You make some tea. I can't think of a better time to read the leaves. I wish I could read my own so I'd be able to see if I'm doing the right thing by going with you."

Eleanor went into her little kitchen and put on the kettle. She heard Maeve say, "Wait there. I don't think she can receive you today, but I'll tell her you're here."

She knew by the sudden nervous contraction of her stomach muscles who her visitor was. Maeve's face appeared around the kitchen door. "It's Thane," she whispered. "Shall I send him away?"

"No, I'll see him." Why not? She could give him the news she was marrying Owain. There was no need to add that they wouldn't be leaving the country. Let Thane discover that for himself *after* she was safely married to a British subject.

Thane stood in the center of her small parlor, studying the boxes in varying stages of being packed with her few pieces of china and cutlery. "I see you're moving," he said, without preamble.

"I'm getting married," Eleanor replied, watching for his reaction and, to her disappointment, seeing no change in his expression.

"Owain Davies?"

"Yes."

He gave a small smile of triumph, one eyebrow raised in mock surprise. "Why, my dear Miss Hathaway, what a loss to the male population. When is the happy event to take place?"

"Tomorrow."

"Am I invited?"

"No. You'd make a better guest at a funeral."

"Probably. But I'll be there tomorrow. To make sure you haven't changed your mind. Good day, Miss Hathaway."

Even after he was gone, his presence seemed to linger in the room. Eleanor shivered and sat down abruptly on one of her trunks. She hadn't said where she was getting married, so she didn't really expect Thane to be there. But his visit had disturbed her deeply. She was still sitting on the trunk when Maeve appeared with the tea tray.

Maeve grinned as she poured the tea. "What did he say when you told him? I hope you rubbed his nose in it."

"Oh, yes," Eleanor replied, as airily as she could manage.

They drank their tea and Maeve said, "Go on, turn the cup around three times."

"If I let you read my tea leaves, will you come north with us?"

"I'll join you after the honeymoon," Maeve promised.

Eleanor turned her cup, thinking that she really would have preferred to have Maeve along on the honeymoon, so that she wouldn't have to be alone with Owain. Tomorrow she would marry a man who had not as yet even kissed her, at least not on the lips. The first time he gave her a brotherly peck on the cheek, he had told her that he realized she needed time to think of him as a husband rather than her good and true friend, and he was prepared to wait.

Maeve was studying the residue in her cup. "Well now, here's an interesting situation. The two men I saw last time are still here, bigger than life, but now I have an initial for one of them . . . it's a V."

"I don't know any V," Eleanor said.

"You're going to, believe me. You're going to know a V very well."

"Are you sure it isn't an O, for Owain?"

"I'm positive." She held the teacup at arm's length and scrutinized it again. "News from across the water."

"Probably a letter from my grandfather's lawyers. The trust fund he left for me will be mine on my eighteenth birthday."

Eleanor shivered noticeably, and Maeve looked up. "Someone walking on your grave?"

"I was just thinking how glad I am that I never had need of Grandfather's money. I could have drawn on the trust any time but his will said I had to go back to Boston to get it. Lucky for me I started earning my own keep at an early age."

"You never told me why you're so afraid of going back."

"No . . . I didn't." Unwilling to tell even Maeve of her fears, Eleanor stood up and started wrapping newspaper around a fragile china figurine that had been a gift from Tristan. Her grandfather had named Franklyn Yarborough executor of his estate. Sooner or later, if she wanted to collect her inheritance, she would have to face the demon of her nightmares, and she was afraid when she did she would kill him.

Maeve was still studying the tea leaves. "No, I don't think the news from across the water is from America, because the United States is part of a continent. I see news from a country surrounded by water. There's an E and a C involved."

"Evan? Charlotte? As far as I know he's up at Glendower, and the Lord knows where Charlotte is. It was strange what happened. She wrote and told me she got married in Italy, had a baby, and then was widowed and going back to Glendower as Evan's housekeeper. She stopped to see me with the handsomest baby and I was supposed to spend that summer at Glendower. But there was the fire and some sort of hushed-up scandal, and then Charlotte was just gone . . . vanished, and I never heard from her again.''

"I think she's coming back," Maeve said. "But not in the way you might expect. What a lot in this cup, Eleanor! I see a grand house and a plainer one, separated by trees.''

"Glendower and the grange," Eleanor said at once.

Maeve looked solemn. "You're going back there . . . and you'll be wearing black . . . mourning.''

Eleanor threw up her hand. "Enough! I don't want to hear any gloom. It's all nonsense anyway. Tomorrow I shall wear white, for my wedding . . . don't talk to me about funerals.''

The church was crowded, thanks to Tristan's legion of friends among the upper classes as well as in the theatrical world. Lord Ramsey had called on Eleanor and said he would be honored to give the bride away, and Eleanor accepted, although she was hurt that Owain had not been invited to meet the Ramseys.

Peter Maitland-Howard was to be Owain's best man, and he proved to be a charming golden-haired man with a magnificent curling moustache. Eyeing her own fair locks, Peter had glanced at the swarthy Owain and remarked, "He does seem to have a penchant for Saxons, doesn't he? Despite his fierce Celtic pride. He'd have bought land in Wales if I'd let him. I had to explain that we'd have had a hell of a job getting the horses over the mountains and onto English racetracks.''

"For a silent partner," Owain had responded good-naturedly, "you talk too much.''

Peeping out of a crack in the vestry door, Eleanor could see Peter's golden head brightening the gloom of the church as he stood waiting in front of the altar.

"Do close that door," Veronica hissed in her ear. "They'll see you.''

Eleanor did so, although she felt like flinging it even wider. She had had to ask Veronica to be her maid of honor, in view of Lord Ramsey giving her away, but it seemed that Veronica must lately have been on a continual eating binge, because she had now grown to an incredible size. Her pale blue gown had been let out several times, and even now threatened to burst at the seams. Eleanor had had nightmares about the gown flying off Veronica in the middle of the ceremony. There had been several arguments—about the color of the dresses as Veronica preferred pink to blue, about the choice of flowers for the bouquets, and a big one about the food at the reception—but the main point of contention had been Eleanor's insistence that Maeve also be a bridesmaid.

"A common servant in the wedding party?" Veronica had gasped in horror. "You're joking."

"Maeve is not a servant, she's my friend."

"She's a *dresser*." Veronica managed to make it sound as if Maeve were an untouchable. Even Delia had tried to persuade Eleanor that Maeve would be more comfortable as a guest, but Eleanor was adamant. There were two other bridesmaids, both lovely young actresses, who giggled together as they all waited in the vestry for the guests to take their places in the pews.

Eleanor found movement in her bridal gown somewhat difficult, as it had a long train, but she hopped nervously from one foot to another until it was time for the bridesmaids to put on her veil. A mirror had been placed on the vestry wall, and Eleanor peered at her reflection, seeing a ghostly, unreal figure with eyes as big as saucers. The misty veil descended over her face, and in the church, the organ began to play.

Oh, God, what am I doing? she thought in sudden panic as Lord Ramsey opened the vestry door and took her arm. Then it was too late, they were walking slowly up an aisle that seemed much longer than she remembered, and Owain stood at Peter's side, his black hair contrasting with Peter's blond hair. They turned to watch her progress, and she saw that Owain looked both proud and solemn. She wished he would smile at her, but he didn't. Peter gave her an encouraging grin and so did Maeve. Veronica looked very red in the face. Perhaps she was holding her breath to keep her gown intact.

Just before she reached Owain, out of the corner of her eye, she caught a glimpse of a lean, chiseled face wearing a mocking smile. Thane. So he had come after all. She didn't look at him.

"Dearly beloved, we are gathered here today . . ."

It's happening, Eleanor thought, oh, no, I can't let it. I don't want to be married, not even to my good and true friend Owain! She had a wild impulse to turn and run, but stood rooted to the spot.

I'll pretend it's a part I'm playing. Yes, that's what I'll do. I'm playing the part of a bride now . . . and later I'll play the part of Mrs. Owain Davies . . .

25

THE SHADOW HURLED itself toward him and Evan seized the man and hoisted him into the air, throwing him back toward the other two. They went down in a jumble of grunting bodies as Evan felt the tip of a knife rip along his arm, slitting his linen jacket cleanly but only scratching his flesh.

Turning, he kicked upward and saw the gleam of the knife blade as it flew from the man's hand. Evan reached into the darkness, attempting to grab the owner of the knife, but his hands met empty air.

The throbbing misery of his head, the blurring of his vision so that the night became a solid black wall, and the burning agony of his stomach were assailants far worse than those who circled him in the narrow alley like a pack of hyenas.

He battled to stay conscious, while the poison in his system inexorably dragged him toward oblivion. He could feel his knees giving way, and he clutched the air as if hoping to hold on to it. Beyond the range of his slowly fading sight, he heard muttered commands, the scraping of feet, and knew those faceless men were preparing for another attack.

Staggering backward, he felt a solid wall behind him and he braced himself against it, using sheer force of will to remain upright and conscious.

The first man who came at him had retrieved the knife, and it ripped his palm as he grabbed a wrist and snapped it. Then he was battered from all sides. He felt the blows but could no longer see, and blindly flailed with his fists to keep his attackers at bay.

In his last lucid moment, he heard a barked command and,

miraculously his assailants stopped beating him. As he crumpled slowly to the ground, he tried to recall whose voice that was . . . but the demons gnawing at his belly did not permit his thoughts to stray far, and so he slipped into a dark void without knowing who had come to his rescue.

Diagonal stilettos of sunlight entering cracks between wooden shutters pierced Evan's closed eyelids, and he raised them slightly. He lay on a mat on an unfamiliar floor, a pillow under his head.

A comfortable mixture of east and west coexisted around him. Wicker chairs, bamboo tables, and beautifully carved mahogany cabinets shared their space on the rattan floor mats with a solid English oak pianoforte, a Chippendale desk and a dresser filled with Wedgwood china. A faint but unmistakable odor of mildew permeated the room.

He was alone. A throbbing headache and a sick stomach that growled menacingly seemed to be the worst of his ailments. His hand was bandaged. He tried to raise his head but, unaccountably, he fell asleep again.

Some time later, he felt a thumb and forefinger prying up his eyelids and a musical voice said, "He's just sleeping." A pair of coppery brown eyes in a smooth brown face came into focus.

"This is Dr. Singh," said a familiar voice. "He took care of you last night. You were drugged, Lord Athmore."

Drackleby came into view, peering over the shoulder of the Sinhalese doctor.

"Drugged? No . . . food poisoning," Evan said. It was an effort to speak—his voice seemed to roll out in slow waves. The doctor offered him some water, and he drank it gratefully.

"Drugged," Drackleby repeated. "The food was perfectly safe. Actually, the curry kills most of the germs, although you do have to watch out for some of the cooks; they like to strain the broth through their loincloths. By the way, you're in my bungalow in Cinnamon Gardens, which is the Hyde Park of Colombo. We brought you here last night, since we were afraid your assailants might have another go at you if we stayed in Dr. Singh's house. You'll be safe here. Sorry about putting you on the floor, but we didn't have a big enough bed."

"I'm grateful to you," Evan said. "Also somewhat embarrassed that you were evidently able to fend off my attackers whereas I was not."

"Ah, but I had the advantage of a gun. A souvenir I picked up in Alexandria, as a matter of fact. I don't usually carry one, even on the job . . . did I tell you I'm a policeman? Anyway, I'd been home on leave and, in fact, am not yet back on duty. Ah, yes, Dr. Singh, I certainly think you could leave now. I shall take good care of our patient."

Evan feared that the slightest movement on his part might cause him to retch, so he lay still and listened. Drackleby opened the shutters, revealing a stone verandah screened by trellised vines and creepers ablaze with blossoms.

"You see, my dear Lord Athmore, a policeman is one of those unfortunate beings who cannot separate his job from the rest of his life, not even when on leave. I was curious as to why a young man who could have spent the long voyage with anyone he chose, including some rather attractive young women, instead went out of his way to make the acquaintance of a man who clearly would have preferred to be alone . . . yourself. Not to mention the fact that most people are reluctant to associate with someone quite exceptionally different from the rest of us."

Evan's head felt as if it would burst. "I'm sorry . . . I don't understand."

"I dogged your footsteps, too, of course, but with less evil intent. By the way, I've already been to the Grand Orient Hotel, and Fenmore's no longer there. But don't worry, I'll find him. I don't believe Keribunda was involved. He appeared with a rickshaw shortly after I arrested two of your attackers."

"Are you saying Fenmore organized the assault? But why? I didn't know him before boarding the ship, and I thought we got along very well at sea."

"According to the two men I have in custody, they were to be paid by Fenmore for killing you, Lord Athmore. If you don't believe Fenmore wants you dead for personal reasons, then I suggest you examine your circle of acquaintances for someone who paid him to get rid of you."

Evan had a quick vision of Stephen coming to see him sail on the *Southern Star*. To make sure both he and Fenmore were aboard? Surely Stephen wouldn't have gone so far . . . but Zoe would, and Stephen needed Zoe like a bee craves nectar.

"Now," Drackleby said brightly, "about your friend Charlotte . . . She calls herself Charlotte Briggs now, not Danforth, but I'm quite sure she is one and the same. She is on a trip up the mountains at present, visiting a village where some of her girls came from, I expect in the hope of sending them home. Some of the Tamil girls come down from the north and then are afraid to return. You'd better stay with me until she gets back to Colombo. I don't want you wandering about until Fenmore is caught. He may have hired other assassins. You do make a rather large target, you know. Now, we must find somewhere for you to sleep. You can't spend another night on my living room floor. You'll need a proper bed and a mosquito net."

The droning voice went on, and even the mention of Charlotte could not stop Evan from falling asleep again.

In the following days, Evan found he frequently dropped off to sleep at inappropriate times. Dr. Singh said it was an aftereffect of the drug he'd received, and it would wear off in time. The doctor became vague and evasive when Evan asked the·nature of the drug, saying only that it was probably a venom.

"Don't press him," Drackleby advised later. "He practices exclusively in the native quarter and is uneasy dealing with a sahib. But if I'd taken you to a European doctor, you'd likely be dead by now."

Evan still didn't particularly like Drackleby, but was beginning to recognize that the man was lonely, and therefore tended to be both over-talkative and belligerent. The aura of hostility he projected was probably his policeman's suspicion of the motives of those with whom he usually dealt. Still, he was an excellent host. His bungalow was comfortable, staffed with a butler he called his *appo,* and several sari-clad women servants.

"Tell me all you've learned about Charlotte Danforth . . . I mean Briggs," Evan said, as they sat on the verandah having a before-dinner drink.

"Originally she went to one of the jungle missions as a teacher. Then, several months later, she returned to Colombo and made inquiries about returning to England. Very unusual, since missionaries have to agree to remain a specified length of time. The serious illness of a family member or bereavement would be about the only reason not to complete the period of service."

"But she didn't return to England," Evan pointed out.

"No. It seems the society didn't believe her story that her baby had died, since it's unlikely that any woman would take such an assignment and leave a baby behind. They refused to pay her way back."

Evan stared straight ahead, unwilling to let Drackleby see his distress. So Charlotte believed her son was dead. Oh, God, if there is any justice in the universe, he thought, surely Zoe must pay for her deeds, sooner or later.

Drackleby continued, "According to Singh, soon after that, Miss Briggs came upon a young prostitute giving birth in the street. She later managed to convince the society that if the missionaries' primary duty was to help sinners, then someone should be caring for, and attempting to save the souls of the prostitutes. Miss Briggs runs a sort of clinic . . . unwed mothers, diseased prostitutes, beggars. A hopeless task, of course, and a dangerous one in these perilous times."

"Dangerous? How so?"

"She refuses to accept the caste system, for one thing. For another she cares for both Sinhalese and Tamils."

"What difference does that make, if she's trying to convert them all to Christianity, anyway? They're just different religions, aren't they, like protestants and catholics?"

Drackleby smiled tolerantly. "Most of the Tamils were originally brought here from India to work as coolies. They are Hindus, whereas the Sinhalese are Buddhist. The Sinhalese are in the majority, and the two groups have coexisted for a couple of thousand years, but the Sinhalese are acutely aware of the proximity of the Indian state of Tamil Nadu, home of fifty million Tamils, with close linguistic and religious ties to the Tamils here. While India is under British rule, the Tamils here are beginning to talk about Sinhalese oppression. We don't want the kind of unrest in Ceylon they're trying to deal with in India."

"So this is why you are so against missionary work."

"No one benefits from civil war."

"Least of all the Raj," Evan remarked.

"Spoken like a Welshman. You Celts have been making nationalist noise for donkey's years."

"You accuse *Lord Athmore* of being a Welshman?" Evan asked with mock incredulity.

"You spoke in Welsh when you collapsed in the alley."

Evan leaned back in his wicker chair, feeling pools of clammy perspiration form on his body in the suffocating heat. "I'm beginning to think I should go to the village where Charlotte is, rather than waiting here."

"Bad idea. The monsoons are coming. The villages will be cut off then. She'll have to return soon. I haven't found Fenmore yet, either.''

The heat seemed even more oppressive at night. It pressed in like a sticky pall, sapping strength, draining will. Charlotte forced herself to step into the rank-smelling hovel.

What appeared to be a pile of rags on the floor shifted and began to stir. A stick-thin arm emerged from the rags, feebly waving in the fetid air as if seeking alms.

As her eyes adjusted to the darkness, Charlotte saw a face at the end of the emaciated arm, with wrinkled skin and eyes so sunken in their sockets and filmed with cataracts that they resembled the sightless stare of a dead fish. The woman's lips and remaining teeth were stained purple from a lifetime habit of betel nut chewing. Worst of all were the shriveled tattoos still gaudily evident on the cheeks of the parody of a face. Charlotte had long ago learned that only prostitutes had their faces tattooed. She tried to close her nostrils against the reek of opium.

Turning to Rhani, who hovered in the doorway, Charlotte said, ''She may be beyond hearing you, but speak to her. It will ease her passing.''

''She isn't my mother. I don't believe you,'' Rhani said sullenly. ''My mother married a wealthy merchant and went to Bombay.''

''The poor soul has been here in Colombo all the time. I had hoped that you would have been more compassionate than your brother. Keribunda refused to even come here,'' Charlotte said quietly.

She kneeled on the dirt floor beside the woman and held a bowl of broth to the stained mouth. ''Try to take a little, please.'' Although Charlotte wasn't aware of the girl's departure, she understood Rhani's terror of facing what would ultimately be her own fate.

Charlotte had given up trying to get the woman to take food and was bathing the skeletal body when a nervous young girl came to tell her that her younger sister was about to give birth.

Plodding wearily through the sodden heat of the night, Charlotte reflected on the hopelessness of attempting to ease the passage from life to death of one prostitute, then helping bring another into the world. But perhaps the child would be a boy.

The clinic was overflowing, as usual, with street girls suffering from every imaginable disease and injury. At least now Charlotte had a bona fide doctor to assist with the worst cases, and, since he was a bachelor, some of the upper caste women had begun to send their servants to help out, in the hope he would reciprocate by accepting their social invitations. When Charlotte originally opened the clinic, she had done most of the work herself. The suffering of these women had been so terrible, that Charlotte's own grief and anguish had been set aside as she devoted every waking hour to the service of others.

But her health was beginning to fail, the attacks of malaria were more frequent, and the task she had embarked upon had become overwhelming. For some time her superiors in the society had urged her to go home. They didn't know that she had no home to return to, no one in the world who cared whether she lived or died. Even Eleanor had cut her out of her life, not even bothering to respond to any of the letters she had sent. Although, recalling her meeting with Lady Ramsey, Charlotte wondered if perhaps her letters had never reached Eleanor.

The instant Charlotte entered the clinic, a turbaned young man sprang into view. His eyes wild, pupils dilated, he raised a finger and pointed at her. "The curse of Allah be upon you. You defile our people. Turn our daughters into whores. Force them to lie with untouchables. Kill their babies. Allah's wrath will strike you dead."

Charlotte squared her shoulders and stared him down. Several of the women screamed at him to leave and, after a moment, he did so. She was accustomed to such incidents and to name-calling. Occasionally, she'd had to minister to women suffering the effects of botched abortions, and this had earned her the name "baby-killer." But there was no time to dwell on the injustice of such accusations. She had not caused the problems of these women, and sought only to ease their suffering.

The young, expectant mother, daughter of a drumbeater, was well into her labor. She and her sister had been turned out into the streets by their father because no suitable husbands could be found for them within their own caste. Each caste kept to its own work and was heartily despised by the caste above them. Even the drumbeaters had a caste under them to do their washing—the pariah caste, who lived in abject filth and poverty. Most of the converts were from the lower castes, further alienating the church from Sinhalese society as a whole.

Charlotte washed her hands to remove the stench of the dying woman and prepared to deliver a baby.

Just after midnight a frail infant girl slept beside her exhausted fourteen-year-old mother, and Charlotte sat in one of the few chairs, too drained by the smothering humidity to sleep. She had traveled back to Colombo the previous day, and within twenty-four hours had cared for a dying woman, beseeched a number of young prostitutes to halt their descent into hell, been reviled by one of the men who no doubt patronized her patients, and delivered a baby. She ached in every limb, and silently prayed that she was not coming down with another attack of malaria.

A sudden violent roar rent the hot still air, tearing the heavens to shreds, reverberating across the canopy of the night. Everyone was startled to wakefulness, as the clinic was lit with the forked intermittent glare of lightning.

The roof shuddered as a clap of thunder like the volley of a cannonade exploded overhead. A distant hissing grew in volume until it became the swishing sound of drenching rain.

The monsoon had burst at last.

Charlotte jumped to her feet to rush around closing shutters, which were already banging in the wind. Gusts of cool air refreshed yet chilled perspiration-soaked bodies. The smell of dampness already carried the threat of imminent mildew. She felt clammy, limp, and knew she would soon find the constant drumming of rain on roof and walls nerve-wracking.

The door rattled and then blew open. Silhouetted against a solid sheet of rain lit by lightning stood a majestically tall figure. He bent his head in order to enter and, as if in a dream, Charlotte moved slowly toward him.

Sweeping his sodden hat from his dripping hair, Evan bowed. "Forgive the rather abrupt entrance, but . . . ."

Charlotte couldn't speak. Long held back sobs threatened to erupt, and she kept them at bay by holding her breath. Wordlessly she held out her hands, and Evan clasped them in his. She noted briefly that one of his hands was bandaged, that there were streaks of gray at his temples, and a new gentleness in his eyes.

They stood looking at one another as the rattle of the rain grew to a roar, then, becoming aware of sleeping bodies on the floor all around them, Evan said, "If we could go somewhere private . . . ?"

"I . . . I live here," Charlotte said.

"Then let us go out to the rickshaw driver, who must be drowning by now, and return to my lodgings."

Fatigue and shock and the onset of the monsoon all overwhelmed her at once, and Charlotte swayed dizzily on her feet. Evan picked her up and carried her out into the tempest.

Long before they reached Drackleby's bungalow in Cinnamon Gardens, Evan said, "Your son is alive, Charlotte. He's a fine boy and he's in boarding school. I've come to take you home to him . . . and to ask you to be my wife."

26

A THUNDERSTORM WAS rumbling in from the channel as Eleanor and Owain arrived at the small hotel on the south coast where they were to spend their wedding night.

Although they raced from the hansom cab, they were drenched to the skin before they reached shelter. In their room overlooking a wildly churning sea, they faced each other breathlessly.

Eleanor glanced nervously at the window, where rain slashed in silver daggers across the black glass. She had been afraid of thunderstorms ever since that day at Glendower when lightning had felled the tree, injuring Owain. The day he had saved her life, and she had incurred an everlasting debt to him. "Pull the curtains, would you, Owain?"

As Owain went to close the curtains, she wondered if the storm inspired any feelings of fear in him, too, but when he turned to face her, his dark eyes told her that all he saw or heard was her. There was both love and concern in his gaze. "Off with those wet clothes, Ellie, *bach*. We can't have you catching another cold."

Ignoring his own dripping suit, he started toward the door.

"Where are you going?" Eleanor asked, removing her sodden cloak.

"To get some coal to light a fire. Summer or no, there's a damp chill in this room."

"Oh, no, don't bother—"

He smiled at her over his shoulder. "You get into your nightgown and into bed. I shan't bring anyone up here. I'll light it myself."

After he left she undressed quickly and put on her white cambric gown, delicately embroidered with white silk roses, a gift from Maeve. Dear Owain, he probably left to give her privacy while she undressed. The room wasn't that cold.

Thunder pounded the sky, shaking the roof, and she leaped into bed and pulled the covers over her head. Minutes later she heard the door open and Owain's soft chuckle. "Are you in there somewhere, Ellie?"

She peered at him over the top of the sheet, grinning sheepishly. He carried a coal scuttle and bundle of kindling wood. She said, "Talk to me, I hate storms."

"You were a lovely bride today, Ellie. My heart almost burst with love." He kneeled in front of the grate and began to lay the fire.

A flash of lightning flicked across the window curtains. Eleanor shivered. "Do you think about that . . . other storm . . . when you hear thunder and see lightning?"

"Only to remind myself that lightning doesn't strike twice in the same place."

When the fire flared to life, he stood up and began to strip off his clothes. Fascinated, Eleanor watched. His shoulders were broad, and when he raised his arms to pull his undershirt over his head, she saw the muscles ripple beneath his skin.

He hesitated before removing his trousers. "Ellie . . . my leg is still badly scarred. Perhaps you should look away."

Blushing, she turned her head. A moment later he turned down the lamp, leaving the room lit by firelight. She felt the bed move and he slipped in beside her. She tensed, lying rigid on the very edge of the mattress. The storm had momentarily distracted her from the coming ordeal of the consummation of her marriage.

Owain's hand, warm, calloused, closed lightly around her arm. "Ellie, *bach*," he whispered. "Let me hold you close to my heart. Don't be afraid of me. There's no need for us to . . . there's no hurry. It's been a long hard day for you, and you were very ill not long ago. You're tired and besides, you need time to get your strength back and to . . . get used to me. We'll have the rest of our lives to be husband and wife."

Gratefully, Eleanor moved into the comforting circle of his arms, feeling the warmth of his body envelop her. She sighed contentedly as the sounds of the storm began to recede. It was very nice to drift off to sleep feeling warm and secure.

The following day fitful sunshine chased away the clouds for a time, and they walked along the windswept promenade and threw bread crumbs to the gulls. It was like old times, and they talked and laughed easily together. That night she again lay close to him, and he stroked her hair and massaged her shoulders and kissed her eyelids lightly, and she felt loved and safe and so relaxed that sleep came without warning.

It rained again the next day, so they went to a seaside revue, which was wonderfully awful, with common-looking dancers, a wobbly tenor and a comedian who relied heavily upon double entendres. Afterwards they had a supper of fish and chips and ale, and took a bottle of wine back to their room.

That night they went to bed slightly tipsy, laughing at nonsensical things and playfully tickling one another. Then Owain pulled her into his arms and kissed her mouth, and his kiss was thrilling in a way she had not expected.

After a moment he drew back, trembling. Wanting him to continue, she pressed her lips to his again, but he seemed tethered somehow, unavailable, and she was disappointed.

His fingers went to her hair, gently separating the strands, and his other hand drifted lightly up and down her back. She clung to him, wanting him to kiss her in that desperately hungry way again, which was ever so slightly rough and demanding. But his mouth was tentative now, as if he were afraid of hurting her. Recklessly she allowed her hands to seek him out, to feel the taut muscles of his back, to travel around to his chest and press hard pectorals.

She felt his hands on her body, under her nightgown, and she squirmed closer, still lost in a rosy haze of wine, warm and drowsy and almost unaware of what was happening.

It seemed that hours passed, but perhaps she was too sleepy to know. His lips brushed every part of her face and throat, his hands traversed gently as a breeze over her flesh as if worshiping her body. When at last he came to her in the act of love she thought that, apart from a single stab of pain which seemed to worry him more than it did her, she had dreaded something that was really quite inconsequential.

She was unprepared for his apparent explosion of pleasure, or for the instant remorse that followed it. "Oh, Ellie, my sweet wife, forgive me . . . I didn't mean to take you so soon. But you're so beautiful, it just seemed to happen. Did I hurt you? Oh, God, don't let me have hurt you!"

Eleanor shut her ears to his apologies, which she felt diminished him and certainly irritated her. When she didn't respond, he said brokenly, "Please don't hate me. For I love you so much. I love you enough to die for you, Ellie, *bach,* and I always will."

Almost asleep, she murmured, "I love you, too, Owain, my good and true friend."

There was a short silence. "I'm your husband now."

"Yes, of course you are. And it's all right, I mean, about making love."

"No, it wasn't all right. You . . . you didn't care for it."

"I'm not supposed to, silly. I'm a woman." She sighed, and turned over and went to sleep.

In her dream she ranted and raved at someone who stood in the shadows, just out of sight, just out of reach. She wasn't sure what it was she screamed at him, because in the way of dreaming there was no sound. But she thought it was something about being handled with kid gloves. It didn't make sense, but the dream lingered in her mind after she awakened.

Owain's farm in Cheshire proved to be a small brick house surrounded by barns and cow sheds. Upon their arrival in the late evening, Eleanor screamed in fright as dozens of gray shadows darted from the haystacks.

"My God, they're rats!" she shrieked, flinging herself into her husband's arms.

Owain gave her an indulgent hug and said, "Hard to get rid of them on a farm. But I'll set some traps to try to keep them out of the house."

They went into a musty smelling house that seemed smaller than her London flat. When Owain lit an oil lamp, Eleanor looked around in dismay.

A dark sideboard with a mottled mirror filled one wall, and a gateleg table was crowded so close to it that when the sideboard drawers were opened, they collided with the chairs around the table. A pair of wooden rocking chairs flanked a black-leaded fireplace. A large aspidistra plant, dense and somber, stood on a stand in front of the window, creating gloom rather than relieving it. This room was evidently used for both dining and sitting.

"It will be more cheerful in here in the daytime. I could light a fire, but it's a bit late," Owain said, a worried note in his voice suggesting that his farm had looked grander before he saw it through Eleanor's eyes. He added hopefully, "There's a nice view from the window of a stream and a copse of birch."

They were tired after their long journey and Eleanor dispirited-

ly followed Owain up a narrow staircase to an equally claustro-
phobic bedroom. She sat on the edge of the bed and promptly
sank deep into a feather mattress.

It occurred to her that now their honeymoon was over they
would have their own bedrooms, and she suddenly felt bereft at
the thought of losing the comfort of falling asleep in his arms. To
mask her distress, she asked briskly, "Where is your room?"

Owain placed the lamp he had carried upstairs on a marble
washstand and turned to look at her. "This is *our* room. Look,
Ellie, *bach*, I know you lived with the upper classes and it's their
habit to sleep in separate rooms, but it's my belief . . . and I'm
not alone in it by any means, that a man and wife should share the
same bed."

Feeling chastised and not liking the feeling, but too exhausted
to clear the air, Eleanor looked around. "Where is my dressing
room?"

"You can undress here. There is no dressing room."

"And where will I bathe?" she inquired icily.

"There's a hip bath downstairs in the pantry. Tomorrow you
can heat some water and put it in front of the fire. Ellie, have a
little patience. I can't give you all you've been used to right away,
but we've more than most young couples start out with. Come on,
let me help you get into your nightgown and take down your
hair."

"I don't need your help. Good heavens, Owain, I'm not
completely helpless, you know. Don't treat me like a child."

Now, why had she snapped at him like that? She supposed it
was the gloom and isolation of her new home, and the fact that
she already missed London's lights and throngs of people. She
couldn't bear the hurt look that crept over his face, but before she
could make amends he said gruffly, "I must go downstairs to see
everything's in order."

Minutes later when he returned, she had undressed, donned her
nightgown, pulled the covers around her chin, and was feigning
sleep.

The following day she learned that there were no servants other
than a boy Owain had hired to help him take care of the horses.
He seemed to think she should be grateful when he said the boy
would also milk the cows and feed the chickens, to relieve her of
these chores.

"But who will do the cooking and cleaning?" she asked.

"You, of course, you little ninny. And you'll have Maeve to

help you when she gets here. Why, you'll have hours to spend
with your books and playacting, at least until the children come
along.''

Eleanor counted the days until Maeve's arrival, knowing true
loneliness for the first time in her life. Owain rose long before
dawn and worked until dusk. She thought perhaps the hard labor
would tire him so that he would only want to sleep after they went
to bed, but his sexual appetite seemed to increase as time went
by. It was she who had to plead tiredness, faintness, or illness, or
else race him to bed and pretend to be asleep.

It wasn't that she didn't enjoy the closeness of hugging and
kissing and caressing, but the sex act itself always left her feeling
vaguely angry; that anger spilled over into the rest of their
relationship, and so it was to be avoided at all costs.

She considered telling him she found it impossible to sleep
with another body in the bed, but there was only one other
bedroom which they would have to give to Maeve, and a tiny box
room that Owain said one day he would convert to a nursery.

Married life, Eleanor decided, was worse than being in prison.
Owain was patient and affectionate, and he promised that once
the stables were renovated, exercise track laid, the fences repaired
and he had acquired the horses he needed for breeding purposes,
that he would be able to spend more time with her. Eventually he
would be able to hire people to ease their burden. He painted a
rosy picture of the future that did little to ease the bleak present.

Two weeks after they moved into the farmhouse, Maeve
arrived, and Eleanor couldn't wait to unburden herself. Maeve sat
quietly at the kitchen table drinking a cup of tea as Eleanor
recounted her woes. ''Look at my hands! They're ruined. I have
to wash Owain's clothes as well as my own, and I have to scrub
the floors and wash dishes, and I never have time to do my hair or
an opportunity to wear a pretty dress and, oh, Maeve, I feel like
an old lady! At night I lie in bed and hear rats running along the
rafters and I'm terrified to go into the chicken pen to get the eggs
because it's full of mice.'' She dissolved into tears.

Maeve's arms went around her, and Eleanor buried her face in
her friend's firm shoulder. ''Is he likely to walk in on us?''
Maeve whispered.

''No . . . he w—won't come back to the house until after
dark.''

''Your voice sounds hoarse. Do you have a sore throat?''

Eleanor sighed. ''Yes. It's so damp here, I've had a cold. I thought I was getting over it, but now I think it's going into my chest.''

"You're going straight to bed," Maeve said. "With a hot water bottle. Have you any rum? We'll put a drop in your tea. You have a nice nap, that will make you feel better.''

"I can't Maeve . . . they'll want dinner soon. They eat in the middle of the day, and they're so hungry when they come in. I've got to get the clothes in off the line, it looks like it might rain—''

Maeve's capable hand touched her brow. "Fever, too. Oh, Eleanor, you're barely over the flu. No more arguments. Off to bed. You leave the dinner and the washing to me.''

"I *can't* be ill again," Eleanor wailed. "And you've only just arrived, I can't let you do all the work—''

But by nightfall a knifelike pain in her chest made every breath a torture, and she hardly had enough strength to raise her head. Maeve sent Owain for the doctor.

The last thing she remembered was the dread word, "Pneumonia.''

Maeve walked slowly down the stairs, so weary that all she could do when she reached the kitchen was to collapse into the wooden rocker and sway gently back and forth.

It was almost dawn, and they had been at Eleanor's beside all night as her illness reached its climax. Owain remained with his wife while Maeve went to prepare breakfast. The horses and cows would need him now, despite his sleepless night.

Eleanor had been deathly ill for weeks, and it was clear that she would not have the strength to get out of bed for some time to come.

The running of the house and care of the invalid had presented no difficulty to Maeve, since she had come from a working class background, and her own father had been an invalid for most of her childhood. While her mother worked as a theatrical dresser, it had fallen upon Maeve to run their household. She had learned to cook and clean and launder at an early age, but she was strong and healthy, and so whisked through her tasks.

Despite her worry about Eleanor, Maeve found her new surroundings and tasks much to her liking. Instead of the dreary terrace house in a working-class neighborhood of the big city where she had toiled as a child, or a dismal room in a boarding house that had been her lodgings as a dresser, she now had the running of what to her was a spacious farmhouse, surrounded by lovely countryside. And Owain was such a kind and considerate man, so hard-working, that Maeve felt Eleanor's complaints about him upon her arrival must surely have been due to the onset of her illness. Then, too, it must have been a shock to leave the bright lights of the theater, a flat that was kept clean by a daily maid, and meals in fancy cafes, to say nothing of her own services in taking care of Eleanor's hair and wardrobe, for life on a farm. Maeve had tried to warn her, but how could the poor little thing have had any concept of what the life of a farmer's wife would be?

Maeve dragged herself to her feet and went into the kitchen, which was aromatic with the pungent scent of drying bunches of thyme and rosemary hanging from the rafters. She lit the stove and carved a thick slice from the side of bacon that also hung from the ceiling. When Owain came downstairs a little while later, she placed a plate of eggs and bacon on the table and poured tea.

"She's sleeping peacefully now," Owain said. He picked up a hefty slice of bread and bit into it.

"Thank the good Lord," Maeve breathed. "The doctor said he'd be back this morning. I'll give her a nice wash when she wakes up."

Owain's tired eyes met hers. "How can we ever thank you? I don't know how I'd have managed without you."

"She's my friend. It wasn't any trouble."

"And in the midst of it all, you found time to bake bread. This is very good, indeed. How did you ever learn to do so many different things? I thought you just knew how to dress my wife."

Maeve smiled, pleased by the praise. "I had to learn to cook when I was little. My Mum worked as a dresser, too, and my Dad was an invalid."

He stuffed food into his mouth and rose. "I must go. The boy can't handle the stock by himself."

That evening, Maeve walked down the lane to meet him as he came back from the fields. Owain saw her coming, a breeze blowing her skirts and the fresh, white pinafore she wore. She always looked so well-scrubbed, her skin and hair burnished clean. She was bigger and stronger than Eleanor, and walked with an unself-conscious stride. She reminded Owain of a sturdy Clydesdale mare, built for comfort and stamina, rather than speed and high spirits. Her capable presence had been a Godsend these past anxious weeks, but more than that, Owain liked Maeve for her honesty and cheerfulness.

When she reached him, she smiled shyly. "I wanted a word with you before you get to the house, just in case Eleanor overheard."

"She's all right? What did the doctor say?"

"She's past the worst, as we thought. But he says she will have to be very, very careful for a while. He doesn't know how well her lungs will heal yet. There's something else . . ." A cloud appeared over Maeve's sunny expression. "He doesn't know if she'll ever be able to sing onstage again."

"She doesn't have to," Owain said promptly. "That's all behind her now."

Maeve fell into step beside him. "You know she misses the theater very much. I think it would do her good to see some of her old friends. Before I left London, I heard Tristan Cressey was going to open a new play in the provinces, and, well . . . I wondered if you'd mind if I wrote and asked him and some of her friends to come and visit her?"

Owain felt a stab of jealousy. Eleanor had assured him that she and Tristan were only friends, but Owain found it impossible to believe that any man on earth could not want her as much as he did. "She won't be strong enough to have company for a long time yet."

"But when she is . . ." Maeve persisted.

Against his better judgment, Owain agreed that she could invite any of Eleanor's theatrical friends to visit her. He silently hoped that it would not be Tristan who accepted.

Maeve had polished the furniture with beeswax until it gleamed and laid the table with Eleanor's best linen and china teacups. She had pulled the curtains back to let in the daylight, and lit a fire in the hearth. But the room still looked dismal, shabby, and small as a coffin.

"Perhaps if we took the aspidistra out of the window?" Eleanor asked despairingly. She sat in the rocking chair, a blanket over her lap.

"Now, don't fret about how the room looks. It's you he's coming to see," Maeve said. "And look, here they come!"

The next moment, Tristan swept into the room and flung himself dramatically at Eleanor's feet, seized her hands and held them close to his heart. "What's all this about your being ill? I thought you'd done that role."

Eleanor smiled ruefully, but her eyes lit up for the first time in weeks. "So did I. But I'm much better, really. Oh, Tristan, I'm so glad to see you!"

Owain, who had gone to the railway station to pick up Tristan, now stood awkwardly in the background. After a moment he said, "I'd better go and see to the stock. I'll be back soon." He limped outside and Maeve, wearing a worried frown, watched him go.

Tristan rose and took the other fireside chair, then immediately began to regale Eleanor with news and gossip of the theater and their mutual friends. After a while, Maeve excused herself and went outside to take down the washing, quite sure they hadn't noticed her exit.

When they were alone, Tristan asked, "When are you going to give up this charade and get back to work? I'm quite sure all this illness is the result of your denying your talent."

Eleanor sighed. "Owain doesn't want me to go back on the stage. I suppose I should have discussed it with him before we were married, but, well . . ."

"Out of the frying pan and into the fire," Tristan said. "Why didn't you confide in me the real reason you married him?"

"What do you mean?" Eleanor asked cautiously.

"You can stop playing the dutiful wife now, love. Maeve told me the whole story. Now don't be cross with her, because she's worried about you, too. Darling Eleanor, that dreadful Thane man couldn't have had you deported."

"Oh, God, Maeve shouldn't have told you that. Besides, that's not the only reason I married Owain."

"Ah, so it was one of the reasons? Eleanor, Eleanor. I hate to pick on you when you're in such a poor state of health, but I do think I need to have a little chat with you. Lately you seem to have gone from one disastrous decision to another, and it occurs to me that you simply don't know instinctively that actors are not people."

"Oh, Tristan, what are you talking about?"

"I'm trying to tell you that whatever it is that causes us to practice our make-believe in front of an audience sets us apart from normal people. Fact is, we shouldn't even associate with ordinary souls."

"That's utter nonsense. Are you saying I shouldn't associate with Owain, or Maeve?"

Tristan leaned forward and regarded her with the brooding gaze that had caused female hearts to flutter for two decades. "For you, acting is more important than anything . . . or anyone.

You'll muck up the lives of everyone who loves you, believe me. You'll make a mess of being a wife and a worse one of being a mother, if you ever fall into that trap. They were never meant to be temporary roles, but that's what you'll make of them."

"Why didn't you tell me this *before* I married Owain?"

"You wouldn't have listened. You never do. But when Maeve told me how ill you were, I decided I'd better speak now or forever hold my peace. Get out now, Eleanor, before it's too late."

"What do you mean?"

"Leave him, before the role of wife becomes the dual role of wife and mother. Come back to Liverpool with me. We're at the Playhouse and doing rather well. We hope to open in London in the autumn. You can stay with me until you're able to go back to work. You can understudy if you like. You've got marriage out of your system now, and it's time to get on with your career. Your real one, not the silly singing one."

"Tristan, that's the most outrageous thing you've ever suggested. If I felt stronger I'd throw something at you. As it is, I think it's best if I forget what you just said."

"Very well, but remember this. When you're ready to become the dramatic actress nature intended you to be, come to me at any time and I'll take care of your financial needs. I won't tolerate your going back to variety shows, but when you're ready to be an actress again . . ."

"Thank you, but I don't need anyone's financial support. My grandfather left me a considerable sum of money that I haven't touched yet."

"Good Lord! Maeve tells me you've been taking care of this farmhouse without help. Why on earth don't you use some of your grandfather's money to make life a little easier for yourself?"

"It won't be mine until I'm eighteen, and I have to go back to Boston to claim it," Eleanor said. She didn't add that Owain had already decided that her inheritance would be invested in horseflesh. Of course, he had no idea that Stansfield Hathaway had been a wealthy man, and was expecting only a small bequest. Eleanor had been vague about the extent of her grandfather's fortune because she had no idea how much of it had been bequeathed to her. Since she had become her husband's chattel upon her marriage, it now belonged to him, anyway.

Tristan said, "This place is as dreary as a tomb. I should have screaming fits if I had to live here. You must come to town and see my play as soon as possible. Maeve could bring you. I shall speak with your husband.''

Owain waited until Tristan had departed and Maeve was in bed before turning to Eleanor with fury on his face. ''Why didn't you ask me in private if you could go and see his damn play? Letting him bring it up, with Maeve there, too, meant I had to give in. We couldn't discuss it.''

''Give in?'' Eleanor said. ''Surely you don't begrudge me having a day in town? A matinee, tea?''

''No, of course not. I just object to being told by an outsider what my wife needs.''

''Tristan isn't an outsider. He's my friend. Just as you used to be . . .'' Eleanor felt her lip tremble and turned her head away.

''I'm your husband now, Ellie *bach*,'' Owain said, his voice softening. ''You and I, we're closer than friends, we have to consider each other's feelings before we go off and do something on our own. I can't leave the stock until I can afford to hire a man, or I'd gladly take you to see a play. Oh, Ellie, I love you so. Be patient, please.''

He picked up her hand and massaged it. ''Besides, you're not strong enough yet to go out.''

She jerked her hand from his. ''Don't you understand? I'm shriveling up and dying in this house. I must leave for a while or I shall go mad. You don't have to come with me; Maeve will accompany me to Liverpool next week and be my chaperone. We'll stay overnight with Tristan.''

His face closed up into tight lines of hurt and anger. ''What if I forbid you to go?''

She felt sparks fly from her eyes. ''I'd be more determined than ever to go. If you wanted an obedient farm wife, you picked the wrong woman.'' Her voice cracked horribly, and she was breathing raggedly. She'd had trouble breathing since the pneumonia, especially when she was upset.

''You're not well enough—'' he began, but Eleanor was on her feet and flouncing from the room. To Maeve's surprise, she crawled into bed with her that night.

Tristan's play was wonderful. Eleanor sat in the audience enthralled by the magic of make-believe. He portrayed the brooding, romantic hero in a Gothic tale of love, betrayal, and vengeance. The actress playing the object of his desire was less than thrilling, however, and Eleanor ached to be up on stage giving as impassioned a performance as Tristan.

The second act ended with the foreshadowing of tragedy, and as the curtain came down Eleanor wiped the tears from her eyes and rose to her feet to go backstage during the interval. At her side, Maeve was weeping openly. "Oh, please don't let her die! Eleanor, do you think Margot is really dying? Have you seen the play before?"

"No, I don't know how it ends," Eleanor answered, sniffling into her handkerchief. "Let's go and have a glass of wine in Tristan's dressing room."

The dressing room was crowded with friends and fellow cast members but upon seeing her, Tristan exclaimed, "There you are, dearest Eleanor. Tell me I was magnificent."

"You were magnificent. The play is the best you've ever done. Who wrote it?"

"A young Irish playwright named Sean Connell. Wait till you see the third act. The ending will surprise you."

Maeve peered at her more closely in the brighter light. "You look awfully pale, Eleanor, and your eyes are very bright. Are you sure you feel all right?"

"Yes, yes. I feel alive again just smelling the greasepaint."

Tristan handed her a glass of wine. "You're not really going back to that dreadful farmhouse tomorrow, are you?"

"I promised I would." She drank the wine quickly, hoping to drive away the specter of Owain's hurt expression, dismal rooms and endless chores. At her side, a male voice said, "I say, you're Eleanor Hathaway, aren't you? I heard you sing in London. You have an enchanting voice."

Smiling, she turned to face a handsome young man wearing the familiar stagestruck expression of rapture. He was no doubt one of Tristan's upper-class friends. Oh, how wonderful it was to be dressed up and surrounded by exciting people and to be admired again! To think all this had been going on all the while she was slaving away over washboards and scrubbing brushes.

Tristan had taken a large house in Princes Park for the duration of the play, and several actors were staying with him. Servants had been hired, and Tristan lived in his usual extravagant style even in the provinces. He had a substantial private income, so was not dependent upon his earnings as an actor. Eleanor thought perhaps that was the true measure of happiness. To spend one's life doing what one loved, regardless of whether one could make a living at it.

The following day, when Maeve packed their bags for their

return to Cheshire, Eleanor felt hollow, disconsolate. Maeve, on the other hand, couldn't wait to return to the farm, confessing that a little bit of this kind of life went a long way.

"You didn't used to think so," Eleanor said. "This was the way we always lived."

"Ah, but that was before we knew how nice it would be to live in the country."

"Speak for yourself," Eleanor growled. Damn, her voice was now so low and had a breathy, husky quality since her bout with pneumonia.

"Put your coat on, love, or we'll miss the eleven o'clock train."

"There's plenty of time. I want to stop at the theater and say good-bye to Tristan on the way. He's rehearsing some changes for the first act."

Maeve frowned. "I think we should go straight to the station. Remember what I saw in your tea leaves yesterday?"

"Illness. I know. But I feel well, honestly. Don't pay any heed to my voice, I think it's always going to be like this. I think what you saw in the tea leaves was the consumption that Margot died from in Tristan's play. You know how you cried over that scene. But his leading lady looked a little too sturdy to be on her deathbed, didn't she?"

Later Eleanor wondered about Maeve's psychic powers, but decided it was just a coincidence that, on that morning, both the leading lady and her understudy should eat breakfast at a certain cafe and become the victims of spoiled food.

When Eleanor arrived at the Playhouse, Tristan was screaming instructions at a terrified second understudy. Catching sight of Eleanor, he thrust a copy of the play into her hands. "Take this home with you and learn every part. When we open in London I want the security of knowing that you could go on at a moment's notice."

"I wouldn't let Owain see that, if I were you," Maeve said as Eleanor read the play on the train.

Eleanor clasped the bound manuscript to her breast and stared out the window. "I was born to play the part of Margot in *Last Love*. Oh, how I wish I could have gone on tonight . . ."

Maeve's fingers closed with unexpected ferocity around her arm. "Now you listen to me, miss, you've got a good, hardworking man for a husband, and he worships the ground you walk on. That's what life's all about. All the rest is smoke in a strong breeze. Any woman alive would give anything to have a man like your Owain. So put the stage out of your mind and concentrate on your husband. My God, if you gave half as much attention to him as you do to pining for the theater, why . . .'' She broke off, flushed, and released Eleanor's arm. After a moment, she said, ''I'm sorry. I don't know what came over me. After all, I was the one who arranged this whole thing with Tristan.''

Stunned, Eleanor leaned back against the starched antimacassar adorning the back of her seat. Maeve had never spoken to her so harshly and had certainly exceeded the bounds of their friendship in making such statements, but Eleanor bit back an angry retort, sensing more to Maeve's outburst than appeared on the surface.

Still, upon their return to the farm, Eleanor studied Tristan's play in secret. There was no need for Maeve to know that during Eleanor's afternoon naps, a necessary legacy to her recent illness, she pored over the part of Margot until she had practiced every line twelve different ways, and had died of consumption a hundred times.

It really was most peculiar about Maeve. She had been the one who voiced grave misgivings about giving up the theater and coming to the farm, yet now she embraced their new life with far more enthusiasm than Eleanor expected, especially since her role of dresser had been diminished to that of housekeeper, almost of farm wife, since Eleanor was still too weak to do much in the way of household or farmyard chores. Eleanor missed their former confidence-sharing, since now she dared not utter a word of criticism about Owain or the farm without incurring Maeve's wrath. Maeve treated Owain like the lord of the castle, rushing to anticipate his every need, hanging on to his every word, spending hours scrubbing and ironing clothes he immediately covered with mud and worse.

But Eleanor was too wrapped up in Tristan's play to give too much attention to the changes in Maeve. The characters were constantly on her mind, no matter what she was doing. Often she found herself responding to some trivial question or mundane situation in the way she thought Margot, the heroine of *Last Love*, would respond.

Several times Owain regarded her anxiously and asked if she were feeling ill, and she consciously had to restrain herself from thinking about the third act and Margot's death when he was with her. The playwright had wrought a small miracle in writing what was essentially a tragedy, yet had managed to leave a sense of hope with the audience, a feeling that the dying girl had left a legacy of love that would live on. Rehearsing the role of Margot in her mind gave Eleanor a sense of purpose, and she no longer felt so trapped and isolated.

Everything seemed to be running smoothly, until one evening Owain came back from a visit to the post office in town looking very grave. Maeve had dinner ready and fussed back and forth from kitchen to dining table and didn't notice how worried and withdrawn Owain looked, but Eleanor, already seated at the table, did. "Something's wrong," she said. "What is it?"

He shook his head, glancing toward the kitchen then back, indicating they could talk later.

At that moment Maeve appeared, carrying a pot of stew. "There's no need to keep it from Maeve," Eleanor said. "She knows all there is to know about us, anyway."

Owain flushed, perhaps thinking of the number of times Eleanor had refused to make love because "The walls are thin as paper and Maeve might hear."

Maeve took her place at the table, looking a little uncomfortable as she always did when that particular tone crept into Eleanor's voice, and began to ladle stew into their bowls.

"I had a letter from Peter," Owain said to Eleanor.

"Oh? And how are things in Kentucky?"

"He . . . had to shoot our prize racehorse. He stumbled and broke a leg. Then apparently Peter lost a great deal of money betting on other horses."

"How dreadful," Eleanor exclaimed, upset more about the shooting of the horse than the lost bets.

"Yes." Owain stared at his stew. "Oh, I almost forgot. There's a letter from London for you."

Eleanor recognized Tristan's scrawl instantly, but carelessly tossed the unopened envelope onto the sideboard.

Owain looked at her sharply. "Aren't you curious about who it's from?"

"Oh, it's probably a note from Delia or Veronica. I'll read it later. I don't want Maeve's stew to get cold."

The meal was eaten in silence and, with her usual tact, Maeve quickly excused herself, saying she wanted to take a walk before retiring and would do the dishes in the morning.

"No need for that, Maeve," Eleanor said. "I'm feeling fine tonight. I'll do them." It would give her an opportunity to read Tristan's letter in private.

But after Maeve left, Owain came into the kitchen right away and picked up a tea towel. "There's more I need to tell you, Ellie, about Peter's letter. You see, it's a lot worse than just losing the horse and making bad bets. Peter's been making the mortgage payments on this farm until it starts supporting itself. He won't be able to do that in future. I invested my winnings from the Kentucky Derby, so that when we were ready I could buy some good breeding stock. But if I have to use the money to pay the mortgage . . . well, it's a setback and no mistake.''

"Perhaps we should give up the idea of a stud farm—'' Eleanor began hopefully.

"It will be your birthday in a couple of months,'' Owain went on. "You said your grandfather's money would be yours then . . .'' He broke off, obviously embarrassed at having to suggest that they needed the inheritance, no matter how little it proved to be.

"You think we should go to Boston and get it?''

"I thought you said the lawyers would send you a steamship ticket—I don't think we could afford another passage to America for me. Besides, I'd have to stay and take care of the place.''

Eleanor scrubbed furiously at the stew pot, unsure how she felt about this turn of events. She'd hoped for an escape from the dreariness of her life on the farm, but not at the expense of having to face Franklyn Yarborough. A terrible anger filled her when she allowed childhood memories into her mind. Yarborough had not only molested her and had had Charlotte dismissed, but Eleanor also blamed him for the loss of her parents. It was his improperly constructed railway bridge that had washed out, plunging her parents to their deaths.

"The ocean voyage might do you good,'' Owain went on. "They say it's a fine way to convalesce after an illness.''

"And Maeve could stay and take care of you,'' Eleanor said, her voice bristling with anger as she suddenly saw with revolting clarity why Maeve constantly defended Owain . . . oh yes, all those carefully prepared meals, the fussing with his shirts, the way Maeve gazed at him, enraptured, every time he opened his mouth, no matter how banal the remark he made.

The stew pot clattered to the tile floor as Eleanor spun around to face her husband. "You want me out of the way so you and Maeve—oh, oh, I should have guessed! There had to be a reason why she suddenly changed her tune. It was the oldest one on earth, wasn't it? I was ill, practically unconscious for days at a time. Tell me, what were you and Maeve up to while I practically lay on my deathbed?''

Owain reeled away from her, his face ashen. He shook his head, as if in disbelief. "What are you saying? Good God, Ellie, you can't believe that Maeve and I . . . why, you must be mad if you let a thought like that enter your head. She's your best friend and I'm your husband, and we both love you more than anyone else on earth. How could you even suggest such a thing? I'm ashamed of you."

"*You're* ashamed of *me!* How dare you be ashamed of me? If anyone has any reason to feel . . ." She stopped herself in the nick of time, but Owain had already finished the thought.

His look of hurt disbelief vanished, replaced by a cold fury that Eleanor had never seen before. "To feel that you had stepped down in life? To feel shamed by a marriage that was beneath you? Is that what you were going to say?"

Eleanor took off her apron and flung it into the sink. "Those are your words, not mine. But you might as well know that I didn't expect you to bury me on this farm. I thought after we were married I'd still be able to act. I didn't think you'd want me to give up the theater forever."

"You can't be a wife and an actress. I thought you'd chosen to be a wife." His voice now had a flat stillness that was more threatening than any shouted outrage.

She said calmly, "I'll write to Boston immediately. Make the arrangements to go and collect my inheritance. It will give us both a chance to think about the situation, away from one another."

"Will you tell Maeve that she'll have to leave, or shall I?" He asked the question quietly, in an almost offhand manner, as though the issue hadn't been the one that had caused this most serious breach in their relationship.

Oh, God, Eleanor thought despairingly, we're not shouting anymore, we're too calm, almost disinterested . . . does that mean we don't care any longer? Aloud she said, "I think I hear her coming now. Why don't you tell her?"

Much later, sometime after midnight, she remembered the unopened letter from Tristan and crept downstairs to read it by the dim light of an oil lamp turned low.

"Dearest Eleanor . . . We have a date for the London opening of *Last Love*. But alas, no one to play Margot. You *must* come immediately, as we begin rehearsals on the ninth . . ."

27

DRACKLEBY'S MANSERVANT BROUGHT a china pot of Ceylon tea and a crystal dish of figs. He placed them on a low mahogany table and asked, "Will the memsahib pour?"

The rain still pounded the roof and a damp circle had formed around the shuttered windows. It had been past midnight when Evan brought Charlotte back to the bungalow in Cinnamon Gardens, but Drackleby had received them graciously. Now he said to the *appo*, "Yes, thank you. You may retire."

He smiled at Charlotte, thinking how frail she looked in the oversized man's dressing gown she wore, with long damp strands of hair streaming over her shoulders. Her complexion was still translucently pale, despite her years in the tropics. Such a delicate little woman, so quiet and refined. It was hard to believe that she could have associated with the most depraved of females and remained apparently unaffected by it. He said, "And I shall also be off to bed. Just ring the bell and one of the women will show you to your room when you're ready."

"What a charming man," Charlotte remarked when she and Evan were alone. "He reminds me of a smiling Toby jug. Or a rather wizened baby. So jovial and friendly, he doesn't seem at all one's idea of a policeman. Where did you meet him?"

"Aboard the ship from England. Charlotte . . . I know it was foolish of me to blurt out a proposal of marriage like that. I can't imagine why I did it. I suppose the exotic setting, the fury of the storm . . . the memory of so many lost opportunities."

Drackleby had insisted they both take a warm bath and put on dry clothing, so Charlotte had had time to digest the electrifying news Evan had brought to her. So far, her joy that her son was still alive completely eclipsed any anger or sorrow she felt at the years that had been wasted because of Zoe's cruel lie. Perhaps that would come later. Evan's abrupt proposal of marriage had been almost as much of a surprise, and she felt an agony of shyness now.

She said, with more coyness than she intended, "If you wish to withdraw your impulsive proposal . . ."

"Not at all!" Evan said at once. "I just wish I'd given you time to get used to me again."

"You have never been far from my thoughts."

"Would you . . . would you come and sit beside me?"

Charlotte rose and went to the wicker couch where he sat, and he took her hand. She watched her small pale fingers disappear beneath his great palm and felt curiously comforted by his touch, safe and secure as she had never felt before in her entire life.

He said, "I began to love you long ago. I was afraid to declare my love. I still hesitate to tell you all that is in my heart. I think perhaps if I had not grown to love Geoffrey . . . your son . . . I would never have had the courage to tell you how I feel."

"I have always held you in the highest regard," Charlotte responded. "You do me a great honor in asking me to be your wife. I must confess that at this moment it seems that all of my prayers are being answered . . . for Gwyn to be alive, for a kind and gentle man to want to take care of both of us. I never dared hope for such miracles."

"You must be very anxious to see him. We'll sail for England on the next steamer. We can be married before we leave, or en route, or after we return, whatever you wish. Charlotte, will you be my wife?"

Shyly she laid her cheek against his arm and whispered, "Yes . . . oh, yes. But I cannot leave right away, as much as I want to. I must find someone to continue my work here. And you have not seen any of the wonders of this beautiful island. The mountains and forests are breathtaking. It would be a shame for you to see only Colombo, although, of course, the monsoons are here now, making travel impossible . . ."

The fingers of his bandaged hand reached tentatively for her face, and he pushed one damp strand of hair behind her ear with the tip of his forefinger in a gesture that was so infinitely tender, she could have wept. He said softly, ''All I came for is here beside me.''

Edmund Fenmore eased the bulk of his body onto its side and batted ineffectively at a whining mosquito that had managed to invade the sanctity of the gauzy net swathing his bed. He hated sleeping under the mosquito net. He felt like a trapped fish.

He harbored great resentment about his current situation—a small room in a miserable hotel next to a native bazaar, where no amount of Keatings powder could keep the insect population at bay.

The constant drumming rain played on his nerves and added to his illusion of drowning in a sea of misadventure that had begun when his family had committed him to a private hospital for the mentally unbalanced some eight years earlier. It was there he had first met Zoe Athmore.

She had appeared on the grounds one day, walking toward him through a grove of elms. She wore a white dress, and fingers of sunlight slashed through the branches of the trees and played upon her voluptuous figure and jet-black hair, creating the illusion of a goddess rising from the woods to tempt him.

After several months of total isolation from other human beings, followed by more months of the company of only men, the sight of a woman, especially one as beautiful as she, seemed at first to be a hallucination.

He glanced about, but none of the other patients were near, so he quickly rose and went to meet her. He took her arm and drew her back into the shelter of the trees. ''Where did you come from, lovely figment of my imagination? How did you get into this walled compound?''

She laughed, a low sultry sound that caused him instant tumescence, that familiar stirring of his groin that could make almost as much turmoil in his brain as the sudden rages that flared out of nowhere. She answered, ''I wanted a man, *cherie*. Any man. You will do nicely. I like big strong-looking men with eyes that offer no quarter. Do you find me a tasty treat? Would you like to play the great game of sex with me?''

A dream, of course. Very well, he would enjoy it until he awoke. The women's wing of the hospital lay beyond a high wall topped with broken glass imbedded in cement. She could not possibly have climbed that wall. Perhaps she wasn't an inmate, but a women's attendant who had exchanged her nurse's garb for a dress from one of her charges.

He didn't care. He dragged her back against the wall, behind the trees, and pulled up her dress. He'd never had a woman who was ready for him before he touched her, nor one who took her own pleasure as savagely as any man. They had sex standing up against the wall, then on a bed of withered leaves, several times. They were still ravaging one another when they were discovered by one of the doctors.

Zoe had looked up calmly and announced, "You may take me back to my room now. If you report this incident to anyone, I shall tell my husband that the hospital allowed a patient to rape me."

She had airily patted Fenmore's cheek before she was led away by the red-faced doctor.

He thought he'd never see her again, but she appeared at the same time the following day. "How did you manage to get in here?" he asked. "Didn't they punish you in any way? Lock you up, put manacles on your wrists?"

"Is that what they do to you?" she responded, ignoring his other questions.

"Yes. I've been manacled to my bed. Of course, lately I've learned to say what they want to hear and do what they want me to do."

She gave a throaty chuckle. "Except for yesterday."

"Yes . . ." His hands went greedily to her waist, to pull her close to him, but she evaded him by twisting gracefully away.

"Tell me your name and why you are here."

"I am Edmund Fenmore, and I'm here because I lost my temper and thrashed a man a little too soundly."

"You killed him?"

He nodded. "My family managed to get me committed instead of standing trial. What about you?"

"I am Lady Zoe Athmore and I'm here because my dear husband needs a rest from me from time to time. But I shall be leaving soon. We have a house in London and you must visit me when you're released."

"I doubt that happy event will take place in the near future."

She smiled seductively. "You see that window up there in the women's wing? The one the sunlight is catching right now? I have watched you from that window. My nurse told me that the men who were allowed out in the garden unattended were the ones who were only slightly unbalanced. They perhaps believed they were someone else, or said they heard voices, or went through peculiar rituals. Except for you, Edmund Fenmore. You, she said, did not belong here. She said that you were normal, the victim of a vindictive family . . . I was surprised when you confessed to me that you had killed a man.''

''I would have invented a story similar to the one your nurse told you,'' he responded, ''had I not recognized that I had met a woman who was like me in every respect. I knew the moment you threatened the doctor yesterday that you were almost as clever as I in getting people to do what you want.'' He laughed. ''Look at us, did you ever see a more handsome pair? And does not good looks signify great intelligence? How easy to get lesser mortals to worship us!''

He tried to touch her breast, but she caught his hand, digging her fingernails into his flesh. ''Not now. Tonight you can come to my room.''

''And how do I get out of my locked quarters?''

''The doctor who caught us yesterday will bring you to me. He's new here and fearful of losing his position.''

He didn't really expect it to happen, but shortly after the patients were locked in for the night the young doctor came for him, avoiding his gaze.

Zoe had a private room, and when the doctor unlocked her door she was nude except for a pair of ostrich feather trimmed mules. The doctor's face turned dull red when she chuckled softly and said, ''Why don't you join us, Doctor?''

Fenmore shoved the doctor through the door and grabbed her. Later he wondered about the hold she had on the doctor and decided it was probably sexual. For a lady, she certainly knew some whore's tricks.

That night, and the ones that followed, were the most exciting of Fenmore's already far-from-ordinary life. Like himself, Zoe liked to receive and inflict pain as well as give pleasure. They went at each other like ravening beasts, and he didn't realize how addicted he had become to her until the night he was greeted by a fully dressed Zoe standing beside her packed trunk.

''I'm leaving this place. My husband will be here for me within the hour. Now, I'm going to tell you where you can find me when you get . . .''

No! He couldn't let her go. He needed her. He wasn't ready to give her up.

But, of course, he had to. By the time he was released, years later, she no longer resided at the London address she'd given him, but he quickly learned that the Athmores had an estate in North Wales.

Zoe wasn't pleased when he appeared on the doorsteps of her ornate Creole-style house. "You are never to come here again, do you understand? Go to the village at once, and I'll meet you at the inn later tonight."

That night it was he who was naked when she knocked at his door. She glanced downward at his tumescence, smiled, and shrugged off her furs. He was inside her with a brutal thrust before she finished undressing. Later she climbed on top of him, in the superior position she loved so much. She was as insatiable as he remembered, and when he faltered she commanded him, using her mouth in a way no whore had ever mastered. Later he showed her the specially made miniature cat-o'-nine-tails he'd brought.

At dawn, exhausted, he fell asleep. Zoe, looking as if she had slept eight hours instead of making violent love all night, sallied forth to Glendower to her husband.

Under the terms of his release from the private asylum, it was necessary that he report for periodic checkups to his personal physician in London, and also that he spend time at his parents' home in Norfolk. Not wishing to return to the asylum, he complied with these conditions, although it often meant long periods when he could not see Zoe, especially since she and her husband traveled abroad a great deal.

Then, at last, she had come to him with the news he'd eagerly awaited for so long. "There is a way we can be together permanently," she said, her fingers sliding down his belly as they lay naked together on the bed.

The hotel room they were in went slightly out of focus. "Your husband is dead!" he exclaimed.

"Darling, don't be ridiculous!" She laughed. "Stephen isn't the obstacle in our path. His uncle is. But I have a plan to change that."

"Don't call me ridiculous. I hate to be called names," he muttered, angrier than she knew.

She glanced at him, trying to assess his displeasure, then caressed him in the way only she knew, setting his nerves on fire.

"Come away with me," he said hoarsely. "We can't go on like this. Just seeing one another every blue moon. I can't stand it any longer, Zoe. I've already told you, I'll kill your husband for you if you must have his fortune."

She pushed him away from her, rose from the bed, and paced about the room, and his eyes followed every voluptuous movement. She said, "Will you listen to me? Stephen doesn't have a fortune, I keep trying to tell you—it's his uncle's. First we must get rid of Evan."

"But I have enough money. My family is more than generous, so long as I behave myself."

"It's not just the money. I hate Evan Athmore. His presence on earth is an abomination to me, don't you understand? I have old scores to settle with him."

In the sweltering room in Colombo, Fenmore finally succeeded in smashing the mosquito that had invaded the net over his bed. He slapped his forearm and regarded the resulting smear of blood with satisfaction. Funny, but he could no longer remember exactly what the sequence of events was to be after he killed Evan Athmore. Not that it mattered, because the blighter was still very much alive. But not for much longer. All being well, tomorrow night Edmund Fenmore would transform himself into a Sinhalese. He would darken his skin, don native clothes, including a turban to cover his hair, and slip into the club where Rhani worked. The Eurasian dancing girl knew the whereabouts of the missionary woman Evan Athmore had come to Ceylon to find.

28

ELEANOR GAZED AT her powder-whitened face in the dressing room mirror and added a little more kohl to her lower eyelids, making her eyes look enormous. Behind her, Frieda, her formidable new dresser, stitched up a tear in the gauzy white gown that Eleanor would wear for Margot's death scene.

Opening night jitters assaulted Eleanor more fiercely than ever before. It was not just that this was her first dramatic lead, or Tristan's first London play since he flopped so horribly as Hamlet, with everything depending for both of them on tonight being a resounding success. More than anything else, Eleanor felt that tonight, her whole life hovered on the brink of either triumph or disaster.

If the audience loved her, if the play was a success, then perhaps everything else would be justified. Especially the shattered look Owain had given her when she told him that she was going to London to act in Tristan's play and would have to delay going to America to collect her inheritance.

His body tensed and his jaw tightened, and for an instant Eleanor saw a savage Celt ready to fight the Roman legions to the death. In that split second, as her imagination ran riot, she had the wild notion that he might sweep her into his arms and vow to keep her prisoner rather than let her leave him. Instead, he'd neither argued nor pleaded with her, but said simply, "I'll be here, waiting for you, when you're ready to come home. Just don't make me wait too long."

Overwhelmed with guilt and temporary remorse, she had

foolishly blurted out, "Don't worry about the mortgage. Tristan has promised a handsome stipend, and I'll send you money—"

Thunderclouds claimed his eyes. She saw his fists clench at his sides. "I'll not be supported by a woman, like some gigolo."

Bewildered, Eleanor protested, "But you wanted me to go and get my inheritance so you could spend it on your damn farm. What's the difference between that and the money I'll receive for acting?"

"The difference," he replied coldly, "is that you didn't have to *earn* your grandfather's money."

They had parted on uneasy, distant terms, and exchanged only one brief letter each during the past weeks while the play had been in rehearsal. Maeve had accompanied her to the railway station, called her a fool, burst into tears, hugged her, and refused to resume her duties as dresser. In view of Maeve's emotional state, Eleanor had not inquired about her own plans for the future.

Her new dresser, who had come to London from a Berlin cabaret, bit off the thread she had been using to mend the tear in the costume and announced in her guttural accent, "Is done. Is also time for putting on first costume."

Eleanor's heart thudded against her ribs and her mouth dried completely. Frieda clucked her tongue, yanked in the laces of Eleanor's corset to confine her already slim waist even further, then handed her a glass of water. "No wine, ya?"

Nodding dutifully, Eleanor sipped the water. A moment later, when Tristan knocked on the door, Frieda ordered him to leave.

Feeling faint, Eleanor whispered, "I can't breathe. I think the corset is too tight."

"Nonsense," Frieda thundered. "Come. We go to wings now."

After that, everything became a blur. She recalled Frieda's substantial arm linked through hers, propelling her out of the dressing room. There was that awful moment on the darkened stage before the curtain rose, and a worse one still when the lights came on and she was certain she had forgotten her lines.

Then, before she knew it, she was reclining on Tristan's prized chaise longue, lent as a prop to give her confidence, murmuring Margot's dying words to her lover. By the middle of the last act, Eleanor's voice was not merely a throaty contralto, but was so low and breathless that, to her dismay, she was forced to cough. To compensate, she breathed as deeply as she could and concentrated on speaking her lines clearly. As Margot lay dying, there was complete silence in the crowded theater, except for a muffled sobbing somewhere on the balcony.

She was unprepared for the storm of applause when the final curtain came down. Or for the way the audience surged forward when she took her bow, becoming a sea of smiling, crying faces just beyond the glow of the footlights. Or for the flowers that rained down on the stage. Or for the chant that began, somewhere in the core of that great milling, adoring throng. *"El-ean-or, El-ean-or,"* they chanted, over and over again.

"Tristan," she whispered urgently, tugging at his sleeve as he made a sweeping bow toward her, acknowledging the perfection of her performance. "I think I'm going to faint."

Evidently reading her lips, Frieda, who stood in the wings, glared and mouthed the words, *"Nein!* Don't you dare!"

Tristan beckoned for the author, Sean Connell, a red-haired, freckled Dubliner with a melancholy, nearsighted gaze, to join them on stage, and the applause wafted momentarily in his direction before returning to the star of the evening, "El-ean-or."

At last, Tristan signaled for the curtain to be brought down and swept her away to his dressing room, which was already packed with people. Someone popped a champagne cork, and she took a glass and drained it.

Conversation around her was a noisy babble of congratulations and compliments, everyone speaking at once, no one listening, everyone in accord that *Last Love* was a tremendous, unstoppable success.

"Are you happy, love?" Tristan bellowed in her ear. "You are the brightest comet in the heavens tonight, and probably will be for a long time to come. Oh, God, you broke my heart! Would you believe there was a moment when I thought you were really dying?"

"I thought I was, too. I could hardly breathe."

"The cough—that was masterful! What made you think of it? It sounded so realistic. If any other actress had attempted it she would have been laughed off the stage for overdoing it, but you actually made it sound like the consumptive hack of a dying woman."

She didn't remind him that her own pneumonia had left her with restricted bronchial passages, and she'd coughed to clear them. Let him, and the audience, believe in Margot's tuberculosis.

"But do you think the critics will like it?" she asked, not yet ready to let go of that fear of failure that had been her constant companion for weeks.

"It's not going to matter. The audience loved us, especially you, my sweet precious." Tristan turned to receive a kiss of homage from one of his admirers.

In view of the noise level in the dressing room, it was astonishing that one voice abruptly made itself heard above all the rest, especially since that voice was not raised.

"So, Miss Hathaway, you return to London in triumph. What happened to our bargain?"

Turning her head slightly, Eleanor looked into the glacial stare of Thane.

For an instant everyone else in the room receded, the din around her faded, and only he stood out in sharp, sinister relief. He stood so close to her in the crush that she was aware of a pulse beating in his temple. His cheekbones looked as if they had been hewn from solid granite, and his mouth, although unmoving, managed to express disdain.

She met his icy gaze for only a split second, seeing little in those cold blue eyes beyond her own terrified reflection. It took her a moment to remember that there was no longer any reason to fear him.

"Mrs. Davies," she croaked, her voice still raspy.

One black eyebrow went up questioningly.

"I'm Mrs. Davies and my husband is a British subject," she yelled, into an inexplicable pause that fell in the conversation around them at that moment. Several people raised their glasses in an amused toast.

"Come, we must talk." Thane took her arm and led her through the crowd, which fell back to let them pass. She heard Tristan call after her the name of the supper club where the celebration party would be held. At any time, she could have jerked her arm free and refused to accompany Thane, but her feet just kept moving beside his until at last they were out of the theater and in his carriage.

He dropped the window curtains to shut out the night and then said, "Your accolades were well-deserved. A superb performance tonight. Will you be able to sustain it?"

"Yes. If my voice doesn't let me down."

"Ah, so the bronchial distress was real. I wondered. You

realize that it's only a matter of time before HRH hears you're back and presents himself at the stage door?''

"I'm married now."

He gave a small, explosive laugh.

"I don't know why I came out to your carriage."

"You came because you couldn't help yourself. Because you wanted to remove yourself from that fawning pack of fools back there and be with a man who would tell you the truth about your acting . . . about yourself."

"And you believe you are the only champion of truth I know?"

"The only one not afraid of losing you by telling you what you need to hear about yourself, yes. Does your black-eyed Welshman tell you the truth? Of course not. He loves you to distraction and will let you walk all over him on the strength of the merest, flimsiest hope that you will return to him. But we know that the stage is your first, last, and only love, don't we?"

"No! My God, I hope there's more to me than that! I love my husband. I do, I do!"

"One 'I do' would have been enough. You repeated the vow at your wedding, too. Were you aware of that?"

"No. I expect I was hoarse and thought the minister hadn't heard me the first time."

Abruptly he said, "You haven't said what you intend to do about HRH."

"Nothing. I shan't see him, at least, not alone. So there'll be no need for you to hound me in the future."

"But my hounding you, as you call it, is the spice that adds excitement to your life."

"How you flatter yourself!"

"I've often wondered if actors choose their profession because real life is so dull, and rarely makes any kind of sense, whereas the playwright gives them exciting personalities, noble motives, and a purpose for being. Actors are empty people, I believe, who must be filled up by imagined words and feelings, or they wouldn't exist at all."

"I'm quite sure you have similar cynical feelings about every profession. I understand you were a soldier. A man molded to obey orders without question. A more deadly puppet than any actor, I'd say."

"Ah, I get a brief glimpse of spirit—even native intelligence again. I've seen that spark in you before, Miss Hathaway, but you always manage to extinguish it before it gets a chance to flare into a noticeable flame.''

''*Mrs*. Davies, not Miss Hathaway.''

''I was using your stage name.''

''I really don't know why I'm sitting in this carriage with you, having this conversation, when I could be at a party.''

''Where you would be toasted and adored and thoroughly bored. You surely must find a man like me a challenge in a world of worshiping swains.''

''Why does it give you such pleasure to mock me?''

''My dear child, how can anyone take seriously a person who spends all their time worrying about how they look?''

''I'm not a child, I'm an adult woman. And I don't spend all my time worrying about how I look,'' Eleanor protested angrily.

''Of course you do, all actors do. While they play out little scenes for whomever is near to observe. It didn't take you long to tire of playing the wife of a horse breeder, did it? Tell me, what would happen if one day you simply had to be yourself? No playacting, no prearranged lines to speak, no role created for you. What if you were forced to think your own thoughts, feel your own feelings?''

''My present feeling is one of anger, and my thought is that I should like to learn how to use a pistol and challenge you to a duel.''

Thane threw back his head and laughed, and for once it sounded like genuine amusement. ''I believe you might just mean that. So, there's hope for you yet. Some basic, primitive instincts remain.''

Eleanor reached for the carriage door, afraid that at any moment she might slap his face, or, worse, burst into frustrated tears because she was no verbal match for him.

His hand closed over hers on the carriage door, firmly but not roughly. He asked, ''Shall I tell the driver to take you to your party?''

''Yes.''

They rode in silence, and when they reached the supper club, Thane alighted and helped her down, then placed his hand under her elbow and escorted her to the door. He touched his hat and said, ''Good night.''

At that moment, a woman emerged from the club. Her sable coat brushed against Eleanor as she cried, ''Why, Victor! Is it really you? I thought you were still thrashing Riffs in the desert somewhere. Lord, I can't believe someone had the bad judgment to unleash you on London society."

"My dear Mrs. Summerleigh," Thane murmured.

"Victor Thane," she responded. "You know where to find me, don't you? I shall be expecting you to call."

Eleanor didn't hear his reply. She was trying to digest the fact that his first name was Victor. The initial V that Maeve had seen in her tea leaves.

Thane appeared in a private box at the theater almost every performance, but did not attempt to see her privately. Eleanor wondered if he were making sure that she kept her word about not seeing HRH, but then HRH had not yet come to see the play. After a week or so, she began to look for Thane's decadent profile up there in the box, and to feel vaguely uneasy on the odd nights he was not there.

The critics had been unanimous in their praise for her performance, while dismissing the play itself as a bit of fluff unworthy of attention and castigating Tristan for playing a parody of himself. Still, it was clear they were due for a long run.

Eleanor wondered if Owain had read the reviews. He'd sent a telegram wishing her well and a short note telling her that he'd bought a champion stallion. He didn't say what he'd used for money. Nor did he mention coming to London to see the play. Eleanor felt disappointed, although even she could not think of a way Owain could leave the farm. She could travel north, taking the midnight train after the Saturday performance and returning Monday morning before the matinee, since there was no Sunday performance. It would involve many hours on the train for a very short visit, but she surely owed her husband that. But so far, she had been so exhausted by Sunday that she slept all day, ignoring the plays that were sent to her and the great pile of adoring letters.

It was Frieda who fished out the heavy parchment envelope with the royal crest and brought it to her flat one Sunday afternoon. The note from His Royal Highness was brief. His wife wanted to see the play all London was talking about, and they would be coming to see *Last Love*. Should Her Royal Highness wish to come backstage to meet the cast, he would appreciate Eleanor not acknowledging that they had met previously.

Tossing the note aside, Eleanor said, "How weak and devious men are. I mean, if they're going to do something, why don't they do it openly? They sneak around and . . ." She broke off, realizing that Frieda had no idea what she was talking about. How she missed Maeve's wise counsel, not to mention the often delicious little prophesies that came from the tea leaves.

The stolid Frieda with her flaxen hair wrapped in tight, unyielding braids around her ponderous skull merely waited for instructions, her face bland as a summer moon.

Thane did not come to the theater for nearly two weeks, during which time the royal party attended a performance but did not come backstage to meet the cast. By the time Thane appeared in his usual box one evening and then presented himself at her dressing room door, she had forgotten her instructions to Frieda to take a note requesting him to visit her, and waited for him to speak first.

At length he bowed slightly, his expression indicating that he was concealing impatience, or irritation, or some other annoyance that was all her fault. "You wanted to see me, I believe?"

"Oh . . . yes. But that was nearly a fortnight ago when I got HRH's note."

Instantly his expression changed. "He wrote to you? What did he say?"

She told him exactly what the note contained.

"You'd better give it to me."

"I don't have it. I threw it away."

"Don't lie to me. You just related it word for word."

"I don't know that I recited it word for word, and neither do you, but if I did, well I'm an actress, used to memorizing lines. Why are you making such a fuss about it?"

"From now on you are to burn any notes he sends. In the wrong hands, they could cause a great deal of trouble. He'll undoubtedly be back to see you . . . alone."

"What makes you think so?"

"He won't be able to resist. Your acting . . . your stage presence is mesmerizing. You have the ability to melt a heart of stone. His is made of a less impervious substance."

She couldn't stop herself from asking, "Is that why you keep coming back to see the play?"

"I keep coming back because, irrationally, I keep hoping for a different ending to the play. That this time . . . tonight . . . Margot won't die."

Astonished, Eleanor said, "But you know she will."

"Yes. I'm flabbergasted by my own stupidity."

They regarded each other silently for a moment, and then he asked abruptly, "Will you have supper with me?"

Eleanor felt a surge of triumph. There! I've got him! But then she saw the look in his eyes, that of a watchful hunter with a cornered prey, a look that should have belonged to her. How had he managed to claim it for himself? Knowing that a cool refusal was the correct response, she was amazed to hear herself say, "All right. You can wait for me at the stage door. I'll need about half an hour after the last curtain call so that I can change."

Usually she went straight home to bed after a performance, all energy drained, all emotion spent. Not that she was able to fall asleep for hours, but as Maeve would have said, she could at least rest her bones. Tonight she felt wide-awake, alert, filled with a sense of challenge.

Recalling the matronly dress she'd worn the last time he took her out, she dressed carefully in a pale blue silk gown cut low to show the perfection of her throat and upper bosom. She slipped sapphire earrings into her ears and decided against wearing a necklace. She'd been told by more than one admirer that this particular shade of blue turned her eyes into infinite lakes and made her gold hair sparkle like the sun.

Thane's eyes flickered over her as she emerged from the stage door, but he made no comment. His carriage whisked them swiftly to a fashionable restaurant and, upon entering, several patrons recognized Eleanor and clamored around her.

Thane said quietly, "Miss Hathaway prefers to be left alone." His eyes raked the intruders with silent, steely menace, and they all backed away, apologizing. A nervous maître d' led them to a secluded table.

Eleanor liked having a powerful protector ward off the wolves. On several occasions since the opening of the play, she had ventured forth on shopping expeditions and had been recognized. She had been frightened by the way people jostled close and even touched her, as if she had become public property.

"Would you care for champagne?" Thane asked. "That seems to be the standard drink of actors. The bubbles are, I suppose, a constant celebration of their triumphs which they feel will keep the specter of failure at bay."

Eleanor had been about to order champagne, but now said, "I rather like the German wines."

"A good choice." To the hovering waiter he said, "Bring us a bottle of Niersteiner."

"Why did you invite me to supper?" she asked.

"You know why."

"I assume to discuss what to do about HRH."

"What an accomplished liar you are."

Eleanor flung her napkin on the table and started to rise. "If you are going to call me names—"

"My abject apologies. Will you sit down and sample this excellent wine if I promise to play the part of a gentleman?"

"That is a masquerade I would find alarming."

He grinned, and the resulting change in his countenance was surprising. Why, Eleanor thought, he can look quite attractive when he wants to.

"I asked you out," Thane said, "for the same reason you sent me a message that you wished to see me. Because we are fascinated with one another."

Eleanor's sense of conquest returned. It occurred to her what sweet revenge it would be to have this man on his knees, declaring his love for her, as so many others had done with very little encouragement from her. Why, if she were to lead him on . . .

"Don't do that," he said sharply.

Startled, she asked, "Do what?"

"Indulge yourself in the futile contemplation of conquest."

She caught her breath. Surely he couldn't have known what she was thinking? "Don't flatter yourself," she retorted. "You would be the last man on earth I'd attempt to . . . to . . ."

"To seduce?" he finished for her, his voice velvet soft.

She could feel herself blushing and could not think of anything insulting enough to say, so merely shrugged. "I shan't dignify that remark with a comment."

"Meaning you have no idea what to say. We should have invited your sad-eyed Irish playwright along so he could write a few lines for you. Allow me to expand on your train of thought for you. Now that we know one another a little better than we did upon our first acquaintance, I believe seduction, either one-sided or mutual, might be an interesting experience for both of us. In fact, I believe it's inevitable."

If there was such a thing as an icy thrill, Eleanor decided she felt it now. She said quickly, "You seem to be forgetting that I'm married."

"A marriage doomed from the start, wouldn't you say?"

"How can you suggest such a thing? I've loved Owain since I was a little girl. Why, he saved my life! If you think I only married him in order to remain legally in the country—'' she stopped, aghast, but it was too late.

Thane leaned forward, his eyes slicing her in two. ''I thought so. And having married him, you realized your mistake. Marriage for an actress must be a terrible burden. What you needed was a man to awaken the woman within the actress, while not interfering with the muse. A man like me, for instance. I have no wife, like HRH, to make trouble for you. But I do possess sufficient wealth and power to protect you. Tell me, how would you like to be my mistress?''

Rising to her feet, Eleanor picked up her glass and flung the wine in his face. He didn't follow as she ran to the door and demanded that the maître d' hire a cab for her at once. The following weekend, she bought a train ticket to Cheshire.

29

THE DANCER, RHANI, paced restlessly about the small, curtained-off area of the club in the native quarter of Colombo, anxious for the time to pass so she could go on stage. She was only truly comfortable when she danced. Then there was no time to dwell on the grim realities of her life and the future she faced, because it was necessary for her mind to give itself as completely to her art as did her body.

But the long, empty hours between performances had lately become unbearable, because Rhani was haunted by the specter of that bundle of filthy rags dying on the floor of a stinking hovel. Was it true—could that hideous skeleton have been her mother? Keribunda said no, the missionary woman lied. But Rhani wasn't sure.

She ran her hands through her hair, shook her head so that the dark waves fell freely, and with her fingertip touched the ruby that hung suspended on her forehead. The stone was valuable, the gift of a wealthy merchant. The gold coins about her throat, wrists and ankles were also expensive presents, and she had plenty of other jewelry, and a nicely furnished flat.

But it wasn't enough to protect her from the same fate as that dying bundle of rags with tattooed cheeks and betel nut-stained mouth.

Rhani needed a husband. A certain kind of husband. No Sinhalese would marry her; she was Eurasian, and therefore would not be acceptable to his family. She needed a husband who would take her away from Lanka. Away from the caste system, away from her past and her occupation. She needed a sahib.

She'd heard that light-skinned Eurasians like herself often went unrecognized in the northern European countries. It seemed fortuitous that at this particular time in her life, the fates had provided Edmund Fenmore. He was a sahib of high birth whose family supported him without the necessity of his working for a living. He was new to Lanka, and therefore unfamiliar with either the caste system or her own blemished past. Most importantly, he was now in trouble and hiding in the native quarter. Fenmore had come to see her the previous evening to inquire about Charlotte Briggs, and Rhani had seen the opportunity to make her own escape.

One of the street girls had told her that a great giant of a sahib had carried Charlotte Briggs off to the home of the policeman in Cinnamon Gardens. But to deliver that information to Edmund Fenmore would be to end their acquaintance, so Rhani merely promised to look into the matter.

Fenmore would return for her performance this evening, and a private rendezvous afterwards. Rhani knew exactly what would take place then—absolutely nothing except conversation. She would tell him whatever was necessary to keep him here in the native quarter, in hiding, and accessible to her.

She would not make the mistake with this particular sahib of sleeping with him too soon. When she eventually "gave in," she would weave her spell very carefully, keeping her goal always in mind, waiting to spring the trap until he had become addicted to her. By then he would be so maddened with desire that he would be ready to promise anything she asked.

With this sahib it would be a pleasure. He was big, strong, handsome . . . and young. Oh, yes, a young man's body would be a joy after the sagging flesh and hairy skin of so many old men. Rhani smiled in anticipation, momentarily forgetting her anxiety.

When at last it was time for her to dance, she slipped from behind the embroidered curtain and, swaying sinuously, scrutinized her audience from beneath lowered eyelashes. Yes, there he was, in a corner of the room, looking almost like a native in his disguise. Tonight she would dance only for the sahib Fenmore. She would make love to him with her body in full view of the entire assembly, then behave as chastely as a missionary when they were alone.

Keribunda had warned his sister not to have anything to do with this sahib. "He is dangèrous, Rhani. I see him in Grand Hotel, smiling, laughing, backslapping, being friend to everyone. But look into his eyes. He has the eyes of a cobra."

Fortunately, Keribunda did not know what Rhani knew, that Fenmore had hired men to kill the big sahib. That knowledge was going to insure her passage to England as his wife. In England, she could begin a new life, untainted by the old, and never have to fear the loss of youth and beauty. Hadn't she seen aging memsahibs still attended by devoted husbands, still wallowing in luxury—not forced out onto the street as her mother had been?

As she reached Fenmore's table, she began a slow backbend which would culminate in her lowering herself to her knees, her head touching the floor behind her, in an attitude of surrender. In the instant before she dropped her head, she looked into his eyes. Keribunda was right. Fenmore did have the flat, merciless stare of a serpent.

The cluster of tiny bells on Rhani's ankle tinkled softly, making a sound no more intrusive than the rustling of leaves. She arched her body, stretching like a cat.

In the suffocating heat her skin glistened, yet felt cool to his touch. The persistent scent of incense, overlaid with the musk and sandalwood Rhani touched to the most intimate parts of her body, did little to disguise the smell of recent sex.

Fenmore propped himself up on one elbow and looked down at her. His good looks had attracted a constant supply of willing women, but only Zoe Athmore had ever truly satisfied him sexually. Until now. For the past several hours he had been practically mindless with ecstasy. Even now, sated, he could hardly recall who he was or what he was doing here, he was so besotted by the dancer.

How many nights had he lain with her, enclosed in her silken embrace? How many frustrating nights had she refused him admittance? The masquerade of wearing native clothes and darkening his skin was becoming tiresome, since it meant stepping aside for white men in the bazaar or watching them receive preferential treatment in the club. Yet, still, he remained in the native quarter in disguise, unsure any longer whether he was more interested in seeing the dancer or in killing Evan Athmore. Several times the policeman Drackleby had come close to discovering his hiding place, but Fenmore had taken the precaution of paying the hotel proprietor to warn him of imminent searches.

Rhani had told him that until the monsoons ended the missionary woman would not return from the mountains, therefore the giant would have to remain in Colombo. Besides, the poison Fenmore had slipped into his drink had caused a lingering recurrent illness that still might cause his death. "Be patient," Rhani urged. "Perhaps you've already achieved what you set out to do."

She turned her head to look up at him, and her hair fell back from one ear. For the first time he saw the ruby earring, the stone set in silver and as large as the forehead ruby she wore while dancing.

"Where did you get those earrings?"

"These? Oh, I've had them for ages."

"I've never seen them before."

"They were my grandmother's. My Hindu grandmother, of course. I have nothing from my English grandmother."

"You're a liar. I've seen every piece of jewelry you own, and I wouldn't have missed rubies that size."

He allowed his hand to drift to her throat, then quickly, afraid he might choke the lie out of her, slid his fingers to her breast.

In the semidarkness of her room, she smiled, her teeth very white. She moved slightly under his caressing hand, inviting a firmer touch.

He said, "That Arab trader who stuffed all that money into your costume while you danced the other night . . . did he give you the rubies? Or the man who imports the coolies to send to the plantations . . . the one who pretends to be my friend? Was it him? Where were you last night? You disappeared from the club immediately after you danced, and I waited for you until dawn."

Abruptly she sat up, twitching her head to send her long hair flying back over her shoulder. "You do not own me. I do not have to account to you."

He regarded her through a red haze that consisted of equal parts anger and desire. No, damnit, no native dancer was going to do to him what Zoe had done. He would not share her with another man.

For a moment he fought an inward battle to remain calm. At the asylum, an attendant had taunted him once by pointing out the difference between sane men and the inmates. "You madmen have no control over your impulses. You are ruled by that snake between your legs. Sane men can control themselves, but you can't. You're a willing slave to your genitalia.'' The remark had so enraged him that he'd wanted to choke the life out of the man.

Fenmore smiled apologetically at Rhani, adopting the ingratiating manner that worked so well with everyone else. "I'm sorry. I didn't mean to sound so possessive. It's just that I wonder what you're doing and who you're seeing, when I'm not with you."

She lay down again beside him and pressed her lips to his chest. "Sometimes I must be alone, just to rest. Night after night I dance until I'm ready to drop with exhaustion. Until Keri brought you to me, I didn't bother with men. I think perhaps I hated men. They were simply leering faces in the darkness beyond that small pool of yellow light where I dance. They weren't . . . whole to me. They were clutching hands, wet lips, eyes that burned with lust. And I—what was I to them? What am I to you, Edmund Fenmore? Certainly not a protected woman, not a wife, although I give you more than any wife would. I'm a body, a receptacle, a vessel to receive you. But, of course, only when you choose. I have no say in the matter. You could vanish from my life tomorrow if you wished."

"I shan't vanish. At least not until I do what I came to do."

"And what then?" Her voice was soft, almost a feline purr.

"Why, I—" He broke off. He hadn't planned anything beyond finishing off Athmore and sailing for home. Now he wondered about the possibility of taking her with him. Her mixed blood would be an affront to his family that he would enjoy immensely. Even more, it would be a pleasure to inform Zoe that he had tired of waiting for her.

His mind raced. Zoe owed him a great deal. Hadn't he come halfway around the world, at considerable risk to himself, to do her bidding? Oh, yes, Zoe would spend the rest of her life making it up to him. But was there any reason to give up Rhani? Why not have both women? He could keep Zoe as his mistress. And Rhani as his wife? Now where had that thought come from? But, of course, he had to either make her his wife or kill her. She knew too much about him.

Rhani swung her slender legs over the edge of the bed, rising in a swift, graceful way. Although he reached for her, she eluded him, twisting away from his grasping hands. She walked to the window, moving with the effortless grace of a panther. The breaking dawn did little to lighten the cloudy sky, and the rain still fell in a solid sheet. The soft light of the lamp caught her face as she turned to look at him, and her eyes flashed like polished copper.

There was a half-smile on her sensual lips as she said softly, "It's time for you to go home, Edmund. Time to say good-bye to Rhani forever."

"What?"

"The man you came here to kill . . . Lord Athmore . . . died yesterday afternoon from the poison you gave him."

Fenmore rose and walked slowly to her side. He seized her bare arms and held her, shaking her slightly. "Why didn't you tell me before?"

A tear glistened on her black eyelashes. "Because I knew then you would leave, and I would never see you again. Oh, Edmund, never to make love with you . . . to worship your magnificent body."

She sank slowly to her knees, teasing his already hardening member with her lips and tongue. Even though he had climaxed several times that night, he felt himself soaring to new erotic peaks of feeling. What Rhani did with her lips, tongue, teeth, breasts, and fingers surpassed even Zoe's skill. With Zoe it had amazed him that a lovely, cultured, aristocratic woman was willing and eager to give and receive the most uninhibited sensual delights. But he'd quickly realized that Zoe's charms were available to many men. Rhani's allure lay in the fact that, by her own admission, she really hated men, and little wonder, considering the way they pawed her while she danced. But he had been able to transform her from a frigid marionette to this wildly sexual partner. She, in fact, belonged to him. He had invented her.

He gasped as she brought him to climax and, triumphant, rose to take his face between her long cool fingers and hold it firmly, forcing him to look down into the copper glow of her eyes as though to mesmerize him. "It will be a week before the next ship arrives, so you can't escape from the island until then. You have to stay in Colombo at least that long. You could easily be caught in that length of time. Take me home to England with you, Edmund. Or I shall tell Drackleby everything I know."

The rain pounded the roof overhead, the sound reverberating around the room, beating a relentless, monotonous tattoo in his head until he wanted to scream at the heavens to make it stop.

The hot, humid air suffocated him, and the weeks of living like a native suddenly became unbearable. Something burst inside his mind; he felt the shackles break and rage poured out. The stupid little fool! He had already decided he'd take her home with him, but now she'd spoiled it all by daring to threaten to betray him.

His hands slid up her back and encircled her throat.

30

CHARLOTTE MOPPED THE sweat from Evan's brow and looked up as Drackleby entered the room. Their host's round, pink-cheeked face, so incongruous for his profession, wore a worried expression. "Is he any better?"

"I think the fever is breaking."

"Thank God. You know, it's ridiculous and perhaps I've been here too long and heard too much native mumbo jumbo, but I actually wondered last night if I'd brought about Evan's illness by spreading the word that he was dead. Superstitious nonsense on my part, of course. But, well . . ."

"It was a good idea," Charlotte replied. "With a ship coming into port it was the one way to flush Fenmore from his hiding place. He'll surely attempt to leave Ceylon aboard that vessel."

Drackleby looked down at Evan, who now slept more peacefully. "I'd have sworn it was malaria."

"It *was* malaria. Hasn't he improved since we started giving him quinine?" Charlotte said firmly. "Your Sinhalese doctor was mistaken about it being the residual effects of the poison Evan ingested. I've nursed enough malaria patients, and suffered enough attacks of my own, to recognize it when I see it."

"Then that's both a blessing and a curse."

"Yes. Tell me, Mr. Drackleby, did you learn when the ship will depart?"

"As soon as its cargo is discharged and the tea is loaded. I should think it will be here about a week."

"Then I believe Evan will be well enough to sail aboard her."

"You do realize the vessel is a merchantman? The passenger accommodations will be Spartan, and there will be no doctor aboard."

Charlotte smiled. "Yes. But we shall manage. As long as you keep Fenmore from getting aboard."

"Believe me, no one will get on that ship without my knowledge." He went to the window and opened the shutters. "Look! The monsoon is beginning to break."

A pale, silvery beam of sunlight slipped into the room and fell across the bed. Evan opened his eyes. Catching sight of Charlotte, he smiled. "I didn't intend for you to be forever taking care of me. I wanted to be the one who takes care of you."

"Hush," Charlotte whispered. "From now on, we will take care of one another."

His hand reached for hers and, heedless of Drackleby's presence, he raised it to his lips. "Ah, Charlotte, how I love you."

Drackleby had tactfully started toward the door when scurrying footsteps in the hall and a frantic knocking heralded the approach of his *appo*. The manservant's turbaned head appeared before Drackleby had finished bidding him enter.

"A murder, sahib!" the *appo* announced excitedly. "You are wanted at once. They just found a dancing girl named Rhani, strangled to death."

The train's ascending speed slowed to eight miles an hour due to the steep gradient. Fenmore looked down at a valley filled with luxuriant masses of dense forest, vivid green terraces of rice fields, festoons of flowering creepers, ravines, and foaming waterfalls. Above was a mighty crag, a thousand feet high.

He stared out the train window, uncomfortably aware of the crush of unwashed humanity sharing his compartment. His clothes were as rank as theirs, and he thought perhaps the dye had become a permanent part of his skin, like a tattoo. Or perhaps it was just that it didn't wash off now that the rains had stopped.

Despite the end of the monsoon, it still seemed to be raining inside his head, pounding against his skull until he wanted to scream. Clutching the overhead strap as he swayed with the movement of the train, he assured himself, over and over again, that he could endure this exile. After all, it wouldn't be forever.

The tea plantations were situated in the mountainous central province of Ceylon, some as high as seven thousand feet. At least the climate would be pleasant there, after the sticky heat of Colombo. Each plantation, he'd learned, had a *cangany,* or taskmaster, in charge of the coolies. Since the Sinhalese disdained to work in the fields, Tamils had been imported from India. Their white masters rarely had any dealings with them, and Fenmore was confident that a *cangany* would not be able to pick him out as being different from the rest of his coolies. One thing he had learned since coming to Ceylon was that upper castes never really saw lower castes. They were invisible. Only the tasks they performed were briefly noted.

As the train began to pick up speed again, Fenmore congratulated himself on his fortitude. A lesser man would have attempted to leave the island immediately by ship. Only a man of his strength and cunning would have considered remaining to work as a coolie. He would stick it out as long as necessary, until Drackleby gave up searching for him, or until it was safe to board a ship. He would not sail for England, however. Too dangerous.

First he would sail to India with a shipload of returning Tamils, then make his way home from there. For one thing, he'd need to send word to his parents in England that he needed money, since he hadn't dared collect the funds he had deposited in the safe of the Grand Orient Hotel, in case Drackleby was watching it. He wondered how long it would take to save enough for a passage from Ceylon to India on a coolie's pay.

He shuddered at the thought of the manual labor he'd have to perform. When he eventually returned to his native land . . . ah, then, there were accounts to be settled.

Charlotte and Evan were married in a simple civil ceremony before leaving Colombo, with only Drackleby and a fellow officer for witnesses. Charlotte wore a spray of orange blossoms pinned to her simple, floral cotton gown and, beneath the wide brim of a straw hat, her face was prettily flushed and her eyes shone with happiness.

Evan never took his eyes off her, and he made his vows in a low, clear voice. There was time for a short wedding breakfast at Drackleby's bungalow in Cinnamon Gardens afterwards, before they set off to board the ship that would take them back to England.

Drackleby shook Evan's hand and kissed Charlotte's cheek. "I wish I could have found Fenmore, but rest assured I shall watch that ship until it sails. There is absolutely no possibility he can

slip aboard. Let's get you on your way before too many people
see you. I'm hoping Fenmore believes the story that you're dead,
but we don't get too many men of your height here, and we don't
want anyone mentioning your departure."

At sunset the ship slipped out of the harbor, and they stood on
deck looking at the serrated silhouettes of coco palms against the
fiery brilliance of the sky.

When the island faded into the twilight, Charlotte murmured,
"I'm going to our cabin. Would you mind . . . waiting a little
while before joining me?"

"Of course not," Evan replied, but as she turned to leave his
hand lingered on her arm, as if reluctant to let her go.

Their cabin steward had placed their baggage in a corner, and
she quickly found what she was seeking. Slowly she pulled a
brilliant length of magenta silk from beneath her white cotton
underwear. The sari had been a wedding gift from some of the
prostitutes she had cared for, brought to Drackleby's bungalow
with much giggling by the sister of the girl whose baby Charlotte
had delivered the night Evan found her.

Charlotte undressed and sponged her body from the pitcher of
water the steward had left. She unpinned her hair and brushed it,
then returned to her bags to find the small bottles of sandalwood
and musk oil she had packed. She massaged the fragrant oil into
her skin, paying particular attention to her pulse spots. Finally,
she carefully draped the sari about her body, sighing at the
sensuous caress of the silk.

Looking back on her years of toil and deprivation, it occurred
to her that never in her wildest dreams could she have foreseen
that the time would come when she would imitate some of the
ways the ladies of the evening made themselves alluring to men.
Perhaps there was a grand design to life, after all, and a purpose
for every experience lived through, no matter how harrowing it
seemed at the time. Although she had learned not to judge or
condemn the unfortunate women she cared for, there had been
times when she wished she were not observing so many of their
ways. Now it seemed that knowledge had been acquired in
preparation for her marriage.

She felt eager, happy, excited. She was a mature woman who
had borne a child and known the pleasure of a man's body, not a
virginal girl, and she looked forward with joy to the consummation of her marriage. In these past days, she and Evan had not
only recaptured their previous friendship, but had formed a more

subtle attachment that promised a greater fulfillment than she had ever imagined. The long sea voyage back to England, without distractions, would provide a perfect interlude for learning how to be intimate with one another.

There was a knock on the cabin door, and Evan entered. Smiling, Charlotte rose to her feet and opened her arms to welcome her husband. He picked her up very gently, raising her until her face was level with his, then kissed her lips. She placed her arms around his neck and returned his kiss, thinking how warm and wonderful his mouth felt against hers.

Her hands stroked the luxuriant mass of his hair, and she realized then that the top of his head was pressed to the upper bulkhead. Their cabin, the largest aboard the ship, must seem cramped as a coffin to him. She had already given some thought to the size of the bed, and decided that they could pull a chair to the foot of the bed to give him some extra length.

The deck swayed under his feet with the motion of the ship, and he sat down abruptly, with Charlotte on his lap. "For a moment I forgot we were at sea," he said. "I think, perhaps, the taste of your sweet lips would have made the earth roll as much for me. How lovely you look. And what a charming way to dress. How did you learn to wrap a sari?"

"From watching the women of Ceylon. I learned a great deal from them. I'm afraid I wasn't very good at converting souls, I was more interested in learning their ways than in teaching them ours. I was sent to a mission in the mountains at first, to work with a doctor and his wife, who were medical missionaries. I suppose I wasn't prepared for how intelligent and reasonable the questions of the prospective converts were. Far from accepting answers in a childlike manner, often a lively discussion ensued. They would ask me, 'Why did God place the forbidden fruit in the garden if He knew Adam would disobey?' and 'Why was Jacob blessed instead of Esau?' and, most troubling, 'What are the external evidences that Christ, rather than Mohammed and Buddha, was a revelation of God?' What logical answer could I offer to the question, 'If the doctrine of transmigration is not true, why are men born blind or deformed, if not for some former sin?' "

"You found yourself wavering in your faith?"

"No. But I became less inclined to want to force it upon others. Eventually the Missionary Society gave up on me, I think, and allowed me to do as I pleased. I pointed out that in helping the pariahs, the beggars, and street women, perhaps by example rather than by stern admonition, I could bring some lost souls into the fold.''

She had spoken at length on purpose, having seen that Evan was nervous and on edge, undoubtedly wondering how to proceed. How glad she was that she was not a man, for so much more was required of them when it came to lovemaking. She raised her hand and caressed his cheek. ''But this is far too deep a conversation for our wedding night, my love.''

Evan turned his face so that he could kiss the palm of her hand and murmured, ''Charlotte . . . now that we're alone, I have a great fear . . .''

She placed two fingers against his mouth to silence him. ''You must never feel awkward, or in any way ill at ease with me, my darling husband. I love you and know that you love me.''

''But . . .'' There was a catch in his voice. ''Oh, God, I'm such a monster, and you are so tiny, so fragile. Yet I want you so desperately. I want to love you physically as well as with all my heart and soul, yet I know it cannot be.''

''And what is to prevent our physical intimacy?'' Charlotte asked gently.

''I'm afraid that . . . that I would crush you.''

''Evan, my dearest, you did not live until your present age without ever making love to a woman.''

''No . . . but they were not ladies like you. I could not expect . . . could not ask you to . . . do anything that was not the usual way of a man and woman coming together.''

Charlotte stood up and slowly began to unwrap the sari. The yards of magenta silk began to form a shimmering pool at her feet. ''Between a man and woman who love one another, there is no physical joining that is not good and right. There is no shame, no holding back. Nor is there a correct and an incorrect way of loving. Evan, dearest, I told you I learned much from the women I associated with . . . Although I have not put any of that knowledge into practice, if you will be patient with me . . .''

She stood naked before him and, worshiping her with his eyes, he raised his hands as if in supplication, and drew her to him.

31

THE MIDNIGHT TRAIN from London was interminably slow, and by the time Eleanor reached the farm it was long past sunrise. She felt tired and cross because Owain had not met her at the station, and she'd had trouble finding anyone to take her out into the country. Eventually a farmer returning after delivering milk to the town gave her a ride on his cart. Was it possible her letter had not arrived, and Owain didn't know she was coming?

Pushing open the door, she went into the house. There were dirty dishes in the sink and mouse droppings on the tiled floor. In the living room, a thick film of dust coated the furniture, and the aspidistra had died.

Eleanor bent to pick up a soiled shirt. There were piles of dirty clothes, crumpled bills, almanacs, a couple of pairs of mud-caked boots, a partially repaired saddle, and some tools on the table. The fireplace was piled high with gray ashes, and ivy growing on the outside of the house had insinuated its vines through the window and now snaked across the wallpaper.

She looked around with growing concern, sensing more here than careless bachelor living habits. There was a feeling of despair, of having given up. A bubble of fear formed in her throat. Owain would never live like this . . . not in this utter chaos . . . not unless he were ill. Oh, God . . . what if he'd become ill and he were all alone . . .

Stumbling through the disarray of the room, she rushed upstairs to the bedroom. Except for the unmade bed and more piles of unwashed sheets and clothes, the room was empty.

Puzzled, she went slowly back downstairs. Surely, knowing that she was arriving today, he was not out in the fields? She went outside and began to walk toward the stable, giving the haystacks a wide berth to avoid any lurking rats.

A pair of well-groomed mares grazed in a buttercup-strewn meadow. Fences and paths were neat and orderly, a style connecting two fields was in good repair, leaves and debris had been raked. In contrast to the upheaval in the house, the stable was clean and fresh-smelling. She felt a twinge of resentment. The horses evidently were more important than the humans.

In the last stall, Owain knelt on a bed of straw, a horse's head in his lap. The animal lay on his side, panting, and Eleanor could see the look of suffering and impending death in the stallion's glazed eyes. As she stood silently watching, the horse shuddered violently and then was still. Owain slid the head to the straw and buried his face in his hands.

"Oh, Owain," Eleanor said. "I'm so sorry . . . what happened?"

He turned and looked at her over his shoulder, not startled by her sudden appearance exactly, but rather staring at her as if unsure who she was. She could see tears glistening in his dark eyes, but apparently he was able to keep them from sliding down his cheeks. His unshaven face and the state of his clothes testified to a long vigil with the sick horse.

Rising to his feet, he moved toward her like a sleepwalker. "How did you get here?" he asked in a hollow voice.

"One of your neighbors brought me in his milk cart from the station. Didn't you get my letter?"

"Oh . . . yes. Is it Sunday morning?"

She felt another stab of resentment, more intense this time. It was sad that the horse had died, but surely she deserved more of a welcome than this, after having traveled all night long. She had been unable to get a sleeper and so had to sit up. Then there had been no one to bring her from the station, and she'd walked into the worst mess she'd ever seen. And all he could ask was, is it Sunday morning? No hello, how are you, or sorry I didn't come to meet you.

As if she wasn't there, he looked back at the stallion. "He went off his feed about three weeks ago. I got the vet right away, but he didn't know what ailed him. He just got weaker every day . . . I haven't slept for four or five nights."

Eleanor turned on her heel and ran back outside.

Owain caught up with her halfway back to the house. "Ellie, I'm sorry. This isn't much of a homecoming for you, is it? I'm just so weary I can't seem to think clearly."

"Please don't apologize. After all, horses have always been your first love. I knew that. I should have expected to take second place to a horse."

He grabbed her arm and spun her around to face him. "You seem to have forgotten that I took second place to your acting all these months. I was beginning to think you were never coming back. I'm sorry, but you planned this reunion for the worst possible time. You wouldn't have wanted me to let him die all by himself, would you?"

"You left me standing all by myself at the railway station. You didn't even pick up the disgusting litter in the house—"

"I haven't had time to eat or sleep, never mind do housework. The boy who was working for me broke his arm, so I've had to do everything myself. Ellie, there's worried I've been . . . I invested our last penny in that stallion. Now he's dead, and I don't know how I'll make the next mortgage payment."

He stopped and ran his hand through his hair distractedly. "Look, Ellie, *bach,* I am glad to see you. Truly, I am. Let's not quarrel. Come on, we'll have breakfast and I'll help you clean the house."

Eleanor's mouth opened into a wide O. For an instant she was speechless, then her words tumbled from her mouth in an angry torrent. *"You'll* help *me?* That isn't my mess, it's yours. Great buckets of turds! You really expect me to sit on a train all night long and then scrub floors when I arrive?"

"I didn't mean it like that," Owain said miserably. "I meant we could clean it up together."

Pulling her arm free of his grasp, she continued walking to the house. When they reached the door, she said, "Will you please harness one of the mares to the cart and take me to town?"

"Oh, Ellie, please don't go. There's no train until this afternoon."

"I need to sleep. You can take me to an inn or a boarding-house. I can't possibly get into that filthy bed upstairs."

He blinked, as if trying to bring her into focus. "Yes, that's a good idea. That will give me a chance to do some chores and . . . see about the stallion. I'll come to the inn in time for supper. We need to talk on neutral ground, I think."

"I'll get my bag while you bring the cart." Eleanor turned

away before he saw her tears. Oh, how could everything have gone so desperately wrong? Why, why, did she have to choose this particular weekend to visit? Why did the stallion have to sicken and die? Why today? Why, *why?*

She asked unanswerable questions of herself all the way to a Tudor-style country inn just outside of town. Owain took her up to her room and said, "Rest well, Ellie. I'll be back as soon as I can."

He closed the door quietly, and she flung herself on the bed and cried. Then, exhausted, she fell asleep.

The long shadows of late afternoon were filling the room when she awakened. Owain, washed, shaved, and wearing clean clothes, was sitting beside the bed watching her.

In that waking instant, before memories of hurts and disappointments intruded, she stretched sleepily, smiled at him and murmured, "Owain . . . are you really here, or is this a dream?"

He let out his breath in a swift gasp that could have been relief or joy and, moving to the bed, took her in his arms. His mouth was already on hers and his kiss one of famished need, before she remembered her disastrous arrival that morning. But it was too late, he was fully aroused and she not completely awake. He had removed her shoes and stockings and loosened her gown while she slept. Now he slid her dress down from her shoulders and kissed her breasts.

Eleanor lay limply on her pillow, not resisting his fevered mouth nor shrinking from his caresses, yet not really a part of his madness. She helped him remove her underwear and lay still as he tore off his own clothes and returned to her.

At the moment of his shuddering zenith, the thought drifted into her mind that one of the reasons she loved playing the part of Margot in *Last Love* was that Margot's love was pure and unsullied by lust. It didn't occur to her until much later that the price Margot paid for such a love was early death.

Owain murmured, "Oh, Ellie, *bach,* how I love you. How I missed you. You'll never know how much."

For once she was able to resist the impulse to retort that he certainly hadn't shown any evidence of such feelings that morning. Perhaps for now it would be better to pretend all was well between them. She said, "All at once I'm ravenously hungry. I haven't had anything to eat since last night."

He sat up immediately. "Then we must feed you at once. Come on, let's get dressed and go and have supper."

For a little while the tension had eased, and neither of them wanted to precipitate another quarrel, so they spoke of nothing more serious than the cozy furnishings in the three-hundred-year-old inn, the wonderful collection of gleaming horse brasses that adorned a massive brick fireplace, the magnificence of the landlord's steaming Cornish pasties and mellow golden ale.

There were few other people in the dining room this Sunday evening, and they sat near the fire and ate heartily. When there was no more food to consume, or small talk to exchange, Owain said, "The house is more or less clean and tidy again. Shall we go home?"

Eleanor cleared her throat and glanced about her. All of the other diners had left and they were now alone. "I . . . have to be on the morning train. I have a matinee tomorrow. Perhaps it would be better if I just stayed here tonight. It would save you having to take me to the station."

He stared at his half-empty glass. "You're going back to London," he said, resignation in his voice.

"I have to, Owain."

"What's to become of us, Ellie? We can't go on like this."

Under the table her hands kneaded the soft wool of her dress, and her gaze roved about the room rather than meet his. When the silence became unbearable, she blurted out the most difficult words she had ever had to speak. "I can't live with you in that miserable farmhouse, Owain. I'm sorry. I know I promised to love honor and obey, but I can't live like that."

He looked up. "What if I were to sell the farm?"

"I couldn't ask you to do that."

"It's not a question of your asking . . . it's a question of necessity. Without Peter's financial help, and now with losing the stallion, well, there's nothing else for it but to sell."

"But if you sell, what would you do then?"

"I was thinking of going back to America. I heard from Peter. He's bought some land in Texas. Said I could pick up some acres fairly cheap." He leaned forward, his expression becoming eager. "There'll be a little from the sale of the farm, and if there was enough in your grandfather's bequest, perhaps we could buy some land and some stock."

She tried to keep her voice steady. "The play I'm in is a success. We're expecting a long run. Owain, how can I explain to you? I love acting. I can't imagine not doing it."

"I think I've come to realize that. But settlers are pouring into the American West. There'll be theaters there, too. I'm not asking you to give it up—I'm just asking that you come with me. I can't go back to working as a groom here. I'd feel I was going down in defeat. We could have a fresh start with your inheritance —which you can't get unless you go back, anyway. Please, Ellie, I'm trying to work out a life for both of us.''

"You didn't hear a word I said, did you? *Last Love* is going to run for months, maybe years. I don't want to leave the cast. I can't leave while the play is still running. The part of Margot was written for me. It's my part. It's *my* play, my life!''

"It's not your life, Ellie. It's make-believe.''

"Tristan was right. You don't understand, you'll never understand.''

"Damn Tristan. I don't want to know what Tristan said. You'd no business discussing our personal affairs with him. I wish I'd never let him come to my house. Are you still my wife? Are you going to come to America with me or not?''

"I'm still your wife, Owain. But I can't go to America with you, not now.''

"The two things go together, Ellie.''

The door from the saloon bar opened at that moment, and a noisy group of people entered the dining room, talking and laughing. Owain rose to his feet. "There's not much more to be said, is there?''

Thane regarded her over the rim of his wineglass and said, "Why don't you tell me what happened in Cheshire, and then we can decide what to do about it.''

"It's none of your business,'' Eleanor replied moodily.

He shrugged indifferently, picked up a cracker, and spread caviar lavishly.

Eleanor said, "I don't know why I'm even here with you. Wasting a perfectly good Sunday evening when I could be home washing my hair.''

He motioned to the waiter. "Bring me a dozen oysters and another bottle of Niersteiner.''

"They don't go together,'' Eleanor commented.

"Neither do we, but here we are. Are you going to eat, or continue sulking? It's immaterial to me, but our waiter is about to have a nervous breakdown.''

"I'll have Dover sole. And another glass of wine.''

"Not until you've eaten. Anything more to drink and you'll become maudlin. I can't stand maudlin women."

"And I can't stand domineering men. So pour my wine or I'll move to another table."

He hesitated, noted the tilt of her chin and the set of her mouth, then poured a very small quantity of wine into her glass. "Is he coming to London?"

"Yes. As soon as he's sold the farm."

"Ah, then he's giving up his dream to help you pursue yours? The gravest error any man can make."

"He won't be staying. He's going back to America."

Thane looked at her sharply. "You're not going with him?"

Eleanor gave a mirthless laugh. "I can remember a time when you wanted me to leave the country. How things do change."

"At that time I was charged with the task of making sure HRH didn't make a fool of himself over you."

"Oh? It seemed to me you were more of a procurer than a protector."

He smiled. "Nice attempt at an insult. However, I was not employed by HRH to contact women for him. I was working for his superiors. Even a prince of the realm is answerable to someone above him in the hierarchy."

"I take it you no longer have that job? What exactly do you do nowadays?"

"Anything I wish. Except, apparently, coax you into my bed."

She raised her eyebrows in exaggerated surprise. "What, and spoil a perfectly good vendetta?"

"Is that what we're having?" he asked good-humoredly. "We could have fun in bed, you and I."

"You told me once that copulation without affection is a vastly overrated pastime."

He considered this with mock seriousness. "Do you suppose it's not you but the ethereal Margot I'm lusting after? Yes, I think perhaps it is. The doomed, virginal Margot . . . going to her grave and never knowing carnal ecstasy."

The waiter brought the fish, and as he moved away Eleanor hissed, "I think he heard. Must you say such things in public?"

"You won't give me a chance to say them in private. How many times have I asked you to dine at my house? Or suggested we go to your flat?"

"With what end in mind? No, don't answer, I already know. I've told you many times, I won't sleep with you. Not ever. As far as I'm concerned, copulation even *with* affection is vastly overrated." Damn, she thought, what possessed me to say that?

His eyes gleamed. "I thought so! Your adoring Celt hasn't awakened the woman in you. He probably loves you too much, so handles you with kid gloves."

Startled, she almost dropped her fork. His words seemed to echo something she had heard before, but she couldn't recall where.

Thane went on, "I believe you need a man to be a little more ruthless, a little more dangerous. You need a man who will sweep you away."

"You, for instance."

"Of course. I'm told I'm quite accomplished in that regard."

Eleanor decided this line of conversation had gone far enough. "You never answered my question about HRH. Are you still a royal vassal?"

His eyebrow shot up. *"Vassal?"*

"Oh, you don't like that description any better than procurer?" she asked innocently.

"I'm no longer associated in any way with the royal family. My sense of duty and obligation to my country is impeccable, but I lack the necessary awe of royalty to continue in their service. You probably understand that, being an American."

"Well . . ." Eleanor responded cautiously.

"Don't misunderstand," Thane said. "I am wholly in favor of the monarchy. What did Samuel Johnson tell Boswell? That a civilized society requires some invariable measurement of value, and that the 'higher' class must rest its claims on qualities above and beyond the rivalries of the marketplace. Members of the royal family fill that need and create no jealousy in their subjects because they attain their rank simply by virtue of birth. They are accidental winners in life. Having surrendered the desire to govern us, they rule by charm, rather like children and domestic pets. They are creatures for display only, protected from chance and loss. They live lives that are fantasy ideals for the rest of us."

Eleanor giggled. "Did you tell HRH he's about as useful as a child or a pet hound?"

"Something like that. Fortunately I'm no longer in the army, so he couldn't have me sent to some godforsaken desert."

She had mangled her Dover sole without eating any of it and, noticing this, he said, "You were off your feed the last time we dined together. You're also looking a little pale. You're not ill, are you?"

"No," Eleanor said abruptly. "But I am tired. Will you take me home, please?"

Sometimes when she closed her eyes and feigned death, Eleanor felt herself floating away into a misty netherworld, and the roar of applause intruded rather than gratified. She was so tired that the idea of a very long slumber was appealing, and she didn't want to rise from her deathbed to take her curtain calls. How nice it would be to simply stay here on stage and sleep on Tristan's chaise until it was time to rise for tomorrow's matinee.

She realized that Tristan was shaking her and opened her eyes. "Good Lord, you frightened me! I thought you'd really died," he whispered as he helped her to her feet.

After they had taken their bows, Tristan marched her to her dressing room, ordered Frieda to leave, and locked her door. "All right, young lady, we're alone. I want to know what's wrong with you."

Eleanor rubbed her eyes sleepily, smearing kohl all over her cheek. She bit her lip. "I think I'm . . . in the family way."

Tristan groaned and clapped his hand to his forehead. He walked a small frantic circle around the dressing room, then exclaimed, "You can't be! You mustn't be. Eleanor, I warned you . . . Surely you're mistaken? Your husband is still up north." Another thought struck him. "Oh, God! It isn't Thane's, is it?"

"Of course not! I'm not sleeping with Thane and never have. Don't you remember, I went to visit Owain that weekend . . ."

"Perhaps you're mistaken?" he suggested again, hopefully.

"I'm not. I've been so horribly sick in the mornings and . . . I'm not mistaken."

"This will mean the end of *Last Love*. No audience is going to accept another Margot."

"It's probably the end of my career, too," Eleanor said tearfully. "I have to accept it as a sign that I should go back to Owain."

There was a knock on the dressing room door, and Frieda's voice called, "There is ein messenger here with letter for Miss Hathaway. Is insisting no one else can accept."

Eleanor unlocked the door and took the envelope. She recognized Owain's handwriting immediately. Tearing open the envelope, she read:

ELLIE, *BACH*,
   BY THE TIME YOU READ THIS I SHALL BE ON A STEAMER ON MY WAY TO AMERICA. I SOLD THE FARM AND CAME TO LONDON AND SAW YOUR PLAY. I INTENDED TO COME BACKSTAGE AFTERWARDS, BUT DIDN'T BECAUSE AFTER I SAW THE MAGIC OF YOU UP THERE ON THE STAGE, I KNEW IT WAS HOPELESS. WHAT CAN I OFFER YOU THAT WOULD COMPARE TO YOUR MAKE-BELIEVE WORLD? THANK YOU FOR SHARING A LITTLE BIT OF YOUR LIFE WITH ME. I'LL LET YOU KNOW WHERE I LAND, IN CASE YOU NEED ME FOR ANYTHING. I LOVE YOU.
   OWAIN.

32

CHARLOTTE'S EYES MISTED as she watched the young boy race across the tree-shaded quadrangle of the boarding school in Buckinghamshire and hurl himself into Evan's arms.

Gwynfor, her son . . . she must remember to call him Geoffrey now, since he'd never been called by any other name, looked like an ungainly colt clad in the school uniform of dark gray.

Feelings of gratitude and pride flowed through her, and she was content to wait until Evan and the boy greeted one another, even though her arms ached to embrace her son.

It was clear they were more than fond of one another and that the child had missed Evan desperately. More than that, their features even seemed to look a little alike. But that, of course, was simply the family likeness that Evan also shared to some degree with Stephen. Evan's features were a more rugged, elongated version of his half brother's, lacking Stephen's almost-too-perfect handsomeness. Then, too, Evan had the high, domed forehead and lantern jaw typical of gigantism. The little boy had inherited many of the Athmore features, and his face was less rugged than Evan's, though not quite as handsome as that of his father. But when Geoffrey glanced shyly at Charlotte, she saw that he had her eyes.

Evan ruffled Geoffrey's hair and placed him back on his feet. He was of average height for his age, and perhaps a little thin, but then Charlotte reminded herself that she had small bones that never acquired a spare ounce of flesh, and he'd no doubt inherited his slight frame from her.

The letter Evan had written from Ceylon stated simply that he was bringing Charlotte home to England as his wife. She had worried ever since about what they would tell Geoffrey.

"We'll tell him the truth," Evan said. "About his birth, about how Zoe told you he was dead."

"But the shock of learning I am his mother, and the circumstances of his birth . . . I gave my word that I would never divulge that. If Zoe were to find out that Stephen is Geoffrey's father—"

"Geoffrey needs to know the truth, about everything," Evan said firmly. "Your son is wise for his age, Charlotte, he'll understand that it would be better if Zoe were kept in ignorance of some things."

"But we'll have to tell him of her treachery . . . otherwise he'll believe I abandoned him."

"In the end, the bare truth always hurts less than a sugarcoated lie."

He was right, of course.

Up in the school's bell tower a clock chimed the hour, and Geoffrey offered Charlotte his hand. "I'm very glad to meet you. I was wondering what I should call you?"

Charlotte felt tears trembling on her eyelashes, and for a moment she held her son's hand, unable to speak.

Evan's arm tightened around her shoulder and he said, "We are going for a walk around the school grounds, Geoffrey. They're lovely this time of year, aren't they? And while we walk, we have a great many things to tell you. After that, we shall go to a tea shop and have cream buns and black currant tarts and discuss what we are going to do in the future. You see, we three are going to be a family."

Stephen glanced over his shoulder to be sure he had not been followed, then lifted the loose floorboards in the corner of the summer house.

He hesitated for a second, then reached under the floor for a large, tin box. Placing it beside him, he lifted the lid, hoping the rust was only superficial, and took out a wooden crate. He pried the slats apart and then began to unwrap layers of sacking.

As the layers of cloth came away and he drew near the precious contents, he moved more slowly and carefully. He'd been a fool to leave it here for so long, but had never dared come for it before, fearing ridicule if anyone ever learned of his deception.

Drawing a deep breath, he peeled away the last layer and looked at the rolled canvas. It seemed undamaged, despite the length of time it had been hidden here. As he'd hoped, the tin box had offered protection from the elements and the attentions of any marauding rodents.

Slowly he unrolled the canvas, and a moment later looked down at the nude of Charlotte. His *Passionate Virgin*.

Stephen caught his breath, overcome by the beauty of his own work. The mellow afternoon sunlight spilling through the trellises of the summer house gilded Charlotte's pale complexion, bringing her to life. He'd captured perfectly that shy, sad, eager, brave quality in her eyes, and added the breathless excitement of erotic longing. It was there in her eyes, in her parted lips and the exquisitely fragile curves of her slender body, which even in repose suggested passion and surrender.

The years flew away and he remembered that afternoon when he had made love to her. Strange how so many events that followed were no longer clear in his mind, yet every detail of that first joining now haunted him. He was filled with regret, at what might have been, had he not come to his senses too late.

He was unsure how long he sat there on the dusty floor, admiring the painting and thinking about Charlotte. There had never been a mysterious suitor who paid an enormous sum to own the painting, of course. The truth was that Stephen simply couldn't bear to part with it. After exhibiting it in London, he'd spread the story of the wealthy collector and then hid the canvas, confident that the value of his work would soar, and it did.

Because of this one painting, his reputation had been made. There was no longer any need for him to rely on his allowance from the estate. His commissions for portraits and the various other paintings he sold commanded handsome prices. But, of course, it wasn't enough for Zoe. Nothing on earth was ever enough for her.

Stephen had even been prepared to leave Glendower forever, although the sacrifice would have been akin to amputating a part of his body. At least if they left he'd never have to suffer the humiliation of seeing Evan in possession of everything that was rightfully his . . . the estate, the boy . . . now even Charlotte, his passionate virgin, too.

But Zoe had adamantly refused to leave. She taunted him for his cowardice and said she intended to stand and fight. Stephen had held her as she screamed in frustration because Evan and Charlotte had remained in the south of England near Geoffrey's boarding school until the term ended, then all three of them left for a holiday in Spain without ever returning to Glendower.

"They can't take the boy with them," Zoe had cried. "He's ours! We can stop them."

"No," Stephen said. "That's the last thing we'll do. This is a private matter and will be settled within the family. I will never allow this mess we've created to become public knowledge."

"He'll take away my house! My beautiful mansion."

"Nonsense. He hates this house. He's not even terribly fond of the grange, it was just a refuge from the world. But now, apparently, he no longer fears being out in the world."

"All the more reason he should give Glendower to us. Damn him, and damn that little servant woman. How dare they come back as man and wife?" Zoe had ranted and raved for hours, and then suddenly exclaimed, "And if I ever see Fenmore, he'll pay dearly for letting me down . . ."

"Who is Fenmore? And how did he let you down?"

Zoe had chosen that moment to retreat into one of her long silences. She had remained in her room for several days now, so did not know about the letter that had arrived bearing a Spanish postmark. Evan had written that he and Charlotte and Geoffrey were coming home. They would be at Glendower for Christmas, and that various and sundry problems could be discussed at that time.

Stephen reached toward the painting and with one finger followed the long column of Charlotte's throat to the pale pink areola of her breast. Then he rose reluctantly, picked up the canvas, and went outside.

There was a hint of frost in the air, overlaid with wood smoke coming from the direction of the fields where leaves, branches and other refuse were being burned. He walked slowly, savoring the scents and sounds, feasting his eyes on his surroundings. How he loved Glendower. The stark grandeur of the mountains against the sky, the sparkling clarity of the lake, the gaudy clash of autumn colors layered upon tree branches as if by an artist drunk with the power of his fiery palette.

He sometimes thought he only went away from Glendower in order to have the pleasure of returning. To have to leave forever was unthinkable, yet that was surely what Evan would demand.

Stephen felt his melancholy mood press down upon him like a yoke. He had not slept for almost a week, but he thought his mind was remarkably clear. He wasn't sure the precise moment he had looked at Zoe and seen evil instead of beauty, or at himself and recognized how he had enabled her to perpetrate that evil. He knew only that he had to put a stop to it.

At the top of the hill he paused and looked down at the valley. The diamond sparkle of sunlight on the lake blinded him, and he turned to look in the other direction, at the plume of wood smoke rising from a harvested field like a funeral pyre.

He was aware of the turf beneath his feet as he approached the pile of burning branches, and of the song of a lonely finch somewhere in the woods, but his eyes saw only the bonfire. A young gardener piling on dead branches spoke to him as he drew near, but Stephen was unsure what was said. He stood looking at the flames for a moment, then threw the oil painting of Charlotte into the molten core of the fire.

As the canvas curled, then flared and was consumed, Stephen wished that he could as easily erase both Zoe and himself from existence. When nothing remained of *The Passionate Virgin* except falling ash, he turned away and walked briskly back to the house.

Evan was right, the house was a gaudy monstrosity No doubt after their departure he would tear it down. Stephen felt calm now, and he smiled pleasantly at a passing footman, and made his way to the trophy room. Selecting a shotgun from the gun case, he found a box of shells and loaded it.

He would have preferred to make the whole thing look accidental, for the sake of his son. In fact, he had considered simply taking Zoe out on the lake and sinking the boat. But she could swim and so could he, and he couldn't think of any way to ensure they both drowned. Jumping from an upper story was also risky, in case they were maimed rather than killed. No, it would have to be the shotgun, to be quick and certain. He didn't want her to suffer.

In the hall he was confronted by the housekeeper, Mrs. Carmichael, who gave the gun a startled look before he said quickly, "I saw a wild boar down by the lake."

"Oh, yes," she said uncertainly, then went on hurriedly, "I'm worried about her ladyship, sir. I went down to the village to do some shopping. I wouldn't have left her alone, for the world, and I know I told that flighty Lizzie to stay with her, even though she says I didn't."

"Yes, yes, Mrs. Carmichael," Stephen said impatiently. "What is it?"

"My lady left the house, sir. While I was gone. No one saw her leave."

Stephen sighed. "No doubt she awakened feeling better. You know how abruptly her silent spells end and how energetic she is afterwards. I expect she went riding. Have you inquired at the stables?"

Mrs. Carmichael's pinched features seemed to close still further. "We've searched all over the house and grounds. We've looked everywhere, but we can't find her. There's something else, Lord Athmore. The butler told me he answered the door to a foreign gentleman shortly after I left. He asked for Lady Athmore."

"A foreign gentleman?"

"A Hindu gentleman, I believe. He had dark skin and a beard, and wore a turban. He wouldn't give his name and became very agitated when he was told her ladyship was indisposed. The butler had to call for help to prevent the man from entering the house."

Stephen frowned. "We don't know any Hindu gentleman. Did he say what he wanted?"

"No, just that it was urgent he speak with her ladyship. It just seems strange that this man came and shortly afterwards Lady Athmore vanished from her room."

Stephen looked down at the gun in his hand and said, "I'm going to look around again. You'd better send for the police."

It was well past midnight when Mrs. Carmichael brought the village policeman to Stephen's study. He sat near the window, staring out into the darkness, the shotgun propped against his chair. He had searched the house and grounds over and over again, then ordered the staff to continue searching. But Zoe had vanished without a trace.

As the white-faced housekeeper and the police constable entered the room, Stephen knew, even before they spoke, that Zoe was gone forever. Strange that he himself had arisen that very morning knowing that this would be the last day of Zoe's life. He'd believed it would be his last day on earth, too.

"Very, very sorry, Lord Athmore," the constable was saying. "The man had been seen in the village, but we couldn't arrest him simply for being a foreigner, could we? I did ask him his business and he said he had something to deliver to Glendower, and sure enough, he showed me a letter with your crest on the envelope, imprinted with her ladyship's name. It was addressed to Edmund Fenmore, Esquire. I thought the Hindu was a manservant of this Mr. Fenmore. I would have stopped him, if I'd had any inkling of what he was up to."

Mrs. Carmichael began to sob.

"What happened to my wife?" Stephen asked quietly.

"The Hindu took her to the inn where he had a room. An hour later the gentleman left . . . alone. The innkeeper waited a little while, and when her ladyship didn't come down, he went and knocked on the door. When she didn't answer, he opened the door and . . ."

"She's dead?"

"Yes, sir. I'm sorry. The work of a madman. He had both strangled and stabbed her."

"You have the man in custody?"

"Not yet. But he won't get far. There's no train from Llanrys until morning, and we'll have him by then."

"Where is my wife now?"

"Still at the inn, sir."

"I'm going to her. Mrs. Carmichael, will you bring my coat?" Stephen looked down at the shotgun. "You can put that back in the case. I shan't be needing it now."

Fenmore peered at his reflection in the mirror. He had scrubbed his face until the skin was raw, but still some of the dye seemed to remain. Perhaps it was simply that his skin was tanned from the long hours of working in the sun. He had shaved off his beard and discarded the turban, and in a new, tweed suit he looked like any other Englishman who might have spent some time in the tropics. He was much thinner than when he'd left, and he decided the slightly gaunt look was interesting.

His reflection danced dizzily for an instant, and he had to lean on his washstand to steady himself. He hadn't felt well for some time, and blamed his diet and the poor hygiene of his living quarters on the coolie line of the tea plantation. He'd lost a great deal of weight and had been troubled with skin eruptions, headaches, and pains in his joints.

When he thought of the months he'd toiled as a coolie before saving enough for his passage to India, where he was able to send word to his family that he needed money to come home, Fenmore went into uncontrollable rages. He felt one coming on now. That urge to make someone pay for what had been done to him.

Recalling the satisfaction he'd felt in crushing the life out of Zoe Athmore no longer eased his anger. He wished he'd made her suffer more. If it hadn't been for her, he'd never have gone to Ceylon.

Even though he was home now, in his own room at his parents' estate, he had abruptly awakened from an afternoon nap thinking he could hear the *cangany* chastising him. Often he thought he could still hear the sound of the afternoon horn blowing to call him back to the dismal, mud-floored compartment he shared with three other coolies. Sometimes the sounds in his head, and the voices he heard, made him want to bang his skull against a wall.

There had been plenty of opportunity to regret killing the dancing girl, Rhani. He should at least have let her help him escape from the island, pretended to be willing to marry her, and then dealt with her threat of betrayal. But deferring his pleasures had never been possible for him. He needed instant gratification of his every wish, and at the time, Rhani had inspired a fury in him that demanded appeasement.

A tentative knock on his bedroom door and his mother's voice calling, "Edmund? May we come in?" interrupted his reverie.

"What do you want? I'm just finishing dressing and then I'm going down to the pub for an hour."

"Had you forgotten, dear? It's Tuesday. Dr. Hill is here."

"Tell him to wait."

He frowned, remembering that his mother had been concerned about his poor health and his father had insisted he must be examined by the family doctor, in case he had picked up some lingering tropical disease.

At present he didn't dare go against their wishes, until it was certain no one could connect him with Zoe Athmore's death. Or with the death of the old farmer whose horse he'd stolen and ridden until it collapsed. But then, how could they? A turbaned, dark-skinned foreigner had gone to North Wales, but Edmund Fenmore, son of a well-to-do landowner, had eventually boarded a train for southern England.

He'd always been able to wrap his parents around his little finger. He had been born to them late in life and felt ashamed of their elderly appearance, their gullibility and weakness. They never believed he was guilty of any of the things others accused him of, and on the rare occasions when the proof was incontrovertible, he was able to convince them it was not his fault, or that it had all been a mistake.

But that damn doctor had been his nemesis. Dr. Hill had wanted to send him to an asylum years before the courts finally insisted upon it. The doctor had even tried to persuade his parents not to let the asylum release him into their care. Fenmore hated and feared the old doctor, who would probably jump at the chance of sending him to a hospital or a rest home on the flimsiest of medical excuses. Anything to get him confined somewhere. Fenmore had never been able to charm the old devil the way he could everyone else. Hill looked right into his mind and hated what he saw there. The doctor's voice called through the closed door now, "I'm coming in, Edmund."

Fenmore managed to contain his anger during the examination.

"Well?" he asked when it was finished, furious at the deliberate slowness of the doddering old fool.

Dr. Hill looked him in the eye for an interminable minute.

Fearing the silence, Fenmore said, "I have not been subject to high fevers. So don't tell me I contracted malaria."

"I wouldn't dream of it. Tell me, how long have you had this general run-down feeling?"

Fenmore scratched his scalp. "Oh, I don't know. I think it began about a month after I arrived in Ceylon."

"I see. So you've had the symptoms for several months?"

"I know it can't be serious, because I'm definitely feeling better since I came home. You wouldn't be here now if it weren't for my parents, so stop beating about the bush and tell me what you think it is."

"Oh, it's probably some little tropical germ that will need time to work its way out of your system. I'll prescribe a tonic for you and be back to see you in a few days. Meantime, I'd recommend that you get plenty of bed rest, and don't leave the house."

"What? I'll go mad cooped up here."

Dr. Hill's faded eyes glittered a warning. "Don't leave the house, Edmund. In fact, I don't want anyone other than your mother coming into your room . . . you . . . er . . . well, this is the cold season and I'm afraid if you catch a cold or the flu before we get you back to normal health, it would complicate things."

The old man wasn't usually hesitant in his speech, even if he was slow in his movements, and something in the look in his eyes troubled Fenmore. At least Hill had not suggested the hospital. "Oh, very well. I'll follow your orders, you old quack."

That night his headaches and the pains in his joints seemed worse. Probably due to the poking and prodding of the damned doctor. But it was true that they were not as bad as formerly, and he was improving with each passing day. The skin eruptions had all healed, too. Fenmore drank most of a bottle of whiskey and fell into an inebriated slumber.

He awakened sometime the following day in a vile temper and, feeling imprisoned by his room, decided to go downstairs. Halfway down the staircase, he stopped. He could hear his mother crying, and several voices in urgent conversation. They were in the drawing room, and the door was ajar.

Listening intently, he recognized the voice of Dr. Hill saying, "There is no mistake, Mrs. Fenmore. I'm sorry, but we must act at once, before he has a chance to infect anyone else."

His father's voice, tense, horrified, exclaimed, "For God's sake, stop crying, woman. It's too late for tears. He brought it on himself. Who knows what kind of women he associated with in Ceylon. Or here, for that matter."

"No," his mother begged. "Please . . . Dr. Hill, there must be some other way."

Hill's raspy voice continued, "He's mentally unbalanced now. Oh, he puts on a good act, but the fact is, he can't be treated like a normal, responsible man. He can't be trusted not to spread his filthy disease. Eventually he'll become even more insane. I'm sorry to be so blunt, madam, but you must realize there is no cure. He is terminally ill. He faces possible blindness, diseases of the heart and internal organs . . . and ultimately, dementia paralytica, that is paralysis of the insane."

On the staircase, Fenmore stood rooted to the spot. Below the hall spun crazily out of focus, and he sank down on a stair, clutching the balustrade.

His father's voice spoke again, "You gentlemen go ahead and do what must be done. I want my son locked up immediately. Even if my wife does not fully understand the nature of his illness, I do. All I ask is that you do not tell Edmund that he has syphilis."

Fenmore was on his feet, bellowing at the top of his lungs, screaming like a trapped animal, when the four burly attendants came running up the stairs and seized him.

They dragged him from the house, cursing, shrieking, damning her . . . Rhani, the voluptuous dancing girl . . . may her soul burn in hell. She had succeeded in betraying him after all. He'd killed her, but she had sentenced him to a death more horrible than her own.

33

As Maeve had seen in her tea leaves, Eleanor returned to Glendower wearing black, for Zoe's funeral. The graveside service was conducted in a biting wind, and Eleanor wondered if the frozen ground was reluctant to accept Zoe's remains.

In view of the severe cold, the number of mourners present surprised her. The entire village had turned out, the Ramseys and many other friends of Stephen had come from London, including Veronica, whose hideously fat body looked less overwhelming in her floor-length black coat.

Eleanor studied Stephen, noting that his handsome features were as gray as the December sky. His eyes, which had always appeared to express great sorrow, were now more mournful than ever and seemed to stare down an endless corridor of time, as if wondering what to do with the rest of his life. He seemed aloof, not part of the crowd, as though he had already withdrawn from the rest of the world.

Afraid she might faint, since her pregnancy grew more physically taxing every day, Eleanor tried to concentrate on the minister's words. "Ashes to ashes . . . dust to dust . . ."

She shut him out again, feeling an icy chill that did not originate with the weather gripping her. This was the reality of death, being sealed up in a wooden box in the ground, not the gentle drifting off to dreamy sleep on a satin chaise as the stage lights were dimmed and the audience sobbed.

A wave of dizziness caused her to sway on her feet, and Tristan's arm went around her to steady her. He gave her one of

340

his I-told-you-so looks. He had warned her that she should not corset herself so tightly, that that was what caused her weakness and fainting spells. But the truth was, she wasn't wearing a corset at all. She had lost so much weight she was smaller than ever. Aware of exactly when she had conceived, she knew that she was now over three months along. Frieda had said women often felt better later on in their pregnancies. Only Frieda and Tristan knew her secret.

On the opposite side of the open grave, the family formed a somber semicircle. Evan's big hands tenderly held the small ones of Geoffrey and Charlotte. The little boy's cheeks were tear-stained. Eleanor knew that even a seldom-present mother was grieved for, and for the first seven years of his life Geoffrey had believed Zoe to be his mother. Eleanor herself had never completely stopped grieving for her own mother, despite the fact that it had been Charlotte who brought her up.

Eleanor's glance returned time and time again to Charlotte. Even though she surely couldn't be far from her fortieth birthday, she looked radiantly young. Mrs. Carmichael had remarked to Lizzie, within Eleanor's hearing, that it was really disgusting to see Mr. Evan and his new wife carrying on like carefree newlyweds, in view of the tragedy. To Mrs. Carmichael, the worst tragedy of all was that her late mistress's murderer still remained at large.

At last, the coffin was lowered into the grave. Eleanor stared at it for a moment, thinking of all the mischief Zoe had done during her lifetime. But she was beyond all reproach or retribution now. Delia Ramsey, on the other hand, was not. Eleanor had been appalled to learn of the number of letters Charlotte had sent her which she had never received. She and her old nanny had sat up for hours last night, sharing the missing pieces of their interwoven lives.

Charlotte had made one particularly poignant remark. "I always loved you, Eleanor, as if you were my own daughter. Parting from you was, for me, like tearing off some of my own flesh, even when I had to go . . . as when Geoffrey was born, or when Delia threatened to write to your grandfather if I tried to see you."

Eleanor had hugged her and said, "I know I shouldn't hate a dead woman . . . so I won't say what I think about Zoe. But one of the conspirators who kept us apart is still alive. I'm going to tell Delia Ramsey exactly what I think of her."

"Don't," Charlotte said gently. "It won't change anything, and will only alienate you from Tristan. He's very close to Lord Ramsey. Forgive and forget, my dear."

"I suppose Delia really has been punished enough . . . having Veronica for a daughter." Eleanor had giggled.

Charlotte hadn't said anything about Eleanor's marriage to Owain, but then, there hadn't really been time.

The family and closest friends returned to Glendower and stood around a blazing fire drinking port and brandy to banish the cemetery chill from their bones. Eleanor sank into a chair and Tristan brought her some sandwiches and a cup of tea.

"I'd prefer sherry—" she began, but Tristan silenced her with a threatening look.

He bent over her and whispered, "I'm going back to London on the evening train, but why don't you stay and rest a couple of days? Your understudy can handle things for a few performances. I'll let the gentlemen of Fleet Street know you've been bereaved. Audiences will forgive you for that."

"Yes, I think I will stay on another day or so. I need a rest and besides, I'd like to spend some time with Charlotte."

How wonderful it was to unburden herself to Charlotte, and how fascinating to learn that her former nanny's life had taken her along such exotic paths. The biggest shock came when Charlotte confessed that Stephen had been her son's father. This she did not admit until the day after he departed from Glendower on a pilgrimage to Zoe's former home in New Orleans.

The two women were alone at the breakfast table, since Evan and Geoffrey had gone for an early morning ride. As Eleanor digested this revelation, Charlotte went on, "We've told Geoffrey the truth, and Stephen knows this. Naturally, for the time being we aren't letting anyone outside of the family know, but I wanted you to know the truth because . . . Eleanor, you haven't told me why your husband went to America without you . . . or why you haven't brought up the subject of the child you're carrying."

"How did you know? I'm not showing, am I?"

"No, dear. But I've had a great deal of experience with young mothers-to-be, many of whom were less than overjoyed to find they were with child. Especially when the father was not present. I fear you are wearing that same look of dismay."

"I suppose I didn't mention it because I'm pretending it doesn't exist."

"Your marriage, or the child?" Charlotte asked gently.

"Both, I think. Oh, Charlotte, I've made such a mess of things. I never should have married Owain. I feel so guilty about how I've treated him, yet I can't seem to stop hurting him. I haven't written and told him about the baby . . . I could go to America and join him, but I don't. I just seem to let everything drift."

"Hoping the problems will solve themselves? My dear child, believe me, they won't. Tell me, if the only person you had to please was yourself, what would you do?"

"I'd continue acting. It's all I ever wanted to do, you know that. But it's so difficult for a woman alone to do anything. Now that I think about it, I believe you are the only woman I've ever met who managed to spend a good portion of her life without the protection of a man."

"You speak of protection . . . what about love?"

"I've loved some people . . . you, Maeve, even Owain, before we were married. But I honestly don't know what romantic love is. I'm not sure I want to." She smiled apologetically. "I love acting. I can be in love for a little while on stage and not have to endure all that romantic love involves. The disgusting intimacies."

Charlotte stared at her for a long moment, her expression sympathetic yet surprised, as if she personally had not found physical intimacy disgusting. "Then my advice to you would be to plan your future with that in mind. You will, of course, have to give up acting for a while, but you only need to stay off the stage for a few months. With your present reputation as an actress, you'll soon find another part. But you must be honest with Owain and tell him everything. He has to be consulted about the future of the child. By the way, I should be delighted if you would come to Glendower for your confinement."

Eleanor sighed. "Thank you. I know you're right. I just hate to let Margot die forever."

"What a very strange regret."

"I suppose it is."

"Tell me more about this man Victor Thane you mentioned. He sounds like a very dangerous person to allow into your life."

"I really don't know how I became so involved with him. He's just . . . there. I like the way he's able to cut a swath through the world . . . no one gets in his way, no one bothers me, when he's near. We have supper together after the play, he takes me shopping, or riding in the park. I can say anything at all to him and he isn't shocked. Perhaps it's his freedom to do and be anything he pleases that I envy. I suppose we have a friendship of sorts.''

"But he doesn't look upon you as a friend. He sees you as a possible conquest.''

Surprised, Eleanor exclaimed, "How did you know?''

Charlotte smiled faintly. "I'm well aware of the power a ruthless man wields over a woman. Stephen is such a man. You see, there are the nice, safe men of the world . . . my beloved Evan is one of them . . . oh, I know he used to growl and rampage like an angry bear, but under that facade was a very gentle, compassionate man, deeply sensitive, easily hurt. I think I recognized that immediately. And then there are those dangerously attractive men like Stephen, who caught me unawares. A woman has to choose whether she wants the heady excitement, which will certainly be only temporary, or if she wants lifelong devotion, which . . . for some women, can be just a trifle dull. Others see it as security. For myself, having known both kinds of men, I would urge any woman to run from the dangerous, ruthless, exciting men and settle for a more quiet and steady happiness. I'd advise you to send Thane packing, just as you did Owain, and concentrate on your first love, the theater.''

"Oh, if only I weren't in the family way! I shall never sleep with any man, ever again. I'm too afraid of the consequences.''

"But then, you will miss a great deal.''

Eleanor felt herself blush. "Why, Charlotte, I can't believe you're saying these things.''

"We are both married women. I see nothing wrong with being straightforward. Besides, whether you realize it or not, you are attracted to this man Thane. I recognize the look in your eyes when you speak of him. He's exciting because he's forbidden, you must constantly remind yourself of that. And never forget that if you submit to him, he'll leave you. The excitement of the chase is what keeps him with you now. You know, what surprises me most is that you didn't find Owain Davies the same type of man. He always seemed to me to be so. That wild, Celtic air he had about him. His bravery, both when you ran off that night into the storm and when Evan was shot. I can scarcely reconcile the Owain I knew with the rather hesitant and adoring husband you describe, who apparently did not assert himself with you at all.

Did it occur to you that his manner might have reflected the depth of his love for you?''

Eleanor didn't respond, as at that moment they heard Evan and Geoffrey out in the hall. Just before they came into the room Eleanor whispered, ''Was it difficult . . . telling Geoffrey the truth?''

Charlotte smiled, a hint of sadness in her eyes. ''I believe Geoffrey's main concern was that he not be separated from his beloved Uncle Evan. Like yourself, Geoffrey was brought up by his nanny until he went to boarding school, in fact, he still sees her frequently. Zoe, and myself . . . we're just vague figures somewhere in the background of his life.''

''I'm fascinated by the Athmore saga,'' Thane said. ''Did Stephen find the man, Edmund Fenmore, employer of the mysterious Hindu?''

''I believe the police found his parents, but apparently their son had gone abroad and was still there. They thought perhaps the Hindu had worked for him—that would explain him showing the constable a letter from Zoe addressed to Edmund Fenmore.''

''Abroad where?''

''India, I think.''

''I believe if I'd been investigating the case, I'd have probed a little more deeply.''

''I've no doubt you would. But Stephen went to America after Zoe's funeral, there's no one to demand that the police do anything. Frankly, no one is anxious to have the scandals of Zoe's life come to light. You'll have to go now, I must change for the next act.''

''Go behind the screen if you must.''

''Frieda won't dress me if you're here.''

''Supper later?''

''Yes.'' Eleanor hesitated for a moment then added, ''There's something I want to ask you.''

He raised an eyebrow suggestively. ''At last! The answer is yes.''

Eleanor smiled. ''You're an absolute fool.''

When the performance ended and they went to their favorite cafe, however, her courage faltered. It took several false starts before she at last whispered, ''I was wondering if you knew a doctor who might . . . discreetly treat a friend of mine.''

His face was a mask. He said calmly, "You're speaking of an abortion and it's for yourself, so don't be coy. Tell me, how far along are you?"

"Nearly four months. But I wasn't going to ask you to arrange an illegal operation. I'll never forget a young actress bleeding to death after having one. No, I'll have this baby even if it kills me. It will certainly kill my career as an actress for a while. I need a doctor because I haven't felt well and I think something might be wrong. It's too soon to go to a midwife, and you know how reluctant doctors are to see women who are *enciente*."

"Does your husband know?"

She shook her head. "If I'd told Owain he'd have made me go to Texas, and I'd be trapped forever. I have to stay here and manage somehow. I thought you . . . well, you're so worldly."

"What you mean is, that I've undoubtedly impregnated dozens of hapless young things so have vast experience in such matters. Tell me, what symptoms cause you to think something is wrong? Many women feel ill during the early months."

Eleanor was not about to tell him about her blood-smeared underwear, or the cramping in her lower abdomen, and fortunately did not have to answer the question, as at that moment a man with a pair of opera glasses hung around his neck and a carnation in his buttonhole paused beside their table and stammered, "M—M—Miss Hathaway . . . I've seen *Last Love* seven times. I j—j—just wanted you to know—"

"Yes, yes," Thane said, waving him on his way.

"I would have been glad to sign his napkin," Eleanor said. "He seemed polite and sincere."

"He was also rude to interrupt our meal."

"We've finished . . . Why are you angry? Is it because I told you about the baby?"

"I'd suspected for some time."

"You *are* angry. Is it because you won't be able to believe in Margot any longer? I don't suppose you would accept an immaculate conception—"

"Shut up," Thane snapped, and she recoiled from the cold fury in his tone. "Don't joke about something this serious."

"It's no joke to me, believe me," Eleanor said in a small voice. "I'll have to bow out of *Last Love,* find a hiding place somewhere, and disappear for several months. You don't think I'm looking forward to that, do you?" She glanced up and saw another man bearing down on their table. "Oh, no!" she muttered under her breath. "Sean Connell's coming over. He's the playwright who wrote *Last Love*. Please don't be rude to him."

"Dear heart, how nice to see you," Sean said in his soft Irish brogue. "I can never get near you at the theater, and it's been too long since I've told you that your performance as Margot makes me weep . . . me, who created her out of thin air!"

"Thank you. Have you met Victor Thane?"

To her amazement, Thane rose and offered the playwright his hand, then invited him to join them. Before long, they were engaged in a conversation about the play. Thane asked several questions, which Sean answered. They had a drink, then Thane said, "The process of writing fascinates me. I always wonder how much is truth . . . culled from the playwright's own life and experience, and how much is a carefully constructed lie."

"An odd way of putting it," Sean said, smiling. "I'd have preferred you to ask how much came from my imagination."

"Tell me, had you met Eleanor before you wrote the role of Margot?"

"No, I hadn't."

"Is there a real Margot?" Thane persisted.

Eleanor laughed. "He's in love with her and wants to meet her."

Ignoring her, Thane said, "I don't believe a creature as perfect as Margot could ever have existed. She's your own ideal woman. So lovely, so exquisitely flawless that—in your play—you had to destroy her rather than let her be corrupted."

Sean stared at him. "Tell me, are you a critic? Or one of those anonymous theatergoers who writes to castigate me for Margot's untimely death? You know, neither the critics nor the irate letter-writers seem to realize that if Margot hadn't died, the play might have been quite forgettable."

"I merely wondered," Thane replied slowly, "if you ever knew a woman like Margot."

Sean rose to his feet. "I must be going. To answer your question, Margot was made up of bits and pieces of several women I've known. Most fictional characters are. One can't use real people, they're too inconsistent. Of course, occasionally there is the exception . . . Thank you for the brandy. Good night, sweet Eleanor."

As he walked away, Thane snapped his fingers to summon their waiter and said to Eleanor, "I'd better get you home to bed.

I'll get in touch with a doctor I know and let you know tomorrow when he can see you.''

Eleanor took his arm as they walked out of the restaurant. As always she felt content to let him take charge of matters, and now that he was going to take her to a doctor, she felt vast relief.

They had walked to a restaurant not far from the theater, and Thane's carriage was still at the stage door. The night air was cold, and Eleanor huddled inside her fur-collared coat. She was thinking about Thane's questions about Margot and was unprepared for the sudden melee into which they stumbled.

One minute the street was quiet and deserted, and the next shadowed figures were scuffling directly in their path. There was the sound of bone striking flesh, a sharp cry of pain. The yellow orb of a gas lamp illuminated three men in the act of robbing a fourth. Eleanor saw instantly that it was Sean Connell.

She screamed as Thane grabbed her around the waist, spun her around and pushed her behind him. "Get out of here," he ordered. "Go on, run."

He waded into the group, swinging his silver-knobbed cane with lethal accuracy.

Eleanor stood rooted to the spot, staring in wide-eyed terror. Sean was obviously stunned, and when his attackers released him to turn their attention to Thane, Sean slumped to the pavement. Thane was obviously more than a match for the three men. He fought like no man she had ever seen. Instead of raising his fists, he used his feet, elbows, knees, all the while whacking heads with his cane.

As they crashed about, their boots came perilously close to Sean's head. He was now prone on the cold ground, unconscious. Eleanor thought, if they kick his head, or fall on him . . . they're such big bruisers . . .

She hesitated a split second, then darted in to seize him by the shoulders and pull him to safety. He was heavier than she expected in view of his slight frame, and she released his shoulders in order to crouch lower and try to get a better grip.

The blow to her side winded her, but for a second the pain didn't register. Then she was part of the tangle of flailing fists and kicking boots. The last thing she remembered was the body of a man crashing down on her, and the back of her head hitting the pavement with a resounding thud. Stars spun dizzily and, in the second before she lost consciousness, she thought she heard Thane shouting her name in a tone of such anguish that it hardly resembled his voice at all.

34

"STOP IT! DAMN you, do you hear me? You are *not* Margot. You're not going to die. I won't allow it."

The voice frightened her, and she wanted to go back to that misty dream where everything was so peaceful. Poor Margot, to die so young . . . She must whisper words of comfort to her faithful lover before she left him forever . . . but that persistent, bullying voice wouldn't let her remember what it was she had to say before she could slip away.

"Eleanor, Eleanor listen to me. There are many other parts waiting for you to play. Wonderful roles that no one but you can bring to life. But first you must fight to live, Eleanor. Don't give in."

The pain intruded then. Terrible, tearing pain that was beyond endurance. She whimpered, terrified, wanting it to stop, willing to do anything if it would just go away.

Strong, masculine hands gripped hers so tightly that her body seemed to receive his strength, seemed almost to accept his will. The respite lasted only a moment before the assault of another onslaught of pain.

Panting, too weak to utter more than a long-drawn moan, she forced her lips to move, to say the words that would end the agony and bring down the curtain.

"Don't . . . grieve for me, my love. For I shall live forever in your heart. Where there is love, there can be no death . . . but only a brief parting . . ."

"No!" that terrible, commanding voice thundered. "I won't

let you repeat that damned death scene. You are Eleanor, not Margot.''

She had to go on, there was more to be said before they could bring down the curtain and the pain would end. She wished he wouldn't keep interrupting her, spoiling the most emotional part of the play. Play? But it wasn't a play, it was the few short precious years of Margot's life coming to an end.

''I could not have loved you more, had I been . . .'' She stumbled, unable to remember the next words she was supposed to say. ''I could not have loved you more . . .''

An arm, unyielding as iron, slid under her shoulders, raising her head from the pillow. Lips, bruising, relentless, closed over her mouth, stifling the words. If the touch of his hands had infused strength into her failing body, then the hot breath of his kiss was a life force that was even more difficult to resist. It surged through her body, inciting it to battle the pain and weakness, dragging her back from the brink of oblivion.

His voice, lower now, more ragged, murmured against her mouth. ''If you speak one more of Margot's lines, Eleanor, I shall kiss you again. I won't stop kissing you until you swear to me that you will fight for your life.''

She clung to him as a knot of pain grew, writhing like a snake through her body. Then there was merciful oblivion.

Owain? Owain, please come and find me. I'm so frightened and I need you. She called his name over and over again, but he didn't come.

Eleanor opened her eyes but saw only darkness. She screamed, ''Charlotte! I want Charlotte.''

A dearly familiar voice responded, ''I'm here, dear. Rest now.'' A cool cloth wiped her brow, and the soothing voice murmured, ''I shan't leave you.''

Then she was running as fast as she could because bolts of lightning were striking the earth all around her, and if she didn't reach the house in time, Owain was going to die. Great, black clouds clashed overhead, plunging the world into darkness.

Her grandfather's face intruded into the nightmare. He wanted her to recite for him. Franklyn Yarborough was licking his oily lips and waving at her with his big radish-finger hands. *By the shores of Gitche Gumee, by the shining Big-Sea-Water* . . .

No good! her grandfather roared. No good at all. You shan't have my money. Mr. Yarborough's moon face floated closer, and he laughed and laughed.

If she could just be someone else, even if for only a little while, then neither her grandfather nor Mr. Yarborough would be able to find her. She could hide inside that other person. Eleanor was such a bad little girl, it was all her fault. Not like beautiful Margot . . . so pure in mind, body, and spirit.

Maeve's voice, sharp and distinct, said, "I'm going to make a pot of tea. That will put you back on your feet. Then I'm going to read your tea leaves." But then, inexplicably, she changed into a big, black horse and galloped off into the night.

She tried to call her back, but everything faded again.

Someone was sobbing. They did that, out there in the audience in the darkness of the theater, they cried for the dying Margot.

"Do not grieve for me, my love . . ."

Soon, very soon now, she would be able to slip away.

They sat in a silent row in the hall outside the sickroom, while the doctor and his nurse examined Eleanor.

Charlotte contemplated the motley group. Victor Thane, who had insisted upon bringing Eleanor to his house and adamantly refused to allow her to be taken to a hospital. Tristan, ill at ease, desperately worried, yet reluctant to linger, as if he already smelled death in the air. Sean Connell, the melancholy-looking playwright, a black eye making a livid statement on his pallid face, his nose broken. Maeve, Eleanor's former dresser who had flown to her friend's side even as the new dresser found other employment.

After a moment, Thane rose and began to pace noiselessly up and down the carpeted hall. Charlotte watched him, marveling at the way he was able to hide whatever it was he might have been feeling. She put it down to military stoicism, that blank-faced imperviousness to either mental or physical torture that some men acquired in the army—an almost inhuman discipline. It was impossible to say whether his restless pacing expressed impatience with the slowness of the doctor and the frailty of women, or genuine concern for Eleanor. Despite his long vigil, Thane was immaculately dressed and groomed, and showed no sign of fatigue. Tristan, on the other hand, looked distraught, unkempt, ravaged. Maeve's eyes were red and swollen in her well-scrubbed face, and her lips moved constantly in silent prayer, while Sean occasionally scribbled something in a notebook and then looked around apologetically, as if he'd committed some breach of etiquette.

Charlotte rose, too, and whispered to Thane, "I must have a word with you. Could we go downstairs?"

He glanced toward the sickroom door as if about to refuse, and Charlotte said, "The doctor has only just gone in."

Thane nodded and gestured for her to go downstairs.

His house, Charlotte decided, was as spartan as a barracks. His manservant, who had been his army batman, kept everything in spit and polish condition, but there was that cold, impersonal emptiness to the rooms that had characterized the grange at Glendower prior to her return as its mistress. Evan had indulged her every wish, and she had begun to alleviate the darkness and gloom with bright rugs and draperies, a flash of copper here, the sparkle of a crystal vase there. Thane's house was badly in need of a similar woman's touch.

He opened the drawing room door for her and then made straight for the cabinet which held spirits. "Is it too early for you? I'm going to have a brandy."

"Nothing for me, thank you. Colonel Thane, as I have remarked previously, I really feel we must send for her husband. I realize that, with the distances and time involved, there isn't much hope he would arrive in time, but we would at least have tried."

He turned and looked at her. "And as I have pointed out previously, Lady Athmore, no one has any idea where Mr. Davies is. Eleanor said he was going to Texas to buy land. He may still be on the overland journey."

"But she calls for him constantly. If we could just tell her he was on his way . . . It occurred to me that Owain's former partner, Peter Maitland-Howard, has a family here. We can surely find them and get Peter's address, then send word to Owain in his care."

Thane's pale blue eyes sometimes acquired a metallic gleam, and it was evident now. "Do as you wish."

"I also feel," Charlotte continued, "that it would be improper to notify Eleanor's husband of her current address. Her staying in your house could be misunderstood."

"She's too ill to be moved." There was a dangerous edge to his voice.

"She should go to a hospital, Colonel Thane."

"No."

"You have no right to decide that."

"Neither do you." He placed his empty brandy glass on a table and said, "Excuse me. I want to be on hand as soon as the doctor is finished."

Charlotte remained in the drawing room after he left, too upset to join the others upstairs. Damn the man for his high-handedness. Was it possible he and Eleanor had been lovers? His air of propriety over her surely indicated more than the casual friendship Eleanor had mentioned. Charlotte was quite sure that if Eleanor had not called for her in her delirium, he would never have sent word of the accident to Glendower. Thane barely tolerated Tristan and Maeve's presence, and would not allow anyone else to visit Eleanor. For some reason, Thane welcomed Sean Connell, and was more inclined to be civil to him than to any of the others.

After a few minutes, Tristan's head appeared around the door. "Ah, so that's where you're hiding."

"Has the doctor come out yet?"

"Yes, but don't go up yet. She isn't conscious, anyway, and Thane is with her."

"Did the doctor . . . did he say . . ."

Tristan brushed his fist across his eyes. "She's very weak. He doesn't hold out much hope. The fever . . . the amount of blood she lost . . . Oh, God, it's such a waste. She never should have married, let alone tried to bear a child."

"Pull yourself together," Charlotte said sharply. "And do be careful what you say when you go in to see Eleanor. I believe she drifts in and out of consciousness, and I don't want her to hear any pronouncements of gloom and despair."

Tristan gave her a hurt look. "I adore that talented, lovely child. Don't chastise *me, I* wasn't the one who took her along a back alley late at night."

"Somehow I don't think the formidable Colonel Thane would have been in any danger of being accosted by street thieves. And I understood from Mr. Connell that Colonel Thane ordered Eleanor to run to safety before he went to his aid."

Tristan shivered noticeably. "I'm still in a state of shock that Thane killed one of them. Can you believe it? With his bare hands."

"I hope it was the one who caused Eleanor to lose her baby, and may have killed her, too," Charlotte said with uncharacteristic savageness, then added, "may God forgive me."

"I must go. I'm reading for a new play. I'll look in on Eleanor before I leave."

Charlotte went back into the hall and had started up the stairs when she heard the clatter of hooves and the sound of carriage wheels and voices out on the street. The next moment the door knocker pounded an urgent summons.

Thane's manservant hurried to respond. The moment he opened the door a babble of loud voices assaulted the quiet house. Charlotte could see a crowd of pushing, shoving people led by a man holding note pad and pencil. Oh, no, she thought, someone has told the newspapers. Now there will be no peace.

She was firmly pushed aside as Thane came running down the stairs, two at a time, to deal with the intrusion.

Eleanor sat on a deck chair, wrapped in blankets, watching a pair of swans gliding on the placid surface of a pond. To her right was a stone cottage flanked by trees just beginning to show spring buds, and to her left a craggy cliff overlooked the vast, whispering presence of the ocean. For the first time in what seemed an eternity, her mind and body felt as if they belonged to her.

She said, "To answer your question, I remember bits and pieces of days and conversations and hot broth and you bullying me and Maeve weeping over me . . . and Charlotte shooing both of you out of my room . . . and me wanting nothing more than to sleep." She looked down at her hands folded limply on her lap and added, "I also remember you telling me you were bringing me to Cornwall, but at the time I was too weak to argue. But I must admit, it's very peaceful here."

Thane replied, "My grandfather built this cottage as a retreat. He'd come here to recuperate after a particularly bloody campaign. I've never spent much time here."

"The men in your family were all soldiers?"

"Yes. I'm the first to leave the service of my country while still in my prime and in one piece."

"I seem to recall HRH telling me you had earned your respite."

He leaned over and tucked the blanket around her feet. "Are you warm enough?"

She nodded. "I miss Charlotte and Maeve already. Did you order them to leave? Oh, I know Charlotte had to get back to her husband and son, but did Maeve really have to go?"

"If I'd known she was up to that nonsense with the tea leaves, I'd never have let her come in the first place."

"I'd like to know who appointed you my keeper," Eleanor

said, injecting a note of indignation into her tone because Thane expected it. There was no need for him to know she'd asked Maeve before she left to reopen her London flat and deliver a letter to Tristan, who hadn't been invited to Cornwall.

"The cottage is too small to accommodate a harem," Thane said. "I allowed them to stay until the doctor pronounced you to be out of danger."

"Out of danger," Eleanor repeated. "Am I?"

He flashed her a sinister smile. "Not while you're with me, no." He gave her a long glance of assessment. "Now that I've convinced the doctors to stop dosing you with laudanum, and you seem to be more or less rational again, do you remember what the doctor in London told you?"

"About what?"

"He said that you must never have another child. *Never,* do you understand? Another pregnancy would kill you."

Eleanor was silent, digesting this. The fact was, she didn't particularly want another child, and it would be a relief not to have to worry about it. It occurred to her, too, that she really wouldn't mind living with Owain on a brother and sister basis. Except for the disgusting physical intimacy of marriage, she really did like being with him, and she missed him dreadfully, now that she no longer portrayed Margot's life on stage every day. There was a great deal to be said for having a husband one could trust completely, knowing that he would never, ever do anything to hurt her. "Was there a letter from Owain today?"

"No. I instructed my man in London to pick up the post at your flat, but there's been nothing from America."

She sighed. Owain had given up on her, and who could blame him? "But Charlotte sent word to him that I was ill?"

"She sent a letter to Maitland-Howard in Texas."

Eleanor lay back and closed her eyes, feeling spring and rebirth in the air, hearing the insistent murmur of the sea. Distanced now from that other Eleanor, who had been so discontented on the farm, it seemed inconceivable that she could have allowed Owain to exit from her life. When she was strong again, she would go to America, settle her grandfather's estate and then find Owain.

Even from behind closed eyelids, she became aware that Thane was watching her and, because she found his silences unnerving, she opened her eyes and said, "I suppose I have thanked you for taking care of me?"

"No, but it's not necessary. After all, it's my fault this

happened to you. I should have rushed you away that night and left Connell to his fate.''

"They might have killed him if you had."

"They almost killed you, which would have been a greater loss."

"Would it? Would you have missed me?"

"Now you're fishing for compliments. The loss would have been to the theater, not to me. The world is full of pretty women. But a great actress comes along only rarely."

"Do you really think I am a great actress?"

"I just said so, didn't I?"

"You used to say terrible things about actors."

"I say some things for effect, to goad an honest reaction out of someone. I learn a lot about a person that way. A trick I picked up while commanding men."

"Don't try to command me, Victor Thane. I have a husband who tried that, and it didn't work."

He regarded her with a lazy stare. "Is it really possible you had a husband? Look at you, you're still such a child."

"With a woman's body. If a man had to endure pregnancy and all that it entails . . . especially miscarriage . . . the human race would have died out centuries ago."

He yawned.

Eleanor said, "Sometimes I dislike you intensely."

"Good. It's indifference I can't stand."

"I want to return to London as soon as possible. Do you have a railway timetable?"

"Of course." He sat up, suddenly alert. "There were a number of newspaper articles about you while you were ill. Your face is probably known to everyone in England. When you open in a new play, you will be even more famous. I'd like to offer you my protection. Move into my house and live with me."

"That's out of the question. It's one thing being hidden away here with you, but in London . . . Thane, I'm married."

"Do you know what the basic law of the universe is?"

"No, but what's that got to do with—"

"It is that everything should disintegrate, deteriorate, collapse. Nothing grows together, it falls apart. The sea erodes the land, the desert reclaims the forest. If you put oranges and apples in a box, divided by type, and shake it up, you have a mixed box of oranges and apples, and all the shaking in the world won't rearrange them into six oranges and six apples neatly side by side."

"I haven't the slightest idea what you're talking about, but it's certain to be the view of a cynic."

"I'm telling you that, left unattended, a marriage will fall apart, too. Rather than growing together, a couple will drift apart. Absence *doesn't* make the heart grow fonder. The rule is out of sight, out of mind. Don't let your ill-conceived marriage to Owain Davies—which for all intents and purposes is over— prevent you from accepting my offer."

"Your offer is to have me as your mistress, and the answer is no. Didn't you just tell me I can't ever sleep with a man again?"

His eyes twinkled. "Ah, so that's the only problem. My sweet child, the doctor said no more children, but he didn't say no more lovemaking. There are ways to prevent conception. Look at the advantages to living with me . . . I would protect you from worshiping hoards and amorous swains. I inherited a comfortable sum of money when my father died, and I invested it well, so you could have any luxury you desired. You could pick and choose your parts, and I would never come between you and your acting. Believe me, no other man on earth is going to be that understanding."

Eleanor thought his tone was a trifle too studied, too casual. Like a bad actor, he was straining to project false emotions in order to conceal real ones. She wanted to say to him, the only way you will be believable is to submerge yourself so thoroughly in the part that your own feelings no longer exist. He really wanted her, but how much? Some inner demon goaded her to find out.

"What if I were to obtain a divorce from Owain? Would you marry me?"

He hesitated for a second, raking her with eyes that ripped away pretense. "No, I'd never marry you."

She couldn't keep her wounded pride nor her pique from her tone. "Why? Aren't I good enough to marry?"

"I could give you a number of excellent reasons, but I doubt you'd accept any of them. Your vanity would get in the way."

She threw aside the blanket that had been covering her. "I wouldn't have married you, anyway, Victor Thane. I hate you too much."

Unfortunately, as she attempted to stand up, waves of dizziness caused her to sway toward him, and the next second she was swept up into his arms and carried to the cottage.

Thane's grandfather had packed the cottage with an embarrassing assortment of military memorabilia, hunting trophies, and souvenirs of his service in foreign lands. Thane had in the past visited the cottage so infrequently that he hadn't bothered to clear out his grandfather's possessions, but he promised himself he would do so before leaving Cornwall to take Eleanor back to London.

Sean Connell did not share his dislike of bric-a-brac, and the playwright prowled about the room examining various items. Neither man had mentioned the reason for Sean's visit during dinner, waiting until Eleanor retired to her room before bringing up the subject foremost on both of their minds.

When Thane returned to the living room after giving instructions to his manservant in the kitchen, Sean was standing in front of a mirrored cabinet, peering at his reflection and adjusting a dusty solar topee to a different angle on his head. Seeing Thane, he whipped it off and said sheepishly, "I've never been to the tropics. Never been anywhere, really. My parents brought me to London from Dublin when I was six, and here I've stayed."

"You can have the topee, if you want it," Thane said. "Perhaps someday you'll wear it."

"Oh, I couldn't . . . well, thank you. If you're sure . . ."

Thane poured cognac into two glasses and handed one to Sean. "Did you bring the play?"

"It's not finished, you understand . . . I'm fairly happy with the first act, but the second is a disaster, and I don't know where to go with the third. I've never attempted to write someone else's ideas before and frankly, I'm foundering. If it weren't for my obligation to you . . ."

"Let me see what you've written."

Sean went into the small entry hall and retrieved the pages he had concealed in the inside pocket of his overcoat, which was hanging on the hallstand.

He also took his pipe and tobacco pouch, and puffed anxiously while Thane scanned the pages. After a minute or two, Sean said, "I don't think any producer will touch it. The eroticism is too blatant, no matter how much I try to disguise it. The trouble is, you've described the woman in such graphic detail that now she exists for me, too . . . I'm after thinking Amorette is based on a real woman. Is she? Well, none of my business, of course. But with that strong a character, it's hard not to relinquish control of the plot to her.''

Thane glanced up at him. "You'll be paid, and the play will be produced. I shall put up the money myself. But if Eleanor ever learns of this, I'll probably finish the job those thugs started on you."

Sean chewed on the stem of his pipe. "Eleanor Hathaway is completely wrong for the part of Amorette. She is neither old enough nor sophisticated enough."

"One day soon, Eleanor will be one of the few truly great actresses of our time. Her power of absorption into her characterization is so complete that she became Margot in *Last Love,* and damned near died from it. She will become Amorette. But this time, instead of playing a tragic heroine, she will be a vibrant, uninhibited woman ready to embrace all that life has to offer."

"I haven't written the third act yet," Sean pointed out gloomily. "It could still turn into a tragedy."

"I've told you how I want it to end."

"You don't understand . . . a playwright cannot always manipulate his characters toward the resolution he seeks."

"In this play," Thane said, "the playwright will follow the course I have mapped for him." He turned his attention back to the first act, nodding in approval as he read.

"We won't really know what we have until we put the play on its feet, anyway," Sean commented. "We could have a staged reading after I finish the first draft."

He began to prowl the room again, examining the treasures collected by Thane's ancestor. He fingered a lethal-looking sword hanging on a wall beside a curio cabinet packed with pistols of every conceivable size, shape, and origin. Like most passive men, Sean was fascinated by the exploits of adventurous, active men. *Last Love* had been the first romantic tragedy he had written. Prior to that, his plays had all been about violent men caught up in disastrous and earth-shattering events, which unfortunately did not translate well to the confines of a theater stage.

A scarlet jacket hung from a hook in the wall, and he touched the cloth, imagining the man who had worn it riding fearlessly to face the enemy, his saber glinting in the sun. Vicariously experiencing the adventures of Thane's grandfather momentarily distracted Sean from his nagging worry about Victor Thane's motives for commissioning him to write this new play.

There was little doubt in Sean's mind as to whom the two principal male characters in the play represented. The meek, adoring, cuckolded husband of the magnetic Amorette was Eleanor's missing husband, who appeared to be more interested in breeding horses than protecting his wife from the attentions of other men, while the ruthless and domineering lover who swept Amorette away was undoubtedly Thane himself. What had Thane just said? That Eleanor absorbed herself into her characterization . . . was that why Thane had ordered him to write of a woman's sexual awakening and capitulation?

No, he must be wrong to think it was an elaborate means of transforming the rather sweetly naive young actress into a sensual creature lacking all moral restraint. Surely since they were sharing living quarters, Thane must already have seduced her? But she had been so deathly ill . . . perhaps not. And if not, was Sean in fact using his talent to procure her for Thane? Sean shuddered, suddenly afraid of this man who had befriended him, and had in fact saved his life. It may be that the price he would pay to settle that debt would be far more dear than he had anticipated. Besides, if a man were so obsessed with a woman that he would go to such lengths to possess her, then the woman was possibly in grave danger.

35

CHARLOTTE WALKED UP a flagstone path lined with daffodils to the door of a modest house in Llanrys. She paused for a moment, looking at a weathered and barely readable wooden plaque that proclaimed this to be the home of Dr. Huw Thomas.

Raising her hand to lift the brass door knocker, she wished she had sent a note to announce her arrival, but she hadn't known how to put her fears into words that would not be misunderstood.

The young woman who came to the door had an ink stain on her cheek, and her auburn hair was carelessly drawn into a bun from which several tendrils had escaped. Her gown was out of style and rumpled. But she was one of those women the gods had blessed with an attractiveness not easily disguised.

Large jade-green eyes regarded Charlotte with a keenly intelligent gaze, and her smile of welcome lit up the gloomy vestibule of the house. "I'm sorry, if you're looking for a doctor, my grandfather doesn't practice anymore. He's bedridden."

"No, Megan, I came to see you. You don't remember me, do you? But perhaps you remember Lord Evan Athmore?"

Megan looked more closely. "Why, of course I remember you! Mrs. Danforth—"

"Lady Athmore now. Evan and I were married."

"But that's wonderful. Please, come in."

She led the way into a clean but untidy parlor, moved a stack of books from a chair for Charlotte and took an iron teakettle from the hob and placed it on the coals in the fireplace. "I was just thinking of having a cup of tea, and Grandfather always wants one when he wakes up from his nap. What a surprise this is. How many years has it been since I came running up the mountain to warn you they were coming to arrest your friend?''

Charlotte sat down. ''It's been a long time. I've been abroad, or I would have come to see you before this. I was so grateful to you. I see you're still taking care of your grandfather, what a blessing for him. But a pretty girl like you should be thinking about a family of your own.''

''I'm getting a bit long in the tooth.'' Megan grinned. ''In Llanrys, a girl is an old maid at twenty, and I'm a year past that.''

''My life didn't really begin until I was thirty. I'm now nearly forty and I'm a new bride.''

''You said you were abroad, where?''

Charlotte spoke briefly of her years in Ceylon, and Megan listened with rapt attention. When she got up to make the tea, Charlotte noted that many of the books littering the room were medical texts, including a well-worn copy of *Gray's Anatomy*.

Megan excused herself to take a cup of tea to her grandfather's room, apologizing that he never received visitors nowadays. While she was gone, Charlotte looked around her and saw that a writing desk in one corner of the room was covered with notebooks and still more medical texts. Many of the books had sheets of paper tucked into them, indicating that Megan had made notes about specific diseases.

When the younger woman returned, Charlotte said, ''I couldn't help noticing your interest in medicine. Are you thinking of entering the nursing profession?''

''I can't leave Grandfather. Besides, I don't want to be a nurse, or a midwife. I'm afraid I wouldn't last a day because I'd be trying to tell the doctors what to do. I'd really like to be a doctor myself, but that's impossible, of course, since I was born into the wrong gender.''

''Yet you study your grandfather's books. That seems to indicate that you harbor the hope that one day soon women may breach the male bastion of medicine?''

''Not really. I study because I can't stop myself.'' Megan poured two cups of tea and handed one to Charlotte, who noticed that the saucer was chipped. Megan seemed as oblivious to the state of her china as she was to the disarray of the room.

Charlotte said, ''Perhaps one day you might consider using your knowledge in one of the remote corners of the world where doctors are unknown. I'm sure there are overworked medical missionaries who would welcome your help."

Megan looked startled. "How odd that you should suggest that. You see, my father went abroad to practice medicine after my mother died." She was silent, reflective, for a moment. "I was just a baby so I never knew him. Grandfather believes he's dead, because he never heard from him. But I keep hoping he'll come home one day."

"I'm sorry," Charlotte said. "I didn't mean to open old wounds."

"Oh, it's all right. I've accepted the fact that he's gone forever. I just wish sometimes I knew what happened to him."

Charlotte said quickly, "I remembered your interest in medicine from the time you helped my husband, of course. As a matter of fact, I was hoping that either your grandfather or you might be able to give me some answers to questions that both puzzle and frighten me. And I do insist upon paying a consultation fee."

Megan perched herself on the arm of a sofa that was crowded with books and papers. "To tell you the truth, Grandfather is senile. He couldn't help you. And I'm not licensed, so officially I can't either. But tell me the problem and perhaps I can recommend someone."

"I've already spoken to our family physician and to several other doctors, none of whom were able to answer my question. Most of them were shocked that I asked it."

Megan's green eyes expressed understanding, and she exclaimed, "Then I'm quite sure your question concerns female problems."

Charlotte studied her teacup for a moment. "Well, originally I did inquire if it would be possible for me to have another child at my age."

"If you want to know how to prevent pregnancy, you've come to the right place," Megan said at once.

Although Charlotte had spent many years in the company of the street women of Colombo, she felt herself blush at the candor of this young woman. "Actually, no . . ."

"You can conceive a child—possibly several more, right on into your forties. But I wouldn't if I were you. The mortality rate for both the babies and the older mothers is fearful."

Charlotte picked up her teaspoon, then laid it back in her

saucer. "Megan . . . you met my husband. I have been unable to attach a name to . . . to his affliction or learn anything about it. I wondered . . . is it hereditary? Is there a possibility his child would also be a giant?"

Megan got up and started rummaging through her books. "Let's look it up. But keep in mind that at your age, childbirth could be risky for you, even apart from hereditary factors for the baby. There was a medical paper published a few years ago. I was interested because of having met your husband." She flipped over a page and ran her finger down it. "Here it is . . . acromegaly, gigantism."

At that moment a bell rang in the next room, and Megan said, "Grandfather wants something. Here—read it for yourself."

Charlotte looked at the paragraph Megan indicated and read: "Acromegaly . . . also known as Marie's syndrome, after Pierre Marie (1853—) who first described it in 1886. Gigantism is a related condition . . ."

The brief description of the symptoms of the rare condition, which was not referred to as a disease, did not mention whether it was hereditary or otherwise, but Charlotte felt a cold hand close around her heart when she came to the statement, *"victims of this rare condition rarely live past their fortieth birthdays."*

The room spun out of focus, and the next thing she knew, Megan was holding smelling salts under her nose. "Are you all right? Here, let me loosen your collar. Put your feet up. Do you still feel faint?"

"No, I'm all right," Charlotte whispered.

Realization dawned in Megan's eyes. "You're already carrying his child, aren't you?"

Charlotte nodded. She did not know how to express what she had been feeling lately. It was more than the fatigue of early pregnancy, it was a premonition that her happiness with Evan could not last. Was the revelation in the medical book really a surprise, or had she suspected she would lose him soon? The weariness that she saw in his eyes sometimes, the way he straightened up and became more alert when he thought she was watching him, as if he were really too tired but felt he must continue to pretend to be his former vigorous self.

Megan's eyes fell on the open page of the medical book. She sat down beside Charlotte and held her hand. "From the local legends I've heard, your husband is the only Athmore to attain such height, so I doubt the condition is hereditary."

Charlotte noticed that the younger woman made no comment about the death sentence mentioned in the medical text. Evan was already well past his fortieth birthday.

"What do you suppose your mother's mysterious visit to Llandrys is all about?" Evan inquired of Geoffrey. They had walked down to the summer house, and Evan pretended he wanted to sit and admire the view of the lake for a while, although in truth the walk had exhausted him.

The boy was home from school for the Easter holidays and filled with the boundless energy of youth, which he curbed admirably in order to slow his pace to his Uncle Evan's. He probably thinks I'm beginning to dodder, and I am, Evan thought.

"Oh, I expect she went to buy us a treat for tea and it's to be a surprise. I hope it isn't hot cross buns. I detest them," Geoffrey replied, swinging up onto the wooden balustrade of the summer house and walking the precarious tightrope of the narrow rail. "Or perhaps she's buying a new hat for Easter Sunday. You know how women are."

Evan hid his smile at the boy's attempt at man-to-man camaraderie, and murmured in agreement. How rich my life is, how precious every minute I spend with the two who have given me happiness that I once scarcely could have imagined.

"Did you read the letter from your father, Geoffrey?"

The child knitted his brows, perplexed. "Yes. He says he's well and intends to stay in New Orleans for the time being. You know, Uncle Evan, sometimes I get very mixed up about you and father and Char—Mother." His eyes clouded over and he slid to the wooden deck beside Evan, then hung over the rail looking out over the valley.

"In what way?"

"I don't understand why Mother didn't marry you so I could be your real son."

"I feel you are my son, Geoffrey, more dear than any child of my own flesh could have been to me. Your father once loved your mother, too, and that's why you were born. But he was already married to Zoe. I know it's difficult for you to understand now, but one day it won't seem so."

Geoffrey's lower lip trembled slightly and he resolutely bit down on it. Evan's heart ached for the child. He was simply too young to understand the passion of adults. "But we've been over this before. Something else is bothering you, isn't it? Geoffrey, now that we're alone, you can tell me what it is.''

He spun around, guilt on his face. ''Oh! I didn't mean—I didn't want you to know. It's all right, honestly it is.'' His face was pink and he was close to tears.

Evan reached for the boy's arm to draw him gently closer to his chair. ''You're not too big to sit on my lap, are you? Come on, we haven't had one of our secret talks for a long time.''

He was surprised at how fiercely the boy flung his arms around his neck and hugged him. ''Could we run away together, just the two of us, Uncle Evan? Could we find a desert isle?''

''Well, I don't know. Let's discuss it. I should miss your mother dreadfully if we didn't take her along, wouldn't you?''

''But it's all her fault!'' Geoffrey burst out, then bit his lip.

''What is all her fault?'' Evan asked quietly.

''The boys at school call me a bastard.''

Evan wrapped the child in a protective embrace and held him, trying desperately to think of something to say to ease his pain and humiliation. All at once Evan had a glimmer of what Stephen had suffered, and he felt a deep compassion for his half brother. He had believed his own banishment to an orphanage was the worst sentence a parent could impose, but perhaps there were other equally cruel burdens placed on the fragile shoulders of childhood.

''Geoffrey, listen to me. I'd like to go and tear the tongues out of the heads of the boys who called you names, but there's a better way to protect yourself from them. Learn to ignore them. You'll be surprised how soon the clods of the world find something else to occupy their tiny minds when they don't get any response to their taunts. I've been called giant, monster, freak of nature . . . all of which were directed at me personally. But what those boys are saying to you is only that your parents weren't married when you were born. You can hardly be held responsible for that, now can you?''

Forgetting his own troubles, Geoffrey regarded his uncle with amazement. ''I didn't think anyone would ever dare call you names. Why, you could have smashed them to pieces.''

''I would never have given them the satisfaction of knowing I cared one whit about what they called me.''

Geoffrey whispered, ''Is it still all right to tell you I love you, Uncle Evan?''

''Don't ever stop, for I love you and your mother more than

anything or anyone on earth. And Geoffrey, I want you to promise that you'll always be kind to your mother, and take care of her."

"I do like her," Geoffrey said earnestly. "But I don't know her very well."

"You'll get to know her better in time. Never let yourself forget that the most difficult and painful thing she ever had to do was to go away and leave you . . . and she did it because she loved you so much."

The child sighed. "I just wish she hadn't made me into a bastard."

Evan said sharply, "Don't ever call yourself that. There are no illegitimate children, only illegitimate parents. You are Geoffrey Stephen Phillip Athmore, heir to a title and a considerable fortune, and will one day be master of Glendower."

Geoffrey's eyes widened. "I will?"

"Yes. Your father and I had our solicitors make arrangements for me to legally adopt you, in order that I could name you my heir. You have all the rank and privileges of my firstborn son."

"Then you are my father now?" The boy's eyes shone.

"I'm your adopted father, yes. But I want you to keep a place in your heart for your real father, too."

"But I am truly your son?"

"My son and heir. I signed the final documents just before you came home from school."

"And nothing can ever change that? Are you sure?"

"Nothing," Evan assured him. "Even if your mother and I were to have another child—which at our ages is not very likely—you would still be our firstborn son and heir. You see, Geoffrey, I think in a way I'm endeavoring to right some of the wrongs of the past. You're too young to understand our somewhat tarnished family history now, but I think you know how much your father loves Glendower. Indeed, I believe his present self-imposed exile is his way of doing penance—" He broke off, realizing that the boy had no idea what he was talking about.

"What I'm trying to say is, that perhaps your grandfather should have made your father master of Glendower, instead of me. Your father loves Glendower in a way I never have. I hope that it is a comfort to him now in his time of grief to know that one day his son will inherit the estate and all that goes with it."

"Will he ever come back?"

"Yes, one day I believe he will." Evan allowed his gaze to drift across the verdant valley, where wisps of mist were forming above the lake and sending ghostly tendrils to circle the trees. It still caused an ache in his heart to remember the passion Stephen and Charlotte had once shared, even though she was his now, wholly and completely, and their love was unique unto itself. Evan loved her so unselfishly that he could not bear to think she would ever be unhappy again as long as she lived, and, caring so much, he worried about leaving her alone in the world if he should die first. Oh, she'd have Geoffrey and Glendower and no financial worries, but Evan realized, as perhaps few people did, that without a companion, a human being slowly withered away. Charlotte was too loving and warm to spend her remaining days as a widow and, when Evan felt a great weariness press upon him, which he had of late and which he put down to his illnesses while in Ceylon—the poisoning and the malaria—he comforted himself with the thought that if he were gone, then Stephen would surely return to Glendower. And when he did, that old passion between him and Charlotte might flare once again, to ease their shared loneliness and grief.

"Father?" Geoffrey's voice intruded into his thoughts.

"What did you say?"

"I said Father. I want to call you Father, is that all right?"

"It would make me very happy."

"Were you dreaming, just now?"

"Yes, I think I was. A romantic dream for a spring day."

"What about?"

"Oh, what we'll all be doing years from now. All the happy memories we'll have collected."

"Do you think your dreams will come true?"

Evan ruffled Geoffrey's hair and smiled. "They already have. No man alive is happier than I am. Well . . . perhaps there is one more thing I would wish for."

"What's that?"

"That your mother won't bring hot cross buns back from the confectioners. I detest them, too."

36

ELEANOR AND THANE rode in an open carriage through the park, the spring sunshine and fresh air making her body feel alive again, and the prospect of playing the lead role in *Amorette* foremost in her mind, despite the fact that a nagging voice in the back of her mind warned that she should be paying more attention to the reality of her life.

Sean Connell, who was producing his play himself, had told her he was in no hurry to open, as he wanted a long rehearsal period in order to do a great deal of rewriting on stage. Besides, he had yet to write the last act. Once she had learned her part, there might be time before opening night for her to go to America and spend some time with Owain. Perhaps she could persuade him to return to London for the run of the play if she promised to go back with him, if the play didn't close, after a certain specified period.

"Maeve told me you weren't home yesterday afternoon, although I know damned well you were," Thane remarked. "I almost kicked in your front door."

Eleanor turned her head so he wouldn't see her smile. After all, it had been Thane's idea that she would have more privacy in the mews house she had rented, and he had called a carpenter to install a tiny iron-barred peephole in the front door so that Maeve could determine who their callers were before admitting them. He hadn't anticipated his barricade being used against himself, but Eleanor had decided that Victor Thane could no longer be allowed to dictate how she should live, nor monopolize her time.

Why, if she hadn't allowed Owain that privilege, she certainly wasn't going to grant it to Thane.

"You've been avoiding me," he said. "Why?"

"I've been reading Sean's new play, and I became engrossed in it. I doubt a character such as Amorette has ever appeared on a London stage before. I'm not even sure if—in her present incarnation—she'll be allowed there. She's far too bohemian."

"So you are considering the role?" he asked offhandedly.

"It would be quite a challenge. Amorette is as different from Margot as I am from Cleopatra . . . it will take me some time to immerse myself in the part . . . if I decide to play it."

"Is it a good play?"

"Too early to tell. You see, a good actor can bring to life words that might sound empty on paper. Of course, that's not to say the playwright didn't plan the effect. That's what makes the theater so exciting. Every production of a play is a new one; it doesn't matter how many times it's been performed in the past, because of a particular actor's interpretation of his role. But with a completely new, untried text, one never knows how it will be received. Besides, he hasn't even finished writing it yet. I can't believe he was able to get financial backing, but I suppose he did because of the success of *Last Love*."

Thane called to his driver, "We'll stop at the pavilion and listen to the music for a while." Then, turning back to Eleanor, he asked, "What's it about?"

"Rather a simple theme, really. A beautiful, passionate woman married to a rather dull husband, meets a mysterious stranger who becomes her lover."

"Ah, *Anna Karenina* revisited."

"No . . ." Eleanor replied slowly, "Tolstoy made Anna's husband a brute, didn't he? The husband in Sean's play is really very nice, one feels sorry for him."

"Perhaps his play would be stronger if the husband were less sympathetic, then?"

"I think perhaps it's the character of the lover that must be changed. Reading the play, I felt the fascination he had for Amorette, but I was somewhat troubled also by a sense of . . . menace he exuded. I wonder if he needs to be quite so ruthless and calculating, even cruel."

She turned to look at Thane, who regarded her with a small inscrutable smile, and she realized that she had been so intent upon studying Amorette that she had not recognized that the part of her lover, Nicholas, bore a strong resemblance to Thane. But then, he and Sean had become friends and Thane was such a dominant male, it was probaby inevitable that the playwright would base a character upon him. She would perhaps have been more concerned if the part of Amorette resembled herself in any way, but it didn't. Oddly, she had the uneasy feeling that Amorette was also based on a real person, probably the sort of woman Thane was accustomed to. But that was impossible, since Thane knew nothing about Sean's play.

The carriage came to a halt beside a rolling lawn dotted with deck chairs. A military band was tuning up in a wooden pavilion. As Thane helped her from the carriage, she glanced up unexpectedly and saw a disturbing glint in his eye, which he quickly extinguished. She remembered once at Glendower coming across one of the estate cats stalking an unwary field mouse, and in the instant before the cat pounced, he had worn a look in his eyes very similar to the one Thane just had.

At the first onstage reading of Amorette, Eleanor felt she was probably utterly ridiculous in the role. Sean had cast a quiet, sandy-haired young actor as Amorette's husband, David, and a continental actor as Amorette's lover, Nicholas. Both gave adequate readings, and Sean seemed not to notice how poor her own performance was.

As rehearsals got under way more seriously, Eleanor noticed that something peculiar seemed to be happening to her. She became acutely aware of her senses. She noticed first that food had acquired an appeal it never had before, and the gauntness left in the wake of her illness disappeared. As her sense of taste improved, so did her sense of touch. One day as she slipped a silk gown on, she had an uncontrollable urge to know what the cool silk would feel like next to her skin rather than insulated by cambric underwear.

The touch of the silk was even more exciting than she had imagined. To her astonishment, the tiny peaks of her nipples grew taut against the material, while her body felt languid, pliant, yielding. Her thoughts were dreamy, and she felt as if she were floating in some unfocused universe where exquisite sensations made her acutely aware of her body, indeed of every nerve.

Before long she had replaced her cotton nightgowns and underwear with silk and satin, and enjoyed the sheer pleasure of the taut softness against her skin, particularly against the sensitive

areolas of her breasts. This was how Amorette would feel. She
was a woman enamored of her own body. All of her thoughts
were directed toward physical pleasure, and she was willing to
risk everything in order to satisfy her insatiable need for gratification of the flesh—the loss of her husband, her position in society,
even her home. In a way, she was a modern version of the biblical
women stoned to death for committing adultery. But was it not
possible that Amorette's sexuality was a part of the makeup of
every woman—the Victorian matron who repressed it, along with
the courtesan who flaunted it? As Eleanor strove to become
Amorette and her thoughts led her along these disturbing paths, it
was simply easier to feel rather than think.

Maeve shook her head and compressed her lips disapprovingly
at the changes in Eleanor's wardrobe, and asked constantly when
she should start packing a trunk for America.

One afternoon when Eleanor returned from rehearsing, she
found Maeve had been to the Cunard offices and obtained a
schedule of steamer sailings for America.

Unpinning her hat and peeling off her gloves, Eleanor, who
had just rehearsed an angry confrontation between Amorette and
David, found she was enraged by Maeve's taking matters into her
own hands.

"I didn't ask you to go to Cunard," she said coldly.

"I just thought you might like to know when the sailings are,"
Maeve replied. "You did say you wanted to go before the play
opened, and you're getting well along with the rehearsals."

"You can't wait to see Owain again, can you, Maeve? Oh,
don't pretend you weren't half in love with him. But what makes
you think you're going with me?"

Maeve's clear hazel eyes expressed her hurt, and Eleanor
instantly regretted her harsh tone. Maeve said quietly, "I didn't
expect to go. I just wanted you to be with your husband again,
where you belong. I didn't even know if you'd ever come back,
and if you don't I shall miss you. But I want you to go. I want you
to get away from Colonel Thane. I want you back with Owain,
because you need him, even though you don't think you do." She
turned and fled.

Aghast at the sudden flare-up, Eleanor stared at the steamship
brochure for a moment, thinking of Maeve's loving care during
her illness, then went after her friend. She found her placing
neatly folded clothing into a bag on her bed.

"Oh, Maeve," Eleanor said miserably. "I'm sorry, I didn't mean it about you being in love with Owain. Please don't leave."

Maeve raised tear-drenched eyes. "But you were right," she said, her voice barely audible. "I think I do love him. But I love you, too, and I'm afraid for you. I can't stay here and watch what's happening with Colonel Thane, and Owain so far away in America . . . I . . . just can't. I'll still be your dresser at the theater if you want me, but I wish you'd forget about this new play. There's something . . . evil about it."

Eleanor sat down on the edge of the bed and stared at a small, neatly darned hole in one of Maeve's stockings. "Why, Maeve, I didn't think you'd even read it."

"I've read enough to know Amorette is an immoral woman. I heard Sean telling you she is a creature of the senses. And I see you . . . changing in front of my eyes into someone I scarcely recognize. There's a way you have of walking, and looking at people from under your eyelashes . . . and turning your head. You . . . touch yourself all the time, like you're calling attention to your body. Oh, I can't describe it, but it's going to take you up the primrose path if you're not careful, and I can't stand by and let you do that to Owain."

Stung by Maeve's accusing tone, Eleanor felt her hackles rise. "What nonsense! I'm an actress preparing for a performance. It has nothing to do with my real self. And I do resent this . . . this keeper attitude you have. Besides, for your information, Charlotte wrote to Owain in care of his business partner, to let him know I was ill. There's been no reply, from either of them."

"Owain wanted you to go to America with him. You should have gone."

"How do you know that?"

Flushing scarlet, Maeve turned away, but Eleanor seized her arm, forcing her to turn back and face her. "You saw him, didn't you? After I left the farm you went to see him . . . sneaking around behind my back."

Maeve glared at her defiantly. "He needed a woman there to help him. He needed a wife. To put a meal on the table and take care of his house and listen to his hopes and his dreams and his fears. It should have been you."

Eleanor's fingers fell from Maeve's arm, and she stared at her, not wanting her to go on with a recitation of betrayal.

But Maeve had said too much to retreat now. "You might as

well know . . . I'd have jumped at the chance to be with him, any way he wanted me, whether or not I could have been his wife. Oh, I've no shame when it comes to my feelings for Owain. Yes, I'd even have betrayed our friendship if I could have taken your place with him. But he sent me away. He said he was selling the farm and coming to London to persuade you to go back to America with him.''

Maeve's lips were trembling and her eyes were bright with unshed tears. With a flash of insight, Eleanor realized how much it must have cost Maeve to throw herself at Owain and the humiliation she must have felt at his rejection. But Eleanor's own hurt at her friend's betrayal was too great for her to sympathize with her. After all, she had deliberately tried to come between a husband and wife, and surely there was no greater sin than that.

"You'd better finish packing and leave. There's nothing more to be said, is there?''

Maeve asked humbly, "Can I still be your dresser?''

Eleanor gave her an icy glance of disinterest. "No. I don't think so.''

"Please, Eleanor, forgive me. I've hated myself for what I did, no punishment you could think of would be worse than what I've done to myself. But try to understand . . . I'd never have offered myself to Owain if you hadn't walked out and left him. I felt you didn't deserve him. Oh, Eleanor, he loves you so!''

Maeve took a step toward her, her hands raised in a pleading gesture. "Let me work for you at the theater at least. Let me make up for what I did in some way.''

"You destroyed our friendship . . . over a man. My God, the world is full of men.''

"Not like Owain," Maeve said. "Not even for you, Eleanor, who can have any man you want.''

"Get out," Eleanor shouted. "I want you out of my house and out of my life.'' She left the room, slamming the door behind her.

The actor playing the role of Nicholas, Amorette's lover, had been born of an English mother and a Greek father and had begun his stage career in France. Although he was swarthier of complexion and more foreign-looking, he reminded Eleanor of a young Tristan Cressey, with the same brooding eyes that he could make smolder at will.

He walked across the darkened stage and stood looking down

at Eleanor, who lay on a couch placed center stage. "It has to be settled, once and for all. I won't share you with him. I won't share you with any other man. I'd rather see you dead." He paused, one hand caressing her face and throat. "I believe I would kill you rather than let you go back to him."

"Please, Nicholas, don't say such things. You frighten me. How can I leave David? He is blameless, why should he suffer for our sins? I can't be so cruel. I should feel I was doing something unspeakable."

Nicholas fell to his knees beside her and pulled her roughly into his arms. "Does he make you feel like this? You know that he does not, nor can he . . ."

Eleanor no longer heard the words. Tonight she was a woman torn between loyalty and desire, and desire was winning the battle. Nicholas was very attractive to Amorette, hypnotically so. In the dim lighting, it was easy to forget that Sean and the stagehands were out there watching and listening. It was easy to immerse herself in this role and give in to wanton yearnings.

Perhaps her feelings were due to the rehearsal in the late evening rather than morning, because Sean had added new dialogue and called for an onstage rehearsal this Sunday evening, when the theater was closed; or the feeling of spring in the air; or the fact that, for weeks, she had been filled with vague longings that before now had no name. As her health improved, Eleanor found she thought frequently of Owain, remembering his companionship, his laughter, his loving touch, the way it felt to lie in his arms and drift off to sleep. She closed her eyes and imagined it was Owain who was there with her on stage, instead of an actor playing the part of Nicholas.

A coil of tension sprang into place in the secret core of her being and from it radiated feelings she had never before experienced. Oh, there had been suggestions of those feelings . . . the first time Owain kissed her mouth, and several times when he had entered her body, but always she had been left disappointed, as if he had opened a door and there had been nothing on the other side. She had thought this was Owain's fault, but lately she had begun to see that she had waited for him to awaken in her feelings that she herself could have conjured at any time. Perhaps that day, long ago, when an evil old man had hurt a little girl, that child had closed herself to further hurt by disconnecting the feelings that would have opened the portals of womanhood for her.

But Amorette had no life prior to her first entrance on stage, no painful childhood memories. Amorette was free to feel erotic arousal. There was no Franklyn Yarborough lurking in Amorette's nightmares. Had Amorette and Eleanor blended into one, and was that why her senses were now so finely tuned?

Why, passion was always there, inside me, Eleanor thought wonderingly. I'm the one who had to release it, not anyone else, not even my dear Owain, whom I love with all my heart. How could I not have known that? How could I have allowed my own arrested emotions to prevent the love that was so nearly ours?

On the dimly lit stage, Nicholas bent closer, his lips brushing Amorette's mouth. Her eyelids felt heavy and began to droop, her breath became uneven and her arms wrapped around his neck, although Amorette was supposed to resist him in this scene.

Eleanor was so lost in the part that it was several moments before she realized Sean had called for a halt in the rehearsal, turned up the lights and now said, "Let's all go home. It's late, and I want to think about the last act."

It took Eleanor several minutes to adjust to the fact that Nicholas no longer held her in his arms, and only when she realized the stagehands were waiting to remove the couch upon which she lay did she rouse herself and go to her dressing room to get her hat and coat. She felt strangely incomplete, as if she had been interrupted after taking only the first couple bites of a delicious meal. By the time she reached the stage door where Sean was waiting, her feelings had changed to irritation.

Before Sean could say a word, she snapped, "I can't continue as Amorette unless I know what happens in the third act. Which man will she be with in the end? Surely by now you must have some idea how you're going to end the play?"

"I think she should return to her husband, but—" He paused, frowning. "I'm not sure our audience would accept Amorette getting off scot-free. Our dear old queen seems to have imbued all of us with her own stern and unyielding morals, hasn't she? The sinner must pay for her sins. I wonder if Amorette must die at the hands of her lover."

Eleanor shuddered, remembering Margot's death in *Last Love*. "But surely those aren't the only alternatives. Why can't she run away with Nicholas?"

"I just told you. Our Victorian society would be outraged." He held the door for her and they went outside to a sultry summer evening, the sun not yet set at ten o'clock.

"Don't become so wrapped up in the part that you lose yourself," Sean began. He broke off as he saw Thane's carriage waiting for her. "Eleanor," he said urgently. "Go home. You're very emotional tonight and I—"

Thane moved smoothly between them and took Eleanor's arm. "Rehearsal's over, Sean. Good night."

Eleanor allowed herself to be helped into Thane's carriage, still feeling both irritated yet strangely expectant, although for what, she wasn't sure. She wished Owain were not so far away. Tonight she needed the sanctuary of marriage to protect her from herself.

"You didn't come inside to watch the rehearsal tonight. Why?" she asked when he joined her.

"I was there until Sean stopped the scene." He arched an eyebrow quizzically. "At the point where you melted into your lover's arms, rather than resisting his advances. Your improvisation gave both the actor and the playwright quite a turn, I might add."

Embarrassed, Eleanor said, "If you were watching, why didn't you announce your presence? Or wait for me inside the theater? I hate it when you do things like this. I feel as if you're spying on me."

He didn't reply, but his hand fell lightly on her shoulder, slid down her arm and enclosed her fingers. One finger stroked her palm, then he raised her hand to his lips and kissed her wrist. "You were Amorette tonight. You were inside her skin, weren't you? I think you still are."

"What are you doing?" she asked, in vague astonishment.

"I'm nibbling your fingers," he murmured. "In a moment I am going to kiss you . . . here, in the curve of your throat. Then find my way to the décolletage of your gown and—"

"Hush! The driver will hear. Behave yourself. We're in an open carriage, and it's still daylight."

"Ah, so it would be all right if we were in the concealing darkness?"

"No! Stop it, at once."

"You don't really want me to stop. You find it exciting that I'm so bold. I watched you on stage tonight. You were ready, impatient even, for a sexual encounter. Why do you suppose I made Sean stop the rehearsal? Another moment and you'd have ravaged your fellow actor right there on stage."

"You are the most vile and filthy . . . ." She broke off as his words registered more fully. "*You* made him stop? You really are the giddy limit, Victor Thane. I've never known anyone who took charge of matters that were none of their business, the way you do."

"You are my business, Eleanor. You have been for some time. I want you, I've wanted you for a long time, but I've curbed my lust. I never did that for any other woman. She either gave in or I moved on. But for you I've waited with more patience than I was aware I was capable of. But I'm not prepared to wait any longer. I mean to have you, one way or another."

She gasped as he leaned over and, as he'd threatened, pressed his lips to the curve of her throat. She pushed him away, only to have him kiss the hollow between her breasts. The movement of the carriage caused her to lurch toward him and she distinctly felt his tongue, hot and wet, insinuate itself beneath the silk of her gown.

"You're not wearing a shift," he murmured. "Are you wearing anything at all under this gown? Don't tell me you're not ready to have me take you. I know better."

Casting a frantic glance at the rigid back of his manservant, who drove the carriage, Eleanor realized they were now in the park. The long shadows of approaching nightfall slanted through the trees, creating a disturbing contrast between dark and light that suggested day yielding to night. Sunbeams penetrating the canopy of branches overhead in darting thrusts created a rhythm oddly like the movement of Thane's tongue against her burning flesh.

She felt as if she were going down into a whirlpool from which there would be no return, and she frantically tried to direct her thoughts toward resisting her own surging emotions, fearing he would take her right there in the carriage, with the possibility of others passing by, or at least of the driver turning and observing. "Stop it, or I'll scream for help," she said, loud enough for the driver to hear.

Laughing softly, Thane sat up and pulled her across his lap. He bent and kissed her mouth, his hand closing over her exposed breast, massaging the exquisitely sensitive nipple until it thrust against his palm. His tongue invaded her mouth and, for an instant, she closed her eyes and surrendered to all of the demands her body was making of her.

His tongue probed more deeply, and his hand roamed freely

about her body. Her nostrils were filled with his masculine scent, and she felt as weak and pliant as a rag doll, ready to conform to any demand he might make upon her. Each second she delayed resisting took her closer to capitulation, yet even as she realized that inescapable fact, she lay in his arm and allowed him to overwhelm her.

Only when the carriage lurched to a halt did she realize that they were outside her mews house. She sat up abruptly, trying to rearrange the disarray of her gown, seeing that the lace ruffles around the deep V-neckline had torn under the onslaught of his hands. She had lost her hat, and her hair had partly come down.

Thane opened the carriage door and leaped down to the pavement. He turned to lift her into his arms, and she looked into his eyes and saw raw, undisguised lust, undiluted by any tender or loving thoughts.

In that revealing instant she recognized that, for Thane, their association had always been in this arena. His intent had been to pursue and conquer. He had stalked her, even played the role of her protector when he felt it suited his purpose, yet he had never wanted more from her than to possess her. For him it was a battle to be won or lost, and he had no intention of losing; therefore he would use any means necessary to win. Looking back, she wondered if part of her allure lay in the fact that there had been rivals to dispose of . . . HRH at first, then Owain. A man like Thane didn't like an easy conquest.

Eleanor looked into his eyes and wondered fearfully if she had allowed him to go too far to stop him now. Ignoring his out-stretched arms, she jumped to the ground and ran toward the house. She heard him laugh, then start after her, not hurrying, his footsteps falling on the pavement in a measured, leisurely beat.

She reached the front door and, miraculously, the maid she had hired to replace Maeve opened it as she approached. "I thought I heard a carriage, Mrs. Davies," the girl said excitedly. "I'm glad you're home early, because you've got someone waiting for you. Been here all evening . . . he's in the sitting room."

Scarcely comprehending, Eleanor slammed the front door and slid the bolt into place, then leaned against it, breathing heavily. The maid regarded her in astonishment. "Are you all right, Mrs. Davies?"

At that moment the sitting room door opened, and Eleanor

looked across the hallway at Owain. For an instant she thought he was nothing but a figment of her imagination, conjured out of her need for him. But he was real, he was here in the flesh. His dark eyes locked with hers, and his solidly muscular frame dominated the cramped hall.

Before either could speak, Thane pounded the door knocker.

37

ELEANOR SAID BREATHLESSLY, "Don't open the door." She looked at her husband, her glance sweeping from his handsome leather boots to his deeply tanned face and dark eyes that for the first time did not light up when they saw her. "Owain . . . Owain, I'm so glad to see you. Why didn't you let me know you were coming?"

"Hello, Ellie." He walked across the hall toward her, and she noticed that he managed to do so with only the merest hint of a limp that perhaps would have been unnoticeable to anyone else. His clothes were well-fitted, substantial, tailored unashamedly for rugged outdoor wear rather than drawing room show. "Excuse me," he said, taking her by the shoulders and firmly moving her to one side, then opening the door to Thane's insistent pounding.

Thane, his face livid, started to push his way into the house, but seeing Owain, stopped.

Feeling as if she were watching a scene in a play, Eleanor moved behind Owain. For a split second no one spoke, then Thane regained his composure and said, "Mr. Davies, I presume? Your wife left her hat in my carriage. Here it is."

Owain looked at Thane for a long, unnerving moment, then took the hat from his hand and, without a word, closed the door in his face.

When he turned to face her, Eleanor felt a chill creep along her veins. For an instant his anger leapt from his eyes like the glint of a knife, but as his gaze focused on her, it became impersonal, detached. "I realize it's late, Ellie, but we must talk." He gestured toward the sitting room.

In a daze, Eleanor walked ahead of him and sat down on the sofa. He didn't sit beside her, choosing instead to take a chair on the opposite side of the room. The space between them took on the ominous quality of an unnavigable gulf.

There had been no greeting, no embrace, and Eleanor felt afraid. Ever since she had been a little girl Owain had been on her side, her good and true friend. He had been the one constant being in all the world she could count on to love her, even when she was at her worst. Even when he was far away, it was comforting to think that she could send for him at any time and he'd be there when she needed him. But he sat across the room and looked at her with a stranger's eyes.

"You seem to be in good health. Perhaps a little careless in appearance, but . . ."

Glancing downward, she saw the delicate ruffles of lace on the bodice of her silk gown that had torn under Thane's relentless hands, and she felt a flush stain her cheeks. "Owain . . . Colonel Thane brought me home from the theater . . . he is a friend, nothing more."

Ignoring the explanation, Owain said, "I came as soon as I received Charlotte's letter telling me you were ill. I gather the illness wasn't quite as serious as everyone believed?"

She wanted to tell him that her illness had followed the miscarriage of his child, and that she'd nearly died from it, but his hard, blank look stopped her. Besides, it would be better not to go into detail about what had brought about the miscarriage, in view of the incident with Thane at the door. Instead she replied, "Charlotte sent that letter to Peter ages ago. I'm fully recovered now, but when she wrote it I was very ill."

"It took some time for the letter to chase me about the country." He paused. "I didn't know that theaters opened on Sunday evenings nowadays."

"They don't. Sean . . . the playwright wanted an onstage reading, and we have to go whenever we can get into the theater. We usually rehearse in the mornings, but . . . oh, what does it matter? Owain, you seem so different . . . distant."

"I hope my attitude is one of reasonableness. I came to tell you that you can have your freedom. Rather than having you wait seven years to divorce me for abandonment, I'm willing to give you grounds to divorce me as soon as possible."

"But . . . the only other grounds are . . . adultery." Her mouth was suddenly very dry and her stomach contracted. "Why—why are we talking about divorce? I don't want a divorce."

"But I do."

She jumped to her feet, wanting to fling herself at him, but he leaned back, folding his arms as if to place a barricade between them. She felt tears spring to her eyes. "You don't mean it! I don't believe you came all this way to ask me for a divorce. You came because you were worried about me, because you love me."

He shook his head sadly. "Ellie, *bach*, you're still such a child. You think if you cry and beg for forgiveness then all's well again. That the people who care about you can be put away somewhere, and retrieved when you want them. Like actors in a play. Was I supposed to come on stage in response to a cue, then vanish into the wings when it became tiresome to be with me?"

"Please don't be cruel to me, Owain. I can't bear it, not from you."

He stared at her for a minute, and she felt herself cringe under the impersonal scrutiny. "Cruel? I'm being honest, which is more than you deserve, Ellie. I waited for months for a word from you. And every day of our parody of a marriage, I waited for you to show me by one small word or deed that you cared for me. But all I ever heard was complaints about the farm, about living in the country, and all the hard work. There didn't seem to be anything about our life together that pleased you. All you talked about was the theater and how much you missed it. If it had been another man that came between us, I think it would have been easier to deal with. I'd have killed him. But how did I fight your love of the stage? I never knew when you were acting, even with me. I'm not sure that you did. Why, you were never even there when I made love to you. Did you think I didn't know?"

She felt her lip quiver again, and she compressed her mouth to hold back a sob that threatened to escape. This wasn't happening, it couldn't be. Owain loved her, he always had, she had always been able to count on that, even when they were separated by an ocean. He couldn't withdraw that love now. Not now when she had finally come to realize how to put into their marriage what had been missing from it.

As if reading her thoughts, Owain said, "Even the most faithful and adoring heart can't stand being neglected and ignored forever. It breaks eventually. Mine did. And after that, well, I learned to live without one. It's a lot easier not to care about anything, believe me.''

"Owain, you can't mean that,'' she said miserably, and at the same moment recalled what Thane had said about leaving a marriage unattended, that a couple would inevitably drift apart. "Is there someone else? Someone you met in America?''

"Someone like your Colonel Thane, you mean? No. My only mistress was a few acres of scrubland, a small herd of cattle and a few horses. Peter went to Texas and I did join him there for a while, but then I decided to go and see what I could salvage of our stud farm in Kentucky. But the place had been sold to pay the taxes, so I headed west again, and ended up in the New Mexico territory. That's why it took so long for Charlotte's letter to reach me.''

"How strange,'' Eleanor said. "That's where my parents were going when their train derailed.''

"Not so strange. I remembered your telling me that. I suppose for a time I kept clinging to memories of you . . . trying to go to the places you might want to be, trying to find a place where we could be together again. I can't tell you how many little theaters and opera houses I went to, trying to imagine you on the stage there . . .''

Hope quickened again and she said, "I was going to come to you. I really was. As soon as I'd mastered my part in the new play—'' She broke off, realizing her mistake. "I'm sorry, I didn't mean—''

He looked at her with tired eyes. "Don't apologize. I've accepted that I always came second, after your playacting. I used to think that if I loved you enough I could change you, but you'll always choose imitation emotions over real ones. You'd rather have pretended passions and false conflicts than have to endure real day-to-day living. You wanted a life that was framed by neat little segments, like acts in a play, with everything resolved, and everybody giving dramatic speeches, and the curtain coming down to a roar of applause. You couldn't seem to see that real life is far more dramatic than any three-act play. Two people together solving the little problems, enduring the big hardships, knowing that no matter what comes along, they never have to face it alone. I know you found that dull, Ellie. There was no one to applaud, only me, and my devotion was too easily won, wasn't it? You didn't have to learn a part, all you had to do was just be yourself.''

The look in his eyes unnerved her, while his words struck her like a physical blow. She wanted to crawl away and hide. She cast about desperately for words that would drive away his contempt, but there were none. All she could whisper was, "Owain, please don't hate me."

"I don't hate you, Ellie. I just don't care about you, one way or the other anymore. Talk to a solicitor about a divorce and let me know what he needs from me. I'll be staying at Peter's club in town. I left the address with your maid, in case you didn't come home tonight."

"But I always come home at night," she said forlornly, as if he cared where she slept. It was chillingly clear that he did not. He rose and said, "I'll see myself out."

She glanced at the clock on the mantelpiece and said desperately, "But it's so late, and I think it's started to rain. You won't be able to get a cab at this time of night. Why don't you stay here?"

His eyes flickered over in a glance that was disturbingly reminiscent of the way Thane looked at her, taking in the torn lace of her gown and ruined coiffure, then coming to rest on her daringly low décolletage. She wanted to hold her arms in front of her breasts, afraid he might see the outline of her nipples through the thin silk. He said, "I'd better leave. If I stay I might be tempted to finish what your friend Thane apparently started on the way over here."

Some last trace of pride ended her mute acceptance of the situation. How dare he say such a thing? She took one quick step toward him and slapped his cheek, a stinging blow that surprised her more than it seemed to affect him. He shrugged slightly and walked out.

Eleanor did what she had always done when faced with male wrath. She ran away to hide and lick her wounds. The following morning she sent her maid with a note to Sean Connell, requesting that he make an announcement in the newspapers when he had finished writing *Amorette,* and she would return to London to resume rehearsing. Then, without telling anyone where she was going, she took a train north to Crewe, then west into Wales.

Charlotte welcomed her at Glendower and didn't question her abrupt and unannounced arrival. "How lovely to see you, Eleanor, my dear. How well you look!"

Eleanor glanced about the grange, thinking how much more

cheerful it looked than she remembered, and, as she hugged Charlotte she said, "So do you! Why, you're even getting plump!"

A footman came to take her baggage and Charlotte slipped her arm through Eleanor's, giving her a madonnalike smile as they went into the drawing room. "I'll order a tea tray and we'll have a nice chat before I take you to your room. Evan and Geoffrey took the boat out on the lake and they won't be back for hours, so we shan't be disturbed. We can catch up with all the news and gossip."

Eleanor laughed. "I've never known you to gossip. But if you're interested, Delia Ramsey is trying to buy a husband for Veronica, who is in Switzerland for some new treatment for obesity. Tristan's new play is a tremendous success, but he's talking about retiring while he's still at the height of his career. He's dramatizing himself again, of course."

She prattled on, and Charlotte ordered tea. A maid brought a tray, and they both drank several cups. Charlotte looked so serene that Eleanor was envious. To achieve that perfect state of tranquility must be wonderful. From the vantage point of adulthood, Eleanor pondered upon the fact that her plain little nanny had been loved by two rich and fascinating men, had a handsome son, a beautiful home, an idyllic life, while she, Eleanor, considered the reigning beauty of the English stage, had disastrous relationships with men and a life that was in utter turmoil.

Noting the fact that Charlotte's body had acquired soft curves as well as that dreamy contented look in her eyes, and knowing how she loved children, Eleanor suddenly guessed her secret. "Charlotte, are you . . . in the family way?"

Blushing prettily, Charlotte replied, "Oh, dear, how observant you are. I wanted Evan to be the first to know. I haven't told him yet. But yes, I'm going to have his child."

Eleanor offered her congratulations and then added, "I'm sure Evan will be elated. And Geoffrey, too, as he'll have a little brother or sister."

For the first time Charlotte's smile faded, and Eleanor saw that beyond the surface contentment lurked the shadow of some unresolved sorrow. "I'm a little concerned about how Geoffrey will feel. There have been so many shocks and upheavals in his young life and . . . well, he hasn't really accepted me as his mother yet. Oh, he tries very hard, I think for Evan's sake, but he keeps his distance from me. I'm worried that Geoffrey will see the new baby as a usurper for Evan's affections. Geoffrey adores him so.''

Remembering how Veronica had reacted to her parents taking Eleanor into their family, Eleanor could understand Charlotte's concern.

Charlotte leaned forward. ''But, my dear, we've talked of everything but the reason for that tragic look in your eyes.''

Eleanor felt her lip quiver. ''Owain's back in England.'' She was crying before she finished telling of his wanting a divorce.

''Dear child, I can hardly believe this! But please don't cry. Tell me what you want and then we'll decide the best way to get it for you.''

''I w—want Owain,'' Eleanor sobbed. ''But he doesn't want me. Oh, why couldn't I have known how much I cared about him before it was too late?''

Charlotte lay in Evan's arms in the comfort of the great four-poster bed, feeling blissfully contented and wondrously happy as she always did after they had made love. For a little while she was able to forget the grim prophecy she had read in Megan's medical book. When he made love to her, Evan always seemed so vital, so filled with life.

''My dearest darling,'' Evan whispered, ''when are you going to tell me what has been causing you to smile that secret smile lately, while at the same time clucking after me like a mother hen?''

She sat up, looking down at him. In the candlelight his face looked young and serene, the soft light masking the lines of weariness, the strain around his eyes she sometimes saw. Gently she smoothed the hair back from his brow and bent to kiss his lips. ''I am carrying your child.''

His swiftly indrawn breath and the way his heart began to pound, so strongly that she could feel it against her own body, expressed his feelings more eloquently than any words. ''Oh, my dear wife! Are you sure? But this is wonderful . . . I never thought . . . I'm so happy. Oh, how I love you.''

''My darling,'' Charlotte said softly. ''You say I've been clucking like a mother hen and it's true, I do worry about your health, even more so now that we are going to have a child. You must rest more, and not try to live like a young man, especially when Geoffrey is home. You drive yourself to keep up with him, going beyond fatigue to exhaustion. Riding, boating, hiking, all

those trips to town. Dearest, the years take a toll on all of us, but
you are especially vulnerable because when you were young you
were so very strong, and you believe you can still call upon that
great strength. But it isn't there anymore, not only the passing
years, but your illnesses in Ceylon, have robbed you of much of
it.''

Evan said, "My dear, would you consign me to my rocking
chair? I do get a little tired sometimes, but it's of no consequence.''

"But it is—'' Charlotte heard the fear in her voice, and so did
he. Suddenly alert, he sat up and lifted her to his lap, cradling her
against his chest as if she were a child.

"What is it? Why are you so afraid all at once? Ah, I think I
begin to understand. When you went to Llanrys the other day you
talked to someone . . . a member of the medical profession
perhaps?''

Charlotte nodded and nestled closer to him for comfort.

"Damn him for a meddling fool, whoever he is. He told you
that men like me die young, is that it? Darling Charlotte, doctors
are like fortune-tellers, wrong in their predictions more often
than they're right. Why, when I was a boy, they had no name for
what caused me to grow to this size. How many times do they
change their diagnosis? Besides, we are human beings, not cattle.
We are all different, individual. I believe our strength of will is as
important as our physical strength. Mine, my dear, is indomita-
ble. My life is too happy to leave it. And I do assure you I will be
here to watch my daughter grow to womanhood.''

"Daughter? Don't you want a son?'' Charlotte asked, knowing
he was directing her thoughts away from death toward life.

"A son would be wonderful, too, but a little girl like you, ah,
how I could spoil her! I could give her all the things I want to give
you that you insist you don't need.''

"Darling,'' Charlotte said slowly, "if we do have a son . . .
well, I wonder if you were a little hasty in making Geoffrey your
heir. When I returned from Llanrys the other day, I was surprised
that you'd already told him.''

"The time was right to tell him. I should have waited for you to
be here, I suppose, but, well, he'd had a letter from Stephen
and . . . it was just the right time. And I will never break any
promises to him. Glendower is his. Naturally, I'll make better
financial provision for our child than my father did for Stephen,
but Geoffrey is my heir.''

"It's strange, but I had intended to tell you I was going to have a baby that very day. But, of course, Eleanor's sudden arrival . . ."

"She seems very unhappy."

"Poor child, she is. But we've had a long talk and she's decided upon a course of action." She wanted to talk about their own plans, for their child and their future, and steered their conversation away from Eleanor and the men in her life. For now, she was more concerned with the future of her unborn child. It wouldn't do for Evan to know how dismayed she was that he had made Geoffrey his heir. Of course, that was his privilege and right. She wondered, too, if Geoffrey's lack of warmth toward her was partly the reason she felt as she did, and she chided herself, thinking that his behavior was understandable, in view of her long absence. She resolved to try to bridge the chasm of those lost years, and to endeavor not to notice that with each passing day Geoffrey looked more and more like Stephen, not to feel a stab of envy whenever Geoffrey spoke of "his mother" and meant Zoe. Especially since he had now begun to call Evan "Father."

The following morning Eleanor decided to take a train to Liverpool in order to go to a matinee and insisted Charlotte should stay home and rest, since no doubt there would be a backstage meeting of some of her actor friends and perhaps a late night party. She might even stay overnight. It amused Charlotte that, in the midst of personal heartbreak, Eleanor could draw a veil over reality and lose herself in the theater. Evan had business in Llanrys, and Charlotte decided it would be a good opportunity to tell Geoffrey about the new baby.

He was not in the house, nor had he taken a horse from the stable, but one of the grooms said he thought he had seen the young master walking in the direction of the main house.

Zoe's ornate mansion had acquired a ghostly air since her death. Evan had ordered the furniture covered and the house closed. Charlotte went in the tradesmen's entrance, which was used by a footman who went into the house once a week to be sure rodents had not taken up residence, and to clear dust and cobwebs.

Charlotte had not entered the house since the day of Zoe's funeral, and as she walked through the silent halls, peering into empty rooms, she found she was holding her breath. Her ears were buzzing and her palms felt damp. Surely it was her imagination that Zoe's perfume seemed to linger everywhere?

She called, "Geoffrey? Are you here?" and her voice echoed back to her from the marble floors. Somewhere, deep within the house, it seemed that Zoe's mocking laughter blended with the echo.

Shivering, Charlotte called again, "Geoffrey! Where are you, please answer me."

Pushing open the drawing room door, she was half-blinded by a beam of sunlight coming in through the window and gave a cry of alarm as Zoe materialized amid the floating golden dust motes.

Clutching the door for support, Charlotte realized that she was looking at the full-length portrait of Zoe that had hung over the mantelpiece. Someone had taken it down and propped it against a fireside chair, perhaps to remove cobwebs. Several minutes passed before Charlotte's heart stopped thudding.

Zoe's painted image watched her malevolently, the sloe eyes contemptuous, the full lips curving in a triumphant smile. See, she seemed to be saying, I still have power over you, even from beyond the grave.

She haunts me because I wronged her, Charlotte thought. Or is it my own guilt that causes me to think so? I lay with her husband and bore his son, and for that sin I paid dearly, giving up those first crucial seven years of my son's life. Now he treats me as a polite stranger and you, Zoe, he mourns as his lost mother.

Charlotte's feet felt as if they were nailed to the floor. She wanted to turn and run, but Zoe's eyes pinned her to the spot. All of Charlotte's present happiness was forgotten under the onslaught of that accusing gaze. She tried to wrench her eyes away but succeeded only in staring at the blue-black sheen of Zoe's widow's peak, stark against the pearly translucence of her forehead. Wasn't a woman with a widow's peak supposed to outlive her husband? But was Stephen still alive, really? Hadn't Zoe left behind a hollow shell of a man, the essence of him atrophied, his artistic genius amputated by the same knife that had killed his wife? Charlotte remembered Stephen saying, just before he left for New Orleans, "I shall never paint again."

Nor could Charlotte ignore the fact that, if she had never come to Glendower in the first place, then the fabric of the lives of Stephen and Zoe and Evan would not have unraveled. Now Zoe was dead, murdered, and Stephen was in exile, broken in mind and body. While Evan . . . oh, dear God, don't let him be dying. Please let me have been punished enough, spare me that final unbearable loss . . .

She was unsure how long she stood in the open doorway, staring, mesmerized at Zoe's portrait, while an unseen and evil force reduced her marital happiness and her relationship with her son to rubble. She felt as if all her strength was draining from her, as if all that was left was for her to give up, to admit she was unworthy of joy.

A faint sound, barely distinguishable, somewhere in the house, jolted her out of the black mood that possessed her. Quickly she closed the door and hurried across the hall to the gracefully curved spiral staircase that connected the three stories of the house.

There was no sign of Geoffrey anywhere upstairs, and Charlotte stood for a moment at the top of the staircase, catching her breath. Released from the hypnotic presence of Zoe's picture, Charlotte felt a corner of the smothering cloak of depression that had engulfed her lift slightly. But she was anxious to leave Zoe's house quickly, to escape from the relentless evil that still seemed to pervade these rooms.

She turned to go back downstairs, and the sudden movement, or perhaps the stagnant air in the sealed house, caused in her a wave of nausea. The dizzying spiral staircase writhed, snakelike, before her eyes, and somewhere—was it in her mind only?—Zoe's laughter rang hollowly about the rafters.

Charlotte felt such panic and terror she could hardly breathe, but in that same split second the face of her son flashed across her mind. He was here in the house and she had to find him. There was still one place she hadn't searched for Geoffrey and, instead of taking a step downward, she spun around to go up to the attic floor of the house that had housed Stephen's studio.

Only when she turned her back on the spiral staircase did Charlotte realize that she might have fallen, surely would have, if instead of turning back, she had given in to the urge to run down the stairs to escape from Zoe's presence.

Stephen had installed a heavy oak door at the foot of the attic stairs, which he locked when he wanted to work undisturbed, and this was undoubtedly the reason Geoffrey had not heard his mother calling him.

The studio door at the top of the short flight of stairs was open, and she could see him standing in front of one of his father's easels. A sketch pad was propped on the easel, and Geoffrey was absorbed in his drawing.

Although his back was turned to her, she was startled by the uncanny way the boy had struck the same pose as Stephen, feet astride, left shoulder slightly back and left hand on his hip, head cocked to one side, right arm moving in sweeping arcs as he wielded the charcoal, as if he were conducting an orchestra, or perhaps dueling with a rapier.

He was humming to himself as he sketched, and she recognized the tune as an old Welsh ballad that Evan had undoubtedly taught him. The floor creaked as Charlotte reached the landing outside the studio, and hearing it, Geoffrey spun around, his expression apprehensive. "Oh! It's you, Charlotte."

Breathless, she sank onto a wooden bench beside the wall. "Didn't . . . mean to startle you."

Geoffrey had moved between her and the easel, almost defensively, but she had already seen that he was making a sketch of the house, surrounded by oaks, and that it was very well executed, considering his age. She wondered if Stephen had taught him to draw and reflected sadly that there was so much she didn't know about her son. "I didn't mean to intrude on your privacy. But I wanted to talk to you and . . ."

He looked uncomfortable. "I just felt like drawing, and all the stuff is here."

"Yes. It's quite all right, really. Your sketch is very good. Did your father teach you how to draw?"

Geoffrey stared at his feet. "He used to let me watch him work sometimes. What did you want to talk to me about, Charlotte?"

"Do you think you might start calling me Mother now?"

"My . . . other mother, who died—" He looked at her helplessly.

"Yes. I understand." Charlotte turned her head in order to hide her tears. Zoe's unseen presence loomed between them, as in life she had stood between Charlotte and those she loved. How easy it would be to destroy her memory by telling Geoffrey even the least of her misdeeds. But Charlotte could never do that. The boy remembered a beautiful, extravagantly generous woman who had flitted in and out of his short life like a rare and exotic butterfly. A unique being like no other boy had in his life. A creature so beautiful that to associate such loveliness with evil would be almost sacrilegious. There was no need to burden him with the knowledge of Zoe's true nature.

"Charlotte," Geoffrey said.

"Yes, dear?"

"I do understand that you're really my mother, only—"

"It's quite all right. You may call me Charlotte. Now, let me share my exciting news. You are going to have a little brother, or perhaps a little sister."

Geoffrey's eyes widened. He bit his lip and made a valiant attempt to swallow a sob, but a telltale tear glistened on his eyelashes.

Dismayed, Charlotte wished she had led up to the news more carefully. "My dear, what is it? Aren't you happy? This is wonderful news, for all of us."

"But . . . h—he'll be Uncle Evan's real son."

Oh, why hadn't she waited to break the news when Evan was present? Was it because Evan had told the child of his inheritance while she was away, and she wanted to impart good news also? But this clearly was the worst possible news to Geoffrey. "No one can ever take your place in your Uncle Evan's heart. He loves you so much, more than you can imagine."

The child was obviously unconvinced. Charlotte rose to her feet and moved closer to him. She allowed her hands to rest lightly on his shoulders, and although flight was written all over his face, he suffered her touch.

"Don't you see, Geoffrey, that the baby who is coming will link all of us together . . . your Uncle Evan and me and you . . . uniting us into one family. Because the baby will be a part of all of us. Our child, your brother or sister. You see, love is not something that has to be shared, a piece for you, a slice for someone else. Love grows to accommodate all of the people who are dear to us. So you mustn't fear that in loving another child, we will love you less."

He raised his face to look at her, and she felt that he was really seeing her for the first time. Then, wordlessly, he flung his arms around her and hugged her.

Charlotte sank to her knees and held her son. She closed her eyes in a prayer of silent thanks, feeling all of the different parts of her life fit together again.

At length she said, "Shall we go back to the grange? Evan will be coming home soon."

"Do you think it would be all right if I were to ask him for some paints and charcoal of my own? I really don't like coming here to draw. Oh, it's all right here in the studio, but I feel funny coming through the house. I think that's why I was drawing it today. I wanted it to be just a house, and sometimes when I draw something it's like I can see it in a different way."

So he felt Zoe's eerie presence in the house, too. "Yes, of course. We'll go into Llanrys tomorrow and get you everything you need. May I see some of your other sketches?"

He went to a dusty cupboard and took out several sheets of paper. Charlotte looked in awe at several charcoal sketches and watercolors. The mountains and lake captured in a few bold strokes. A golden dandelion with a mate turned to fluffy seed, one a misty vision of the other and both rendered larger than life, hugely exuberant. There was a soaring, happy quality to the boy's drawing. Unlike his father, he was evidently not interested in drawing people.

"Oh, Geoffrey . . . these are awfully good," Charlotte said. "Why didn't you tell us you loved to draw and paint?"

He avoided her eyes. "I don't know."

"Oh, I think you do. You can tell me."

For a moment he squirmed, obviously reluctant, then answered, "I was afraid to. My mother found one of my pictures when I was little, and she said that there would be only one artist in the family. That I was only . . . only imitating the artist. She burned up my drawings and said I must never let my father see me draw."

Charlotte stared at the wondrous dandelion in the watercolor. What a shock it must have been to Zoe to see that Geoffrey was perhaps even more talented than Stephen . . . and how impossible it would have been for her not to wonder about hereditary factors. Had Zoe suspected that Geoffrey was, indeed, Stephen's son?

All at once, Charlotte revised her mental picture of what Geoffrey's life had been like in this house. His apparent loyalty to Zoe had been born of fear, not love as she'd imagined, and even now, like herself, he felt a superstitious need to cater to the dictates of a dead woman.

Zoe had known, as everyone else had, that without her influence, Stephen would never have achieved success as an artist. It was not that Stephen needed her in order to create, but that he believed he needed her. Zoe must have looked at his son's work and recognized, as Charlotte did now, that here was a different kind of genius. Geoffrey didn't see the world through his father's melancholy eyes, desperately seeking in the human face qualities that would offset the evil he knew could lurk in the mind; instead, he saw with a vision that gloriously enhanced everything around him, even the least of God's creations.

Charlotte wanted to shout into the opulent emptiness of the house, "You shan't stop him, Zoe. You can't. Nor have you destroyed Stephen. His talent lives on in his son." Instead, she said quietly, "Zoe was wrong to burn your sketches. Geoffrey, she's gone now. There is no longer any need to feel you must please her. She was a deeply troubled woman and not all she did and said was right. Your drawings are very, very good. Your father will be so proud of you. And so will your Uncle Evan."

"Uncle Evan said it would be all right . . ." Geoffrey began hesitantly, "if I called him Father. So . . . well, it would be funny to call him Father and you Charlotte, wouldn't it?"

"Oh, dear, yes," Charlotte said, and they laughed as they went down the attic stairs together, not needing to say any more about their future together. And the house did not seem so oppressive any longer, because they both knew they were now simply walking down a rather silly spiral staircase in a house that was only a gingerbread imitation of a real home.

38

Owain ignored the curious stares of the members of Peter's club as he sat in the lounge awaiting the arrival of Victor Thane. Owain had left New Mexico so hurriedly that there had not been time to buy new clothes, and he knew that his western boots and buckskin jacket over a cambric shirt were causing a mild stir amid the conservatively tailored pinstriped suits and black broadcloth jackets of the members of the club.

His overland journey had been at breakneck speed, and he'd taken the fastest steamer from New York. Charlotte's letter had implied that Eleanor might be near death, and every mile of the five-thousand-mile journey had been agonizing. Charlotte had written that Eleanor was staying with friends, but perhaps would be back in London by the time he arrived, and she suggested that if Eleanor were not at her flat, he inquire of Tristan or the Ramseys as to her whereabouts. It seemed odd that Charlotte didn't simply give him the address where Ellie was staying, and this worried him, too, as he feared it was a hospital.

He was told that Tristan was appearing in summer stock but would be back in London shortly. Lord and Lady Ramsey were already at their country estate for the summer, but he found Veronica at the London house, packing for a trip to Switzerland. She greeted him more warmly than a long-lost brother, ushered him into a sheet-draped drawing room and proceeded to inform him of all the sordid details of Eleanor's affair with Thane. Owain listened with growing despair.

"When the newspapers got hold of the story of their being in a street brawl, Thane took her away somewhere,'' Veronica told him. "No one knew where, but they were gone for weeks, living together in some hideaway. Owain, you're not one of us, but you seem a decent sort, and you don't deserve to be chained to a woman completely lacking in morals. Even before Thane, there were other men, many men. Including members of the royal family.''

"If you could tell me where she is now," Owain had said stiffly, wanting to escape, yet unable to move.

"There was a rumor,'' Veronica went on, ignoring him, "that she had a miscarriage.'' Pale eyebrows rose over small, piglike eyes, and she added archly, "Shall we say a *planned* miscarriage? Lord knows whose child it was. Thane's probably. Or perhaps the playwright's—Sean's besotted by her, too. One reporter hinted that the street brawl was contrived to give her an excuse to bow out of *Last Love* so that she could take care of her little personal problem. If you're interested, I could show you some of the newspaper stories. I saved a few of them.''

"No, thank you,'' Owain answered. "I rarely believe anything I read in the papers.'' He stood up. "You didn't say where my wife is now?''

"She took a mews house. I'll get the address,'' Veronica said sulkily, obviously disappointed at his apparent lack of reaction to her scandalous revelations. How could she know the rage and despair he was feeling?

Between his conversation with Veronica and his meeting with Eleanor, Owain went through a gamut of emotions. The first was a primal anger directed at Thane. He wanted to kill the man. He wished passionately that he and Thane were back in the wild New Mexico territory where differences were settled according to the laws of the frontier, with a gun. In his years in the untamed West, Owain had, of necessity, become proficient with a handgun. There had been rustlers and Indians to contend with in the early days, and later a breed of outlaws whose trademark was a swiftly drawn weapon. The fact that Owain had stayed alive during the most lawless period in America's frontier history was itself testimony not only to his marksmanship, but also to his lightning-swift draw. But he could hardly face down Thane on a London thoroughfare.

Owain's anger then turned inward. He shouldn't have left her alone; what did he expect? He should have insisted she go to America with him, or stayed with her in London. But he could not make a living in London, and she had been equally adamant she would not go to America. Still, he'd believed that after he left she would follow. After all, she was American-born, there was her grandfather's estate, however small, awaiting settlement . . . besides, surely she would miss him as much as he missed her. But it was too late to agonize over what might have been. He could never forgive her infidelity. There was nothing else to do but accept that he had lost her, and act accordingly.

There had been no word from her since their meeting, and so he had sent a note to her mews house telling her that he would be returning to America at the end of the month, and if she did not institute divorce proceedings by then, he would be forced to do so himself, naming Victor Thane as correspondent. He was not surprised to receive a note from Thane requesting a meeting.

Glancing at the grandfather clock that stood ponderously near the double doors of the lounge, Owain saw that it was exactly four o'clock, the appointed time. Almost the instant the clock started to chime, a steward entered the lounge. He approached Owain and whispered that a visitor awaited him.

A small room off the main entry hall had been set aside for business meetings of a private nature, and Thane stood in front of a huge globe of the world set on a wooden pedestal, idly turning it with a silver-knobbed, ebony cane. He turned as Owain entered the room, icy blue eyes raking him from head to toe in a contemptuous glance that no doubt intimidated most people who encountered it.

Owain resisted the urge to smash his fist into the man's jaw. He merely met his eyes and refused to be the first to look away, or the first to speak.

The ebony cane stopped turning the globe, and at length Thane said, "Eleanor is out of town. You will deal with me."

"Nothing would give me more pleasure," Owain said, in a deadly quiet voice. "However, I can be as much of a civilized savage as you. We'll settle this in the courts. I gave my wife the option of instituting proceedings herself, but I can't remain in England indefinitely. I have obligations in America."

Thane momentarily lost his composure. "Divorce?"

So he hadn't known, after all, and hadn't come in response to the note to Ellie. Owain himself was somewhat taken aback. Where was she? More to the point, had she left Thane? "I wanted to spare my wife any embarrassment, so I offered to provide her with grounds for divorce. However, I've changed my mind about that. Tell her I intend to file myself, and you will be named correspondent.''

Owain felt a certain satisfaction in observing the various expressions that ravaged the usually impassive face Thane presented to the world. Dismay, anger, apprehension. A man named as correspondent in a divorce action was ruined, socially and professionally. He was branded a cad, a sneak, a cheat, and, worst of all for a man like Thane, a fool for getting caught.

Not waiting for a reply, Owain left the room and went back into the lounge. Before he reached his chair he heard footsteps behind him on the polished wood floor. He stopped and turned around.

Peeling off one of his kid gloves, Thane slapped Owain's cheek. The soft leather inflicted no more than a glancing blow. Thane said, in a voice loud enough to be heard all around the lounge, ''Since you're of the lower classes and may not understand the symbolic slap with the glove, let me explain. I'm challenging you to a duel.''

Owain shook his head in disbelief. ''And since you're of an archaic breed that belongs in a museum, perhaps I should point out to you that dueling was outlawed years ago in this country.''

''Nevertheless,'' Thane said, ''there will be a duel. My seconds will call upon you to make the arrangements.''

They were to meet in a lonely part of Hampstead Heath, at dawn, as was the tradition. Two of Peter's fellow club members who had overheard Thane's challenge had quickly volunteered to act as Owain's seconds, and to provide dueling pistols.

''I have a gun of my own,'' Owain had said, not knowing how to stop the flow of events. And Thane had replied, ''Good. So do I. We'll each bring our favorite weapon.''

That evening Owain pondered deeply, part of him relishing the idea of shooting the arrogant swine, while his own inborn sense of fair play told him that, no matter how proficient with a gun Thane was, he would be no match for a man who had learned the art of the fast draw and accurate first shot. Owain would have squeezed the trigger long before Thane had raised his arm and had his target in his sights. Then, too, there was the legal aspect of the duel. The winner would be guilty of murder in the eyes of the law.

So . . . Owain could either flee from the country and have everyone, including Ellie, think him a coward, or he could kill Thane and be arrested for murder. A poor set of choices, indeed.

At last he decided that, since he had no idea where Ellie was staying, he would have to at least tell one of her friends his side of the story. He considered looking up Maeve, but remembering their last meeting, when she'd made it clear how she felt about him, he quickly discarded that idea.

Tristan's manservant informed Owain that his master was due to arrive at any minute, having taken a train from Brighton, and invited him to wait. A short time later, Tristan appeared. "Ah, Eleanor's fierce-eyed Celt. Mr. Owain Davies. Where is your good wife?"

"I hoped you'd know," Owain replied honestly.

"Oh, dear. Am I to be privy to your marital squabbles? My dear fellow, if you're going to unburden yourself on me, you'll have to take me out for supper. My man is the worst gossip in town and will surely eavesdrop if we eat here."

Considering Tristan's rather fragile appearance, Owain was amazed by the size of the supper he tucked away. He waited as patiently as he could for the actor to finish eating, watching a huge dish of pickled herring disappear, along with cold roast beef smothered with chutney, a generous wedge of gorgonzola, several balm cakes and half a bottle of port wine. While Tristan ate, Owain sipped a tankard of ale.

"No gloomy pronouncements while I eat," Tristan warned. "This is my only meal of the day. I can't eat before I perform, and I did a matinee today and had to rush straight to the railway station from the theater. So tell me where you've been . . . Mexico, do I recall Eleanor saying?"

"The New Mexico territory. It belongs to the United States, but is not yet a state."

Tristan held up his fork. "No politics, dear boy. Too boring."

"The country is beautiful, mountains, rivers, forests . . . even the desert areas have a stark appeal of their own. But the territory is not quite civilized yet. Peter visited me once and said he thought there was something in the dry, intoxicating air that makes men prone to violence, because everyone seemed to be at loggerheads. But I believe that New Mexico is a catch basin for human refuse. They come from Texas and Kansas and Colorado and the Indian Territory. The Indian wars lasted longer in New

Mexico and Arizona than anywhere else in the country. Most of the native population was uneducated and didn't speak English. It seemed that every immigrant was more lawless than the last. They stole land from one another, jumped mining claims, and settled their differences with a gun.''

"Good gracious! Why did you make your home in such a place?''

"I was looking for cheap land. But when I arrived in Silver City . . .''

Owain recalled in vivid detail his first impression of the Blue Goose Saloon where he had stopped to slake his thirst. Although hours from sundown, gamblers sat behind stacks of silver and bags of nugget ore. An orchestra imported from San Francisco played expensive music. Money seemed to float in the air, changing hands, wafting in and out in such a careless manner that it seemed almost as if the Silver City miners wanted to get rid of it, they gambled with such reckless abandon. Owain soon learned that, in addition to the seemingly endless supply of silver that poured out of local mines, there was gold in the Mogollon mountains, turquoise in the Burro mountains, and iron nearby. Huge cattle ranches were springing up now that ranchers could ship their beef to market by rail rather than on long and hazardous overland cattle drives. Owain decided to take a risk and instead of buying land, he invested in a silver claim.

But it was Peter's arrival that was the catalyst that changed Owain's fortunes. The golden-haired Englishman had observed the fever pitch of gambling and remarked, "Taffy, my friend, why are you grubbing in the earth for a stake, when you could be relieving these gentlemen of their spare cash?''

"I don't know anything about card games," Owain replied.

"Ah, but I do. I shall teach you."

Owain was astonished at their poker winnings. He learned from Peter how to bluff and, more importantly, how to recognize when the other players were bluffing. Peter soon had enough money to return to Texas, where he'd bought land and hoped to resume breeding racehorses. But Owain decided to stay in the territory. He found some prime grazing land along one of the tributaries of the Gila river, bought a small herd of cattle and a few blooded horses. He also invested in a copper mine. Having once put everything he owned into racehorses, he decided never again to rely on a bow with only one string.

By the time Charlotte's letter found its way from England to Texas and then on to New Mexico, Owain's fortunes were at flood tide.

Tristan listened to his story with obvious admiration. "But you left it all behind for the sake of love!" He sighed dramatically. "How wonderfully, stupidly romantic!"

"I left a competent foreman in charge of the ranch and a business manager I can trust looking after the mines," Owain growled, irritated by Tristan's remark.

"No offense, old man," Tristan murmured, unperturbed. He refilled his wineglass. "But you did come a very long way to find your wife involved with another man, and I do sympathize. I don't understand such mad passions, but I do sympathize. But, you know, Eleanor assured me that she and Thane were only friends. And I believe her. Oh, I know she's wearing the look of lust lately, but my dear fellow, it's the part she's rehearsing. She's preparing to play a wanton in Sean's new play."

"I'd prefer not to talk about the parts Ellie plays. I don't understand the compulsion to act. I think it might have something to do with not being able to accept life as it is."

"You surprise me greatly, Mr. Davies. Knowing of your—forgive me—humble origins, you have acquired a certain gritty polish, almost an education. Not only has your Welsh accent been tamed, but your conversation is filled with original ideas."

"Peter's influence," Owain replied. "Along with my travels and the books I've read." He gave a short, mirthless laugh. "I worked hard to be more of a gentleman, to impress my wife. I shouldn't have bothered, should I?"

Tristan had now finished his gargantuan meal. "Of course you should. For your own enjoyment of life. But tell me, what do you intend to do about the lovely Eleanor?"

"I want you to give her a message for me," Owain said. "I'm not sure what will happen tomorrow morning, but I want her to know that this duel was not my idea."

"Duel? Good God, man, dueling is against the law." Realization dawned in Tristan's eyes. "Ah, I see. Thane. He would do something like that. But you refused, of course?"

"How could I refuse? He challenged me in public. I'd have been branded a coward, law or no law." He told Tristan briefly of asking Eleanor for a divorce, and how Thane had reacted to the news that he would be named correspondent.

"Tristan, I don't expect to die tomorrow, but . . . well, Ellie has no idea of what I'm worth or even where my holdings are, and of course, everything will go to her if anything happens to me. There wasn't time to see a solicitor, but I've written a will, and I want you to witness it and give it to her.''

Tristan's brooding gaze expressed shock. ''You're facing death at dawn and worrying about getting your assets to a wife who will undoubtedly—'' He broke off.

Owain knew he had been about to say Ellie would undoubtedly fly to Thane's arms. But how could he explain to Tristan how he felt about her, when he could not explain his feelings to himself? He reached into his inside pocket and withdrew an envelope. ''The will is in here, and a letter to Ellie. Will you see that she gets them?''

Tristan stared at the envelope in Owain's hand. ''Yes, of course. But what if you kill Thane?''

''I still want her to have this letter and my will. By this time tomorrow, I'll either be dead, or in hiding . . . trying to get to a ship to take me back to America. In either case, I want Ellie to know my side of what happened.''

Tristan shuddered. ''Bloodshed appalls me. There must be some other solution.'' He snapped his fingers. ''Of course. We must find Eleanor and she will talk some sense into you two hotheads. I'm quite sure she doesn't want either of you to die because of her.''

''It's too late for that. Even if we knew where she went, I've given up trying to make our marriage work.'' Owain gestured for the waiter. ''Would you like something else to eat?''

''No, thank you. Having come to realize that I've been talking with a dead man has quite ruined my appetite. You do know that Thane was a much-decorated military hero who was the crack shot of his regiment?''

A thin ground mist swirled over the heath as the last stars faded and the night sky began to lighten. The group of men stood together under a tree, nervously glancing about to be sure they were unobserved, and discussing the rules by which the duel would be fought.

''Ten paces, turn and fire,'' one of Thane's seconds insisted. ''The pistol in your hand *before* you start to walk.''

Owain had strapped on his holster and tied it to his thigh. ''My gun stays here. I don't want to commit murder, but if I have to defend myself I will.''

"He'll shoot you down like a dog then," the man remarked.

One of Owain's seconds said, "There's still time to resolve your differences. An honorable solution can be found, and we can all go home to bed and forget this madness."

Thane, who stood apart from the others, his head tilted slightly backward in a superior attitude, now said, "I insist we proceed. Nothing less will satisfy me."

"What if he agrees not to name you as correspondent—and apologizes publicly?"

"I won't do that," Owain said.

"Then what if he just goes back to America? Fades right out of the picture?"

"I'll agree to that," Owain said. "But only after he publicly withdraws his challenge."

"No," Thane said coldly. "We settle it here and now. Are you going to take your pistol from that stupid holster or not?"

"No, I'm not."

"You gentlemen are my witnesses that the holstered pistol is his choice. Come now, we've wasted enough time here. It will soon be daylight."

"Take your positions, gentlemen. Back to back. When I give the signal, you will start walking. I will count the paces. At ten, you will turn and fire. One shot each. No more."

Owain pushed his coat back, behind his holster, as he turned his back to Thane. For an instant the misty heath vanished and in its place a dusty street, baking under a New Mexico sun, appeared. There had been several men who would not listen to reason. Disgruntled gamblers, would-be claim jumpers, outlaws bent on robbery. Owain had never been able to fire first. Even the most degraded life was sacred to him, yet he had no desire to die, either, and so he had learned to respond instantaneously to the movement of a man's finger on a trigger. But as the dawn crept across the heath, in the gray and sullen light, he was unsure that he would see Thane's finger tighten on the trigger.

". . . three, four, five . . ." the second's voice called.

What the hell am I doing? Owain thought. Am I doing this for Ellie's honor? My own? Out of hurt pride? Loss of face? Revenge? Bravado?

". . . six, seven, eight . . ."

He thought of Ellie briefly. She had run off to hide, from both Thane and himself. Did that mean her feelings for Thane were no deeper than for him? But no, whatever else she felt for Thane, there was no denying that erotic longing that was written all over her the night he had waited for her to come home. She had the look of a woman in the throes of sexual awakening, and that had been Thane's doing. But wait, what had Tristan said about the new play she was rehearsing? It was about a wanton . . . and in *Last Love* she had played a dying girl . . . and was so immersed in the part that she had almost died herself, according to Charlotte. Was it possible . . . ?

". . . nine, ten."

The ball of Owain's foot connected with a large stone on the ground, and he stumbled, regained his balance, and wheeled around. He heard the explosion of Thane's pistol, saw the smoke, and then his own weapon was in his hand and he fired.

Afterwards, he was never sure if he deliberately aimed for Thane's hand, or if the stone under his foot had not only caused him to move slightly out of range of Thane's bullet, but also had thrown off his own aim. His bullet struck Thane's hand, sending the pistol flying into the air. As it fell to the ground, Thane started after it, ignoring the shouts of the seconds, "One shot! One shot only!"

Owain fired again, this time at the gun on the ground. There was a metallic ping as the bullet found its mark and the pistol jumped, sending up a shower of dirt. He sent four more bullets in rapid succession after the gun, each one striking it.

As the last shot reverberated about the heath, then faded into silence, Owain looked at Thane. His right hand dripped blood onto the turf below, but he ignored it. He stood looking at Owain, a curious mixture of hatred and respect on his face.

39

How STRANGE IT was to be back in Boston after all these years. To stand in front of her grandfather's house and look up at the lavender-tinted windows that regarded the outside world like blank, unseeing eyes.

The house was larger than Eleanor remembered, in itself odd, since she would have imagined that as she grew, it would have shrunk. But the four-story house with its arched Georgian doorway and handsome Corinthian portico, externally at least, bore little resemblance to the bleak prison of childhood memory.

She had expected the house to be closed and shuttered, but it was not. Having come directly here after taking the train from New York, where her ship had docked, she had not yet spoken with the estate lawyers, but had written them from England, advising them of her arrival and requesting that they meet her at the house on this date. Perhaps a caretaker had been left in charge, or perhaps only the exterior and grounds had been cared for, and inside she would find an empty shell.

She was surprised to find that the nearest neighbor on the hill, the house that belonged to Franklyn Yarborough, had disappeared. Oh, not completely. There were remnants of the foundations protruding from the overgrown grounds, even a portion of a wall and chimney stack. From the charred brick it appeared that the house had burned to the ground, and from the way the grass and bushes were healing the scars, this had happened some time ago.

After a moment, she walked up to the front door of her

grandfather's house and rang the bell. The door was opened by a stern-looking woman with iron gray hair, wearing the black gown of a servant, her cap and apron bristling with starch. She regarded Eleanor with vague surprise.

"I was formerly Eleanor Hathaway—" she began.

The woman's mouth slackened and she blinked, as if trying to comprehend.

"This was my grandfather's house. I believe it is now mine. I was supposed to meet the lawyers here. Have they arrived yet?"

"Oh, yes, of course, miss. Please come in. Excuse me for being so slow . . . I was expecting a little girl. Mr. Yarborough always talks about you as if you were only about ten years old."

"Mr. Yarborough?" Eleanor followed the woman into the hall, feeling a chill at the mention of his name. "You know him?"

The woman looked at her in astonishment. "I'm Mrs. Soames. I've looked after him ever since he became ill. That was just before his house burned down."

"You mean he's living here?" Eleanor said faintly, fighting an impulse to turn and leave.

"Yes, miss. Ever since the fire."

"I don't want to see him," Eleanor said. "Oh, I know he's the executor of my grandfather's estate, but—"

A door across the hall opened and a corpulent man with a florid face appeared. "Did I hear the doorbell? Ah, I see I did." He came toward her. "You must be Mrs. Davies, nee Hathaway?"

"If I'd known Franklyn Yarborough was in residence here, I'd never have come. Why wasn't I informed of this?"

"My dear Mrs. Davies, we felt you would not object, in view of the circumstances of Mr. Yarborough's tenancy. Mrs. Soames, here, is the caretaker of the house. Originally she and her husband looked after it until your grandfather's untimely demise. It seemed only a matter of courtesy, or perhaps human charity, especially since your estate prospered because of Mr. Yarborough's tireless efforts all these years, to allow him to move in here . . . temporarily, of course, when his own house burned to the ground."

"And how long ago was that?" Eleanor inquired. "And wouldn't it have been common courtesy to let me know? I understood I was my grandfather's sole heir?"

The lawyer looked uncomfortable. "Well, yes . . . But Mr. Yarborough was his best friend, as well as being the executor of his will and . . . well, he became ill shortly before his house burned down. But please, won't you step into the library and we'll go over the terms of your inheritance.''

"No. I won't stay in this house if Franklyn Yarborough is here.''

"Excuse me, miss," Mrs. Soames interrupted. "But I think you should go up to Mr. Yarborough's room and look in on him.''

"I'll do no such thing.''

"He's helpless as a baby, and . . . well, not quite right in the head," Mrs. Soames said. "He won't know you. He doesn't know anybody.''

Eleanor looked questioningly at the lawyer, who nodded. "It's true. He had a series of disastrous financial reverses, even before the fire, that began with the train wreck that killed your parents. Your grandfather left explicit instructions as to how your investments should be handled, but Mr. Yarborough managed to put his own money into one financial flop after another. Eventually, he went into bankruptcy and lived on his fees for handling your grandfather's estate.''

"But surely there was great risk to my inheritance in entrusting it to a bankrupt? Especially one obviously going out of his mind. Is there anything left, beside this house?''

The lawyer gave her a pained look. "Naturally, our firm took over the administration of the estate when Mr. Yarborough became incompetent. You are a wealthy young woman. But, please . . . I have documents to go over with you, if you will step into the study.''

"I want to see him," Eleanor said, abruptly. She turned to Mrs. Soames. "Will you show me his room?''

It was time to face him, Eleanor thought as she followed Mrs. Soames up the stairs. Time to bury the ghosts of the past. Her hands and feet felt ice-cold, and she could hardly breathe, but she told herself there would never be another opportunity to erase his sinister influence from her life.

Halfway up the staircase, they heard the study door close firmly in the hall below. Mrs. Soames paused and whispered to her, "I keep him locked in his room, so you need have no fear he's done any damage anywhere else in the house. And I don't let him have a lamp or candles. Soon as it's dark, I give him a good dose of medicine to make him sleep.''

"He burned down his own house?" Eleanor asked.

"Well, we don't know for sure. But Mr. Yarborough was acting peculiar long before the fire. He'd run around the house and yard with a lantern, shouting that the bridge was washed out and that we had to stop the train. We think he dropped a lantern and started the fire accidentally. Here, this is his room." She fished a key from her apron pocket and opened the door.

The room was bare, except for the bed. Devoid of curtains or rugs, with blank walls that gave the appearance of an institution.

For a moment, Eleanor stared at the man who squatted on the floor next to the bed. Yarborough's former bulk had shriveled, leaving folds of loose skin that were obvious beneath the soiled nightshirt he wore. His hair had all but vanished, leaving a few gray sprouts standing on his scalp. His mouth hung open and he muttered unintelligibly. But Eleanor's attention was riveted upon what he held in his hands. A tattered but still recognizable doll. A few strands of golden hair still clung to the china head, but the dress was gone and so was one arm.

Eleanor recognized it as one of her own dolls, left behind years ago when she and Charlotte fled from this man, this house. Behind her, Mrs. Soames said, "That's the last of the dolls. He wore all the others out."

"Take it away from him," Eleanor said through clenched teeth. The woman hesitated. "Do as I say, immediately. Take that doll downstairs and burn it."

"But, miss—"

Eleanor turned, her eyes blazing. "Now, Mrs. Soames."

As the doll was pried from his fingers, Yarborough looked up, bewildered, then looked at Eleanor with a vacant stare. Mrs. Soames hurriedly departed.

"I am Eleanor Hathaway, do you remember me?"

Ignoring her, he began to scrabble about the dusty floor, searching for the doll.

"You molested me when I was a little girl. For that you will roast in hell, Mr. Yarborough. You think you are in hell now? That you're paying for your sins? Why, your punishment has hardly begun. Were there other little girls whose lives you came as close to ruining as you did mine? How many of us did you rob of our innocence? How many nightmares did you cause? I wish they could see you now. I wish they could have the opportunity to tell you that you're a monster and a fiend . . . that what you did was unforgivable. I wish they could see that justice is always served in the end . . . maybe not in the way we think, but ultimately the spoilers have to pay.''

He looked up at her with blank, unseeing eyes that reminded her, unnervingly, of the lavender-tinted windows of the house that had become his prison. After a moment, he held out his hands, looked down at them, and began to cry.

Eleanor closed the door and locked it.

At the foot of the stairs, Mrs. Soames was waiting. ''I burned the doll, like you said.''

''Good. Come with me.'' Eleanor led the way into the study where the lawyer and a clerk awaited her.

Before anyone could speak, Eleanor said, ''I wanted Mrs. Soames present to hear what I have to say. First, Franklyn Yarborough is to be taken immediately to an asylum. I want him out of this house today. Secondly, the house is to be sold. Mrs. Soames, there will be a year's salary for you, to help tide you over until you find another position.''

''But, your grandfather—'' the lawyer began.

''Is dead. I make the decisions now. I intend to liquidate all of my assets and leave Boston. As quickly as possible.''

Hooves thundered and dirt flew as the thoroughbred hurtled around the track. Peter exclaimed, ''My God, he's going to be a winner. Have you ever seen a more noble beast?''

Eleanor shivered in the cool Texas air and said, ''Actually, yes, I have. But could we please discuss it over breakfast?''

As the first light of the new day gilded Peter's golden hair, he murmured apologetically, ''Of course, come on. I tend to forget not everyone gets as excited as I do over horseflesh.''

They walked back to the newly built ranch house, which sprawled across the raw scar of the ground that had been cleared to accommodate it. Everything was new, bleakly so, and the treeless land stretched in flat monotony to the distant horizons. But Peter's enthusiasm for his new home and the string of racehorses he now owned brightened the vacant landscape considerably.

Eleanor had arrived late the previous evening, and had not expected to be dragged out at the crack of dawn to watch a horse exercise. Still, the walk down to the track had given her an appetite, and although she demurred when offered an enormous steak and fried potatoes by Peter's cook, she did accept a stack of hot cakes that once would have daunted her.

Peter drank coffee strong enough to corrode metal, devoured his steak, and said, "Being of an incurably curious nature, before I decide to go along with your intriguing plan, I absolutely insist upon knowing everything. The whole story, Eleanor. No omissions."

"All right. I suppose I have to start with Victor Thane."

"I know about him. At least, I know what Owain told me about him."

"Owain jumped to conclusions about him. Oh, not that I blame him, but . . ." She told Peter how she met Thane before Owain ever returned to England and, not sparing herself, explained everything that occurred until Owain demanded a divorce and she ran away to hide at Glendower.

"I didn't learn of the duel until Tristan sent me a telegram. I took the next train back to London, but by then Owain was gone."

Peter smiled, relishing what had taken place that morning on Hampstead Heath. "I know all about the duel, too. A pair of my old school chums acted as Owain's seconds, and one of them wrote me in detail. Owain shot the pistol out of Thane's hand, then proceeded to make the damn thing dance all over the heath . . . oh, forgive the language. Tell me, did you see Thane again?"

"Yes, briefly." Eleanor gave him only the barest details of that illuminating meeting. Thane, his right hand encased in a thick bandage, had called Owain an ill-mannered colonial, a misbegotten Welshman without honor, and several other even less complimentary names. Owain, he said, had not abided by the rules.

"He told me he wants a divorce," Thane had added. "Before that occurs, you should be aware that I feel no obligation to marry you."

"Nor I to marry you," Eleanor had responded sweetly.

"I shall be leaving the country shortly."

"Oh?"

"I've accepted a diplomatic post." He hesitated. "If your husband intends to name me correspondent, it will have to be in absentia. It's ironic, to be accused of seducing the only woman I waited in vain for . . . when London is full of cuckolded husbands who had cause to name me correspondent."

Eleanor saw no reason to relieve Thane of his concern about being a correspondent in a divorce action, so did not share with him the details of the letter Owain had given to Tristan for her. In it, Owain had written that if he prevailed in the duel, he would immediately return to New Mexico. He would leave the divorce proceedings up to her. She decided Thane might as well worry about that a little longer, it would serve him right.

"I suppose HRH suggested you disappear to avoid a scandal?"

His silence suggested she was correct in the assumption. Just before he bade her good-bye, Thane had looked at her with an expression of deep regret. "It could have been exciting, you and I together, you know."

"But only temporary," she had replied, and he'd laughed and said she was probably right.

To Peter she said, "Thane was a member of a family that had served the royal family for generations, and I'm quite sure his friend HRH arranged for his discreet disappearance."

"I haven't seen Owain since he came back. I didn't know there was a possibility of divorce."

"There won't be one, if I can help it. Peter, you must help me. I don't know anyone else who can."

He regarded her thoughtfully. "You could be throwing away your money, you know. Not to mention your career."

"I need Owain. I have for a long time. I can't give him up. You know, Peter, there were years when I didn't see him and we just exchanged letters occasionally, but he was still a part of my life. After we married, I foolishly thought we could be separated again, and it wouldn't make any difference. That he'd always be there if I needed him. But I was wrong, and now I must make it right."

"So your intention is to go to some godforsaken little town in New Mexico, a territory populated by ignorant miners, uneducated cowboys, outlaws, railroad men, Indians and Spanish-speaking Mexicans . . . and build a theater."

"Yes."

"And put on plays."

"I've already found a director, and he's auditioning actors willing to come west. I'll produce the plays myself."

"And who will round up an audience for you? If you must throw your money away on such a foolhardy venture, at least build your theater in some established town. Sante Fe, or Albuquerque or Silver City."

"It has to be the little town closest to Owain's ranch."

"You haven't even seen Los Coyotes, population: one hundred. It can't support a saloon, let alone a theater."

"I don't care. I'm going to build one. And put on plays."

A slow smile spread over Peter's handsome face. "And why not? All right, my lovely. I'll go to Silver City and hire carpenters and laborers, and get your theater built. I'll lie low and use an assumed name, so Owain won't have any inkling of who is behind such a harebrained scheme. You can stay here until it's finished, if you like."

"Thank you, Peter. You're a good friend. But while you're getting my theater built, I'd like to go back to New York to rehearse our first production."

"There's just one thing I must ask of you, Eleanor." He was suddenly serious.

"Anything. Anything at all."

"Please don't break Owain's heart again."

40

THE IDENTITY OF the eccentric who built a theater with a seating capacity of five hundred in a town with a population of one hundred was solved when the first posters announcing opening night appeared.

Owain's foreman had ridden in with the news that London's most celebrated actress, Eleanor Hathaway, would be appearing at the Los Coyotes Playhouse in a production of *East Lynne*. Unable to believe Ellie could possibly be coming to New Mexico, Owain rode into town to see the posters for himself.

Painters were putting the finishing touches to the theater, which stood in regal splendor at the end of a dusty boardwalk on the only street in town, not far from a small, adobe jailhouse and a now abandoned Butterfield Stage station.

The theater entrance was flanked by handsome columns, the brick facade topped by a row of gargoyles of the traditional tragicomic variety. It had been reported that plush seats had been imported from the east, and that a crystal chandelier hung in the carpeted foyer.

But Owain saw nothing beyond the life-size photograph of Ellie adorning the poster. "Eleanor Hathaway, the toast of London," he read, "who captivated audiences in *Last Love, Amorette*, and played before the crowned heads of Europe, now comes to New Mexico . . ."

Several different emotions washed over him, and he dealt with them by reminding himself that sometimes it's enough just to be free of an obsession. He had filled his hours with work and achieved a certain peace, if not contentment, since his last meeting with Ellie, which now seemed so long ago.

He didn't want to open old wounds by even seeing her. After all, how long would she stay in a town this size? But as opening night approached, he couldn't bear the thought of her performing to all those empty seats in the theater and, at the last minute, decided to go and see *East Lynne*.

Several weeks elapsed between the time he rode into Los Coyotes to see the posters and opening night. When at last the appointed night arrived, he bathed, shaved and dressed in his best suit, allowed plenty of time for a leisurely ride so that he would not collect trail dust on the way.

Long before he reached the weather-beaten straggle of buildings on the single street of the town, he realized how foolish he'd been to think Ellie would play to an empty house.

Carriages, buggies, and buckboards jammed every clearing. All around the town, campsites had been set up. Tents had been pitched so that visitors could spend the night, and campfires twinkled in the hills like fallen stars.

By the time Owain made his way through the crowded main street of town and reached the theater, he found not only that every seat had been sold, but there was no longer any standing room, either.

The first available tickets were for two weeks hence, and Owain bought one, overlooking the fact that Ellie obviously didn't need anyone to help fill up empty seats.

He assured himself that it would not be like meeting Ellie herself again, after all, she would be playing a part. But when, two weeks later, Ellie walked onto the stage, as Lady Isabel Vane, his heart turned over and then began to thump painfully.

Although *East Lynne* had been dismissed by critics as having no literary merit, in transition from novel to drama, its emotional impact on audiences had been stunning. The story concerned Lady Isabel Vane's mistakenly believing her husband had been unfaithful, and leaving him for another. Later, she returns in disguise as a nurse for her own children and, on her deathbed, receives her husband's forgiveness.

Eleanor was perhaps a little young for the part, but from the moment she appeared on stage, it was clear the audience suspended all disbelief. They might have been observing real people live their lives, because it was clear that real emotions were plucking at the heartstrings of the audience. When the second act ended, Owain saw his neighbors, men and women alike, wiping their eyes or weeping openly.

Only Owain seemed to realize that it was all make-believe, but perhaps that was because he was oblivious to anyone but Ellie. In the concealing darkness, he was able to feast his eyes on her and marvel that once she had belonged to him, if only for a little while. Her beauty had a radiance that lit up the stage, while her fragile air of vulnerability contrasted compellingly with the sensual appeal of the unspoken invitation in her eyes and her low, husky voice. The combination aroused both lust and an urge to protect her, and Owain wondered if the man had been born who would willingly share her with the rest of the world.

When the final curtain came down, he looked around and saw that the people in the audience were on their feet, still applauding wildly. He slipped out of the theater, feeling drained, numb, wishing he'd followed his instincts and stayed away from her.

Eleanor drew in the reins and her buggy rolled to a stop in front of a rambling, adobe house. A wide-eyed ranch hand came slowly toward her, stumbling over his feet. He took the reins from her hands before helping her down.

She had worn a simple linen skirt which emphasized her tiny waist and slender hips, with a matching short jacket of palest blue. Her hair was drawn into a knot on top of her head and shielded by a wide-brimmed hat of natural straw, trimmed with blue and white ribbons.

"Is Mr. Davies at home?" she inquired. "He isn't expecting me, but—"

"Oh, yes, ma'am, he sure is," the man breathed fervently. "Y'all just go right on up to the house. I'll take care of the buggy for you."

Eleanor walked up a gravel path to the old adobe house Owain had acquired with his land, a legacy left from the time the ranch had been a Spanish hacienda. She'd heard that Owain had lovingly restored the house to its original condition.

A stout door of weathered oak was slightly ajar, and she pushed it open and stepped into the surprising coolness beyond. Fifteen-inch-thick adobe walls effectively shut out the hot New Mexico sun.

Carved mahogany furniture of Spanish colonial style furnished a spacious living room directly in front of her, and she saw that one room flowed into the next through wide archways. In the center of the house, an open courtyard, visible through a wrought iron gate, was bright with flowers and bougainvillea vines surrounding a tiled fountain. The sound of running water added to the feeling of coolness.

She called, "Owain? Are you there?"

A shadow fell across the tiled floor of the living room, and Owain appeared, framed by the archway leading to the atrium. "Hello, Ellie. What brings you here?" His voice was coolly detached and in a setting so exotically foreign, it was difficult to associate this self-assured stranger with the young groom who had befriended her at Glendower. She felt her heart sink. He had greeted her with the polite interest given to a casual acquaintance.

"Aren't you going to offer me a chair?"

"Please, come in and sit down," he said, an uncharacteristic hint of sarcasm in his tone. "And forgive my lack of manners. I don't get many visitors. Stay for dinner, if you like, although I'd better warn you that I've got a Mexican cook and his chile peppers will make your eyes water."

She sat on a leather cushion on a sanctuary bench in an alcove, with a narrow slit of a window above her head emitting a mellow beam of late afternoon sunshine. He took a tall-backed armchair next to an open hearth, his legs sprawled in front of him in a relaxed attitude. She noted that he wore spurs, which clinked against the tile, and a white kerchief loosely knotted at the neck of his cambric shirt emphasized his deep tan and coal-black hair. He had never looked more handsome, nor more unreachable.

Clearing her throat, she asked, "Did you like the play?" She had searched the audience every night to see if he was present, and had known the instant the curtain went up that he had finally come. He had vanished at the end of the play, and she had waited in vain to hear from him.

"You were very good. But you know that. They came from all over the territory to see you. I understand the newspapers in all the big cities were full of stories about you and speculation about which of your admirers built a backwoods theater for you. I heard that one circuit judge sends you a bouquet of flowers and a proposal of marriage every single day."

"Owain, I . . ."

Ignoring her, he went on, "Who built the theater for you, Ellie? How does it feel to have such power? Surely you don't need another love-struck swain? That can't be why you came to see me."

"Stop it!" Eleanor cried, jumping to her feet. "I built the damn theater myself, with my inheritance. Just to be near you. Oh, Owain, I want to try again. I want another chance. I know I don't deserve one, but I promise it will be different in future. I'll have the theater in Los Coyotes, but I don't have to always be on stage myself, just occasionally."

"Ellie, *bach*," Owain said softly, "I can't suffer through another attempt at married life with you. I don't have a big enough capacity for pain. Oh, I don't doubt that you mean what you say . . . now. You're like every other actor on earth, you need a strong spirit of competitiveness in order to succeed, and you'll do anything to get the part you want. Right now, you want the part of my wife, but it isn't available."

"Then can we at least be friends? See each other—"

"No. I don't think so. We can never go back to being just friends. Besides, I've come to love this land, I'd never want to leave it. But you'll soon tire of living in a backwater."

"I love it here, too. I've never felt so well in my life. I haven't had a single cold since I came to this climate, and you know how I used to be."

"I'm glad, but I still say you'll start missing the crowds and excitement of a big city before long."

Unable to keep still, she walked around the living room, stopped before a cabinet to examine a wooden statuette of a hooded monk. "I know there is no other woman in your life, Owain."

"I assume at the moment there is no serious suitor in yours, or you wouldn't be wasting your time with me."

"I hope neither of us will waste any more time." She paused. "I swear to you that I never had an affair with Victor Thane, or anyone else."

"It doesn't matter now."

"Yes, it does. Owain, you fought a duel over me. I can't believe you don't care. And the letter you left with Tristan . . . your will leaving everything to me . . . I was deeply moved by that. Despite everything, you wanted me to have all your worldly goods. I *must* still mean something to you."

"I didn't have anyone else to leave it to. Peter's doing so well in Texas that he certainly didn't need any more money. I don't have any relatives. As for the shooting, I'm sorry now I let Thane goad me into it."

She felt a rising desperation. This was not the scene she had rehearsed in her mind when she had made her careful plans, what seemed like ages ago, with Charlotte at Glendower. Owain simply wasn't giving the right responses. Perhaps she should have left for America then, rather than giving in to the temptation to appear as Amorette. The play had been a sensation for a few weeks, until Eleanor caught a cold which turned into bronchitis, and left the cast. She had recuperated on the ocean voyage to America. The trouble was, during the run of a play, she always lost track of time, as if the weeks or months she acted a part didn't count, or were not deducted from her allotted life-span. Had she waited too long to come to New Mexico?

Feeling Owain's eyes on her, she said quickly, "I wish I could make you understand how much I've changed."

"The golden round of royalty now crowns her brow," he quoted quietly, "and royal robes enfold her form; but the peace that passeth all understanding is lost to her forever, and the worm that never dies already gnaws her heart . . ."

Startled, Eleanor stopped pacing and turned to look at him. "Macbeth? Good heavens, Owain! How you do surprise me."

"I'm not an ignorant groom at Glendower any longer. Thanks to you, I think, Ellie. I might have been content if I hadn't known you. I wanted to be my own master to be worthy of you. Then I wanted to acquire at least a little surface polish so you wouldn't be ashamed of me. Mainly, I wanted to appreciate your art, and perhaps succeed in understanding you. Now I wonder if I came to understand you too well."

"You only know the me that was, not the one that is. I learned something, too. That I used to allow the spirit of the drama to possess me, mind and body. I quite literally became the character I was playing. When I realized that it was easier to separate the parts I played from my real life, I played Amorette, but I didn't become a fallen woman."

"I'm happy for you, Ellie. But you see, while you were changing, so was I. There's an orderliness to my life now, and I've no wish to disrupt it. No more frantically seeking a way to win you back. No more dragging myself around the world to be with you. No more agonizing about how to make you happy. I can't make you happy, only you can do that."

"I know, I know! And I will be happy, if you'll just let me be with you." She went to him, sank down on the hard tile of the floor and clasped his hands. "I need you, Owain. I need someone always to be there. Someone I can count on. All my life the people I cared about deserted me. First my parents left me with my grandfather, then Charlotte abandoned me to the Ramseys, and they in turn cast me out when I was no longer a sweet, obedient child. If you abandon me, too, I shan't survive."

"Don't turn your life into a melodrama. You don't need anyone, Ellie, *bach*," he said gently. "All you need is a playwright to put words in your mouth and the boards under your feet."

"I've lost you, then," she said forlornly. "There's no hope."

He leaned forward and cupped her cheek in his hand. "This scene doesn't become you, don't go on with it. You're acting like a child who only wants what she can't have."

There was pity in his eyes, and Eleanor recoiled from it. Oh, God, she thought, what am I doing? Why am I begging him? Surely no man ever wanted a woman who clung so desperately?

She pulled away and rose to her feet. "You're quite right, Owain. I can't seem to stop acting, can I? Why, I do believe I may still be playing Lady Isabel Vane in *East Lynne* . . . seeking a deathbed reconciliation with her husband. Well, enough of that."

The pity in his eyes was replaced by a glimmer of respect.

Smoothing her skirt, she deliberately avoided looking at him, peering instead at her own reflection on a large copper plaque over the fireplace. She adjusted the brim of her hat in what she hoped was a nonchalant manner. "I probably would have come to New Mexico eventually, whether or not you were here. My parents were on their way here when they were killed, and I always wondered what their life here might have been like, had they lived."

He stood up. "I'm forgetting my manners. You had a thirsty journey out here. Would you like something to drink?"

"No, thank you. I believe it's time to make my exit." She gave him a shadow of a smile, although she was choking on tears. "No need to applaud. Or to worry that I'll throw myself at you again. Good-bye, Owain."

He accompanied her out to her buggy, helped her into it, and handed her the reins. "What will you do now?"

"What I planned to do. Bring dramatic theater to the West. I've invested a great deal of money in a playhouse, remember? And as you've pointed out, acting is my whole life."

* * *

Some of the citizens of Los Coyotes claimed that the town began to boom with the coming of the railroads to southern New Mexico, but others insisted that it was the Playhouse that put the town on the map.

At first audiences traveled from nearby Silver City, the local mines, and sprawling cattle ranches, but as word spread of the quality of the dramatic productions performed at the Playhouse, they came from all over the state, and even from as far away as Texas and Arizona. A hotel was built to house overnight visitors, quickly followed by several saloons and, ultimately, a post office, bank, lumberyard and a newspaper. Houses were built, settlers poured in, a sheriff was appointed, and a schoolhouse was built.

The Hathaway Players performed to packed houses, and noted actors and actresses journeyed from both coasts for the honor of appearing with Eleanor Hathaway.

Eleanor did not appear in every production, since she became interested in directing, but audiences could always count on seeing her in her private box and in the foyer afterwards, mingling with the departing crowd, always a gracious hostess.

She built a house on the edge of town, hired a Mexican couple to run it for her, and became known for her charitable works, as well as for taking in any wandering thespian who drifted into town. All a vagrant had to do was to tell her he was an actor down on his luck, and he could count on room and board, at least until he was proved to be a fraud. She gave lavish parties, to which Owain was never invited. A society page in the newspaper was devoted almost solely to her activities and to the visiting dignitaries she attracted.

Despite his vow to avoid contact with her, Owain went to see each new play, sometimes twice. He saw her occasionally dining at the hotel, or driving her buggy to the railroad station to pick up a new batch of actors arriving to appear at the Playhouse.

They always greeted one another, sometimes exchanged small talk. A comment on the weather, or the incredible beauty of the New Mexico sunsets; speculation on the possibility of statehood; news of the latest outrage committed by the last of a fortunately vanishing breed of gunfighters who still occasionally terrorized the state. Owain warned her several times not to wander too far afield alone, especially at night.

Although it was frequently rumored that Eleanor might marry one of the men who constantly proposed to her, she was rarely seen twice in the company of the same man. No one in town knew that the beautiful actress was married, and it would have caused a sensation had anyone suspected that the quietly spoken, successful rancher, horse breeder, and copper mine owner, Owain Davies, was her husband.

Owain expected every day to hear that Eleanor had sold the Playhouse and was leaving to go back east, or even back to England. But she didn't. He waited for her to approach him with the news that she wanted a divorce in order to remarry, convincing himself that it was inevitable she would.

As time went by, it became more difficult for him to pretend indifference toward her when their paths crossed, and he found himself pacing the floor at night, no matter how exhausting his day had been, unable to sleep for thinking of her or worrying about the way she drove herself around town unaccompanied. How drab the town would be when she left, as she undoubtedly would.

Then, just as he reached the point where he could no longer tolerate the tension, wanting something to happen, anything, that would put an end to the stalemate of his relationship with Eleanor, a letter arrived from England.

Owain looked at the unfamiliar handwriting, a large, rather childish script, and tore open the envelope. A glance at the last page revealed that the letter was from Maeve. Owain sat in his saddle, outside the post office, and read it.

"I got your address from Lady Charlotte Athmore," Maeve had written.

> I'M WORKING AS A DRESSER NOW FOR THE ACTRESS WHO IS APPEARING WITH TRISTAN CRESSEY. THEY'RE TRYING TO DO LAST LOVE AGAIN, BUT NOBODY CAN PLAY MARGOT, NOT LIKE ELEANOR.
>
> LADY ATHMORE WAS IN LONDON WITH HER HUSBAND AND TWO SONS. THEY LOOKED WELL AND HAPPY, AND THE YOUNGER BOY IS A LIVELY CHILD, NOT A BIT LIKE HIS MOTHER AND FATHER WHO SEEM VERY RESERVED.
>
> I EXPECT YOU'RE WONDERING WHY I'M WRITING TO YOU AFTER ALL THIS TIME. I KNEW THAT ELEANOR BUILT A THEATER NEAR YOUR RANCH, AND I THOUGHT YOU WOULD BE BACK TOGETHER AGAIN BY NOW, BUT LADY ATHMORE TOLD ME THAT YOU AREN'T. (SHE AND ELEANOR WRITE TO ONE ANOTHER.)

SO I DECIDED THAT SOMEBODY NEEDED TO TELL YOU A FEW HOME TRUTHS, OWAIN. LIKE THE FACT THAT ELEANOR NEARLY DIED WHEN SHE LOST YOUR BABY. SHE WAS ILL FOR MONTHS, SO WEAK, THE POOR LITTLE THING, AND HOUNDED NEARLY TO DEATH BY NEWSPAPER PEOPLE, SO COLONEL THANE TOOK HER AWAY TO THE COUNTRY. CHARLOTTE AND I HELPED HIM TAKE CARE OF HER FOR A TIME. THAT WAS WHY YOU NEVER HEARD FROM HER WHEN YOU WENT BACK TO AMERICA. WHY, SHE DIDN'T EVEN HAVE THE STRENGTH TO WRITE TO YOU, LET ALONE COME TO YOU.

NOW, I'LL ADMIT I DIDN'T LIKE COLONEL THANE ANY MORE THAN ANYBODY ELSE. HE FRIGHTENS PEOPLE, EVERYBODY, WELL, EVERYBODY BUT YOU, I SUPPOSE. (I HEARD ABOUT YOUR DUEL.) BUT WE HAVE TO GIVE THE DEVIL HIS DUE. HE CAME TO SEE ME SHORTLY AFTER YOU AND HIM HAD THAT MEETING ON HAMPSTEAD HEATH.

HE SAID, "I KNOW YOU DON'T LIKE ME, MAEVE, BUT HEAR ME OUT. YOU'RE A GOOD, HONEST GIRL AND I'M SURE EVERYONE YOU KNOW TRUSTS YOU TO TELL THE TRUTH. SO I WANT YOU TO TELL THE TRUTH TO ELEANOR'S HUSBAND. TELL HIM THAT I DID MY DAMNEDEST TO SEDUCE HIS WIFE, BUT I NEVER SUCCEEDED, AND I'M CERTAIN NO ONE ELSE DID, EITHER. IN MY FORMER OCCUPATION, I LEARNED HOW TO UNCOVER EVERY DETAIL OF ANOTHER PERSON'S LIFE, EITHER BY INVESTIGATION OR BY TRICKING THEM INTO CONFIDING IN ME. IT WAS NOT TOO DIFFICULT TO UNCOVER THAT ELEANOR HATHAWAY DAVIES HAS AN INBORN FEAR OF MOST MEN, PERHAPS BECAUSE OF THE MISTREATMENT SHE SUFFERED AT THE HANDS OF HER GRANDFATHER AND HIS FRIEND. I LEARNED THIS WAS THE REASON HER FORMER NANNY BROUGHT HER TO THIS COUNTRY IN THE FIRST PLACE. TELL HER HUSBAND THAT ELEANOR LOVES HIM IN HER OWN WAY, AND IF HE HAS ANY SENSE, HE'LL ACCEPT HER ON HER TERMS."

WELL, OWAIN, I WROTE DOWN EVERYTHING HE SAID, RIGHT THEN, BECAUSE I WAS AFRAID I'D FORGET. I DID INTEND TO TELL YOU, BUT I NEVER SAW YOU AGAIN. I KNOW I SHOULD HAVE WRITTEN BEFORE NOW, BUT, LIKE I SAID, I THOUGHT EVERYTHING WAS ALL RIGHT AGAIN WITH BOTH OF YOU LIVING IN THE SAME TOWN. (TRISTAN

TOLD ME THIS, BUT HE SAID NOTHING ABOUT SEPARATE HOUSES.)

ONE OTHER THING ABOUT COLONEL THANE. JUST BEFORE HE LEFT HE GOT THIS STRANGE LOOK ON HIS FACE AND HE SAID, "I LOVED HER, TOO, YOU KNOW. I SUFFERED MORE AT HER HANDS THAN SHE'LL EVER KNOW. I LIVED IN FEAR OF HER FINDING OUT HOW MUCH I CARED, BECAUSE SHE WOULD SURELY HAVE USED IT AGAINST ME. PERHAPS IN SOME WAY SHE WAS TRYING TO PAY BACK THE MEN WHO HAD HARMED HER AS A CHILD, I DON'T KNOW. I JUST KNOW I'D HAVE GIVEN MY RIGHT ARM TO HAVE HER CARE FOR ME AS MUCH AS SHE CARED FOR HER HUSBAND. EVEN THOUGH SHE THOUGHT SHE ONLY LOVED HIM AS A FRIEND, I RECOGNIZED A MUCH DEEPER BONDING."

Maeve went on to ask Owain's forgiveness again for the tardiness of her letter, and begged him on her behalf to speak to Eleanor and try to end their estrangement. Owain sat up until late that night, reading her letter over and over again.

The following morning, he rode into town and was on his way to the theater when he met Eleanor, riding in her buggy as usual. Reining his horse, he went impatiently through their customary ritual exchange of small talk, then asked if she would care to have a glass of sarsaparilla in the hotel bar.

Her large blue eyes gave him a polite but distant glance. "Oh, I'd love to, but I have an appointment at the bank." She swept on her way, leaving a faint hint of fragrance in the arid air and Owain motionless in the middle of the dusty street, staring after her.

He decided to go to the lumberyard and settle his bill; perhaps she'd be finished in the bank by then. He was dismounting when he saw three horsemen ride into town. Their horses were lathered, although they came up the main street at a slow and deliberate pace. Their hats and faces were trail-dusted, and they wore loose ponchos that didn't hide the fact that they were well armed, with rifles as well as handguns. But it was the way their eyes darted from side to side that caught Owain's attention—they had the look of men bent on mischief. He lingered in front of the lumberyard, waiting to see where they were going.

They disappeared into the livery stable. Still uneasy, Owain went into the lumberyard and paid his bill, then hurried outside again, a sixth sense warning him of impending danger. At midmorning, with the sun climbing high in the summer sky and dust devils dancing on the baked earth, the town seemed almost deserted.

One of the three men, now astride a fresh horse, was in front of the bank, holding the reins of two other horses.

Owain had broken into a run when he heard the first shots. The explosion of sound stilled the buzzing of insects, set dogs barking and brought a deputy running from the jailhouse. Owain gritted his teeth as his bad leg protested the fast pace he forced on it and the boardwalk between the lumberyard and the bank seemed suddenly to stretch to infinity. *Ellie is in the bank. Oh, God, Ellie is in the bank!*

A second man ran from the bank as the lookout fired at the approaching deputy, who spun around and then crashed backward to the ground, blood staining the earth around him. Owain's gun was in his hand and he fired, almost simultaneously, bringing down the lookout horseman. His horse reared, whinnying in terror, and the second man leapt out of the way of crashing hooves. Grabbing the reins, he jumped into the saddle and came hurtling down the street in a cloud of dust, shooting at everything that moved.

Owain dived for cover behind a water trough, and heard a bullet slice through the air over his head. The thunder of hooves faded as the horseman abandoned his partners in crime to their fate, and Owain raised his head in time to see the third man emerge from the bank, his arm around Eleanor's neck as he half-carried, half-dragged her outside.

Everything else within the range of Owain's vision blurred. He saw only the fear in Eleanor's eyes and the coldly desperate look on the bank robber's face. His weapon was pressed to Eleanor's head, the barrel of the gun disappearing into her hair. He was shouting something into the silence that had descended upon the street, but Owain didn't hear the words.

He sprang into the middle of the street, gun in hand, and began to walk toward the bank. The robber saw him and shouted, "Stay away or I'll kill her."

"No habla Inglese," Owain shouted back, continuing toward him.

"Goddamn greaser—*vamos!*"

Eleanor suddenly bent and bit the imprisoning arm, drawing blood, at the same time using the heel of her hand to push the gun upward, away from her head. The gun went off and a bullet ricocheted off the iron bars of the jailhouse across the street. Eleanor, her back to the robber, raised her foot and kicked his calf with all her strength, throwing him off-balance.

Owain took careful aim and fired, the shot going cleanly through the man's cheek. Eleanor broke free and stumbled into Owain's arms as every door on the street opened and men came bursting out to seize the fallen thief and form a posse to follow the one man who had escaped.

There was blood on Eleanor's gown, and her hair hung in her eyes. Her breath wheezed alarmingly in her chest, but she did not appear to be hurt. Owain picked her up, and ignoring the uproar around them, carried her to her buggy.

During the short ride to her house, she sat very close to him, not speaking. He could feel her shaking violently, and he reassured her, over and over again, that she was safe now.

A Mexican woman opened the door, her eyes widening at the sight of Eleanor in his arms. "The senorita's bedroom?" Owain asked. The woman pointed up the staircase. "Bring water to bathe her, and make a pot of tea, *por favor*. Get a bottle of brandy, too. *Comprende?*"

"Si, senor." The woman ran to do his bidding.

He carried Eleanor into the bedroom and placed her on the bed. She wore the dazed, uncomprehending look of one still in shock, and did not protest as he began to unbutton her blood-stained dress. "We're going to get you out of these clothes, Ellie, *bach*, and wash you clean as new. It's all over, and you were very brave. You're with Owain now, your good and true friend, remember?"

She nodded, and a great shudder of relief passed through her body. The Mexican woman returned with a pitcher of hot water and a bowl, then brought the tea and brandy. Owain said, "I'll take care of her. You can go." For a moment, the woman looked ready to argue, but meeting his eye, merely nodded and departed.

He tossed the bloodstained clothing out of the room and dressed her in a robe he found hanging in her closet. After he'd laced the tea generously with brandy and sugar, he watched her drink it, then took off his boots, climbed into bed and pulled her in with him.

Holding her in his arms, he stroked her hair and murmured, "Remember when we were first married and we spent our wedding night like this? Just being close to one another, not even thinking about anything but the comfort of being close together? Put everything but pleasant memories out of your mind, Ellie. There'll be time enough to talk about what happened later.''

She lay quietly in his arms and he spoke to her in a soothing voice, recalling details of happy times, guiding her thoughts to every incident that had ever caused her to smile. She could feel his breath move her hair gently against her brow and his arms were like a pliant fortress, keeping the world at bay. Oh, how she had missed the comfort of these arms!

His voice, along with the brandy, soon drove away the helpless fear she had felt when the robber had seized her. Her trembling stopped, and she pressed closer to him, allowing her hand to creep upward over his chest, feeling the dearly familiar contours of his body suddenly become new and exciting. It had been so long since she felt this nearness, and the magic, healing quality of the human touch; she had missed it more than she had known. But other feelings raced along her veins, too, and it was she who tilted her face up to his and kissed his mouth.

He responded instantly, kissing her with all the passion and intensity of need born of long denial. Once before, he had kissed her with this savage hunger, and she had briefly felt the stirring of these same emotions. But at the beginning of their marriage, he had worshiped her too much to give in to his own desire, and, in deferring to her, he had extinguished the spark of her arousal. She had needed to be swept away, not humbly adored.

There was nothing humble about his caresses now. Her kiss had been all the invitation he needed. He made a slight sound, not quite a groan, before desire erased all reticence.

They joined in a fusion of flesh that conveyed messages requiring no spoken words. As Amorette, Eleanor had learned to listen to her own body, and it spoke to her now of a coiled tension, a satin spring tightening and demanding release. She surrendered completely to sensual pleasure, and marveled at how easy it was for two bodies to blend so perfectly that the rhythm of lovemaking flowed from one to the other, until she was no longer sure where his body ended and hers began.

The approaching crescendo brought a cry of pleasure to her lips. There was an explosion of stars somewhere in the heavens, a languorous drifting back to earth as tremors still rippled through her body, then a delicious, incredible feeling of peace and contentment claimed her.

For a long time, neither spoke. Each lay entwined in the other's arms, too stunned by the unexpected intensity of passion to dare to give voice to any comment that might diminish the moment.

But after a while, as Eleanor lay in her husband's arms, the memory of his last rejection of her attempt at reconciliation brought ugly questions to her mind. Had he made love to her only to drive away the specter of the bank robbery? Was it possible that this afternoon was an act of charity? If it was, she wouldn't be able to bear it. Surely he must have known that today, for the first time, she had truly wanted him, and had experienced a physical release as intense as his.

There was only one way to handle the situation. She would simply not give him an opportunity to reject her again. She murmured, "Would you prefer to live in my house, or yours? Or perhaps we could keep both, for the time being, since mine is in town. I'm really quite flexible about our living arrangements, so long as we're together."

He hesitated for a long time before speaking, and she held her breath. At last he said, "Ellie, *bach*, we both know that sooner or later a new play will come along. A different part, an opening in another town, something you have to do, and you'll be gone again. And maybe I'll wait. I don't know. Maybe I won't. I expect we'd both be taking a chance, because . . . well, history does tend to repeat itself, doesn't it? But perhaps that's no reason to deny ourselves whatever time we'll have together."

Eleanor let out her breath in a long sigh. She nestled closer to him. "That's all I ask, Owain."

After all, had she not always had the power to captivate an audience? All that was required was for that audience to be present. If she could enthrall several hundred people, then surely she could enchant one man? It would be a challenge to win Owain's love again. But, now that she knew how much she wanted it, she had no doubt she would succeed.